Warriors of the Storm

ALSO BY BERNARD CORNWELL
FROM CLIPPER LARGE PRINT

The Pagan Lord
The Empty Throne
1356
Waterloo

Warriors of the Storm

Bernard Cornwell

W F HOWES LTD

This large print edition published in 2016 by
W F Howes Ltd
Unit 5, St George's House, Rearsby Business Park,
Gaddesby Lane, Rearsby, Leicester LE7 4YH

1 3 5 7 9 10 8 6 4 2

First published in the United Kingdom in 2015
by HarperCollins*Publishers*

A CIP catalogue record for this book is available
from the British Library

ISBN 978 1 51003 836 3

Typeset by Palimpsest Book Production Limited,
Falkirk, Stirlingshire

Printed and bound in Great Britain
by TJ International Ltd, Padstow, Cornwall

Warriors of the Storm
is for
Phil and Robert

CONTENTS

PART I	FLAMES ON THE RIVER	1
PART II	THE GHOST FENCE	195
PART III	WAR OF THE BROTHERS	321
HISTORICAL NOTE		427

PART I

FLAMES ON THE RIVER

CHAPTER 1

There was fire in the night. Fire that seared the sky and paled the stars. Fire that churned thick smoke across the land between the rivers.

Finan woke me. 'Trouble,' was all he said.

Eadith stirred and I pushed her away from me. 'Stay there,' I told her and rolled out from under the fleeces. I fumbled for a bearskin cloak and pulled it around my shoulders before following Finan into the street. There was no moon, just the flames reflecting from the great pall of smoke that drifted inland on the night wind. 'We need more men on the walls,' I said.

'Done it,' Finan said.

So all that was left for me to do was curse. I cursed.

'It's Brunanburh,' Finan said bleakly and I cursed again.

Folk were gathering in Ceaster's main street. Eadith had come from the house, wrapped in a great cloak and with her red hair shining in the light of the lanterns that burned at the church door. 'What is it?' she asked sleepily.

'Brunanburh,' Finan said grimly. Eadith made the sign of the cross. I had a glimpse of her naked body as her hand slipped from beneath the cloak to touch her forehead, then she clutched the heavy woollen cloth tight to her belly again.

'Loki,' I spoke the name aloud. He is the god of fire, whatever the Christians might tell you. And Loki is the most slippery of all the gods, a trickster who deceives, charms, betrays and hurts us. Fire is his two-edged weapon that can warm us, cook for us, scorch us, or kill us. I touched Thor's hammer that hung from my neck. 'Æthelstan's there,' I said.

'If he lives,' Finan said.

There was nothing to be done in the darkness. The journey to Brunanburh took at least two hours on horseback and would take longer in this dark night, when we would be stumbling through woods and possibly riding into an ambush set by the men who had fired the distant burh. All I could do was watch from Ceaster's walls in case an attack burst from the dawn.

I did not fear such an attack. Ceaster had been built by the Romans and it was as tough a fortress as any in Britain. The Northmen would need to cross a flooded ditch and put ladders against the high stone walls, and Northmen have ever been reluctant to attack fortresses. But Brunanburh was aflame, so who knew what unlikely things the dawn might bring? Brunanburh was our newest burh, built by Æthelflaed who ruled over Mercia, and it guarded the River Mærse, which offered the Northmen's boats an easy route into central Britain. In years past the Mærse had been busy, the oars dipping and pulling, and the dragon-headed boats surging against the river's current to bring new warriors to the unending struggle between the Northmen and the Saxons, but Brunanburh had stopped that traffic. We kept a fleet of twelve ships there, their crews protected by Brunanburh's thick timber walls, and the Northmen had learned to fear those ships. Now, if they landed on Britain's west coast, they went to Wales or else to Cumbraland, which was the fierce wild country north of the Mærse.

Except tonight. Tonight there were flames by the Mærse.

'Get dressed,' I told Eadith. There would be no more sleep this night.

She touched the emerald encrusted cross at her neck. 'Æthelstan,' she said softly as if she prayed for him while fingering the cross. She had become fond of Æthelstan.

'He either lives or is dead,' I said curtly, 'and we won't know till the dawn.'

We rode just before the dawn, rode north in the wolf-light, following the paved road through the shadowed cemetery of Roman dead. I took sixty men, all mounted on fast light horses so that if we ran into an army of howling Northmen we could flee. I sent scouts ahead, but we were in a hurry so there was no time for our normal precaution, which was to wait for the scouts' reports before we rode on. Our warning this time would be the death of the scouts. We left the Roman road to follow the track we had made through the woods. Clouds had come from the west and a drizzle was falling, but still the smoke rose ahead of us. Rain might extinguish Loki's fire, but not drizzle, and the smoke mocked and beckoned us.

Then we came from the woods to where the fields turned into mudflats and the mudflats merged with the river, and there, far to our west on that wide stretch of silver-grey water, was a fleet. Twenty, thirty ships, maybe more, it was impossible to tell because they were moored so close together, but even from far away I could see that their prows were decorated with the Northmen's beasts; with eagles, dragons, serpents, and wolves. 'Sweet God,' Finan said, appalled.

We hurried now, following a cattle track that meandered along higher ground on the river's southern bank. The wind was in our faces, gusting suddenly to send ripples scurrying across the Mærse. We still could not see Brunanburh because the fort lay beyond a wooded rise, but a sudden movement at the wood's edge betrayed the presence of men, and my two scouts turned their horses and galloped back towards us. Whoever had alarmed them vanished into the thick spring leaves and a moment later a horn sounded, the noise mournful in the grey damp dawn.

'It's not the fort burning,' Finan said uncertainly.

Instead of answering I swerved inland off the track onto the lush pasture. The two scouts came close, their horses' hooves hurling up clods of damp turf. 'There are men in the trees, lord!' one shouted. 'At least a score, probably more!'

'And ready for a fight,' the other reported.

'Ready for a fight?' Finan asked.

'Shields, helmets, weapons,' the second man explained.

I led my sixty men southwards. The belt of young woodland stood like a barrier between us and Brunanburh, and if an enemy waited then they would surely be barring the track. If we followed the track we could ride straight into their shield wall hidden among the trees, but by cutting inland I would force them to move, to lose their order, and so I quickened the pace, kicking my horse into a canter. My son rode up on my left side. 'It's not the fort burning!' he shouted.

The smoke was thinning. It still rose beyond the trees, a smear of grey that melted into the low clouds. It seemed to be coming from the river, and I suspected Finan and my son were right, that it was not the fort burning, but rather the ships. Our ships. But how had an enemy reached those ships? If they had come by daylight they would have been seen and the fort's defenders would have manned the boats and challenged the enemy, while coming by night seemed impossible. The Mærse was shallow and barred with mudbanks, and no shipmaster could hope to bring a vessel this far inland in the dark of a moonless night.

'It's not the fort!' Uhtred called to me again. He made it sound like good news, but my fear was that the fort had fallen and its stout timber walls now protected a horde of Northmen. Why should they burn what they could easily defend?

The ground was rising. I could see no enemy in the trees. That did not mean they were not there. How many enemy? Thirty ships? That could easily be a thousand men, and those men must have known that we would ride from Ceaster. If I had been the enemy's leader I would be waiting just beyond the trees, and that suggested I should slow our advance and send the scouts ahead again, but instead I kicked the horse. My shield was on my back and I left it there, just loosening Serpent-Breath in her scabbard. I was angry and I was careless, but instinct told me that no enemy waited just beyond the woodland. They might have been waiting on the track, but by swerving inland I had given them little time to reform a shield wall on the higher ground. The belt of trees still hid what lay beyond, and I turned the horse and rode west again. I plunged into the leaves, ducked under a branch, let the horse pick its own way through the wood, and then I was through the trees, and I hauled on the reins, slowing, watching, stopping.

No enemy.

My men crashed through the undergrowth and stopped behind me.

'Thank Christ,' Finan said.

The fort had not been taken. The white horse of Mercia still flew above the ramparts and with it was Æthelflaed's goose flag. A third banner hung from the walls, a new banner I had ordered made by the women of Ceaster. It showed the dragon of Wessex, and the dragon was holding a lightning bolt in one raised claw. It was Prince Æthelstan's symbol. The boy had asked to have a Christian cross on his flag, but I had ordered the lightning bolt embroidered there instead.

I called Æthelstan a boy, but he was a man now, fourteen or fifteen years old. He had grown tall, and his boyish mischief had been tempered by experience. There were men who wanted Æthelstan dead, and he knew it, and so his eyes had become watchful. He was handsome too, or so Eadith told me, those watchful grey eyes set in a strong-boned face beneath hair black as a raven's wing. I called him Prince Æthelstan, while those men who wanted him dead called him a bastard.

And many folk believed their lies. Æthelstan had been born to a pretty Centish girl who had died whelping him, but his father was Edward, son of King Alfred and now king of Wessex himself. Edward had since married a West Saxon girl and fathered another son, which made Æthelstan an inconvenience, especially as it was rumoured that in truth he was not a bastard at all because Edward had secretly married the girl from Cent. True or not, and I had good cause to know the story of the first marriage was entirely true, it did not matter because to many in his father's kingdom Æthelstan was the unwanted son. He had not been raised in Wintanceaster like Edward's other children, but sent to Mercia. Edward professed to like the boy, but ignored him, and in truth Æthelstan was an embarrassment. He was the king's eldest son, the ætheling, but he had a younger half-brother whose vengeful mother wanted Æthelstan dead because he stood between her son and the throne of Wessex. But I liked Æthelstan. I liked him enough to want him to reach the throne that was his birthright, but to be king he first needed to learn a man's responsibilities, and so I had given him command of the fort and of the fleet at Brunanburh.

And now the fleet was gone. It was burned. The hulls were smoking beside the charred remnants of the pier we had spent a year building. We had driven elm pilings deep into the foreshore and thrust the walkway out past the low water mark to make a wharf where a battle fleet could be ever ready. Now the wharf was gone, along with the sleek high-prowed ships. Four of those ships had been stranded above the tide mark and were still smouldering, the rest were just blackened ribs in the shallow water, while, at the pier's end, three dragon-headed ships lay moored against the scorched pilings. Five more ships lay just beyond, using their oars to hold the hulls against the river's current and the ebbing tide. The rest of the enemy fleet was a half mile upriver.

And ashore, between us and the burned wharf, were men. Men in mail, men with shields and helmets, men with spears and swords. There were perhaps two hundred of them, and they had herded what few cattle they could find and were pushing the beasts towards the river bank where they were being slaughtered so the flesh could be carried away. I glanced at the fort. Æthelstan commanded a hundred and fifty men there, and I could see them thick on the ramparts, but he was making no attempt to impede the enemy's retreat. 'Let's kill some of the bastards,' I said.

'Lord?' Finan asked, wary of the enemy's greater number.

'They'll run,' I said. 'They want the safety of their ships, they don't want a fight on land.'

I drew Serpent-Breath. The Norsemen who had come ashore were all on foot, and they were scattered. Most were close to the burned wharf's landward end where they could quickly form a shield wall, but dozens of others were struggling with the cattle. I aimed for those men.

And I was angry. I commanded the garrison at Ceaster, and Brunanburh was a part of that garrison. It was an outlying fort and it had been surprised and its ships had been burned and I was angry. I wanted blood in the dawn. I kissed Serpent-Breath's hilt then struck back with my spurs, and we went down that shallow slope at the full gallop, our swords drawn and spears reaching. I wished I had brought a spear, but it was too late for regrets.

The cattle herders saw us and tried to run, but they were on the mudflats and the cattle were panicking and our hooves were loud on the dew-wet turf. The largest group of enemy was making a shield wall where the charred remains of the pier reached dry land, but I had no intention of fighting them. 'I want prisoners!' I bellowed at my men, 'I want prisoners!'

One of the Northmen's ships started for the beach, either to reinforce the men ashore or to offer them an escape. A thousand white birds rose from the grey water, calling and shrieking, circling above the pasture where the shield wall had formed. I saw a banner raised above the locked shields, but I had no time to look at that standard because my horse thundered across the track, down the bank and onto the foreshore. 'Prisoners!' I shouted again. I passed a slaughtered bullock, its blood thick and black on the mud. The men had started to butcher it, but had fled, and then I was among those fugitives and I used the flat of Serpent-Breath's blade to knock one man down. I turned. My horse slipped in the mud, reared, and as he came down I used his weight to drive Serpent-Breath into a second man's chest. The blade pierced his shoulder, drove deep, blood bubbled at his mouth and I kicked the stallion so he would drag the heavy blade free of the dying man. Finan went past me, then my son galloped by, holding his sword Raven-Beak low and bending from the saddle to plunge it into a running man's back. A wild-eyed Norseman swung an axe at me, which I avoided easily, then Berg Skallagrimmrson's spear blade went through the man's spine, through his guts, and showed bright and blood-streaked at his belly. Berg was riding bare-headed, his fair hair, long as a woman's, was hung with knuckle bones and ribbons. He grinned at me as he let go of the spear's ash pole and drew his sword. 'I ruined his mail, lord!'

'I want prisoners, Berg!'

'I kill some bastards first, yes?' He spurred away, still grinning. He was a Norse warrior, maybe eighteen or nineteen summers old, but he had already rowed a ship to Horn on the island of fire and ice that lay far off in the Atlantic, and he had fought in Ireland, in Scotland, and in Wales, and he had stories of rowing inland through forests of birch trees, which, he claimed, grew east of the Norsemen's land. There were frost giants there, he told me, and wolves the size of stallions. 'I should have died a thousand times, lord,' he told me, but he was only alive now because I had saved his life. He had become my man, sworn to me, and in my service he took the head from a fugitive with one swing of his sword. 'Yah!' he bellowed back to me, 'I sharpen the blade good!'

Finan was close to the water's edge, close enough that a man on the approaching ship hurled a spear at him. The weapon stuck in the mud, and Finan contemptuously bent from the saddle to seize the shaft and spurred to where a man lay fallen and bleeding in the mud. He looked back to the ship, making sure he was being watched, then raised the spear ready to plunge the blade into the wounded man's belly. Then he paused and, to my surprise, tossed the spear away. He dismounted and knelt by the wounded man, talked for a moment and then stood. 'Prisoners,' he shouted, 'we need prisoners!'

A horn sounded from the fort and I turned to see men pouring out of Brunanburh's gate. They came with shields, spears, and swords, ready to make a wall that would drive the enemy's shield wall into the river, but those invaders were already leaving and needed no help from us. They were wading past the charred pilings, and edging around the smoking boats to clamber aboard the nearest ships. The approaching ship paused, churning the shallows with its oars, reluctant to face my men, who called insults to them and waited at the river's edge with drawn swords and bloodied spears. More of the enemy waded out towards the dragon-headed boats. 'Let them be!' I shouted. I had wanted blood in the dawn, but there was no advantage in slaughtering a handful of men in the Mærse's shallows and losing maybe a dozen myself. The enemy's main fleet, which had to contain hundreds more men, was already rowing upriver. To weaken it I needed to kill those hundreds, not just a few.

The crews of the nearer ships were jeering at us. I watched as men were hauled aboard, and I wondered where this fleet had come from. It had been years since I had seen so many northern ships. I kicked my horse to the water's edge. A man hurled a spear, but it fell short, and I deliberately sheathed Serpent-Breath to show the enemy I accepted that the fight was over, and I saw a grey-bearded man strike the elbow of a youth who wanted to throw another spear. I nodded to the greybeard, who raised a hand in acknowledgement.

So who were they? The prisoners would tell us soon enough, and we had taken almost a score of men, who were now being stripped of their mail, helmets, and valuables. Finan was kneeling by the wounded man again, talking to him, and I kicked my horse towards him, then stopped, astonished, because Finan had stood and was now pissing on the man, who struck feebly at his tormentor with a gloved hand. 'Finan?' I called.

He ignored me. He spoke to his prisoner in his own Irish tongue and the man answered angrily in the same language. Finan laughed, then seemed to curse the man, chanting words brutally and distinctly, and holding his outspread fingers towards the piss-soaked face as though casting a spell. I reckoned that whatever happened was none of my business and I looked back to the ships at the end of the ruined wharf just in time to see the enemy's standard-bearer climb aboard the last remaining high-prowed vessel. The man was in mail and had a hard time pulling himself over the ship's side until he handed up his banner and held up both arms so he could be hauled aboard by two other warriors. And I recognised the banner, and I hardly dared believe what I saw.

Haesten?

Haesten.

If this world ever contained one worthless, treacherous slime-coated piece of human dung then it was Haesten. I had known him for a lifetime, indeed I had saved his miserable life and he had sworn loyalty to me, clasping his hands about mine which, in turn, were clasped about Serpent-Breath's hilt, and he had wept tears of gratitude as he vowed to be my man, to defend me, to serve me, and in return to receive my gold, my loyalty, and within months he had broken the oath and was fighting against me. He had sworn peace with Alfred and had broken that oath too. He had led armies to ravage Wessex and Mercia, until finally, at Beamfleot, I had cornered his men and turned the creeks and marshes dark with their blood. We had filled ditches with his dead, the ravens had gorged themselves that day, but Haesten had escaped. He always escaped. He had lost his army, but not his cunning, and he had come again, this time in the service of Sigurd Thorrson and Cnut Ranulfson, and they had died in another slaughter, but once again Haesten had slipped away.

Now he was back, and his banner was a bleached skull mounted on a pole. It mocked me from the nearest ship, which was now rowing away. The men aboard called insults, and the standard-bearer waved the skull from side to side. Beyond that ship was a larger one, prowed with a great dragon that reared its fanged mouth high, and at the ship's stern I could see a cloaked man wearing a silver helmet crowned with black ravens' wings. He took the helmet off and gave me a mocking bow, and I saw that it was Haesten. He was laughing. He had burned my boats and had stolen a few cattle, and for Haesten that was victory enough. It was not revenge for Beamfleot, he would need to kill me and all my men to balance that bloody scale, but he had made us look fools and he had opened the Mærse to a great fleet of Northmen who now rowed upriver. A fleet of enemies who came to take our land, led by Haesten.

'How can a bastard like Haesten lead so many men?' I asked aloud.

'He doesn't.' My son had walked his horse into the shallows and reined in beside me.

'He doesn't?'

'Ragnall Ivarson leads them.'

I said nothing, but felt a chill pass through me. Ragnall Ivarson was a name I knew, a name we all knew, a name that had spread fear up and down the Irish Sea. He was a Norseman who called himself the Sea King, for his lands were scattered wherever the wild waves beat on rock or sand. He ruled where the seals swam and the puffins flew, where the winds howled and where ships were wrecked, where the cold bit like a knife and the souls of drowned men moaned in the darkness. His men had captured the wild islands off Scotland, had bitten land from the coast of Ireland, and enslaved folk in Wales and on the Isle of Mann. It was a kingdom without borders, for whenever an enemy became too strong, Ragnall's men took to their long ships and sailed to another wild coast. They had raided the shores of Wessex, taking away slaves and cattle, and had even rowed up the Sæfern to threaten Gleawecestre, though the walls of that fortress had daunted them. Ragnall Ivarson. I had never met him, but I knew him. I knew his reputation. No man sailed a ship better, no man fought more fiercely, no man was held in more fear. He was a savage, a pirate, a wild king of nowhere, and my daughter Stiorra had married his brother.

'And Haesten has sworn loyalty to Ragnall,' my son went on. He watched the ships pull away. 'Ragnall Ivarson,' he still gazed at the fleet as he spoke, 'has given up his Irish land. He's told his men that fate has granted him Britain instead.'

Haesten was a nothing, I thought. He was a rat allied to a wolf, a ragged sparrow perched on an eagle's shoulder. 'Ragnall has abandoned his Irish land?' I asked.

'So the man said.' My son gestured to where the prisoners stood.

I grunted. I knew little of what happened in Ireland, but over the last few years there had come news of Northmen being harried out of that land.

Ships had crossed the sea with survivors of grim fights, and men who had thought to take land in Ireland now sought it in Cumbraland or on the Welsh coast, and some went even further, to Neustria or Frankia. 'Ragnall's powerful,' I said, 'why would he just abandon Ireland?'

'Because the Irish persuaded him to leave.'

'Persuaded?'

My son shrugged. 'They have sorcerers, Christian sorcerers, who see the future. They said Ragnall will be king of all Britain if he leaves Ireland, and they gave him warriors to help.' He nodded at the fleet. 'There are one hundred Irish warriors on those ships.'

'King of all Britain?'

'That's what the prisoner said.'

I spat. Ragnall was not the first man to dream of ruling the whole island. 'How many men does he have?'

'Twelve hundred.'

'You're sure of that?'

My son smiled. 'You taught me well, Father.'

'What did I teach you?'

'That a spear-point in a prisoner's liver is a very persuasive thing.'

I watched the last boats row eastwards. They would be lost to sight soon. 'Beadwulf!' I shouted. He was a small wiry man whose face was decorated with inked lines in Danish fashion, though Beadwulf himself was a Saxon. He was one of my best scouts, a man who could cross open grassland like a ghost. I nodded at the disappearing ships. 'Take a dozen men,' I told Beadwulf, 'and follow the bastards. I want to know where they land.'

'Lord,' he said, and started to turn away.

'And Beadwulf!' I called, and he looked back. 'Try to see what banners are on the ships,' I told him, 'and look for a red axe! If you see a red axe I want to know, fast!'

'The red axe, lord,' he repeated and sped away.

The red axe was the symbol of Sigtryggr Ivarson, my daughter's husband. Men now called him Sigtryggr One-Eye because I had taken his right eye with the tip of Serpent-Breath. He had attacked Ceaster and been beaten away, but in his defeat he had taken Stiorra with him. She had not gone as a captive, but as a lover, and once in a while I would hear news of her. She and Sigtryggr possessed land in Ireland, and she wrote letters to me because I had made her learn writing and reading. 'We ride horses on the sand,' she had written, 'and across the hills. It is beautiful here. They hate us.' She had a daughter, my first grandchild, and she had called the daughter Gisela after her own mother. 'Gisela is beautiful,' she wrote, 'and the Irish priests curse us. At night they scream their curses and sound like wild birds dying. I love this place. My husband sends you greetings.'

Men had always reckoned that Sigtryggr was the more dangerous of the two brothers. He was said to be cleverer than Ragnall and his skill with a sword was legendary, but the loss of his eye or perhaps his marriage to Stiorra had calmed him. Rumour said that Sigtryggr was content to farm his fields, fish his seas, and defend his lands, but would he stay content if his older brother was capturing Britain? That was why I had told Beadwulf to look for the red axe. I wanted to know if my daughter's husband had become my enemy.

Prince Æthelstan found me as the last of the enemy ships vanished from sight. He came with a half-dozen companions, all of them mounted on big stallions. 'Lord,' he called, 'I'm sorry!'

I waved him to silence, my attention with Finan again. He was chanting in fury at the man who lay wounded at his feet, and the wounded man was shouting back, and I did not need to speak any of the strange Irish tongue to know that they exchanged curses. I had rarely seen Finan so angry. He was spitting, ranting, chanting, his rhythmic words heavy as hammer blows. Those words beat down his opponent who, already wounded, seemed to weaken under the assault of insults. Men stared at the two, awed by their anger, then Finan turned and snatched up the spear he had thrown aside. He stalked back to his victim, spoke more words, and touched the crucifix about his neck. Then, as if he were a priest raising the host, he lifted the spear in both hands, the blade pointing downwards, and held it high. He paused, then spoke in English.

'May God forgive me,' he said.

Then he rammed the spear down hard, screaming

with the effort to thrust the blade through mail and bone to the heart within, and the man leaped under the spear's blow and blood welled from his mouth, and his arms and legs flailed for a few dying heartbeats, and then there were no more heartbeats and he was dead, open-mouthed, pinned to the shore's edge with a spear that had gone clean through his heart into the soil beneath.

Finan was weeping.

I urged my horse near him and stooped to touch his shoulder. He was my friend, my oldest friend, my companion of a hundred shield walls. 'Finan?' I asked, but he did not look at me. 'Finan!' I said again.

And this time he did look up at me and there were tears on his cheeks and misery in his eyes. 'I think he was my son,' he said.

'He was what?' I asked, aghast.

'Son or nephew, I don't know. Christ help me, I don't know. But I killed him.'

He walked away.

'I'm sorry,' Æthelstan said again, sounding as miserable as Finan. He stared at the smoke drifting slow above the river. 'They came in the night,' he said, 'and we didn't know until we saw the flames. I'm sorry. I failed you.'

'Don't be a fool,' I snarled. 'You couldn't stop that fleet!' I waved towards the bend in the river where the last of the Sea King's ships had disappeared behind a stand of trees. One of our burning ships gave a lurch, and there was a hiss as steam thickened the smoke.

'I wanted to fight them,' Æthelstan said.

'Then you're a damned fool,' I retorted.

He frowned, then gestured towards the burning ships and at the butchered carcass of a bullock. 'I wanted to stop this!' he said.

'You choose your battles,' I said harshly. 'You were safe behind your walls, so why lose men? You couldn't stop the fleet. Besides, they wanted you to come out and fight them, and it isn't sensible to do what the enemy wants.'

'That's what I told him, lord,' Rædwald put in. Rædwald was an older Mercian, a cautious man who I had posted in Brunanburh to advise Æthelstan. The prince commanded the garrison, but he was young and so I had given him a half-dozen older and wiser men to keep him from making youth's mistakes.

'They wanted us to come out?' Æthelstan asked, puzzled.

'Where would they rather fight you?' I asked. 'With you behind walls? Or out in the open, shield wall to shield wall?'

'I told him that, lord!' Rædwald said. I ignored him.

'Choose your battles,' I snarled at Æthelstan. 'That space between your ears was given so that you can think! If you just charge whenever you see an enemy you'll earn yourself an early grave.'

'That's . . .' Rædwald began.

'That's what you told him, I know! Now be quiet!' I gazed upstream at the empty river. Ragnall had brought an army to Britain, but what would he do with that army? He needed land to feed his men, he needed fortresses to protect them. He had passed Brunanburh, but was he planning to double back and attack Ceaster? The Roman walls made that city a fine base, but also a formidable obstacle. So where was he going?

'But that's what you did!' Æthelstan interrupted my thoughts.

'Did what?'

'You charged the enemy!' He looked indignant. 'Just now! You charged down the hill even though they outnumbered you.'

'I needed prisoners, you miserable excuse for a man.'

I wanted to know how Ragnall had come upriver in the darkness. It had either been an incredible stroke of fortune that his great fleet had negotiated the Mærse's mudbanks without any ship going aground, or else he was an even greater ship-handler than his reputation suggested. It had been an impressive feat of seamanship, but it had also been unnecessary. His fleet was huge, and we had only a dozen boats. He could have brushed us aside without missing an oar stroke, yet he had decided to attack in the night. Why risk that?

'He didn't want us to block the channel,' my son suggested, and that was probably the truth. If we had been given just a few hours' warning we could have sunk our ships in the river's main channel. Ragnall would still have got past eventually, but he would have been forced to wait for a high tide, and his heavier ships would have had a difficult passage, and meanwhile we would have sent messengers upriver to make sure more barricades blocked the Mærse and more men waited to greet his ships. Instead he had slipped past us, he had wounded us, and he was already rowing inland.

'It was the Frisians,' Æthelstan said unhappily.

'Frisians?'

'Three merchant ships arrived last night, lord. They moored in the river. They were carrying pelts from Dyflin.'

'You inspected them?'

He shook his head. 'They said they carried the plague, lord.'

'So you didn't board them?'

'Not with the plague, lord, no.' The garrison at Brunanburh had the duty of inspecting every ship that entered the river, mainly to levy a tax on whatever cargo the ship carried, but no one would board a ship that had sickness aboard. 'They said they were carrying pelts, lord,' Æthelstan explained, 'and they paid us their fees.'

'And you left them alone?'

He nodded miserably. The prisoners told me the rest. The three merchant ships had anchored where the Mærse's channel was narrowest, the place where a fleet faced the greatest danger of running aground, and they had burned lanterns that had guided Ragnall's ships past the peril. The tide had done the rest. Let a vessel drift and it will usually follow the swiftest current in the deepest channel and, once past the three merchant ships, Ragnall had simply let the flood carry him to our wharf. There he had burned both wharf and ships, so that his own vessels could now use the river safely. Reinforcements could now come from his sea kingdom. He had ripped apart our defence of the Mærse and he was loose in Britain with an army.

I let Æthelstan decide what to do with the prisoners. There were fourteen of them, and Æthelstan chose to have them executed. 'Wait for low tide,' he ordered Rædwald, 'then tie them to the stakes.' He nodded at the charred pilings that jutted at awkward angles from the swirling river. 'Let them drown in the rising tide.'

I had already sent Beadwulf eastwards, but would not expect to hear his news for at least a day. I ordered Sihtric to send men south. 'They're to ride fast,' I said, 'and tell the Lady Æthelflaed what's happening. Tell her I want men, a lot of men, all her men!'

'At Ceaster?' Sihtric asked.

I shook my head, thinking. 'Tell her to send them to Liccelfeld. And tell her I'm going there.' I turned and pointed to Æthelstan, 'and you're coming with me, lord Prince. And bringing most of Brunanburh's garrison with you. And you,' I looked at Rædwald, 'will stay here. Defend what's left. You can have fifty men.'

'Fifty! That's not enough . . .'

'Forty,' I snarled, 'and if you lose the fort I'll cut your kidneys out and eat them.'

We were at war.

Finan was at the water's edge, sitting on a great driftwood log. I sat beside him. 'So tell me about that,' I said, nodding at the corpse that was still fixed by the spear.

'What do you want to know?'

'Whatever you choose to tell me.'

We sat in silence. Geese flew above us, their wings beating the morning. A flurry of rain spat past. One of the corpses farted. 'We're going to Liccelfeld,' I said.

Finan nodded. 'Why Liccelfeld?' he asked after a moment. The question was dutiful. He was not thinking about Ragnall or the Norsemen or anything except the spear-pierced corpse at the river's brink.

'Because I don't know where Ragnall's going,' I said, 'but from Liccelfeld we can go north or south easily.'

'North or south,' he repeated dully.

'The bastard needs land,' I said, 'and he'll either try to take it in northern Mercia or from southern Northumbria. We have to stop him fast.'

'He'll go north,' Finan said, though he still spoke carelessly. He shrugged, 'Why would he pick a fight with Mercia?'

I suspected he was right. Mercia had become powerful, its frontiers protected by burhs, fortified towns, while to the north were the troubled lands of Northumbria. That was Danish land, but the Danish lords were squabbling and fighting amongst themselves. A strong man like Ragnall could unite them. I had repeatedly told Æthelflaed that we should march north and take land from the fractious Danes, but she would not invade Northumbria until her brother Edward brought his West Saxon army to help. 'Whether Ragnall goes north or comes south,' I said, 'now's the time to fight him. He's just arrived here. He doesn't know the land. Haesten does, of course, but how far does Ragnall trust that piece of weasel-shit? And from what the prisoners said, Ragnall's army has never fought together, so we hit him hard now, before he has a chance to find a refuge and before he feels safe. We do to him what the Irish did, we make him feel unwanted.'

Silence again. I watched the geese, looking for an omen in their numbers, but there were too many birds to count. Yet the goose was Æthelflaed's symbol, so their presence was surely a good sign? I touched the hammer that hung at my neck. Finan saw the gesture and frowned. Then he grasped the crucifix that hung at his neck, and, with a sudden grimace, tugged it hard enough to break the leather cord. He looked at the silver bauble for a moment, then flung it into the water. 'I'm going to hell,' he said.

For a moment I did not know what to say. 'At least we'll still be together,' I finally spoke.

'Aye,' he said, unsmiling. 'A man who kills his own blood is doomed.'

'The Christian priests tell you that?'

'No.'

'Then how do you know?'

'I just know. That was why my brother didn't kill me so long ago. He sold me to that bastard slaver instead.'

That was how Finan and I had first met, chained as slaves to a bench and pulling on long oars. We still carried the slaver's brand on our skin, though the slaver himself was long dead, slaughtered by Finan in an orgy of revenge.

'Why would your brother want to kill you?' I asked, knowing I trod on dangerous ground. In all the long years of our friendship I had never discovered why Finan was an exile from his native Ireland.

He grimaced. 'A woman.'

'Surprise me,' I said wryly.

'I was married,' he went on as though I had not spoken. 'A good woman, she was, a royal daughter of the Uí Néill, and I was a prince of my people. My brother was too. Prince Conall.'

'Conall,' I said after a few heartbeats of silence.

'They're small kingdoms in Ireland,' he said bleakly, staring across the water. 'Small kingdoms and great kings, and we fight. Christ, how we love to fight! The Uí Néill, of course, are the great ones, at least in the north. We were their clients. We gave them tribute. We fought for them when they demanded it, we drank with them and we married their good women.'

'And you married a Uí Néill woman?' I prompted him.

'Conall is younger than me,' he said, ignoring my question. 'I should have been the next king, but Conall met a maid from the Ó Domhnaill. God, lord, but she was beautiful! She was nothing by birth! She was no chieftain's daughter, but a dairy girl. And she was lovely,' he spoke wistfully, his eyes gleaming wet. 'She had hair dark as night and eyes like stars and a body as graceful as an angel in flight.'

'And she was called?' I asked.

He shook his head abruptly, rejecting the question. 'And God help us we fell in love. We ran away. We took horses and we rode south. Just Conall's wife and me. We thought we'd ride, we'd hide, and we'd never be found.'

'And Conall pursued you?' I guessed.

'The Uí Néill pursued us. God knows it was a hunt. Every Christian in Ireland knew of us, knew of the gold they would make if they found us, and yes, Conall rode with the men of the Uí Néill.'

I said nothing. I waited.

'Nothing is hidden in Ireland,' Finan went on. 'You can't hide. The little people see you. Folk see you. Find an island in a lake and they know you're there. Go to a mountain top and they'll find you, hide in a cave and they'll hunt you down. We should have taken ship, but we were young. We didn't know.'

'They found you.'

'They found us, and Conall promised he would make my life worse than death.'

'By selling you to Sverri?' Sverri was the slaver who had branded us.

He nodded. 'I was stripped of my gold, whipped, made to crawl through Uí Néill shit, and then sold to Sverri. I am the king that never was.'

'And the girl?'

'And Conall took my Uí Néill wife as his own. The priests allowed it, they encouraged it, and he raised my sons as his own. They cursed me, lord. My own sons cursed me. That one,' he nodded at the corpse, 'cursed me just now. I am the betrayer, the cursed.'

'And he's your son?' I asked gently.

'He wouldn't say. He could be. Or Conall's boy. He's my blood, anyway.'

I walked to the dead man, put my right foot on his belly, and tugged the spear free. It was a struggle and the corpse made an obscene sucking noise as I wrenched the wide blade out. A bloody cross lay on the dead man's chest. 'The priests will bury him,' I said, 'they'll say prayers over him.' I hurled the spear into the shallows and turned back to Finan. 'What happened to the girl?'

He stared empty-eyed across the river that was smeared dark with the ash of our ships. 'For one day,' he said, 'they let the warriors of the Uí Néill do as they wished with her. They made me watch. And then they were merciful, lord. They killed her.'

'And your brother,' I said, 'has sent men to help Ragnall?'

'The Uí Néill sent men to help Ragnall. And yes, my brother leads them.'

'And why would they do that?' I asked.

'Because the Uí Néill would be kings of all the north. Of Ireland and of Scotland too, of all the north. Ragnall can have the Saxon lands. That's the agreement. He helps them, they help him.'

'And he begins with Northumbria?'

'Or Mercia,' Finan suggested with a shrug. 'But they won't rest there,' he went on, 'because they want everything.'

It was the ancient dream, the dream that had haunted my whole life, the dream of the Northmen to conquer all Britain. They had tried so often and they had come so close to success, yet still we Saxons lived and still we fought back so that now half the island was ours again. Yet we should have lost! The Northmen were savage, they came with fury and anger, and their armies darkened the land, but they had one fatal weakness. They were like dogs that fought each other, and only when one dog was strongest and could snarl and bite and force the others to his bidding were the invasions dangerous. But one defeat shattered their armies. They followed a man so long as he was successful, but if that man showed weakness they deserted in droves to find other, easier prey.

And Ragnall had led an army here. An army of Norsemen and Danes and Irish, and that meant Ragnall had united our enemies. That made him dangerous.

Except he had not whipped all the dogs to his bidding.

I learned one other thing from our prisoners. Sigtryggr, my daughter's husband, had refused to sail with his brother. He was still in Ireland. Beadwulf would think otherwise because he would see the flag of the red axe and he would think it belonged to Sigtryggr, but two of the prisoners told me that the brothers shared the symbol. It was their dead father's flag, the bloody red axe of Ivar, but Sigtryggr's axe, at least for the moment, was resting. Ragnall's axe had chopped a bloody hole in our defences, but my son-in-law was still in Ireland. I touched my hammer and prayed he stayed there.

'We must go,' I told Finan.

Because we had to whip Ragnall into defeat.

And I thought we would ride east.

CHAPTER 2

The priests came to me early next morning. There were four of them, led by the Mercian twins Ceolnoth and Ceolberht who hated me. I had known them since boyhood and had no more love for them than they had for me, but at least I could now tell them apart. For years I had never known which twin I spoke to, they were as alike as two eggs, but one of our arguments had ended with me kicking out Ceolberht's teeth, so now I knew that he was the one who hissed when he spoke. He dribbled too. 'Will you be back by Easter, lord?' he asked me. He was being very respectful, perhaps because he still had one or two teeth left and wanted to keep them.

'No,' I said, then urged my horse forward a pace. 'Godwin! Put the fish in sacks!'

'Yes, lord!' Godwin called back. Godwin was my servant, and he and three other men had been rolling barrels from one of Ceaster's storehouses. The barrels were filled with smoked fish, and the men were trying to make rope slings that would let each packhorse carry two barrels. Godwin frowned. 'Do we have sacks, lord?'

'There are twenty-two sacks of fleeces in my storeroom,' I told him. 'Tell my steward to empty them!' I looked back to Father Ceolberht. 'We won't get all the wool out of the sacks,' I told him, 'and some of the wool will stick to the fish and then get caught in our teeth.' I smiled at him. 'If we have teeth.'

'How many men will be left to defend Ceaster?' his brother asked sternly.

'Eighty,' I said.

'Eighty!'

'And half of those are sick,' I added. 'So you'll have forty fit men and the rest will be cripples.'

'It isn't enough!' he protested.

'Of course it isn't enough,' I snarled, 'but I need an army to finish off Ragnall. Ceaster will have to take its chances.'

'But if the heathens come . . .' Father Wissian suggested nervously.

'The heathens won't know how big the garrison is,' I said, 'but they will know how strong the walls are. Leaving so few men here is a risk, but it's a risk I'm taking. And you'll have men from the fyrd. Godwin! Use the sacks for the bread too!'

I was taking just over three hundred men, leaving behind barely enough troops to defend the ramparts of Ceaster and Brunanburh. It might sound simple to say I was leading three hundred men, as if all we had to do was mount our horses, leave Ceaster and ride eastwards, but it takes time to organise the army. We had to carry our own food. We would be riding into country where food could be bought, but never enough for all of us. The Northmen would steal what they wanted, but we paid because we rode in our own country, and so I had a packhorse laden with silver coins and guarded by two of my warriors. And we would number well over three hundred because many men would take servants, some would take the women they could not bear to leave behind, and then there were the boys to lead the spare horses and the herd of packhorses laden with armour, weapons, and the sacks of salted meat, smoked fish, hard-baked bread, and thick-rinded cheese.

'You do know what happens at Easter!' Ceolnoth demanded sternly.

'Of course I know,' I said, 'we make babies.'

'That is the most ridiculous . . .' Ceolberht began to protest, then went silent when his brother glared at him.

'It's my favourite feast,' I continued happily. 'Easter is baby-making day!'

'It is the most solemn and joyous feast of the Christian year,' Ceolnoth lectured me, 'solemn because we remember the agony of our Saviour's death, and joyous because of His resurrection.'

'Amen,' Father Wissian said.

Wissian was another Mercian, a young man with a shock of prematurely white hair. I rather liked Wissian, but he was cowed by the twins. Father Cuthbert stood beside him, blind and smiling. He had heard this argument before and was enjoying it. I glowered at the priests. 'Why is it called Easter?' I demanded.

'Because our Lord died and was resurrected in the east, of course,' Ceolnoth answered.

'Horse shit,' I said, 'it's called Easter because it's Eostre's feast, and you know it.'

'It is not . . .' Ceolberht began indignantly.

'Eostre!' I overrode him. 'Goddess of the spring! Goddess of baby-making! You Christians stole both her name and her feast!'

'Ignore him,' Ceolnoth said, but he knew I was right. Eostre is the goddess of the spring, and a merry goddess she is too, which means many babies are born in January. The Christians, of course, try to stop the merriment, claiming that the name Easter is all about the east, but as usual the Christians are spouting nonsense. Easter is Eostre's feast and despite all the sermons that insisted feast was solemn and sacred, most folk had a half memory of their duties towards Eostre and so the babies duly arrived every winter. In the three years I had lived at Ceaster I had always insisted on a fair to celebrate Eostre's feast. There were fire-walkers and jugglers, musicians and acrobats, wrestling matches and horse races. There were booths selling everything from pottery to jewellery, and there was dancing. The priests disapproved of the dancing, but folk danced anyway, and the dances ensured that the babies came on time.

But this year was going to be different. The

Christians had decided to create a Bishop of Ceaster and had set Easter as the date of his enthronement. The new bishop was called Leofstan, and I had never met the man and knew little of him except that he came from Wessex and had an exaggerated reputation for piety. He was a scholar, I had been told, and was married, but on being named as the new bishop he had famously sworn to fast three days in every week and to stay celibate. Blind Father Cuthbert, who revelled in nonsense, had told me of the new bishop's oath, knowing it would amuse me. 'He did what?' I asked.

'He vowed to give up pleasuring his wife, lord.'

'Maybe she's old and ugly?'

'Men say she's comely,' Father Cuthbert said dubiously, 'but our bishop-to-be says that our Lord gave up His life for us and the very least we can do is to give up our carnal pleasures for Him.'

'The man's an idiot,' I had said.

'I can't agree with you,' Cuthbert said slyly, 'but yes, lord, Leofstan's an idiot.'

The idiot's consecration was what had brought Ceolnoth and Ceolberht to Ceaster. They were planning the ceremonies and had invited abbots, bishops, and priests from all across Mercia, from Wessex, and from even further afield in Frankia. 'We need to ensure their safety,' Ceolnoth insisted now. 'We have promised them the city will be defended against any attack. Eighty men isn't enough!' he said scornfully.

I pretended to be worried. 'You mean your churchmen might all be slaughtered if the Danes come?'

'Of course!' Then he saw my smile and that only increased his fury. 'We need five hundred men! King Edward might come! The Lady Æthelflaed will certainly be here!'

'She won't,' I said. 'She'll be with me, fighting Ragnall. If the Northmen come you'd better just pray. Your god is supposed to work miracles, isn't he?'

Æthelflaed, I knew, would come north as soon as my messengers reached Gleawecestre. Those same messengers would then order new ships from the boatbuilders along the Sæfern. I would have preferred to buy ships from Lundene where the yards employed skilled Frisian boatbuilders, but for now we would buy three vessels from the shipwrights on the Sæfern. 'Tell them I want their smaller ships,' I told the messengers, 'no more than thirty oars on each side!' The Sæfern men built heavy ships, wide and deep, which could ride the rough seas to Ireland, but such vessels would be cumbersome in a shallow river. There was no hurry. The men who would man those ships were riding east with me, and in our absence I ordered Rædwald to start rebuilding the wharf. He would do the job well, though slowly.

I had sent my son ahead with fifty men, all mounted on light fast horses. They had left the day before and their job was to pursue the enemy, attack their forage parties and ambush their scouts. Beadwulf was already following Ragnall's men, but his task was simply to report back to me where the army went ashore, and that must happen soon because the river became unnavigable after a few miles. Once ashore, Ragnall's army would spread out to find horses, food, and slaves, and my son had been sent to slow them, annoy them, and, if he was sensible, avoid a major fight with them.

'What if Ragnall goes north?' Finan asked me.

'I told Uhtred not to leave Saxon land,' I said. I knew what Finan was asking. If Ragnall chose to take his men north he would be entering Northumbria, a land ruled by the Danes, and if my son and his war-band followed they would find themselves in enemy land, outnumbered and surrounded.

'And you think he'll obey you?' Finan asked.

'He's no fool.'

Finan half smiled. 'He's like you.'

'Meaning?'

'Meaning he's like you, so as like or not he'll chase Ragnall halfway to Scotland before he comes to his senses.' He stooped to tighten his saddle's girth. 'Besides, how can you tell where Mercia ends and Northumbria begins?'

'He'll be careful,' I said.

'He'd better be, lord.' He put his foot in the stirrup and swung up into the saddle where he settled himself, collected the reins, and turned to look at the four priests. They were talking to each other, heads bowed, hands gesticulating. 'What did they want?'

'For me to leave an army here to protect their damned bishops.'

Finan sneered at that, then turned and stared northwards. 'Life's a crock of shit, isn't it?' he said bitterly. I said nothing, just watched as Finan loosened his sword, Soul-Stealer, in its scabbard. He had buried his son or nephew beside the river, digging the grave himself and marking it with a stone. 'Families,' he said bitterly, 'now let's go and kill more of the bastards.'

I pulled myself up into the saddle. The sun was up now, but still low in the east where it was shrouded by grey clouds. A chill wind blew from the Irish Sea. Men were mounting and the last spears were being tied to packhorses when a horn sounded from the northern gate. That horn only sounded if the sentries had seen something worth my attention and so I kicked my horse up the main street and my men, thinking we were leaving, followed. The horn sounded again as I cantered past Ceaster's great hall, then a third time as I slid from the saddle and climbed the stone steps that led to the rampart above the gate arch.

A dozen horsemen were approaching, spurring their stallions across the Roman cemetery, coming as fast as they could ride. I recognised my son's grey horse, then saw Beadwulf was with him. They slewed to a stop just beyond the ditch and my son looked up. 'They're at Eads Byrig,' he called.

'A thousand of the bastards,' Beadwulf added.

I instinctively looked eastwards, even though I knew Eads Byrig was not visible from the gateway. But it was close. It lay no further to the east than Brunanburh did to the west. 'They're digging in!' my son shouted.

'What is it?' Finan had joined me on the rampart.

'Ragnall's not going north,' I said, 'and he's not going south.'

'Then where?'

'He's here,' I said, still staring east. 'He's coming here.'

To Ceaster.

Eads Byrig lay on a low ridge that ran north and south. The hill was simply a higher part of the ridge, a grassy hump rising like an island above the oaks and sycamores that grew thick about its base. The slopes were mostly shallow, an easy stroll, except that the ancient people who had lived in Britain long before my ancestors had crossed the sea, indeed before even the Romans came, had ringed the hill with walls and ditches. They were not stone walls, as the Romans had made at Lundene and Ceaster, nor wooden palisades as we build, but walls made of earth. They had dug a deep ditch all around the hill's long crest and thrown the soil up to make a steep embankment inside the ditch, then made a second ditch and wall inside the first, and though the long years and the hard rain had eroded the double walls and half filled the two ditches, the defences were still formidable. The hill's name meant Ead's stronghold, and doubtless some Saxon called Ead had once lived there and used the walls to defend his herds and home, but the stronghold was much older than its name suggested. There were such grassy forts on high hills throughout Britain, proof that men have fought for this land as long as men have lived here, and I sometimes wonder whether a thousand years from now folk will still be making walls in Britain and setting sentries in the night to watch for enemies in the dawn.

It was difficult to approach Ead's stronghold. The woods were dense and an ambush among the trees was all too easy. My son's men had managed to get close to the ridge before Ragnall's numbers forced them away. They had retreated to the open pastureland to the west of the forest, where I found them watching the thick woods. 'They're deepening the ditches,' one of Beadwulf's men greeted my arrival, 'we could see the bastards shovelling away, lord.'

'Cutting trees too, lord,' Beadwulf added.

I could hear the axes working. They sounded far off, muffled by the spring foliage. 'He's making a burh,' I said. Ragnall's troops would be deepening the old ditches and raising the earth walls, on top of which they would build a wooden palisade. 'Where did the ships land?' I asked Beadwulf.

'By the fish traps, lord.' He nodded to the north, showing where he meant, then turned as a distant crash announced a tree's fall. 'They went aground before that. They took a fair time to get their ships off the mud.'

'The ships are still there?'

He shrugged. 'They were at dawn.'

'They'll be guarded,' Finan warned me. He suspected I was thinking of attacking Ragnall's ships and burning them, but that was the last thing I had in mind.

'I'd rather he went back to Ireland,' I said. 'So leave his ships alone. I don't want to trap the bastard here.' I grimaced. 'It looks as if the priests will get what they want.'

'Which is?' my son asked.

'If Ragnall stays here,' I said, 'then so must we.' I had thought to take my three hundred men eastwards to Liccelfeld where I could meet the forces Æthelflaed would send from Gleawecestre, but if Ragnall was staying at Eads Byrig then I must stay to protect Ceaster. I sent all the pack-horses back to the city, and sent more messengers south to tell the reinforcements to abandon their march on Liccelfeld and to come to Ceaster instead. And then I waited.

I was waiting for Æthelflaed and her army of Mercia. I had three hundred men, and Ragnall had over a thousand, and more were joining him every day. It was frustrating. It was maddening. The garrison at Brunanburh could only watch as the beast-prowed ships rowed up the Mærse. There were two ships the first day and three the second, and still more every following day, ships heavy with men who had come from Ragnall's furthest islands. Other men came by land, travelling from the Danish steadings in Northumbria, lured to Eads Byrig by the promise of Saxon silver, Saxon land, and Saxon slaves. Ragnall's army grew larger and I could do nothing.

He outnumbered me by at least three to one, and to attack him I needed to take men through the forest that surrounded Eads Byrig, and that forest was a death-trap. An old Roman road ran just south of the hill, but the trees had invaded the road, and once among their thick foliage we would not be able to see more than thirty or forty paces. I sent a party of scouts into the trees and only three of those four men returned. The fourth was beheaded, and his naked body thrown out onto the pastureland. My son wanted to take all our men and crash through the woodland in search of a fight. 'What good will that do?' I asked him.

'They must have men guarding their ships,' he said, 'and others building their new wall.'

'So?'

'So we won't have to fight all his men. Maybe just half of them?'

'You're an idiot,' I said, 'because that's exactly what he wants us to do.'

'He wants to attack Ceaster,' my son insisted.

'No, that's what I want him to do.'

And that was the mutual trap Ragnall and I had set each other. He might outnumber me, but even so he would be reluctant to assault Ceaster. His younger brother had attempted to take the city and had lost his right eye and the best part of his army in the attempt. Ceaster's walls were formidable. Ragnall's men needed to cross a deep, flooded ditch spiked with elm stakes, then climb a wall twice the height of a man while we rained spears, axes, boulders and buckets of shit on them. He would lose. His men would die under our ramparts. I wanted him to come to the city, I wanted him to attack our walls, I wanted to kill his men at Ceaster's defences, and he knew I wanted that, which is why he did not come.

But we could not assault him either. Even if I could lead every fit man through the forest unscathed I would still have to climb Eads Byrig and cross the high ditch and clamber up the earthen bank where a new wall was being made, and Ragnall's Northmen and Irishmen would outnumber us and have a great killing that their poets would turn into a triumphant battle song. What would they call it? The Song of Ragnall the Mighty? It would tell of blades falling, foemen dying, of a ditch filled with blood, and of Uhtred, great Uhtred, cut down in his battle glory. Ragnall wanted that song, he wanted me to attack him, and I knew he wanted it, which is why I did not oblige him. I waited.

We were not idle. I had men driving new sharpened stakes into the ditch around Ceaster, and other men riding south and east to raise the fyrd, that army of farmers and free men who could man a burh wall even if they could not fight a Norse shield wall in open battle. And each day I sent a hundred horsemen to circle Eads Byrig, riding well south of the great forest and then curling northwards. I led that patrol on the third day, the same day that four more ships rowed up the Mærse, each holding at least forty warriors.

We wore mail and carried weapons, though we left our heavy shields behind. I wore a rusted coat of mail and an old undecorated helmet. I carried Serpent-Breath, but left my standard-bearer behind in Ceaster. I did not ride in my full war-glory because I did not seek a fight. We were scouting, looking for Ragnall's forage parties and for his patrolling scouts. He had sent no men towards Ceaster, which was puzzling, so what was he doing?

We crossed the ridge four or five miles south of Ragnall's hill. Once on the low crest I spurred my horse to the top of a knoll and stared northwards, though I could see almost nothing of what happened on that distant hilltop. I knew the palisade was being built there, that men were pounding oak trunks into the summit of the earthen bank, and just as surely Ragnall knew I would not waste my men's lives by attacking that wall. So what was he hoping for? That I would be a fool, lose patience and attack anyway?

'Lord,' Sihtric interrupted my thoughts. He was pointing north-east, and I saw, perhaps a mile away, a dozen horsemen. More riders were further off, perhaps a score of them, all of them heading eastwards.

'So they've found horses,' I said. From what we had seen, and from our questioning of the prisoners we had taken, the enemy had brought very few horses on their ships, but the forage parties, I assumed that was what the horsemen were, proved that they had managed to capture a few, and those few, in turn, could ride further afield to find more, though by now the countryside was alerted to their presence. There were few steadings here because this was border country, land that belonged neither to the Danes of Northumbria nor to the Saxons of Mercia, and what folk lived here would already have left their homes and driven their livestock south to the nearest burh. Fear ruled this land now.

We rode on eastwards, dropping from the ridge into wooded country where we followed an overgrown drover's path. I sent no scouts ahead, reckoning that Ragnall's men did not have enough horses to send a war-band large enough to confront us, nor did we see the enemy, not even when we turned north and rode into the pastureland where we had glimpsed the horsemen earlier.

'They're staying out of our way,' Sihtric said, sounding disappointed.

'Wouldn't you?'

'The more he kills of us, lord, the fewer to fight on Ceaster's walls.'

I ignored that foolish answer. Ragnall had no

intention of killing his men beneath Ceaster's ramparts, not yet anyway. So what did he plan? I looked back in puzzlement. It was a dry morning, or at least it was not raining, though the air felt damp and the wind was chill, but it had rained hard in the night and the ground was sopping wet, yet I had seen no hoofmarks crossing the drover's path. If Ragnall wanted horses and food then he would find the richer steadings to our south, deeper inside Mercia, yet it seemed he had sent no men that way. Perhaps I had missed the tracks, but I doubted I could have overlooked something so obvious. And Ragnall was no fool. He knew reinforcements must join us from the south, yet it seemed he had no patrols searching for those new enemies.

Why?

Because, I thought, he did not care about our reinforcements. I was staring northwards, seeing nothing there except thick woods and damp fields, and I was thinking what Ragnall had achieved. He had taken away our small fleet, which meant we could not cross the Mærse easily, not unless we rode even further eastwards to find an unguarded crossing. He was making a fortress on Eads Byrig, a stronghold that was virtually impregnable until we had sufficient men to overwhelm his army. And there was only one reason to fortify Eads Byrig, and that was to threaten Ceaster, yet he was sending no patrols towards the city, nor was he trying to stop any reinforcements reaching the garrison. 'Is there water on Eads Byrig?' I asked Sihtric.

'There's a spring to the south-east of the hill,' he said, sounding dubious, 'but it's just a trickle, lord. Not enough for a whole army.'

'He's not strong enough to attack Ceaster,' I said, thinking aloud, 'and he knows we're not going to waste men against Eads Byrig's walls.'

'He just wants a fight!' Sihtric said dismissively.

'No,' I said, 'he doesn't. Not with us.' There was an idea in my head. I could not say it aloud because I did not understand it yet, but I sensed what Ragnall was doing. Eads Byrig was a deception, I thought, and we were not the enemy, not yet. We would be in time, but not yet. I turned on Sihtric. 'Take the men back to Ceaster,' I told him. 'Go back by the same path we came on. Let the bastards see you. And tell Finan to patrol to the edge of the forest tomorrow.'

'Lord?' he asked again.

'Tell Finan it should be a big patrol! A hundred and fifty men at least! Let Ragnall see them! Tell him to patrol from the road to the river, make him think we're planning an attack from the west.'

'An attack from the . . .' he began.

'Just do it,' I snarled. 'Berg! You come with me!'

Ragnall had stopped us from crossing the river and he was making us concentrate all our attention on Eads Byrig. He seemed to be behaving cautiously, making a great fortress and deliberately not provoking us by sending war-bands to the south, yet everything I knew about Ragnall suggested he was anything but a cautious man. He was a warrior. He moved fast, struck hard, and called himself a king. He was a gold-giver, a lord, a patron of warriors. Men would follow him so long as his swords and spears took captives and captured farmland, and no man became rich by building a fortress in a forest and inviting attack.

'Tell Finan I'll be back tomorrow or the day after,' I told Sihtric, then beckoned to Berg and rode eastwards. 'Tomorrow or the day after!' I shouted back to Sihtric.

Berg Skallagrimmrson was a Norseman who had sworn loyalty to me, a loyalty he had proven in the three years since I had saved his life on a beach in Wales. He could have ridden north any time to the kingdom of Northumbria and there found a Dane or a fellow Norseman who would welcome a young, strong warrior, but Berg had stayed true. He was a thin-faced, blue-eyed young man, serious and thoughtful. He wore his hair long in Norse fashion, and had persuaded Sihtric's daughter to make a scribble on his left cheek with oak-gall ink and a needle. 'What is it?' I had asked him as the scars were still healing.

'It's a wolf's head, lord!' he had said, sounding indignant. The wolf's head was my symbol and the inked device was his way of showing loyalty, but even when it healed it looked more like a smeared pig's head.

Now the two of us rode eastwards. I still did not

fear any enemy war-band because I had a suspicion of what Ragnall really wanted, and it was that suspicion that kept us riding into the afternoon, by which time we had turned north and were following a Roman road that led to Northumbria. We were still well to the east of Eads Byrig, but as the afternoon waned we climbed a low hill and I saw where a bridge carried the road across the river, and there, clustered close to two cottages that had been built on the Mærse's north bank, were men in mail. Men with spears. 'How many?' I asked Berg, whose eyes were younger than mine.

'At least forty, lord.'

'He doesn't want us to cross the river, does he?' I suggested. 'Which means we need to get across.'

We rode east for an hour, keeping a cautious eye for enemies, and at dusk we turned north and came to where the Mærse slid slow between pastureland. 'Can your horse swim?' I asked Berg.

'We'll find out, lord.'

The river was wide here, at least fifty paces, and its banks were earthen bluffs. The water was murky, but I sensed it was deep and so, rather than risk swimming the beasts over, we turned back upstream until we discovered a place where a muddy track led into the river from the south and another climbed the northern bank, suggesting this was a ford. It was certainly no major crossing place, but rather a spot where some farmer had discovered he could cross with his cattle, but I suspected the river was usually lower. Rain had swollen it.

'We have to cross,' I said, and spurred my horse into the water. The river came up to my boots, then above them, and I could feel the horse struggling against the current. He slipped once, and I lurched sideways, thought I must be thrown into the water, but somehow the stallion found his footing and surged ahead, driven more by fear than by my urging. Berg came behind and kicked his horse faster so that he passed me and left the river before I did, his horse flailing up the far bank in a flurry of water and mud.

'I hate crossing rivers,' I growled as I joined him.

We found a spinney of ash trees a mile beyond the river and we spent the night there, the horses tethered while we tried to sleep. Berg, being young, slept like the dead, but I was awake much of the night, listening to the wind in the leaves. I had not dared light a fire. This land, like the country south of the Mærse, appeared deserted, but that did not mean no enemy was near, and so I shivered through the darkness. I slept fitfully as the dawn approached, waking to see Berg carefully cutting a lump of bread into two pieces. 'For you, lord,' he said, holding out the larger piece.

I took the smaller, then stood, aching in every bone. I walked to the edge of the trees and gazed out at greyness. Grey sky, grey land, grey mist. It was the wolf-light of dawn. I heard Berg moving behind me. 'Shall I saddle the horses, lord?' he asked.

'Not yet.'

He came and stood beside me. 'Where are we, lord?'

'Northumbria,' I said. 'Everything north of the Mærse is Northumbria.'

'Your country, lord.'

'My country,' I agreed. I was born in Northumbria and I hope to die in Northumbria, though my birth had been on the eastern coast, far from these mist-shrouded fields by the Mærse. My land is Bebbanburg, the fortress by the sea, which had been treacherously stolen by my uncle and, though he was long dead, the great stronghold was still held by his son. One day, I promised myself, I would slaughter my cousin and take back my birthright. It was a promise I made every day of my life.

Berg gazed into the grey dampness. 'Who rules here?' he asked.

I half smiled at the question. 'Tell me,' I said, 'have you heard of Sygfrothyr?'

'No, lord.'

'Knut Onehand?'

'No, lord.'

'Halfdan Othirson?'

'No, lord.'

'Eowels the Strong?'

'No, lord.'

'Eowels wasn't that strong,' I said wryly, 'because he was killed by Ingver Brightsword. Have you heard of Ingver?'

'No, lord.'

'Sygfrothyr, Knut, Halfdan, Eowels, and Ingver,' I repeated the names, 'and in the last ten years each of those men has called himself King of Jorvik. And only one of them, Ingver, is alive today. You know where Jorvik is?'

'To the north, lord. A city.'

'It was a great city once,' I said bleakly. 'The Romans made it.'

'Like Ceaster, lord?' he asked earnestly. Berg knew little of Britain. He had served Rognvald, a Norseman who had died in a welter of bloodshed on a Welsh beach. Since then Berg had served me, living in Ceaster and fighting the cattle-raiders who came from Northumbria or the Welsh kingdoms. He was eager to learn though.

'Jorvik is like Ceaster,' I said, 'and like Ceaster its strength lies in its walls. It guards a river, but the man who rules in Jorvik can claim to rule Northumbria. Ingver Brightsword is King of Jorvik, but he calls himself King of Northumbria.'

'And is he?'

'He pretends he is,' I said, 'but in truth he's just a chieftain in Jorvik. But no one else can call himself King of Northumbria unless he holds Jorvik.'

'But it's not strong?' Berg asked.

'Eoferwic's walls are strong,' I said, using the Saxon name for Jorvik, 'they're very strong! They're formidable! My father died attacking those walls. And the city lies in rich country. The man who rules Eoferwic can be a gold-giver, he can buy men, he can give estates, he can breed horses, he can command an army.'

'And this is what King Ingver does?'

'Ingver couldn't command a dog to piss,' I sneered. 'He has maybe two hundred warriors. And outside the walls? He has nothing. Other men rule beyond the walls, and one day one of those men will kill Ingver as Ingver killed Eowels, and the new man will call himself king. Sygfrothyr, Knut, Halfdan, and Eowels, they all called themselves King of Northumbria and they were all killed by a rival. Northumbria isn't a kingdom, it's a pit of rats and terriers.'

'Like Ireland,' Berg said.

'Like Ireland?'

'A country of little kings,' he said. He frowned for a moment. 'Sometimes one calls himself the High King? And maybe he is, but there are still many little kings, and they squabble like dogs, and you think such dogs will be easy to kill, but when you attack them? They come together.'

'There's no high king in Northumbria,' I said, 'not yet.'

'There will be?'

'Ragnall,' I said.

'Ah!' he said, understanding. 'And one day we must take this land?'

'One day,' I said, and I wanted that day to be soon, but Æthelflaed, who ruled Mercia, insisted that first we drive the Danes from her country. She wanted to restore the ancient frontier of

Mercia, and only then lead an army into Northumbria, and even then she would not invade unless she had her brother's blessing, but now Ragnall had come and threatened to make the conquest of the north even more difficult.

We saddled the horses and rode slowly westwards. The Mærse made great lazy loops to our left, twisting through overgrown water meadows. No one farmed these lands. There had been Danes and Norsemen settled here once, their steadings fat in a fat land, but we had driven them northwards away from Ceaster, and thistles now grew tall where cattle had grazed. Two heron flew downriver. A light rain blew from the distant sea.

'The Lady Æthelflaed is coming, lord?' Berg asked me as we pushed the horses through a gap in a ragged hedge, then across a flooded ditch. The mist had lifted, though there were still patches above the river's wide bends.

'She's coming!' I said, and surprised myself by feeling a distinct pang of pleasure at the thought of seeing Æthelflaed again. 'She was coming anyway for this nonsense with the new bishop.' The enthronement was the sort of ceremony she enjoyed, though how anyone could endure three or four hours of chanting monks and ranting priests was beyond my understanding, just as it was beyond my understanding to know why bishops needed thrones. They would be demanding crowns next. 'Now she'll be bringing her whole army as well,' I said.

'And we'll fight Ragnall?'

'She'll want to drive him out of Mercia,' I said, 'and if he stays behind his new walls that will be a bloody business.' I had turned north towards a low hill that I remembered from raids we had made across the river. The hill was crowned with a stand of pine trees, and from its summit we could see Ceaster on a clear day. There was no chance of seeing the city on this grey day, but I could see Eads Byrig rising green from the trees on the river's far side, and I could see the raw timber of the new wall atop the fort's embankment, and, much closer, I could see Ragnall's fleet clustered at a great bend of the Mærse.

And I saw a bridge.

At first I was not sure what I was seeing, but I asked Berg, whose eyes were so much younger than mine. He gazed for a while, frowned, and finally nodded. 'They make a bridge with their boats, lord.'

It was a crude bridge made by mooring ships hull to hull so that they stretched across the river and carried a crude plank roadway on their decks. So many horses and men had already used the makeshift bridge that they had worn a new road in the fields on this side of the river, a muddy streak that showed dark against the pale pasture and then fanned out into lesser streaks that all led northwards. There were men riding the tracks now, three small groups spurring away from the Mærse and going deeper into Northumbria, and one large band of horsemen travelling south towards the river.

And on the river's southern bank where the trees grew dense there was smoke. At first I took it for a thickening of the river mist, but the longer I looked the more I became convinced that there were campfires in the woodland. A lot of fires, sifting their smoke above the leaves, and that smoke told me that Ragnall was keeping many of his men beside the Mærse. There was a garrison at Eads Byrig, a garrison busy making a palisade, but not enough water there for the whole army. And that army, instead of making tracks south into Mercia, was trampling new paths northwards. 'We can go home now,' I said.

'Already?' Berg sounded surprised.

'Already,' I said. Because I knew what Ragnall was doing.

We went back the way we had come. We rode slowly, sparing the horses. A small rain blew from behind us, carried by a cold morning wind from the Irish Sea, and that made me remember Finan's words that Ragnall had made a pact with the Uí Néill. The Irish rarely crossed the sea except to trade and, once in a while, to look for slaves along Britain's western coast. I knew there were Irish settlements in Scotland, and even some on the wild western shore of Northumbria, but I had never seen Irish warriors in Mercia or Wessex. We had enough trouble with the Danes and the Norse, let alone dealing with the Irish. It was true that

Ragnall only had one crew of Irishmen, but Finan boasted that one crew of his countrymen was worth three from any other tribe. 'We fight like mad dogs,' he had told me proudly. 'If it comes to a battle then Ragnall will have his Irish at the front. He'll let them loose on us.' I had seen Finan fight often enough and I believed him.

'Lord!' Berg startled me. 'Behind us, lord!'

I turned to see three riders following us. We were in open country with nowhere to hide, but I cursed myself for carelessness. I had been daydreaming, trying to decide what Ragnall would do, and I had not looked behind. If we had seen the three men earlier we might have turned away into a copse or thicket, but now there was no avoiding the horsemen, who were coming fast.

'I'll talk to them,' I told Berg, then turned my horse and waited.

The three were young, none more than twenty years old. Their horses were good, spirited and brisk. All three wore mail, though none had a shield or helmet. They spread out as they approached, and then curbed their horses some ten paces away. They wore their hair long and had the inked patterns on their faces that told me they were Northmen, but what else did I expect on this side of the river? 'I wish you good morning,' I said politely.

The young man in the centre of the three kicked his horse forward. His mail was good, his sword scabbard was decorated with silver panels, while the hammer about his neck glinted with gold. He had long black hair, oiled and smoothed, then gathered with a black ribbon at the nape of his neck. He looked at my horse, then up at me, then gazed at Serpent-Breath. 'That's a good sword, Grandad.'

'It's a good sword,' I said mildly.

'Old men don't need swords,' he said, and his two companions laughed.

'My name,' I still spoke softly, 'is Hefring Fenirson and this is my son, Berg Hefringson.'

'Tell me, Hefring Fenirson,' the young man said, 'why you ride eastwards.'

'Why not?'

'Because Jarl Ragnall is calling men to his side, and you ride away from him.'

'Jarl Ragnall has no need of old men,' I said.

'True, but he has need of young men.' He looked at Berg.

'My son has no skill with a sword,' I said. In truth Berg was lethally fast with a blade, but there was an innocence to his face that suggested he might have no love for fighting. 'And who,' I asked respectfully, 'are you?'

He hesitated, plainly reluctant to give me his name, then shrugged as if to suggest it did not matter. 'Othere Hardgerson,' he said.

'You came with the ships from Ireland?' I asked.

'Where we are from is none of your concern,' he said. 'Did you swear loyalty to Jarl Ragnall?'

'I swear loyalty to no man,' I said, and that was true. Æthelflaed had my oath.

Othere sneered at that. 'You are a jarl, perhaps?'

'I am a farmer.'

'A farmer,' he said derisively, 'has no need of a fine horse. He has no need of a sword. He has no need of a coat of mail, even that rusty coat. And as for your son,' he kicked his horse past mine to stare at Berg, 'if he cannot fight then he too has no need of mail, sword or horse.'

'You wish to buy them?' I asked.

'Buy them!' Othere laughed at that suggestion. 'I will give you a choice, old man,' he said, turning back to me. 'You can ride with us and swear loyalty to Jarl Ragnall or you can give us your horses, weapons, and mail, and go on your way. Which is it to be?'

I knew Othere's kind. He was a young warrior, raised to fight and taught to despise any man who did not earn a living with a sword. He was bored. He had come across the sea on the promise of land and plunder, and though Ragnall's present caution was doubtless justified, it had left Othere frustrated. He was being forced to wait while Ragnall gathered more men, and those men were evidently being recruited from Northumbria, from the Danes and Norsemen who had settled that riven country. Othere, ordered to the dull business of patrolling the river's northern bank to guard against any Saxon incursion across the Mærse, wanted to start the conquest of Britain, and if Ragnall would not lead him into battle then he would seek a fight of his own. Besides, Othere was an over-confident young bully, and what did he have to fear from an old man?

I suppose I was old. My beard had turned grey and my face showed the years, but even so, Othere and his two companions should have been more cautious. What farmer would ride a swift horse? Or carry a great sword? Or wear mail? 'I give you a choice, Othere Hardgerson,' I said, 'you can either ride away and thank whatever gods you worship that I let you live, or you can take the sword from me. Your choice, boy.'

He gazed at me for a heartbeat, looking for that moment as if he did not believe what he had just heard, then he laughed. 'On horse or on foot, old man?'

'Your choice, boy,' I said again, and this time invested the word 'boy' with pure scorn.

'Oh, you're dead, old man,' he retorted. 'On foot, you old bastard.' He swung easily from the saddle and dropped lithely to the damp grass. I assumed he had chosen to fight on foot because his horse was not battle-trained, but that suited me. I also dismounted, but did it slowly as though my old bones and aching muscles hampered me. 'My sword,' Othere said, 'is called Blood-Drinker. A man should know what weapon sends him to his grave.'

'My sword . . .'

'Why do I need to know the name of your sword?' he interrupted me, then laughed again as he pulled Blood-Drinker from her scabbard. He was right-handed. 'I shall make it quick, old man. Are you ready?' The last question was mocking. He did not care if I was ready, instead he was sneering because I had unsheathed Serpent-Breath and was holding her clumsily, as if she felt unfamiliar in my hand. I even tried holding her in my left hand before putting her back in my right, all to suggest to him that I was unpractised. I was so convincing that he lowered his blade and shook his head. 'You're being stupid, old man. I don't want to kill you, just give me the sword.'

'Gladly,' I said, and moved towards him. He held out his left hand and I sliced Serpent-Breath up with a twist of my wrist and knocked that hand away, brought the blade back hard to beat Blood-Drinker aside, then lunged once to drive Serpent-Breath's tip against his breast. She struck the mail above his breastbone, driving him back, and he half stumbled and roared in anger as he swept his sword around in a hay-making slice that should have sheared my head from my body, but I already had Serpent-Breath lifted in the parry, the blades struck and I took one more step forward and slammed her hilt into his face. He managed to half turn away so that the blow landed on his jawbone rather than his nose.

He tried to cut my neck, but had no room for the stroke, and I stepped back, flicking Serpent-Breath up so that her tip cut through his chin, though not with any great force. She drew blood and the sight of it must have prompted one of his companions to draw his sword, and I heard but did not see, a clash of blades, and knew Berg was fighting. There was a gasp behind me, another ringing clash of steel on steel, and Othere's eyes widened as he stared at whatever happened. 'Come, boy,' I said, 'you're fighting me, not Berg.'

'Then to the grave, old man,' he snarled, and stepped forward, sword swinging, but that was easy to parry. He had no great sword-craft. He was probably faster than I was, he was, after all, younger, but I had a lifetime of sword knowledge. He pressed me, cutting again and again, and I parried every stroke, and only after six or seven of his savage swings did I suddenly step back, lowering my blade, and his sword hissed past me, unbalancing him, and I rammed Serpent-Breath forward, skewering his sword shoulder, piercing the mail and mangling the flesh beneath, and I saw his arm drop, and I backswung my blade onto his neck and held it there, blood welling along Serpent-Breath's edge. 'My name, boy, is Uhtred of Bebbanburg, and this sword is called Serpent-Breath.'

'Lord!' He dropped to his knees, unable to lift his arm. 'Lord,' he said again, 'I didn't know!'

'Do you always bully old men?'

'I didn't know!' he pleaded.

'Hold your sword tight, boy,' I said, 'and look for me in Valhalla,' and I grimaced as I dragged the blade back, sawing at his neck, then thrust it forward, still sawing and he made a whimpering noise as his blood spurted far across the damp pasture. He made a choking sound. 'Hold onto Blood-Drinker!' I snarled at him. He seemed to nod, then the light went from his eyes and he fell forward. The sword was still in his hand, so I would meet him again across the ale-board of the gods.

Berg had disarmed one of the remaining horsemen, while the other was already two hundred paces away and spurring his horse frantically. 'Should I kill this one, lord?' Berg asked me.

I shook my head. 'He can take a message.' I walked to the young man's horse and hauled him hard downwards. He fell from the saddle and sprawled on the turf. 'Who are you?' I demanded.

He gave a name, I forget what it was now. He was a boy, younger than Berg, and he answered our questions willingly enough. Ragnall was making a great wall at Eads Byrig, but he had also made an encampment beside the river where the boats bridged the water. He was collecting men there, making a new army. 'And where will the army go?' I asked the boy.

'To take the Saxon town,' he said.

'Ceaster?'

He shrugged. He did not know the name. 'The town nearby, lord.'

'Are you making ladders?'

'Ladders? No, lord.'

We stripped Othere's corpse of its mail, took his sword and horse, then did the same to the boy Berg had disarmed. He was not badly wounded, more frightened than hurt, and he shivered as he watched us remount. 'Tell Ragnall,' I told him, 'that the Saxons of Mercia are coming. Tell him that his dead will number in the thousands. Tell him that his own death is just days away. Tell him that promise comes from Uhtred of Bebbanburg.'

He nodded, too frightened to speak.

'Say my name aloud, boy,' I ordered him, 'so I know you can repeat it to Ragnall.'

'Uhtred of Bebbanburg,' he stammered.

'Good boy,' I said, and then we rode home.

CHAPTER 3

Bishop Leofstan arrived the next day. Of course he was not the bishop yet, for the time being he was just Father Leofstan, but everyone excitedly called him Bishop Leofstan and kept telling each other that he was a living saint and a scholar. The living saint's arrival was announced by Eadger, one of my men who was with a work party in the quarry south of the River Dee where they were loading rocks onto a cart, rocks that would eventually be piled on Ceaster's ramparts as a greeting to any Northman who tried to clamber over our walls. I was fairly certain Ragnall planned no such assault, but if he lost his mind and did try, I wanted him to enjoy a proper welcome. 'There's at least eighty of the bastards,' Eadger told me.

'Priests?'

'There are plenty enough priests,' he said dourly, 'but the rest of them?' He made the sign of the cross, 'God knows what they are, lord, but there's at least eighty of them, and they're coming.'

I walked to the southern ramparts and gazed at the road beyond the Roman bridge, but saw nothing there. The city gate was closed again. All Ceaster's gates would stay closed until Ragnall's men had left the district, but the news of the bishop's approach was spreading through the town, and Father Ceolnoth came running down the main street, clutching the skirt of his long robe up to his waist. 'We should open the gates!' he shouted. 'He is come unto the gate of my people! Even unto Jerusalem!'

I looked at Eadger, who shrugged. 'Sounds like the scripture, lord.'

'Open the gates!' Ceolnoth shouted breathlessly.

'Why?' I called down from the fighting platform above the arch.

Ceolnoth came to an abrupt halt. He had not seen me on the ramparts. He scowled. 'Bishop Leofstan is coming!'

'The gates stay closed,' I said, then turned to look across the river. I could hear singing now.

Finan and my son joined me. The Irishman stared south, frowning. 'Father Leofstan is coming,' I explained the excitement. A crowd was gathering in the street, all of them watching the big closed gates.

'So I heard,' Finan said curtly. I hesitated. I wanted to say something comforting, but what do you say to a man who has killed his own kin? Finan must have sensed my gaze because he growled. 'Stop your worrying about me, lord.'

'Who said I was worried?'

He half smiled. 'I'll kill some of Ragnall's men. Then I'll kill Conall. That'll cure whatever ails me. Sweet Jesus! What is that?'

His question was prompted by the appearance of children. They were on the road south of the bridge and, so far as I could tell, all were dressed in white robes. There must have been a score of them, and they were singing as they walked. Some of them were waving small branches in time to their song. Behind them was a group of dark-robed priests and, last of all, a shambling crowd.

Father Ceolnoth had been joined by his twin brother, and the pair had climbed to the ramparts from where they stared south with ecstatic looks on their ugly faces. 'What a holy man!' Ceolnoth said.

'The gates must be open!' Ceolberht insisted. 'Why aren't the gates open?'

'Because I haven't ordered them opened,' I growled, 'that's why.' The gates stayed closed.

The strange procession crossed the river and approached the walls. The children were waving ragged willow fronds in time to their singing, but the fronds drooped and the singing faltered when they reached the flooded ditch and realised they could go no further. Then the voices died away altogether as a young priest pushed his way through the white-robed choir and called up to us. 'The gates! Open the gates!'

'Who are you?' I called back.

The priest looked outraged. 'Father Leofstan has come!'

'Praise God,' Father Ceolnoth said, 'he is come!'

'Who?' I asked.

'Oh, dear Jesus!' Ceolberht exclaimed behind me.

'Father Leofstan!' the young priest called. 'Father Leofstan is your . . .'

'Quiet! Hush!' A skinny priest mounted on an ass called the command. He was so tall and the ass was so small that his feet almost dragged on the roadway. 'The gates must be closed,' he called to the angry young priest, 'because there are heathens close by!' He half fell off the ass, then limped across the ditch's wooden bridge. He looked up at us, smiling. 'Greetings in the name of the living God!'

'Father Leofstan!' Ceolnoth called and waved.

'Who are you?' I demanded.

'I am Leofstan, a humble servant of God,' the skinny priest answered, 'and you must be the Lord Uhtred?' I nodded for answer. 'And I humbly ask your permission to enter the city, Lord Uhtred,' Leofstan went on.

I looked at the grubby-robed choir, then at the shambolic crowd, and shuddered. Leofstan waited patiently. He was younger than I had expected, with a broad, pale face, thick lips, and dark eyes. He smiled. I had the impression that he always smiled. He waited patiently, still smiling, just staring at me. 'Who are those people?' I demanded, pointing to the shambles who followed him. They were a shambles too. I had never seen so many people in rags. There must have been almost a hundred of them; cripples, hunchbacks, the blind, and a group of evidently moon-crazed men and women who shook and gibbered and dribbled.

'These little ones,' Leofstan placed his hands on the heads of two of the children, 'are orphans, Lord Uhtred, who have been placed under my humble care.'

'And the others?' I demanded, jerking my head at the gibbering crowd.

'God's children!' Leofstan said happily. 'They are the halt, the lame, and the blind! They are beggars and outcasts! They are the hungry, the naked and the friendless! They are all God's children!'

'And what are they doing here?' I asked.

Leofstan chuckled as though my question was too easy to answer. 'Our dear Lord commands us to look after the helpless, Lord Uhtred. What does the blessed Matthew tell us? That when I was hungry you gave me food! When I was thirsty you gave me drink, when I was a stranger, you gave me shelter, when I was naked you clothed me, and when I was sick you visited me! To clothe the naked and to give help to the poor, Lord Uhtred, is to obey God! These dear people,' he swept an arm at the hopeless crowd, 'are my family!'

'Sweet suffering Jesus,' Finan murmured, sounding amused for the first time in days.

'Praise be to God,' Ceolnoth said, though without much enthusiasm.

'You do know,' I called down to Leofstan, 'that there's an army of Northmen not a half-day's march away?'

'The heathen pursue us,' he said, 'they rage all about us! Yet God shall preserve us!'

'And this city might be under siege soon,' I persevered.

'The Lord is my strength!'

'And if we are besieged,' I demanded angrily, 'how am I supposed to feed your family?'

'The Lord will provide!'

'You'll not win this one,' Finan said softly.

'And where do they live?' I asked harshly.

'The church has property here, I am told,' Leofstan answered gently, 'so the church will house them. They shall not come nigh thee!'

I growled, Finan grinned, and Leofstan still smiled. 'Open the damned gates,' I said, then went down the stone steps. I reached the street just as the new bishop limped through the long gate arch and, once inside, he dropped to his knees and kissed the roadway. 'Blessed be this place,' he intoned, 'and blessed be the folk who live here.' He struggled to his feet and smiled at me. 'I am honoured to meet you, Lord Uhtred.'

I fingered the hammer hanging at my neck, but even that symbol of paganism could not wipe the smile from his face. 'One of these priests,' I gestured at the twins, 'will show you where you live.'

'There is a fine house waiting for you, father,' Ceolnoth said.

'I need no fine house!' Leofstan exclaimed. 'Our Lord dwelt in no mansion! The foxes have holes and the birds of the sky have their nests, but something humble will suffice for us.'

'Us?' I asked. 'All of you? Your cripples as well?'

'For my dear wife and I,' Leofstan said, and gestured for a woman to step forward from among his accompanying priests. At least I assumed she was a woman, because she was so swathed in cloaks and robes that it was hard to tell what she was. Her face was invisible under the shadow of a deep hood. 'This is my dear wife Gomer,' he introduced her, and the bundle of robes nodded towards me.

'Gomer?' I thought I had misheard because it was a name I had never heard before.

'A name from the scriptures!' Leofstan said brightly. 'And you should know, lord, that my dear wife and I have taken vows of poverty and chastity. A hovel will suffice us, isn't that so, dearest?'

Dearest nodded, and there was the hint of a squeak from beneath the swathe of hoods, robes, and cloak.

'I've taken neither vow,' I said with too much vehemence. 'You're both welcome,' I added those words grudgingly because they were not true, 'but keep your damned family out of the way of my soldiers. We have work to do.'

'We shall pray for you!' He turned. 'Sing, children, sing! Wave your fronds merrily! Make a joyful noise unto the Lord as we enter his city!'

And so Bishop Leofstan came to Ceaster.

'I hate the bastard,' I said.

'No, you don't,' Finan said, 'you just don't like the fact that you like him.'

'He's a smiling, oily bastard,' I said.

'He's a famous scholar, a living saint and a very fine priest.'

'I hope he gets worms and dies.'

'They say he speaks Latin and Greek!'

'Have you ever met a Roman?' I demanded, 'or a Greek? What's the point of speaking their damned languages?'

Finan laughed. Leofstan's arrival and my splenetic hatred of the man seemed to have cheered him, and now the two of us led a hundred and thirty men on fast horses to patrol the edge of the forest that surrounded and protected Eads Byrig. So far we had ridden the southern and eastern boundaries of the trees because those were the directions Ragnall's men would take if they wanted to raid deep into Mercia, but not one of our scouts had seen any evidence of such raids. Today, the morning after Leofstan's arrival, we were close to the forest's western edge, and riding north towards the Mærse. We could see no enemy, but I was certain they could see us. There would be men standing guard at the margin of the thick woodland. 'Do you think it's true that he's celibate?' Finan asked.

'How would I know?'

'His wife probably looks like a shrivelled turnip, poor man.' He slapped at a horsefly on his stallion's neck. 'What is her name?'

'Gomer.'

'Ugly name, ugly woman,' he said, grinning.

It was a windy day with high clouds scudding

fast inland. Heavier clouds were gathering above the distant sea, but now an early-morning shaft of sunlight glinted off the Mærse's water that lay a mile ahead of us. Two more dragon-boats had rowed upriver the previous day, one with more than forty men aboard, the other smaller, but still crammed with warriors. The heavy weather threatening to the west would probably mean no boats arriving today, but still Ragnall's strength grew. What would he do with that strength?

To find the answer to that question we had brought a score of riderless horses with us. All were saddled. Anyone watching from the forest would assume they were spare mounts, but their purpose was quite different. I let my horse slow so that Beadwulf could catch up with me. 'You don't have to do this,' I told him.

'It will be easy, lord.'

'You're sure?' I asked him.

'It will be easy, lord,' he said again.

'We'll be back this time tomorrow,' I promised him.

'Same place?'

'Same place.'

'So let's do it, lord,' he suggested with a grin.

I wanted to know what happened both at Eads Byrig and at the river crossing to the north of the hill. I had seen the bridge of boats across the Mærse, and the density of the smoke rising from the woods on the river's southern bank had suggested Ragnall's main camp was there. If it was, how was it protected? And how complete were the new walls at Eads Byrig? We could have assembled a war-band and followed the Roman track that led through the forest and then turned north up the spine of the ridge, and I did not doubt we could reach Eads Byrig's low summit, but Ragnall would be waiting for just such an incursion. His scouts would give warning of our approach and his men would flood the woodland, and our withdrawal would be a desperate fight in thick trees against an outnumbering enemy. Beadwulf, though, could scout the hill and the riverside camp like a phantom and the enemy would never know he was there.

The problem was to get Beadwulf into the forest without the enemy seeing his arrival, and that was the reason we had brought the riderless horses. 'Draw swords!' I called to my men as I pulled Serpent-Breath free of her scabbard. 'Now!' I shouted.

We spurred our horses, turning them directly eastwards and galloping for the trees as though we planned to ride clean through the forest to the distant hill. We plunged into the wood, but instead of riding straight on towards Eads Byrig, we suddenly swung the horses southwards so we were riding among the trees at the edge of the woods. A horn sounded behind us. It sounded three times, and that had to be one of Ragnall's sentinels sending a warning that we had entered the great forest, but in truth we were merely thundering along its margin. A man ran from a thicket to our left and Finan swerved, chopped down once, and there was a bright red splash among the spring-green leaves. Our horses galloped into sunlight as we crossed a clearing dense with bracken, then we were back among the thick trunks, ducking under the low branches, and another of Ragnall's scouts broke cover and my son rode him down, spearing his sword into the man's back.

I galloped through a thicket of young hazel trees and elderberries. 'He's gone!' Sihtric called from behind me, and I saw Beadwulf's riderless horse off to my right. We kept going for another half-mile, but saw no more sentries. The horn still called, answered by a distant one presumably on the hill. Ragnall's men would be pulling on mail and buckling sword belts, but long before any could reach us we had swerved back to the open pasture and onto the cattle tracks that would lead us back to Ceaster. We paused in a fitful patch of sunlight, collected the riderless horses and waited, but no enemy showed at the woodland's edge. Birds that had panicked to fly above the woods as we rode through the trees went back to their roosts. The horns had gone silent and the forest was quiet again.

Ragnall's scouts would have seen a war-band go into the forest and then leave the forest. If Beadwulf had simply dropped from his saddle to find a hiding place then that enemy might have noticed that one horse had lost its rider among the trees, but I was certain no sentry would have bothered to count our riderless stallions. One more would not be noticed.

Beadwulf, I reckoned, was safely hidden among our enemies. Cloud shadow raced to engulf us and a heavy drop of rain spattered on my helmet. 'Time to go home,' I said, and so we rode back to Ceaster.

Æthelflaed arrived that same afternoon. She was leading over eight hundred men and was in a thoroughly bad temper that was not improved when she saw Eadith. The day had turned stormy, and the long tail and mane of Æthelflaed's mare, Gast, lifted to the gusting wind, as did Eadith's long red hair. 'Why,' Æthelflaed demanded of me with no other form of greeting, 'does she wear her hair unbound?'

'Because she's a virgin,' I said, and watched Eadith hurry through the spatter of rain towards the house we shared on Ceaster's main street.

Æthelflaed scowled. 'She's no maid. She's . . .' she bit back whatever she was about to say.

'A whore?' I suggested.

'Tell her to bind her hair properly.'

'Is there a proper way for a whore to bind her hair?' I asked. 'Most of the ones I've enjoyed prefer to leave it loose, but there was a black-haired girl in Gleawecestre who Bishop Wulfheard liked to hump when his wife wasn't in the city, and he made her coil her hair around her head like ropes. He made her plait her hair first and then insisted that she . . .'

'Enough!' she snapped. 'Tell your woman she can at least try to look respectable.'

'You can tell her that yourself, my lady, and welcome to Ceaster.'

She scowled again, then swung down from Gast. She hated Eadith, whose brother had tried to kill her, and that was doubtless reason enough to dislike the girl, but most of the hatred stemmed from the simple fact that Eadith shared my bed. Æthelflaed had also disliked Sigunn, who had been my lover for many years but had succumbed to a fever two winters before. I had wept for her. Æthelflaed had also been my lover and perhaps still was, though in the mood that soured her arrival she was more likely to be my foe. 'All our ships lost!' she exclaimed. 'And a thousand Northmen not a half-day's march away!'

'Two thousand by now,' I said, 'and at least a hundred battle-crazed Irish warriors with them.'

'And this garrison is here to stop that happening!' she spat. The priests who accompanied her looked at me accusingly. Æthelflaed was almost always escorted by priests, but there seemed to be more than usual, and then I remembered that Eostre's feast was just days away and we were to enjoy the thrill of consecrating the humble, ever-smiling Leofstan. 'So what do we do about it?' Æthelflaed demanded.

'I've no idea,' I said, 'I'm not a Christian. I suppose you shove the poor man into the church, stick him onto a throne, and have the usual caterwauling?'

'What are you talking about?'

'I honestly don't see why we need a bishop

anyway. We already have enough useless mouths to feed, and this wretched creature Leofstan has brought half the cripples of Mercia with him.'

'What do we do about Ragnall!' she snapped.

'Oh him!' I said, pretending surprise. 'Why nothing, of course.'

She stared at me. 'Nothing?'

'Unless you can think of something?' I suggested. 'I can't!'

'Good God!' she spat the words at me, then shivered as a blast of wind brought a slap of cold rain to the street. 'We'll talk in the Great Hall,' she said, 'and bring Finan!'

'Finan's patrolling,' I said.

'Thank God someone's doing something here,' she snarled, and strode towards the Great Hall, which was a monstrous Roman building at the centre of the town. The priests scuttled after her, leaving me with two close friends who had accompanied Æthelflaed north. One was Osferth, her half-brother and illegitimate son of King Alfred. He had been my liegeman for years, one of my better commanders, but he had joined Æthelflaed's household as a councillor. 'You shouldn't tease her,' he reproved me sternly.

'Why not?' I asked.

'Because she's in a bad mood,' Merewalh said, climbing down from his horse and grinning at me. He was the commander of her household warriors, and was as reliable a man as any I have ever known. He stamped his feet, stretched his arms, then patted his horse's neck. 'She's in a downright filthy mood,' he said.

'Why? Because of Ragnall?'

'Because at least half the guests for Father Leofstan's enthronement have said they're not coming,' Osferth said gloomily.

'The idiots are frightened?'

'They're not idiots,' he said patiently, 'but respected churchmen. We promised them a sacred Easter celebration, a chance for joyful fellowship, and instead there's a war here. You can't expect the likes of Bishop Wulfheard to risk capture! Ragnall Ivarson is known for his bestial cruelty.'

'The girls at the Wheatsheaf will be pleased Wulfheard's staying in Gleawecestre,' I said.

Osferth sighed heavily and set off after Æthelflaed. The Wheatsheaf was a fine tavern in Gleawecestre that employed some equally fine whores, most of whom had shared the bishop's bed whenever his wife was absent. Merewalh grinned at me again. 'You shouldn't tease Osferth either.'

'He looks more like his father every day,' I said.

'He's a good man!'

'He is,' I agreed. I liked Osferth, even though he was a solemn and censorious man. He felt cursed by his bastardy and had struggled to overcome the curse by living a blameless life. He had been a good soldier, brave and prudent, and I did not doubt he was a good councillor to his half-sister, with whom he shared not just a father but a deep piety. 'So Æthelflaed,' I started walking with Merewalh towards the Great Hall, 'is upset because a pack of bishops and monks can't come to see Leofstan made a bishop?'

'She's upset,' Merewalh said, 'because Ceaster and Brunanburh are close to her heart. She regards them as her conquests, and she isn't happy that the pagans are threatening them.' He stopped abruptly and frowned. The frown was not for me, but rather for a young dark-haired man who galloped past, his stallion's hooves splashing mud and rainwater. The man slewed the tall horse to an extravagant stop and leaped from the saddle leaving a servant to catch the sweat-stained stallion. The young man swirled a black cloak, nodded a casual acknowledgement towards Merewalh, then strode towards the Great Hall.

'Who's that?' I asked.

'Cynlæf Haraldson,' Merewalh said shortly.

'One of yours?'

'One of hers.'

'Æthelflaed's lover?' I asked, astonished.

'Christ, no. Her daughter's lover probably, but she pretends not to know.'

'Ælfwynn's lover!' I still sounded surprised, but in truth I would have been more surprised if Ælfwynn had not taken a lover. She was a pretty and flighty girl who should have been married three or four years by now, but for whatever reason her mother had not found a suitable husband. For a time everyone had assumed Ælfwynn would marry my son, but that marriage had raised no enthusiasm, and Merewalh's next words suggested it never would.

'Don't be surprised if they marry soon,' he said sourly.

Cynlæf's stallion snorted as it was led past me, and I saw the beast had a big C and H branded on its rump. 'Does he do that to all his horses?'

'His dogs too. Poor Ælfwynn will probably end up with his name burned onto her buttocks.'

I watched Cynlæf, who had paused between the big pillars that fronted the hall and was giving orders to two servants. He was a good-looking young man, long-faced and dark-eyed, with an expensive mail coat and a gaudy sword belt from which hung a scabbard of red leather studded with gold. I recognised the scabbard. It had belonged to the Lord Æthelred, Æthelflaed's husband. A generous gift, I thought. Cynlæf saw me looking at him and bowed, before turning away and disappearing through the big Roman doors. 'Where did he come from?' I asked.

'He's a West Saxon. He was one of King Edward's warriors, but after he met Ælfwynn he moved to Gleawecestre,' he paused and half smiled, 'Edward didn't seem to mind losing him.'

'Noble?'

'A thegn's son,' he said dismissively, 'but she thinks the sun shines out of his arse.'

I laughed. 'You don't like him.'

'He's a useless lump of self-important gristle,'

Merewalh said, 'but the Lady Æthelflaed thinks otherwise.'

'Can he fight?'

'Well enough,' Merewalh sounded grudging. 'He's no coward. And he's ambitious.'

'Not a bad thing,' I said.

'It is when he wants my job.'

'She won't replace you,' I said confidently.

'Don't be so sure,' he said gloomily.

We followed Cynlæf into the hall. Æthelflaed had settled into a chair behind the high table, and Cynlæf had taken the stool to her right, Osferth was on her left, and she now indicated that Merewalh and I should join them. The fire in the central hearth was smoky, and the brisk wind gusting through the hole in the Roman roof was swirling the smoke thick about the big chamber. The hall filled slowly. Many of my men, those who were not riding with Finan or standing guard on the high stone walls, came to hear whatever news Æthelflaed had brought. I sent for Æthelstan, and he was ordered to join us at the high table where the twin priests Ceolnoth and Ceolberht also took seats. Æthelflaed's warriors filled the rest of the hall as servants brought water and cloths so the newly arrived guests at the high table could wash their hands. Other servants brought ale, bread, and cheese. 'So what,' Æthelflaed demanded as the ale was poured, 'is happening here?'

I let Æthelstan tell the story of the burning of Brunanburh's boats. He was embarrassed by the telling, certain he had let his aunt down by his lack of vigilance, but he still told the tale clearly and did not try to shrink from the responsibility. I was proud of him and Æthelflaed treated him gently, saying that no one could have expected ships to sail up the Mærse at night. 'But why,' she asked harshly, 'did we have no warning of Ragnall's coming?'

No one answered. Father Ceolnoth began to say something, glancing at me as he spoke, but then decided to be silent. Æthelflaed understood what he had wanted to say and looked at me. 'Your daughter,' she sounded disapproving, 'is married to Ragnall's brother.'

'Sigtryggr isn't supporting his brother,' I said, 'and I assume he doesn't approve of what Ragnall is doing.'

'But he must have known what Ragnall planned?'

I hesitated. 'Yes,' I finally admitted. It was unthinkable that Sigtryggr and Stiorra had not known, and I could only presume they had not wanted to send me any warning. Perhaps my daughter now wanted a pagan Britain, but if that was the case, why had Sigtryggr not joined the invasion?

'And your son-in-law sent you no warning?' Æthelflaed asked.

'Perhaps he did,' I said, 'but the Irish Sea is treacherous. Perhaps his messenger drowned.'

That feeble explanation was greeted with a snort of derision from Father Ceolnoth. 'Perhaps your daughter preferred—' he began, but Æthelflaed cut him short before he could say more.

'We mostly rely on the church for our news from Ireland,' she said acidly. 'Have you stopped corresponding with the clerics and monasteries of that land?'

I watched as she listened to the churchmen's limping excuses. She was King Alfred's eldest daughter, the brightest of his large brood, and as a child she had been quick, happy, and full of laughter. She had grown to be a beauty with pale gold hair and bright eyes, but marriage to Æthelred, Lord of Mercia, had etched harsh lines on her face. His death had taken away much of her unhappiness, but she was now the ruler of Mercia, and the care of that kingdom had added streaks of grey to her hair. She was handsome rather than beautiful now, stern-faced and thin, ever watchful. Watchful because there were still men who believed no woman should rule, though most men in Mercia loved her and followed her willingly. She had her father's intelligence as well as his piety. I knew her to be passionate, but as she aged she had become ever more dependent on priests for the reassurance that the Christians' nailed god was on her side. And perhaps he was, for her rule had been successful. We had been pushing the Danes back, taking from them the ancient lands they had stolen from Mercia, but now Ragnall had arrived to threaten all she had achieved.

'It's no accident,' Father Ceolnoth insisted, 'that he has come at Easter!'

I did not see the significance and nor, apparently, did Æthelflaed. 'Why Easter, father?' she asked.

'We reconquer land,' Ceolnoth explained, 'and we build burhs to protect the land, and we rely on warriors to keep the burhs safe,' that last statement was accompanied by a quick and spiteful glance in my direction, 'but the land is not truly safe until the church has placed God's guardian hand over the new pastures! The psalmist said as much! God is my shepherd and I shall lack for nothing.'

'Baaaaa,' I said, and was rewarded by a savage look from Æthelflaed.

'So you think,' she said, pointedly ignoring me, 'that Ragnall wants to stop the consecration?'

'It is why he has come now,' Ceolnoth said, 'and why we must thwart his evil intent by enthroning Leofstan!'

'You believe he will attack Ceaster?' Æthelflaed asked.

'Why else is he here?' Ceolnoth said heatedly. 'He has brought over a thousand pagans to destroy us.'

'Two thousand by now,' I corrected him, 'and some Christians too.'

'Christians?' Æthelflaed asked sharply.

'He has Irish in his army,' I reminded her.

'Two thousand pagans?' Cynlæf spoke for the first time.

I ignored him. If he wanted me to respond then he needed to use more courtesy, but he had asked a sensible question, and Æthelflaed also wanted the answer. 'Two thousand? You're certain he has that many?' she demanded of me.

I stood and walked around the table so that I was

at the front of the dais. 'Ragnall brought over a thousand warriors,' I said, 'and he used those to occupy Eads Byrig. At least another thousand have joined him since, coming either by sea or on the roads south through Northumbria. He grows strong! But despite his strength he has not sent a single man southwards. Not one cow has been stolen from Mercia, not one child taken as a slave. He hasn't even burned a village church! He hasn't sent scouts to look at Ceaster, he's ignored us.'

'Two thousand?' Æthelflaed again echoed Cynlæf's question.

'Instead,' I said, 'he's made a bridge across the Mærse and his men have been going north. What lies to the north?' I let the question hang in the smoky hall.

'Northumbria,' someone said helpfully.

'Men!' I said. 'Danes! Northmen! Men who hold land and fear that we'll take it from them. Men who have no king unless you count that weakling in Eoferwic. Men, my lady, who are looking for a leader who will make them safe. He's recruiting men from Northumbria, so yes, his army grows every day.'

'All at Eads Byrig?' Æthelflaed asked.

'Maybe three, four hundred men there,' I said. 'There isn't enough water for more, but the rest are camped by the Mærse where Ragnall's made a bridge of boats. I think that's where he's gathering his army, and by next week he'll have three thousand men.'

The priests crossed themselves. 'How in God's name,' Ceolberht asked quietly, 'do we fight a horde like that?'

'Ragnall,' I went on remorselessly, talking directly to Æthelflaed now, 'leads the largest enemy army to be seen in Britain since the days of your father. And every day that army gets bigger.'

'We shall trust in the Lord our God!' Father Leofstan spoke for the first time, 'and in the Lord Uhtred too!' he added slyly. The bishop elect had been invited to join Æthelflaed on the high dais, but had preferred to sit at one of the lower tables. He beamed his smile at me then wagged a disapproving finger. 'You're trying to frighten us, Lord Uhtred!'

'Jarl Ragnall,' I said, 'is a frightening man.'

'But we have you! And you smite the heathen!'

'I am a heathen!'

He chuckled at that. 'The Lord will provide!'

'Then perhaps someone can tell me,' I turned back to the high table, 'how the Lord will provide for us to defeat Ragnall?'

'What has been done so far?' Æthelflaed asked.

'I've summoned the fyrd,' I said, 'and sent all the folk who wanted refuge to the burhs. We've deepened the ditch here, we've sharpened the stakes in the ditch, we've stacked missiles on the walls, and we've filled the storerooms. And we have a scout in the woods now, exploring the new camp as well as Eads Byrig.'

'So now is the time to smite Ragnall!' Father Ceolnoth said enthusiastically.

I spat towards him. 'Will someone please tell that drivelling idiot why we cannot fight Ragnall.'

The silence was finally broken by Sihtric. 'Because he's protected by the walls of Eads Byrig.'

'Not the men by the river!' Ceolnoth pointed out. 'They're not protected!'

'We don't know that,' I said, 'which is why my scout is in the woods. But even if they don't have a palisade, they do have the forest. Lead an army into a forest and it will be ambushed.'

'You could cross the river to the east,' Father Ceolnoth decided to offer military advice, 'and attack the bridge from the north.'

'And why would I do that, you spavined idiot?' I demanded. 'I want the bridge there! If I destroy the bridge then I've trapped three thousand Northmen inside Mercia. I want them out of Mercia! I want the bastards across the river.' I paused, then decided to speak what my instinct told me was the truth, a truth I confidently expected Beadwulf to confirm. 'And that's what they want too.'

Æthelflaed frowned at me, puzzled. 'They want to be across the river?'

Ceolnoth muttered something about the idea being a nonsense, but Cynlæf had understood what I was suggesting. 'The Lord Uhtred,' he said, investing my name with respect, 'believes that what Ragnall really means to do is invade Northumbria. He wants to be king there.'

'Then why is he here?' Ceolberht asked plaintively.

'To make the Northumbrians believe his ambitions are here,' Cynlæf explained. 'He's misleading his pagan enemies. Ragnall doesn't want to invade Mercia . . .'

'Yet,' I intervened strongly.

'He wants to be king of the north,' Cynlæf finished.

Æthelflaed looked at me. 'Is he right?'

'I think he is,' I said.

'So Ragnall isn't coming to Ceaster?'

'He knows what I did to his brother here,' I said.

Leofstan looked puzzled. 'His brother?'

'Sigtryggr attacked Ceaster,' I told the priest, 'and we slaughtered his men, and I took his right eye.'

'And he took your daughter to wife!' Father Ceolnoth could not resist saying.

'At least she gets humped,' I said, still looking at Leofstan. I turned back to Æthelflaed. 'Ragnall's not interested in attacking Ceaster,' I assured her, 'not for a year or two, anyway. One day? Yes, if he can, but not yet. So no,' I spoke firmly to reassure her, 'he's not coming here.'

And he came next morning.

The Northmen came from the forest's edge in six great streams. They still lacked sufficient horses, so many of them came on foot, but they all came in mail and helmeted, carrying shields and weapons, emerging from the far trees beneath their banners that showed eagles and axes, dragons and ravens, ships and thunderbolts. Some flags showed the Christian cross, and those, I assumed, were Conall's Irishmen, while one banner was Haesten's simple emblem of a human skull held aloft on a pole. The biggest flag was Ragnall's blood-red axe that flew in the strong wind above a group of mounted men who advanced ahead of the great horde, which slowly shook itself into a massive battle line that faced Ceaster's eastern ramparts. A horn sounded three times from the enemy ranks as if they thought we had somehow not noticed their coming.

Finan had returned ahead of the enemy, warning me that he had seen movement in the forest, and now he joined me and my son on the ramparts and looked at the vast army, which had emerged from the distant trees and faced us across half a mile of open land. 'No ladders,' he said.

'Not that I can see.'

'The heathen are mighty!' Father Leofstan had also come to the ramparts and called to us from some paces away. 'Yet shall we prevail! Is that not right, Lord Uhtred?'

I ignored him. 'No ladders,' I said to Finan, 'so this isn't an attack.'

'It's impressive though,' my son said, staring at the vast army. He turned as a small voice squeaked from the steps leading up to the ramparts. It was Father Leofstan's wife, or at least it was a bundle of cloaks, robes, and hoods that resembled the bundle he had arrived with.

'Gomer dearest!' Father Leofstan cried, and

hurried to help the bundle up the steep stairs. 'Careful, my cherub, careful!'

'He married a gnome,' my son said.

I laughed. Father Leofstan was so tall, and the bundle was so small and, swathed in robes as she was, she did resemble a plump little gnome. She reached out a hand and her husband helped her up the last of the worn steps. She squeaked in relief when she reached the top, then gasped as she saw Ragnall's army that was now advancing through the Roman cemetery. She stood close beside her husband, her head scarcely reaching his waist, and she clutched his priestly robe as if fearing she might topple off the wall's top. I tried to see her face, but it was too deeply shadowed by her big hood. 'Are they the pagans?' she asked in a small voice.

'Have faith, my darling,' Father Leofstan said cheerfully, 'God has sent us Lord Uhtred, and God will vouchsafe us victory.' He raised his broad face to the sky and lifted his hands, 'pour out Thy fury upon the heathen, oh Lord!' he prayed, 'vex them with Thy wrath and smite them with Thine anger!'

'Amen,' his wife squeaked.

'Poor little thing,' Finan said quietly as he looked at her. 'She's got to be ugly as a toad under all those clothes. He's probably relieved he doesn't have to plough her.'

'Maybe she's relieved,' I said.

'Or maybe she's a beauty,' my son said wistfully.

'Two silver shillings says she's a toad,' Finan said.

'Done!' My son held out his hand to seal the wager.

'Don't be such damned fools,' I snarled. 'I have enough trouble with your damned church without either of you plugging the bishop's wife.'

'His gnome, you mean,' my son said.

'Just keep your dirty hands to yourself,' I ordered him, then turned to see eleven riders spurring ahead of the massive shield wall. They came under three banners and were riding towards our ramparts. 'It's time to go,' I said.

Time to meet the enemy.

CHAPTER 4

Our horses were waiting in the street where Godric, my servant, carried my fine wolf-crested helmet, a newly painted shield, and my bearskin cloak. My standard-bearer shook out the great banner of the wolf's head as I heaved myself into the saddle. I was riding Tintreg, a new night-black stallion, huge and savage. His name meant Torment, and he had been a gift from my old friend Steapa who had been commander of King Edward's household troops until he had retired to his lands in Wiltunscir. Tintreg, like Steapa, was battle-trained and bad-tempered. I liked him.

Æthelflaed was already waiting at the north gate. She was mounted on Gast, her white mare, and wearing her polished mail beneath a snow-white cloak. Merewalh, Osferth and Cynlæf were with her, as was Father Fraomar, her confessor and chaplain. 'How many men are coming from the pagans?' Æthelflaed asked me.

'Eleven.'

'Bring one more man,' she ordered Merewalh. That added man, with her standard-bearer and mine, and with my son and Finan as my companions, would make the same number as Ragnall brought towards us.

'Bring Prince Æthelstan!' I told Merewalh.

Merewalh looked at Æthelflaed, who nodded assent. 'But tell him to hurry!' she added curtly.

'Make the bastards wait,' I growled, a comment Æthelflaed ignored.

Æthelstan was already dressed for battle in mail and helmet, so the only delay was as his horse was saddled. He grinned at me as he mounted, then gave his aunt a respectful bow. 'Thank you, my lady!'

'Just keep silent,' Æthelflaed ordered him, then raised her voice. 'Open the gates!'

The huge gates creaked and squealed and scraped as they were pushed outwards. Men were still pounding up the stone steps to the ramparts as our two standard-bearers led the way through the arch's long tunnel. Æthelflaed's cross-holding goose and my wolf's head were the two banners that were lifted to a weak spring sunlight as we clattered over the bridge that crossed the flooded ditch. Then we spurred towards Ragnall and his men, who had reined in some three hundred yards away.

'You don't need to be here,' I told Æthelflaed.

'Why not?'

'Because it will be nothing but insults.'

'You think I'm afraid of words?'

'I think he'll insult you and try to offend you, and his victory will be your anger.'

'Our scripture teaches us that a fool is full of words!' Father Fraomar said. He was a pleasant enough young man and intensely loyal to Æthelflaed. 'So let the wretch speak and betray his foolishness.'

I turned in my saddle to look at Ceaster's walls. They were thick with men, the sun glinting from spear-points along the whole length of the ramparts. The ditch had been cleared and newly planted with sharpened stakes, and the walls were hung with banners, most of them showing Christian saints. The defences, I thought, looked formidable. 'If he tries to attack the city,' I said, 'then he is a fool.'

'Then why is he here?' Æthelflaed asked.

'This morning? To scare us, insult us, and provoke us.'

'I want to see him,' she said. 'I want to see what kind of man he is.'

'He's a dangerous one,' I said, and I wondered how many times I had ridden in my war-glory to meet an enemy before battle. It was a ritual. To my mind the ritual meant nothing and it changed nothing and it decided nothing, but Æthelflaed was evidently curious about her enemy, and so we indulged Ragnall by riding to endure his insults.

We halted a few paces from the Northmen. They carried three standards. Ragnall's red axe was the largest, and it was flanked by a banner showing a ship sailing through a sea of blood and by Haesten's bare skull on its tall pole. Haesten sat on his horse beneath the skull, and he grinned at me as if we were old friends. He looked old, but I suppose I did too. His helmet was decorated with silver and had a pair of raven's wings mounted on its crown. He was plainly enjoying himself, unlike the man whose banner showed a ship in a sea of blood. He was also an older man, thin-faced and grey-bearded, with a scar slashing across one cheek. He wore a fine helmet that framed his face and was crested with a long black horse's tail, which cascaded down his back. The helmet was circled by a ring of gold, a king's helmet. He wore a cross above his mail, a gold cross studded with amber, showing that he was the only Christian among the enemies who faced us, but what distinguished him that morning was the murderous gaze directed at Finan. I glanced at Finan and saw the Irishman's face was also taut with anger. So the man in the gold-ringed horsetail helmet, I thought, had to be Conall, Finan's brother. You could feel the mutual hatred. One word from either, I reckoned, and swords would be drawn.

'Dwarves!' the silence was broken by the hulking man beneath the flag of the red axe, who kicked his big stallion one pace forward.

So this was Ragnall Ivarson, the Sea King, Lord of the Islands and would-be King of Britain. He wore leather trews tucked into tall boots that were plated with gold badges, the same golden plaques that studded his sword belt, from which hung a monstrous blade. He wore neither mail nor helmet, instead his bare chest was crossed by two leather straps beneath which his muscles bulged. His chest was hairy, and under the hair were ink marks; eagles, serpents, dragons, and axes that writhed from his belly to his neck, around which was twisted a chain of gold. His arms were thick with the silver and gold rings of conquest, while his long hair, dark brown, was threaded with gold rings. His face was broad, hard and grim, and across his forehead was an inked eagle, its wings spread and its talons needle-written onto his cheekbones. 'Dwarves,' he sneered again, 'have you come to surrender your city?'

'You have something to tell us?' Æthelflaed asked in Danish.

'Is that a woman in mail?' Ragnall addressed the question to me, perhaps because I was the biggest man in our party, or else because my battle finery was the most elaborate. 'I have seen many things,' he told me in a conversational tone. 'I have seen the strange lights glitter in the northern sky, I have seen ships swallowed by whirlpools, I have seen ice the size of mountains floating in the sea, I have watched whales break a ship in two, and seen fire spill from a hillside like vomit, but I have never seen a woman in mail. Is that the creature who is said to rule Mercia?'

'The Lady Æthelflaed asked you a question,' I said.

Ragnall stared at her, lifted himself a hand's breadth from the saddle, and let out a loud and long fart. 'She's answered,' he said, evidently amused as he settled back. Æthelflaed must have shown some distaste because he laughed at her. 'They told us,' he looked back to me, 'that the ruler of Mercia was a pretty woman. Is that her grandmother?'

'She's the woman who will grant you a grave's length of her land,' I said. It was a feeble answer, but I did not want to match insult with insult. I was too aware of the hatred between Finan and Conall, and feared that it could break into a fight.

'So it is the woman ruler!' Ragnall sneered. He shuddered, pretending horror. 'And so ugly!'

'I hear that no pig, goat, or dog is safe from you,' I said, provoked to anger, 'so what would you know of beauty?'

He ignored that. 'Ugly!' he said again. 'But I command men who don't care what a woman looks like, and they tell me that an old worn boot is more comfortable than a new one.' He nodded at Æthelflaed. 'And she looks old and worn, so think how they'll enjoy using her! Maybe she'll enjoy it too?' He looked at me as if expecting an answer.

'You made more sense when you farted,' I said.

'And you must be the Lord Uhtred,' he said, 'the fabled Lord Uhtred!' He shuddered suddenly. 'You killed one of my men, Lord Uhtred.'

'The first of many.'

'Othere Hardgerson,' he said the name slowly. 'I shall revenge him.'

'You'll follow him to a grave,' I said.

He shook his head, making the gold rings in his hair clink softly together. 'I liked Othere Hardgerson. He played dice well and could hold his drink.'

'He had no sword-craft,' I said, 'maybe he learned from you?'

'A month from now, Lord Uhtred, I shall be drinking Mercian ale from a cup fashioned from your skull. My wives will use your long bones to stir their stew, and my babes will play knucklebones with your toes.'

'Your brother made the same kind of boasts,' I responded, 'and the blood of his men still stains our streets. I fed his right eye to my dogs, and the taste of it made them vomit.'

'But he still took your daughter,' Ragnall said slyly.

'Even the pigs won't eat your rancid flesh,' I said.

'And a pretty daughter she is too,' he said musingly, 'too good for Sigtryggr!'

'We shall burn your body,' I said, 'what's left of it, and the stench of the smoke will make the gods turn away in disgust.'

He laughed at that. 'The gods love my stench,' he said, 'they revel in it! The gods love me! And the gods have given me this land. So,' he nodded towards the walls of Ceaster, 'who commands in that place?'

'The Lady Æthelflaed commands,' I said.

Ragnall looked left and right at his followers. 'Lord Uhtred amuses us! He claims that a woman commands warriors!' His men dutifully laughed, all except for Conall who still stared malevolently at his brother. Ragnall looked back to me. 'Do you all squat when you piss?'

'If he has nothing useful to say,' Æthelflaed's voice was filled with anger, 'then we shall return to the city.' She wrenched Gast's reins unnecessarily hard.

'Running away?' Ragnall jeered. 'And I brought you a gift, lady. A gift and a promise.'

'A promise?' I asked. Æthelflaed had turned her mare back and was listening.

'Leave the city by dusk tomorrow,' Ragnall said, 'and I shall be merciful. I shall spare your miserable lives.'

'And if we don't?' Æthelstan asked the question. His voice was defiant and earned him an angry glance from Æthelflaed.

'The puppy barks,' Ragnall said. 'If you don't leave the city, little boy, then my men will cross your walls like a storm-driven wave. Your young women will be my pleasure, your children shall be my slaves, and your weapons my playthings. Your corpses will rot, your churches will burn, and your widows weep.' He paused and gestured at his standard. 'You can take that flag,' he was talking to me, 'and display it above the city. Then I shall know you're leaving.'

'I shall take your banner anyway,' I said, 'and use it to wipe my arse.'

'It will be easier,' he spoke to me now as if he

addressed a small child, 'if you just leave. Go to another town! I shall find you there anyway, worry not, but you'll live a little longer.'

'Come to us tomorrow,' I said in the same tone of voice, 'try to cross our walls, be our guests, and your lives will be a little shorter.'

He chuckled. 'I shall take a delight in killing you, Lord Uhtred. My poets will sing of it! How Ragnall, Lord of the Sea and King of all Britain, made the great Lord Uhtred whimper like a child! How Uhtred died begging for mercy. How he cried as I gutted him.' The last few words were spoken with sudden vehemence, but then he smiled again. 'I almost forgot the gift!' He beckoned to one of his men and pointed to the grass between our horses. 'Put it there.'

The man dismounted and brought a wooden chest that he laid on the grass. The chest was square, about the size of a cooking cauldron, and decorated with painted carvings. The lid was a picture of the crucifixion, while the sides showed men with haloes about their heads, and I recognised the chest as one that had probably held a Christian gospel book or else one of the relics that Christians so revered. 'That is my gift to you,' Ragnall said, 'and it comes with my promise that if you are not gone by tomorrow's dusk then you will stay here for ever as ashes, as bones, and as raven food.' He turned his horse abruptly and savaged it with his spurs. I felt relief as Conall, grey-bearded, dark-eyed King Conall, turned and followed.

Haesten paused a moment. He had said nothing. He looked so old to me, but then he was old. His hair was grey, his beard was grey, but his face still held a sly humour. I had known him since he was a young man, and I had trusted him at first, only to discover that he broke oaths as easily as a child breaks eggs. He had tried to make himself a king in Britain and I had thwarted every attempt until, at Beamfleot, I had destroyed his last army. He looked prosperous now, gold-hung, his mail bright, his bridle studded with gold, and his brown cloak edged with thick fur, but he had become a client to Ragnall, and where he had once led thousands he now commanded only scores of men. He had to hate me, yet he smiled at me as though he believed I would be glad to see him. I glared at him, despising him, and he seemed surprised by that. I thought, for a heartbeat, that he would speak, but then he pulled on his reins and spurred after Ragnall's horsemen.

'Open it,' Æthelflaed commanded Cynlæf, who slid from his horse and walked to the gospel box. He stooped, lifted the lid and recoiled.

The box held Beadwulf's head. I gazed down at it. His eyes had been gouged out, his tongue torn from his mouth, and his ears cut off. 'The bastard,' my son hissed.

Ragnall reached his shield wall. He must have shouted an order because the tight ranks dissolved and the spearmen went back towards the trees.

'Tomorrow,' I announced loudly, 'we ride to Eads Byrig.'

'And die in the forest?' Merewalh asked anxiously.

'But you said . . .' Æthelflaed began.

'Tomorrow,' I cut her off harshly, 'we ride to Eads Byrig.'

Tomorrow.

The night was calm and moonlit. Silver touched the land. The rainy weather had gone eastwards and the sky was bright with stars. A small wind came from the far sea, but it had no malice.

I was on Ceaster's ramparts, gazing north and east and praying that my gods would tell me what Ragnall was doing. I thought I knew, but doubts always creep in, and so I looked for an omen. The sentinels had edged aside to give me space. All was quiet in the town behind me, though earlier I had heard a fight break out in one of the streets. It had not lasted long. It had doubtless been two drunks fighting and then being pulled apart before either could kill the other, and now Ceaster was quiet and I heard nothing except the small wind across the roofs, a cry of a child in its sleep, a dog whining, the scrape of feet on the ramparts, and a spear butt knocking on stone. None of those was a sign from the gods. I wanted to see a star die, blazing in its bright death across the darkness high overhead, but the stars stayed stubbornly alive.

And Ragnall, I thought, would be listening and watching for a sign too. I prayed that the owl would call to his ears and let him know the fear of that sound that foretells death. I listened and heard nothing except the night's small noises.

Then I heard the clapping sound. Quick and soft. It started and stopped. It had come from the fields to the north, from the rough pasture that lay between Ceaster's ditch and the Roman cemetery. Some of my men wanted to dig up the cemetery and throw the dead onto a fire, but I had forbidden it. They feared the dead, reckoning that ancient ghosts in bronze armour would come to haunt their sleep, but the ghosts had built this city, they had made the strong walls that protected us, and we owed them our protection now.

The clapping sounded again.

I should have told Ragnall of the ghosts. His insults had been better than mine, he had won that ritual of abuse, but if I had thought of the Roman graves with their mysterious stones I could have told him of an invisible army of the dead that rose in the night with sharpened swords and vicious spears. He would have mocked the idea, of course, but it would have lodged in his fears. In the morning, I thought, we should pour wine on the graves as thanks to the protecting dead.

The clapping started again, followed by a whirring noise. It was not harsh, but neither was it tuneful. 'Early in the year for a nightjar,' Finan said behind me.

'I didn't hear you!' I said, surprised.

'I move like a ghost,' he sounded amused. He came and stood beside me and listened to the sudden clapping sound. It was the noise made by the long wings of the bird beating together in the dark. 'He wants a mate,' Finan said.

'It's that time of year. Eostre's feast.'

We stood in companionable silence for a while. 'So are we really going to Eads Byrig tomorrow?' Finan finally asked.

'We are.'

'Through the forest?'

'Through the forest to Eads Byrig,' I said, 'then north to the river.'

He nodded. For a while he said nothing, just gazed at the distant shine of moonlight on the Mærse. 'No one else is to kill him,' he broke the silence fiercely.

'Conall?'

'He's mine.'

'He's yours,' I agreed. I paused, listening to the nightjar. 'I thought you were going to kill him this morning.'

'I would have done. I wish I had. I will.' He touched his breast where the crucifix had hung. 'I prayed for this, prayed God would send Conall back to me.' He paused and smiled. It was not a pleasant smile. 'Tomorrow then.'

'Tomorrow,' I said.

He slapped the wall in front of him, then laughed. 'The boys need a fight, by Christ they do. They were trying to kill each other earlier.'

'I heard it. What happened?'

'Young Godric got in a fight with Heargol.'

'Godric!' He was my servant. 'He's an idiot!'

'Heargol was too drunk. He was punching air.'

'Even so,' I said, 'one of his punches could kill young Godric.' Heargol was one of Æthelflaed's household warriors, a great brute of a man who revelled in the close work of a shield wall.

'I pulled the bastard off before he could do any harm, and then I smacked Godric. Told him to grow up.' He shrugged. 'No harm done.'

'What were they fighting over?'

'There's a new girl at the Pisspot.' The Pisspot was a tavern. Its proper name was the Plover and that bird was painted on its sign, but for some reason it was always called the Pisspot, and it was a place that sold good ale and bad women. The holy twins, Ceolnoth and Ceolberht, had tried to close the tavern, calling it a den of iniquity, and so it was, which is why I wanted it left open. I commanded a garrison of young warriors and they needed everything the Pisspot provided. 'Mus,' Finan said.

'Mus?'

'That's her name.'

'Mouse?'

'You should go see her,' Finan said, grinning. 'Sweet God in His heaven, lord, but she's worth seeing.'

'Mus,' I said.

'You won't regret it!'

'He won't regret what?' a woman's voice asked, and I turned to see Æthelflaed had come to the ramparts.

'He won't regret cutting the big willows downstream of Brunanburh, my lady,' Finan said. 'We need new shield wood.' He gave her a respectful bow.

'And you need your sleep,' Æthelflaed said, 'if you're to ride to Eads Byrig tomorrow.' She laid a stress on the word 'if'.

Finan knew when he was being dismissed. He bowed again. 'I bid you both goodnight,' he said.

'Look out for mice,' I said.

He grinned. 'We assemble at dawn?'

'All of us,' I said. 'Mail, shields, weapons.'

'It's time we killed a few of the bastards,' Finan said. He hesitated, wanting an invitation to stay, but none came and he walked away.

Æthelflaed took his place and gazed at the moon-silvered land for a moment. 'Are you really going to Eads Byrig?'

'Yes. And you should send Merewalh and six hundred men with me.'

'So they can die in the forest?'

'They won't,' I said and hoped I did not lie. Had the nightjar been the omen I had wanted? I did not know how to interpret the clapping sound. The direction that a bird flies has meaning, as does the stoop of a falcon or the hollow call of an owl, but a drumming noise in the darkness? Then I heard it again and something about the sound made me think of the clatter of shields as men made a shield wall. It was the omen I sought.

'You told us!' Æthelflaed was insistent. 'You said

that once you were among the trees you can't see where the enemy is. That they could get behind you. That you'll be ambushed! So what's changed?' She paused and, when I did not answer, grew angry. 'Or is this stupidity? You let Ragnall insult us so now you have to attack him?'

'He won't be there,' I said.

She frowned at me. 'He won't be there?' she repeated.

'Why did he give us a full day to leave the city?' I asked. 'Why not tell us to leave at dawn? Why not tell us to leave immediately?'

She thought about the questions, but found no answer. 'Tell me,' she demanded.

'He knows we're not going to leave,' I said, 'but he wants us to think we have a whole day before he attacks us. He needs that day because he's leaving. He's going north across his bridge of boats and he doesn't want us interfering with that. He's no intention of attacking Ceaster. He's got a brand new army and he doesn't want to lose two or three hundred men trying to cross these walls. He wants to take the army to Eoferwic because he needs to be King of Northumbria before he attacks Mercia.'

'How do you know?'

'A nightjar told me.'

'You can't be sure!'

'I'm not sure,' I admitted, 'and perhaps it's a ruse to persuade us to go into the forest tomorrow and be killed. But I don't think so. He wants us to leave him in peace so he can withdraw, and if that's what he wants then we shouldn't give it to him.'

She put her arm through mine, a gesture that told me she had accepted both my argument and my plan. She was silent a long time. 'I suppose,' she said at last, her voice low and small, 'that we should attack him in Northumbria?'

'I've been saying we should invade Northumbria for months.'

'So you can retake Bebbanburg?'

'So we can drive the Danes out.'

'My brother says we shouldn't.'

'Your brother,' I said, 'doesn't want you to be the champion of the Saxons. He wants to be that himself.'

'He's a good man.'

'He's cautious,' I said, and so he was. Edward of Wessex had wanted to be King of Mercia too, but he had bowed to Mercian wishes when they had chosen his sister Æthelflaed to rule instead of him. Perhaps he had expected her to fail, but in that he had been disappointed. Now his armies were busy in East Anglia, driving the Danes north out of that land, and he had insisted that his sister do no more than reconquer the old Mercian lands. To conquer the north, he said, we would need both the armies of Wessex and of Mercia, and perhaps he was right. I thought we should invade anyway and take back a slew of towns in southern Northumbria, but Æthelflaed had accepted her brother's wishes. She needed his support, she told me. She needed the gold that Wessex gave Mercia, and she needed the West Saxon warriors who manned the burhs in eastern Mercia. 'In a year or two,' I said, 'Edward will have secured East Anglia and then he'll come here with his army.'

'That's good,' she said. She sounded cautious, not because she did not want her brother to join his forces to hers, but because she knew I believed she should strike north long before her brother was ready.

'And he'll lead your army and his into Northumbria.'

'Good,' she insisted.

And that invasion would make the dream real. It was the dream of Æthelflaed's father, King Alfred, that all the folk who spoke the English language would live in one kingdom under one king. There would be a new kingdom, Englaland, and Edward wanted to be the first man to carry the title of King of Englaland. 'There's only one problem,' I said bleakly, 'right now Northumbria is weak. It has no strong king and it can be taken piece by piece. But a year from now? Ragnall will be king, and he's strong. Conquering Northumbria will be far more difficult once Ragnall rules there.'

'We're not strong enough to invade Northumbria on our own,' Æthelflaed insisted. 'We need my brother's army.'

'Give me Merewalh and six hundred men,' I said, 'and I'll be in Eoferwic in three weeks. A month from now I'll see you crowned queen of

Northumbria, and I'll bring you Ragnall's head in a gospel box.'

She laughed at that, thinking that I joked. I did not. She squeezed my arm. 'I'd like his head as a gift,' she said, 'but for now you need your sleep. And so do I.'

And I hoped the message of the nightjar was true.

I would find out tomorrow.

The sun had risen into a sky of ragged clouds and scudding wind by the time we left Ceaster. Seven hundred men rode to Eads Byrig.

The horsemen streamed through Ceaster's northern gate, a torrent of mail and weapons, hooves clattering on the gate-tunnel's stone, the bright spear-points raised to the fitful sun as we followed the Roman road north and east.

Æthelflaed insisted on coming herself. She was mounted on Gast, her white mare, and followed by her standard-bearer, by a bodyguard of ten picked warriors, and by five priests, one of whom was Bishop Leofstan. He was not formally the bishop yet, but would be soon. He was mounted on a roan gelding, a placid horse. 'I don't like riding when I can walk,' he told me.

'You can walk if you prefer, father,' I said.

'I limp.'

'I noticed.'

'I was kicked by a yearling when I was ten,' he explained, 'it was a gift from God!'

'Your god gives strange gifts.'

He laughed at that. 'The gift, Lord Uhtred, was the pain. It lets me understand the crippled, it permits me to share a little in their agony. It is a lesson from God! But today I must ride or else I won't see your victory.'

He was riding beside me, just in front of my great wolf's head banner. 'What makes you think it will be a victory?' I asked.

'God will grant you the victory! We prayed for that this morning.' He smiled at me.

'Did you pray to my god or your god?'

He laughed, then suddenly winced. I saw a look of pain cross his face, a grimace as he bent forward in the saddle. 'What is it?' I asked.

'Nothing,' he said. 'God afflicts me with pain sometimes. It comes and it goes.' He straightened and smiled at me. 'There! Gone already!'

'A strange god,' I said viciously, 'who gives his worshippers pain.'

'He gave his own son a cruel death, why should we not suffer a little pain?' He laughed again. 'Bishop Wulfheard warned me against you! He calls you the spawn of Satan! He said you would oppose everything I try to achieve. Is that true, Lord Uhtred?'

'You leave me alone, father,' I said sourly, 'and I'll leave you alone.'

'I shall pray for you! You can't object to that!' He looked at me as if expecting a response, but I said nothing. 'I'm not your enemy, Lord Uhtred,' he said gently.

'Count yourself fortunate in that,' I said, knowing that I was being boorish.

'I do!' He had taken no offence. 'My mission here is to be like Christ! To feed the hungry, clothe the naked, heal the sick, and to be a father to the fatherless. Your task, if I understand it right, is to protect us! God gave us different missions. You do yours and I will do mine. I am not Bishop Wulfheard!' he said that with a surprising slyness, 'I shall not interfere with you! I know nothing of war!'

I made a grunting sound that he could take as grateful acceptance of his words.

'Do you think I wanted this burden?' he asked me. 'To become a bishop?'

'You don't?'

'Dear Lord, no! I was happy, Lord Uhtred! I laboured in King Edward's household as a humble priest. My duty was to draw up charters and write the king's letters, but my joy was translating Saint Augustine's *City of God*. It is all I ever wanted from life. A pot of ink, a sheaf of quills, and a church father to guide my thoughts. I'm a scholar, not a bishop!'

'Then why . . .' I began.

'God called me,' he answered my question before I finished it. 'I walked the streets of Wintanceaster and saw men kicking beggars, saw children forced into slavery, saw women degraded, saw cruelty, saw cripples dying in the ditches. That was not the city of God! For those people it was hell, and the church was doing nothing! Well, a little! There were convents and monasteries that tended the sick, but not enough of them! So I began to preach, and tried to feed the hungry and help the helpless. I preached that the church should spend less on silver and gold and more on food for the hungry and on clothes for the naked.'

I half smiled. 'I can't think that made you popular.'

'Of course it didn't! Why do you think they sent me here?'

'To be the bishop,' I said, 'it's a promotion!'

'No, it's a punishment,' he said, laughing. 'Let that fool Leofstan deal with the Lord Uhtred!'

'Is that the punishment?' I asked, curious.

'Good Lord, yes. They're all terrified of you!'

'And you're not?' I asked, amused.

'My tutor in Christ was Father Beocca.'

'Ah,' I said. Beocca had been my tutor too. Poor Father Beocca, crippled and ugly, but a better man never walked this earth.

'He was fond of you,' Leofstan said, 'and proud of you too.'

'He was?'

'And he told me often that you are a kind man who tries to hide his kindness.'

I grunted again. 'Beocca,' I said, 'was full of . . .'

'Wisdom,' Leofstan interrupted me firmly. 'So no, I'm not frightened of you and I will pray for you.'

'And I'll keep the Northmen from slaughtering you,' I said.

'Why do you think I pray for you?' he asked, laughing. 'Now go, I'm certain you have more pressing duties than talking to me. And God be with you!'

I kicked back my heels, riding hard to the front of the column. Damn it, I thought, but now I liked Leofstan. He would join that small group of priests like Beocca, Willibald, Cuthbert, and Pyrlig, whom I admired and liked, a group hugely outnumbered by the corrupt, venal and ambitious clerics who governed the church so jealously. 'Whatever you do,' I told Berg, who was the leading horseman, 'never believe the Christians when they tell you to love your enemies.'

He looked puzzled. 'Why would I want to love them?'

'I don't know! Just Christian shit. Have you seen any enemy?'

'Nothing,' he said.

I had sent no scouts ahead. Ragnall would learn soon enough that we were coming, and he would either gather his men to oppose us or, if I was right, he would refuse battle. I would learn which soon enough. Æthelflaed, even though she had decided to trust my instinct, feared I was being impetuous, and I was not so sure that she was wrong and so had attempted to persuade her to stay in Ceaster. 'And what will men think of me,' she had asked, 'if I cower behind stone walls while they ride to fight Mercia's enemies?'

'They'll think you're a sensible woman.'

'I am the ruler of Mercia,' she said. 'Men won't follow unless I lead.'

We followed the Roman road, which would eventually lead to a crossroads where ruined stone buildings stood above deep shafts dug into the layers of salt that had once made this region rich. Old men remembered clambering down the long ladders to reach the white rock, but the shafts now lay in the uncertain land between the Saxons and the Danes, and so the buildings, which the Romans had made, decayed. 'If we garrison Eads Byrig,' I told Æthelflaed as we rode, 'we can reopen the mines.' A burh on the hill would protect the country for miles around. 'Salt from a mine is much cheaper than salt from fire pans.'

'Let's capture Eads Byrig first,' she said grimly.

We did not go as far as the old shafts, turning north a few miles short of the crossroads and plunging into the forest. Ragnall would know we were coming by now and we made no attempt to hide our progress. We rode on the ridge's crest, following an ancient track from where I could see the green slopes of Eads Byrig rising above the sea of trees, and I could see the bright raw wood of the newly-made palisade, then the track plunged leftwards into trees and I lost sight of the hill until we burst out into the great space that Ragnall had cleared around the ancient fort. The trees had been cut down, leaving stumps, wood chips, and sheared branches. Our appearance in that waste land prompted the defenders of the fort to jeer at us, one even hurled a spear that fell a hundred paces short of our nearest horseman. Bright banners flew above the ramparts, the largest showing Ragnall's red axe. 'Merewalh!' I shouted.

'Lord?'

'Keep a hundred men here! Just watch the fort! Don't start a fight. If they leave the fort to follow us then ride ahead of them and join us!'

'Lord?' he called questioningly.

'Just watch them! Don't fight them!' I shouted and rode on, skirting the hill's western flank. 'Cynlæf!'

The West Saxon caught up with me. 'Lord?' The expensive red scabbard with the gold plaques bounced at his side.

'Keep Lady Æthelflaed at the back!'

'She won't . . .'

'Just do it!' I snarled. 'Hold her bridle if you must, but don't let her get caught up in the fighting.' I quickened the pace and drew Serpent-Breath and the sight of that long blade prompted my men to unsheathe their own swords.

Ragnall had not faced us at Eads Byrig. True there were men on the fort's ramparts, but not his full army. The spear-points had been spaced apart, not crowded together, and that told me most of Ragnall's men were to the north. He had landed his ships on the banks of the Mærse and then fortified Eads Byrig to deceive his real enemy, to persuade the feeble king in Eoferwic that his ambitions lay in Mercia, but Northumbria was much easier prey. Dozens of Northumbrian jarls had already joined Ragnall, some no doubt believing he would lead them south, but by now he would have fired them with enthusiasm for the attack northwards. They would be lured by promises of gold, of land taken from King Ingver and his supporters, and, doubtless, of the prospect of a renewed assault on Mercia once Northumbria was secure.

Or so I believed. Perhaps I was wrong. Perhaps Ragnall was marching on Ceaster or waiting at the river with a shield wall. His banner had flown over Eads Byrig, but that, I thought, was a deception intended to make us think he was inside the new palisade. The prickle of instinct told me he was crossing the river. Why, then, had he left men at Eads Byrig? That was a question that must wait, and then I forgot it altogether because I suddenly saw a group of men running ahead of me. They were not in mail. We had been following a newly-made track through the trees, a track that must lead from Eads Byrig to the bridge of boats, and the men ahead were carrying sacks and barrels. I suspected they were servants, but whoever they were they scattered into the undergrowth when they saw us. We pounded on, ducking under branches, and more men were running away from us, and suddenly the green shadows under the trees lightened and I saw open land ahead, land scattered with makeshift shelters and the remnants of campfires, and I knew we had come to the place beside the river where Ragnall had made his temporary encampment.

I spurred Tintreg out into the sunlight. The river was now a hundred paces away and a crowd was waiting to cross the bridge of boats. The far bank was already thick with men and horses, a horde, most of whom were already marching north, but on this side of the river were more men with their horses, livestock, families, and servants. My instinct had been right. Ragnall was going north.

And then we struck.

Ragnall would have known we were coming, but he must have assumed we would ride straight to Eads Byrig and stay there, lured by his great banner into the belief that he was inside the walls, and our sudden and fast ride northwards took his rearguard by surprise.

It was kind to call it a rearguard. What was left on the Mærse's southern bank was a couple of hundred warriors, their servants, some women and children, and a scattering of pigs, goats, and sheep. 'This way!' I shouted, swerving left. I did not want to charge straight into the panicking crowd who were now struggling to reach the bridge, instead I wanted to cut them off, and so I skirted them and then spurred Tintreg along the river bank towards the bridge. At least a dozen men stayed close behind me. A child screamed. One man tried to stop us, hurling a heavy spear that flew past my helmet. I ignored him, but one of my men must have struck because I heard the butcher's sound of sword on bone. Tintreg snapped his teeth as he ploughed into the folk closest to the bridge. They were trying to escape, some scrambling onto the closest boat, some jumping into the river or else pushing desperately back towards the forest, and then I hauled on the reins and swung out of the saddle. 'No!' a woman was trying to shelter two small children, but I ignored her, instead going to where the planks of the bridge stretched down to the muddy bank, and I stood there, and one by one my men joined me and we unslung our shields and clashed the iron rims together.

'Put your weapons down!' I shouted at the panicked crowd. They had no escape now. Hundreds of my horsemen had come from the trees and I had a shield wall barring their path across the Mærse. I had hoped to trap more than this ragged handful, but Ragnall must have marched early, and we had left Ceaster too late.

'They're burning the boats!' Finan called to me. He had joined me, but was still on horseback. Women were shrieking, children screaming, and my men bellowing at the trapped enemy to put down their weapons. I turned and saw that Ragnall's huge fleet was either beached or moored on the Mærse's far bank and that men were hurling firebrands into the hulls. Other men were setting fire to the ships that supported the crude plank roadway. The boats had been readied for burning, their hulls filled with tinder and soaked in pitch. A handful of vessels were upstream of the others, tied with long lines to poles driven into the shelving mud, and I guessed those were the few ships that were being saved from the flames. 'God in His heaven,' Finan said as he dismounted, 'but that's a fortune going up in flames!'

'Worth losing a fleet to gain a kingdom,' I said.

'Northumbria,' Finan said.

'Northumbria, Eoferwic, Cumbraland, he'll take it all,' I said, 'he'll take the whole north country between here and Scotland! All of it, under a strong king.'

The smoke was churning now as the strong flames leaped from ship to ship. I had thought to try to rescue one of the vessels, but the roadway was firmly lashed to the ships, which, in turn, were lashed to each other. There was no time to cut the lashings and prise the nailed planks apart. The bridge would soon be ash, but as I stared at it I saw a single horseman come through the smoke. He was a bare-chested, long-haired, tall rider on a great black stallion. It was Ragnall who rode the burning road. He came within thirty paces of us, the smoke whipping around horse and man. He drew his sword, and the long blade reflected the flames that surrounded him. 'I will be back, Lord Uhtred!' he shouted. He paused, as if waiting for an answer. A ship's mast collapsed behind him, spewing sparks and a burst of darker smoke. Still he waited, but when I said nothing he turned the horse and vanished into the fire.

'I hope you burn,' I growled.

'But why did he leave men at Eads Byrig?' Finan asked.

The sorry rearguard at the river put up no fight. They were hugely outnumbered and the women screamed at their men to drop their weapons. Behind me the bridge broke and burning ships drifted downstream. I slid Serpent-Breath back into her scabbard, remounted, and forced Tintreg into the mass of frightened enemy. Most of my men were now on foot, collecting swords, spears, and shields, though young Æthelstan was still on horseback and like me was pushing his way through the defeated crowd. 'What do we do with them, lord?' he called to me.

'You're a prince,' I said, 'so you tell me.'

He shrugged and looked about him at the frightened women, crying children, and sullen men, and I thought as I watched him how he had grown from a mischievous child into a strong and handsome youth. He should be king, I thought. He was his father's eldest child, son of Wessex's king, a man who should be king himself. 'Kill the men,' he suggested, 'enslave the children, put the women to work?'

'That's the usual,' I said, 'but this is your aunt's land. She decides.' I could see Æthelstan was staring at a girl and I moved my horse to get a better view. She was a pretty little thing with a mass of unruly fair hair, very blue eyes, and a clear unblemished skin. She was clutching an older woman's skirts, presumably her mother. 'What's your name?' I asked the girl in Danish.

Her mother began screaming and begging, then went to her knees and turned a tear-stained face to me. 'She's all I have, lord, all I have!'

'Quiet, woman,' I snarled, 'you don't know how lucky your daughter is. What's her name?'

'Frigga, lord.'

'How old is she?'

The mother hesitated, perhaps tempted to lie, but I snarled and she blurted out her answer. 'She'll be fourteen at Baldur's Day, lord.'

Baldur's Feast was the midsummer so the girl was more than old enough to wed. 'Bring her here,' I commanded.

Æthelstan frowned, thinking I was taking Frigga for myself, and I confess I was tempted, but I called to Æthelstan's servant instead. 'Tie the girl to your horse's tail,' I ordered him, 'she's not to be touched! She's not to be hurt! You protect her, understand?'

'Yes, lord.'

'And you,' I looked back to the mother, 'can you cook?'

'Yes, lord.'

'Sew?'

'Of course, lord.'

'Then stay with your daughter.' I turned to Æthelstan. 'Your household just increased by two,' I told him, and, as I glanced back at Frigga, thought what a lucky bastard he was, except he was not a bastard, but the true-born son of a king.

A cheer sounded from the horsemen watching from

the south. I thrust Tintreg through the prisoners and saw that Father Fraomar, Æthelflaed's confessor, had made some announcement. He was mounted on a grey mare, the horse's colour matching Father Fraomar's white hair. He was close to Æthelflaed, who smiled as I drew near. 'Good news,' she called.

'What news?'

'God be praised,' Father Fraomar said happily, 'but the men at Eads Byrig have surrendered!'

I felt disappointment. I had been looking forward to a fight. Ragnall seemed to have left a substantial part of his army behind the walls of Eads Byrig, presumably because he wanted to hold onto the newly constructed fort, and I had wanted that garrison's death to be a warning to the rest of his followers. 'They surrendered?'

'God be praised, they did.'

'So Merewalh is inside the fort?'

'Not yet!'

'What do you mean, not yet? They've surrendered!'

Fraomar smiled. 'They're Christians, Lord Uhtred! The garrison is Christian!'

I frowned. 'I don't care if they worship weevils,' I said, 'but if they've surrendered then our forces should be inside the fort. Are they?'

'They will be,' Father Fraomar said. 'It's all agreed.'

'What's agreed?' I demanded.

Æthelflaed looked troubled. 'They've agreed to surrender,' she said, looking to her confessor for confirmation. Fraomar nodded. 'And we don't fight Christians,' Æthelflaed finished.

'I do,' I said savagely, then called for my servant. 'Godric! Sound the horn!' Godric glanced at Æthelflaed as if seeking her approval, and I lashed out and struck his left arm. 'The horn! Sound it!'

He blew it hurriedly, and my men, who had been disarming the enemy, ran to mount their horses.

'Lord Uhtred!' Æthelflaed protested.

'If they've surrendered,' I said, 'then the fort is ours. If the fort is not ours then they haven't surrendered.' I looked from her to Fraomar. 'So which is it?'

Neither answered.

'Finan! Bring the men!' I shouted, and, ignoring Æthelflaed and Fraomar, spurred back southwards.

Back to Eads Byrig.

CHAPTER 5

I should have guessed. It was Haesten. He had a tongue that could turn turds into gold and he was using it on Merewalh.

I found the two men, each attended by a dozen companions, a hundred paces outside the fort on the western side where the slope was gentler. The two sides stood a few paces apart beneath their respective banners. Merewalh, of course, had Æthelflaed's flag showing the goose of Saint Werburgh, while Haesten, instead of his usual skull on a pole, was flaunting a new standard, this one a grey flag on which was sewn a white cross. 'He's shameless!' I called to Finan as I spurred Tintreg up the slope.

Finan laughed. 'He's a slippery bastard, lord.'

The slippery bastard had been talking animatedly as we came from the trees, but as soon as he saw me he fell silent and stepped back into the protective company of his men. He greeted me by name as I arrived, but I ignored him, turning Tintreg in the space between the two sides and then sliding from the saddle. 'Why haven't you occupied the fort?' I demanded of Merewalh as I threw the stallion's reins to Godric.

'I . . .' he began, then looked past me. Æthelflaed and her entourage were approaching fast and he plainly preferred to await their arrival before answering.

'Has the bastard surrendered?' I asked.

'The Jarl Haesten . . .' Merewalh began again, then shrugged as if he neither knew what to say nor understood what was happening.

'It's an easy question!' I said threateningly. Merewalh was a good man and a stalwart fighter, but he looked desperately uncomfortable, his eyes flicking towards the half-dozen priests who stood around him. Father Ceolnoth and his toothless twin Ceolberht were there, as was Leofstan, all of them looking extremely discomfited by my sudden arrival. 'Has he surrendered?' I asked again, slowly and loudly.

Merewalh was saved from the question by Æthelflaed's arrival. She pushed her mare through the priests. 'If you have things to say, Lord Uhtred,' she spoke icily from her saddle, 'then say them to me.'

'I just want to know whether this piece of shit has surrendered,' I said, pointing at Haesten.

It was Father Ceolnoth who answered. 'My lady,' the priest said, pointedly ignoring me, 'the Jarl Haesten has agreed to swear loyalty to you.'

'He has done what?' I asked.

'Quiet!' Æthelflaed snapped. She was still in her saddle, dominating us. Her men, at least a hundred and fifty, had followed her from the river bank and now stood their horses lower down the slope. 'Tell me what you have agreed,' she demanded of Father Ceolnoth.

Ceolnoth gave me a nervous glance, then looked back to Æthelflaed. 'The Jarl Haesten is a Christian, my lady, and he seeks your protection.'

At least three of us all began to speak at once, but Æthelflaed clapped her hands for silence. 'Is this true?' she demanded of Haesten.

Haesten bowed to her, then fingered the silver cross he wore over his mail. 'Thank God, lady, it is true.' He spoke quietly, humbly, with convincing sincerity.

'Lying bastard,' I growled.

He ignored me. 'I have found redemption, lady, and I come to you as a supplicant.'

'He is redeemed, my lady,' a tall man standing next to Haesten spoke firmly. 'We are prepared, my lady, nay, we are eager to swear our loyalty,' the tall man said, 'and as fellow Christians we beseech you for protection.' He used the English tongue and spoke respectfully, bowing slightly to Æthelflaed as he finished. She looked surprised, and no wonder because the tall man appeared to be a Christian priest, or at least he was wearing a long black robe belted with rope and had a wooden cross hanging at his breast.

'Who are you?' Æthelflaed asked.

'Father Haruld, my lady.'

'Danish?'

'I was born here in Britain,' he said, 'but my parents came across the sea.'

'And you're a Christian?'

'By the grace of God, yes.' Haruld was stern, dark-faced, with flecks of grey at his temples. He was not the first Dane I had met who had converted, nor was he the first to become a Christian priest. 'I have been a Christian since I was a child,' he told Æthelflaed. He sounded grave and confident, but I noticed his fingers were compulsively clasping and unclasping. He was nervous.

'And you're telling me that piece of rancid lizard shit is a Christian too?' I jerked my head at Haesten.

'Lord Uhtred!' Æthelflaed said warningly.

'I baptised him myself,' Haruld answered me with dignity, 'thank God.'

'Amen,' Ceolnoth put in loudly.

I stared into Haesten's eyes. I had known him all his adult life, indeed he owed me that life because I had saved it. He had sworn loyalty to me back then and I had believed him because he had a trustworthy face and an earnest manner, but he had broken every oath he ever swore. He was a weasel of a man, cunning and deadly. His ambitions far outreached his achievements, and for that he blamed me because fate had decreed that I would thwart him time after time. The last time had been at Beamfleot where I had destroyed his army and burned his fleet, but Haesten's fate was to escape from every disaster. And here he was again, apparently trapped at Eads Byrig, but smiling at me as though we were the oldest of friends. 'He's no more a Christian than I am,' I snarled.

'My lady,' Haesten looked at Æthelflaed and then, astonishingly, dropped to his knees, 'I swear by our Saviour's sacrifice that I am a true Christian.' He spoke humbly, shaking with intense feeling. There were even tears in his eyes. He suddenly spread his arms wide and turned his face to the sky. 'May God strike me dead this very moment if I lie!'

I drew Serpent-Breath, her blade scraping loud and fast on her scabbard's throat.

'Lord Uhtred!' Æthelflaed called in alarm. 'No!'

'I was about to do your god's work,' I said, 'and strike him dead. You'd stop me?'

'God can do his own work,' Æthelflaed said tartly, then looked back to thc Danish priest. 'Father Haruld, are you convinced of Jarl Haesten's conversion?'

'I am, my lady. He shed tears of contrition and tears of joy at his baptism.'

'Praise God,' Father Ceolnoth whispered.

'Enough!' I said. I still held Serpent-Breath. 'Why aren't our men inside the fort?'

'They will be!' Ceolnoth said waspishly. 'It is agreed!'

'Agreed?' Æthelflaed's voice was very guarded, and it was clear she suspected the priests had overstepped their authority in making any agreement without her approval. 'What has been agreed?' she asked.

'The Jarl Haesten,' Ceolnoth spoke very

carefully, 'begged that he might swear his loyalty to you, my lady, at the Easter mass. He desires this so that the joy of our Lord's resurrection will consecrate this act of reconciliation.'

'I don't give a rat's turd if he waits till Eostre's feast,' I said, 'so long as we occupy the fort now!'

'It will be handed over on Easter Sunday,' Ceolnoth said. 'That was agreed!'

'Easter day?' Æthelflaed asked, and any man who knew her well could have detected the unhappiness in her voice. She was no fool, but nor was she ready to discard the hope that Haesten truly was a Christian.

'It will be a cause for rejoicing,' Ceolnoth urged her.

'And who are you to make that agreement?' I demanded.

'It is a matter for Christians to decide,' Ceolnoth insisted, looking at Æthelflaed in hope of her support.

Æthelflaed, in turn, looked at me, then to Haesten. 'Why,' she asked, 'should we not occupy the fort now?'

'I agreed—' Ceolnoth began weakly.

'My lady,' Haesten intervened, shuffling forward on his knees, 'it is my sincerest wish that all my men be baptised at Easter. But some, a few, are reluctant. I need time, Father Haruld needs time! We need time to convince those reluctant few of the saving grace of our Lord Jesus Christ.'

'Twisted bastard,' I said.

No one spoke for a moment. 'I swear this is true,' Haesten said humbly.

'Whenever he says that,' I looked at Æthelflaed, 'you can tell that he's lying.'

'And if Father Ceolnoth were to visit us,' Haesten went on, 'or better still, Father Leofstan, and if they were to preach to us, that would be a help and a blessing, my lady.'

'I would be happy to . . .' Ceolnoth began, but stopped when Æthelflaed raised a hand. She said nothing for a while, but just gazed down at Haesten. 'You propose a mass baptism?' she asked.

'All my men, my lady!' Haesten said eagerly, 'all of them coming to Christ's mercy and to your service.'

'How many men, you turd?' I asked Haesten.

'There's just a few, Lord Uhtred, who persist in their paganism. Twenty men, perhaps, or thirty? But with God's help we shall convert them!'

'How many men in the fort, you miserable bastard?'

He hesitated, then realised that hesitation was a mistake, and smiled. 'Five hundred and eighty, Lord Uhtred.'

'That many!' Father Ceolnoth exulted. 'It will be a light to lighten the gentiles!' he pleaded with Æthelflaed. 'Imagine it, my lady, a mass conversion of pagans! We can baptise them in the river!'

'You can drown the bastards,' I muttered.

'And my lady,' Haesten, still on his knees, clasped his hands as he gazed up at Æthelflaed. His face was so trustworthy and his voice so earnest. He was the best liar I had ever met in all my life. 'I would invite you into the fort now! I would pray with you there, my lady, I would sing God's praises alongside you! But those few of my men are still bitter. They might resist. A little time is all I beg, a little time for God's grace to work on those bitter souls.'

'You treacherous piece of arse slime,' I snarled at him.

'And if it will convince you,' Haesten said humbly, ignoring me, 'I will swear loyalty to you now, my lady, this very minute!'

'God be praised,' Father Ceolberht lisped.

'There's one small problem,' I said, and everyone looked at me. 'He can't swear an oath to you, my lady.'

Æthelflaed gave me a sharp look. 'Why not?'

'Because he swore loyalty to another lord, my lady, and that lord has not yet released him from his oath.'

'I was released from my oath to Jarl Ragnall when I gave my allegiance to Almighty God,' Haesten said.

'But not from the oath you swore to me,' I said.

'But you are also a pagan, Lord Uhtred,' Haesten said slyly, 'and Jesus Christ absolves me of all allegiance to pagans.'

'This is true!' Father Ceolnoth said excitedly. 'He has cast off the devil, my lady! He has spurned the devil and all his works! A newly converted Christian is absolved of all oaths made to pagans, the church insists on it.'

Æthelflaed still pondered. Finally she looked at Leofstan. 'You haven't spoken, father.'

Leofstan half smiled. 'I promised the Lord Uhtred I would not interfere with his work if he did not interfere with mine.' He offered Father Ceolnoth an apologetic smile. 'I rejoice in the conversion of pagans, my lady, but the fate of a fortress? Alas, that is beyond my competence. Render unto Caesar that which is Caesar's, my lady, and the fate of Eads Byrig is Caesar's affair or, more strictly, yours.'

Æthelflaed nodded abruptly and gestured at Haesten. 'But do you believe this man?'

'Believe him?' Leofstan frowned. 'May I question him?'

'Do,' Æthelflaed commanded.

Leofstan limped to Haesten and knelt in front of him. 'Give me your hands,' Leofstan said quietly and waited as Haesten dutifully obeyed. 'Now tell me,' the bishop-elect still spoke softly, 'what you believe.'

Haesten blinked back his tears. 'I believe in one God, the Father Almighty, Maker of heaven and earth,' he spoke scarcely above a whisper, 'and in one Lord Jesus Christ, the only-begotten Son of God, begotten of the Father; God of God, Light of Light!' His voice had risen as he said the last few words, and then he seemed to choke. 'I believe, father!' he pleaded, and the tears ran down his face again. He shook his head. 'The Lord Uhtred is right, he is right! I have been a sinner. I have broken oaths. I have offended heaven! Yet Father

Haruld prayed with me, he prayed for me, and my wife prayed, and, praise God, I believe!'

'Praise God indeed,' Leofstan said.

'Does Ragnall know you're a Christian?' I asked harshly.

'It was necessary to deceive him,' Haesten said humbly.

'Why?'

Haesten still had his hands in Leofstan's grip. 'I was driven to take refuge on Mann,' he was answering my question, but looking up at Æthelflaed as he spoke, 'and it was on that island that Father Haruld converted me. Yet we were surrounded by pagans who would kill us if they knew. I prayed!' He looked back to Leofstan. 'I prayed for guidance! Should I stay and convert the heathen? Yet God's answer was to bring my followers here and offer our swords to the service of Christ.'

'To the service of Ragnall,' I said harshly.

'The Jarl Ragnall did demand my service,' Haesten was speaking to Æthelflaed again, 'but I saw God's will in that demand! God had offered us a way off the island! I had no ships, I only had faith in Christ Jesus and in Saint Werburgh.'

'Saint Werburgh!' Æthelflaed exclaimed.

'My dear wife prays to her, my lady,' Haesten said, sounding so innocent. Somehow the slimy bastard had learned of Æthelflaed's veneration of the goose-frightener.

'You lying bastard,' I said.

'His repentance is sincere,' Ceolnoth insisted.

'Father Leofstan?' Æthelflaed asked.

'I want to believe him, my lady!' Leofstan said earnestly. 'I want to believe that this is a miracle to accompany my enthronement! That on Easter day we will have the joy of bringing a pagan horde into the service of Jesus Christ!'

'This is Christ's doing!' Father Ceolberht said through his toothless gums.

Æthelflaed still pondered, staring down at the two kneeling men. One part of her surely knew I was right, but she was also swayed by the piety she had inherited from her father. And by Leofstan's eagerness to believe. Leofstan was her choice. She had persuaded the Archbishop of Contwaraburg to appoint him, she had written letters to bishops and abbots praising Leofstan's sincerity and glowing faith, and she had sent money to shrines and churches, all to sway opinion in Leofstan's favour. The church might have preferred a more worldly man who could expand the see's land-holdings and extort more cash from northern Mercia's nobles, but Æthelflaed had wanted a saint. And that saint was now depicting Haesten's conversion as a sign of heavenly approval of her choice. 'Think, my lady,' Leofstan at last let go of Haesten's hands, and, still on his knees, turned to Æthelflaed, 'think what rejoicing there will be when a pagan leads his men to Christ's throne!' And that idea seduced her too. Her father had always forgiven Danes who converted, even allowing some to settle in Wessex, and Alfred had often claimed that the fight was not to establish Englaland but to convert the heathen to Christ, and Æthelflaed saw this mass conversion of heathen Danes as a sign of God's power.

She urged Gast forward a pace. 'You will swear loyalty to me now?'

'With joy, my lady,' Haesten said, 'with joy!'

I spat towards the treacherous bastard, walked away, slammed Serpent-Breath back into her scabbard and hauled myself into Tintreg's saddle. 'Lord Uhtred!' Lady Æthelflaed called sharply. 'Where are you going?'

'Back to the river,' I said curtly. 'Finan! Sihtric! All of you! With me!'

We rode away from whatever farce was about to happen outside Eads Byrig.

One hundred and twenty-three of us rode. We rode our horses through the ranks of Æthelflaed's followers, then turned north and rode towards the river.

But once among the trees and well hidden from the fools who surrounded Æthelflaed I turned my men eastwards.

Because I was determined to do the Christian god's work.

And strike Haesten dead.

We rode fast, our horses twisting through trees. Finan spurred alongside me. 'What are we doing?'

'Taking Eads Byrig,' I said, 'of course.'

'Sweet Jesus.'

I said nothing as Tintreg dropped into a gully

of thick ferns, then pounded up the short slope beyond. How many men did Haesten lead? He had claimed five hundred and eighty, but I did not believe him. He had lost his army along with his reputation at Beamfleot. He had not been present at that battle, but if he had as many as one hundred followers I would be surprised, though doubtless Ragnall would have left some men inside the fortress too. 'How big is the fortress?' I asked Finan.

'Eads Byrig? It's big.'

'If you walked around the walls, how many paces?'

He thought about his answer. I had turned slightly northwards, setting Tintreg to a long slope that climbed through the oaks and sycamores. 'Nine hundred?' Finan guessed. 'Maybe a thousand?'

'That's what I reckon.'

'It's a big place, sure enough.'

King Alfred had tried to reduce life to rules. Most of those rules, of course, came from his Christian scriptures, but there had been others. The towns he built were measured, and each plot of land carefully surveyed. The walls of the town were also measured to discover their height, depth, and extent, and it had been that last figure, the length of the wall, which determined how many men were needed to defend the town. That number had been worked out by clever priests rattling wooden balls along wire strings, and their conclusion was that each burh needed four defenders for every five paces of wall. Wessex had become a garrison under Alfred, its borders studded with the newly built burhs and the walls manned by the fyrd. Every large town had been walled so that the Danes, piercing deep into Wessex, would be frustrated by ramparts, and those ramparts would be defended by an exact number of men corresponding to the wall's total length. It had worked, and Mercia was now the same. As Æthelflaed reconquered Mercia's ancestral lands she secured them with burhs like Ceaster and Brunanburh, and ensured that the garrison could supply four men for every five paces of rampart. At the first sign of trouble, folk could retreat into the nearest burh, taking their livestock with them. A whole army was needed to capture a burh, and the Danes had never succeeded. Their way of war was to raid deep, to capture slaves and cattle, and an army that stayed still, that remained camped outside the walls of a burh, was soon struck by disease. Besides, no enemy army had ever proved big enough to surround a burh and starve it into submission. The strategy of the burhs had worked.

But it worked because there were men to defend them. Every man over the age of twelve was expected to fight. They might not be trained warriors like the men I now led through the rising woodland, but they could hold a spear or throw a rock or swing an axe. That was the fyrd, the army of farmers and butchers and craftsmen. The fyrd might not be armoured with mail or carry linden-wood shields, but its men could line the walls of a burh and hack enemies to death if they tried to climb the ramparts. A woodsman's axe in the hands of a strong farmer is a fearsome weapon, as is a sharpened hoe if swung fiercely enough. Four men to every five paces, and Eads Byrig was a thousand paces, and that meant Haesten would need at least seven hundred men to defend the whole length of its ramparts. 'I'd be surprised,' I told Finan, 'if he had two hundred men.'

'Then why is he staying there?'

And that was a good question. Why had Ragnall left a garrison in Eads Byrig? I did not believe for a moment that Haesten had decided to stay south of the Mærse in order to seek Æthelflaed's protection, he was only there because Ragnall wanted him there. We had slowed now, the horses walking uphill, their hooves loud in the leaf mould. So why had Ragnall left Haesten behind? Haesten was not the best fighter in Ragnall's army, he might well have been the worst, but he was certainly the best liar, and suddenly I understood. I had thought Eads Byrig was a deception aimed at the weak king in Eoferwic, but it was not. It was aimed at us. At me. 'He's staying,' I told Finan, 'because Ragnall's coming back.'

'He has to take Eoferwic first,' Finan said drily.

I curbed Tintreg and held up my hand to stop my men. 'Stay mounted,' I told them, then slid out of the saddle and threw the reins to Godric. 'Keep Tintreg here,' I told him.

Finan and I walked slowly uphill. 'Ingver's

support will crumble,' I told Finan. 'He's a weakling. Ragnall will find himself King of Eoferwic without a struggle. Jarls will already be flocking to him, bringing men, swearing allegiance. He doesn't even need to go to Eoferwic! He can send three hundred men to take the city from Ingver, turn around and come back here. He just wants us to think that he's going there.'

The trees were thinning and I caught a glimpse of the raw new timbers of Eads Byrig's eastern wall. We stooped and crept forward, wary of any sentry on the high timber ramparts.

'And Ragnall has to reward his followers,' I went on, 'what better than land in northern Mercia?'

'But Eads Byrig?' Finan sounded dubious.

'It's a foothold in Mercia,' I said, 'and a base to attack Ceaster. He needs a big victory, something to send the signal that he's a winner. He wants even more men to come across the sea, and to bring them he has to strike a heavy blow. Capturing Eoferwic doesn't count. It's had half a dozen kings in as many years, but if he takes Ceaster?'

'If,' Finan said, still dubious.

'If he captures Ceaster,' I went on, 'he destroys Æthelflaed's reputation. He gains territory. He controls the Mærse and the Dee, he has burhs to frustrate us. He'll lose men in the assault, but he has men to lose. But to do that he needs Eads Byrig. That's his base. Once inside Eads Byrig we'll never get him out. But if we hold Eads Byrig then he'll find it damned hard to besiege Ceaster.'

By now we were at the edge of the trees where we crouched in the undergrowth and stared at the newly-made walls above us. They were taller than a man and protected by the outer ditch. 'How many men do you see there?' I asked.

'Not one.'

It was true. There was not a single man or spear-point visible above Eads Byrig's eastern wall. 'There's no fighting platform,' I said.

Finan frowned. He was thinking. There, just a hundred paces from us, was a wall, but no visible defenders. There had to be sentries there, but if there was no fighting platform then those men were looking through the chinks between the newly-felled logs, and those logs were uneven, their tops not yet aligned. The wall had been built in a hurry. 'It's a bluff,' he said.

'It's all a bluff! Haesten's conversion is a bluff. He's just buying time until Ragnall can get back here. Four days? Five?'

'That quickly?'

'He's probably already on his way back,' I said. It seemed obvious now. He had burned his bridge of boats to make us think he had abandoned Mercia, but to return, all he needed to do was march a few miles eastwards and follow the Roman road south to where it bridged the Mærse. He was coming, I was sure of it.

'But how many bastards are inside those walls?' Finan asked.

'Only one way to find out.'

He chuckled. 'And you are always telling young Æthelstan to be cautious before starting a fight?'

'There's a time for caution,' I said, 'and a time to just kill the bastards.'

He nodded. 'But how do we cross that wall? We don't have ladders.'

So I told him.

Twelve of my youngest men led the assault. My son was among them.

The trick was to reach the wall fast and to cross it fast. We had no ladders, and the wall was some nine or ten feet high, but we did have horses.

That was how we had captured Ceaster. My son had stood on his horse's saddle and climbed over the gate, and that is what I told the twelve young men to do. Ride fast to the wall and use the height of the horse to reach the wall's top. The rest of us would follow hard behind. I would have liked to have led the twelve, but I was not as agile as I had been. This was a job for young men.

'And if there are two hundred bastards waiting for them on the other side?' Finan asked.

'Then they don't cross the wall,' I said.

'And if Lady Æthelflaed has just agreed a truce?'

I ignored that question. I suspected that the happy Christians were agreeing to let Haesten stay on the hilltop till Easter, but I was not part of that agreement because Haesten was my man. He had sworn loyalty to me. That oath might have been made a long time ago, and Haesten had broken it repeatedly, but an oath was still an oath and he owed me obedience. Christians might declare that an oath sworn to a pagan had no force, but I was under no compulsion to believe that. Haesten was my man, like it or not, and he had no right to make a truce with Æthelflaed unless I agreed, and I wanted the bastard dead. 'Go,' I told my son, 'go!'

The twelve men spurred their horses, crashing through undergrowth and out onto the cleared land. I let them get twenty or thirty paces ahead, then kicked Tintreg. 'All of you,' I called, 'with me!'

My son was ahead of the rest, his horse pounding up the slope. I saw his stallion drop into the ditch and struggle up the far side where Uhtred reached with both hands for the wall's top. He scrabbled with his feet, swung a leg over and now the rest of the dozen were pulling themselves up onto the logs. One man fell back, rolling into the ditch. The abandoned horses just stood there, in our way.

And then the wall fell.

I had just reached the ditch. It was shallow because Haesten's men had not had time to deepen it again. There were no stakes, no obstacles, just a steep short bank climbing to the earth wall's crest where the logs had been sunk, but they had not been buried deep enough, and the weight of the men on their tops was throwing them down. Tintreg shied away from the noise, and I wrenched him back. Horsemen went past me, not bothering to dismount, just spurring the stallions up the bank and onto the fallen logs. 'Dismount!' Finan shouted. A horse slipped and fell on the logs. The beast was thrashing and screaming, driving other men to the edges of the gap that was not wide enough for the mass of frightened horses and hurrying men. 'Dismount!' Finan bellowed again. 'Come on foot! Shields! Shields! I want shields!'

That was the order to make a shield wall. Men were flinging themselves out of their saddles and flooding over the fallen wall. I led Tintreg by his reins. 'Keep your horse with you!' I called to Berg. In front of me were the fallen logs that had tilted down into the inner ditch, beyond which was the second earth wall. Neither was a formidable obstacle. My men were clambering over the fallen wall, drawing their swords, while ahead of us were three large huts, newly built with rough timber walls and bright thatch, and beyond the huts were men, but those men were a long way off at the fort's further end. As far as I could see there had been no sentries at this end of the fort.

'Shield wall!' I shouted.

'On me!' Finan was standing just beyond the three huts, arms spread to show where he wanted the shield wall to form.

'Berg! Help me!' I called, and Berg cupped his hands and heaved me back into Tintreg's saddle. I drew Serpent-Breath. 'Mount up and follow me,' I snarled at Berg.

I spurred around the end of our hastily forming wall. Now I could see the rest of the fort. Two hundred men? I doubted there were more than two hundred. Those men had been gathered at the fort's far end, doubtless waiting to hear what agreement had been reached with Æthelflaed, and now we were behind them. But closer to us, and even more numerous, was a crowd of women and children. They were running. A handful of men were with them, all of them fleeing our sudden invasion of the fort's eastern end. 'We have to stop those fugitives,' I told Berg. 'Come on!' I spurred Tintreg forward.

I was Uhtred, Lord of Bebbanburg, in my war-glory. The arm rings of fallen enemies glinted on my forearms, my shield was newly painted with the snarling wolf's head of my house, while another wolf, this one of silver, crouched on the crest of my polished helmet. My mail was tight, polished with sand, my sword belt and scabbard and bridle and saddle were studded with silver, there was a gold chain at my neck, my boots were panelled with silver, my drawn sword was grey with the whorls of its making running from the hilt to its hungry tip. I was the lord of war mounted on a great black horse, and together we would make panic.

I charged through the fleeing people, cutting Tintreg in front of a woman running with a child in her arms. A man heard the hooves and turned to swing an axe. Too late. Serpent-Breath drank her first blood of the day and the woman screamed. Berg was threading the crowd, sword low, and my son had remounted his horse and was leading three other riders into the chaos. 'Cut them off!' I yelled at him, and steered Tintreg towards the leading fugitives. I wanted to keep them between my shield wall and the larger number of enemy who were hurrying into their own shield wall at the fortress's further end. 'Drive them back!' I called to my son. 'Back towards Finan!' Then I galloped Tintreg in front of the crowd, my sword low and threatening. I was causing panic, but panic with a purpose. We were herding the women and children back towards our own shield wall. Dogs howled and children screamed, but back they went, desperate to escape the thumping hooves and the light-glinting swords as our horses crossed and re-crossed in front of them. 'Now come forward!' I shouted at Finan. 'But come slowly!'

I stayed close to the crowd which, terrified of our big horses, shrank towards Finan's advancing shield wall. I told Berg to watch my back while I looked at the rest of the fort. More huts stretched down the southern flank, but most of the interior was worn grass on which massive log piles were stacked. Haesten had started constructing a hall at the further end, where his men now formed their shield wall. It was a wall of three ranks and it was wider than our wall. Wider and deeper, and above it was Haesten's old banner, the bleached skull on its long pole. The shield wall looked formidable, but Haesten's men were almost as panicked as their wives and children. Some were shouting and pointing at us, plainly wanting to advance and fight, but others were looking back to the far ramparts which, as far as I could see, was the only stretch of wall that had been given fighting platforms. The men on those platforms were watching Æthelflaed's troops. One man was shouting at the shield wall, but was too far away for me to hear what he said.

'Finan!' I bellowed.

'Lord?'

'Burn those huts!' I wanted Æthelflaed's troops to menace that far rampart and so keep the enemy looking both ways, and the sight of smoke should at least tell them that Haesten's fortress was in trouble. 'And come faster!' I pointed Serpent-Breath towards the enemy line. 'Let's kill them!'

Finan gave the command and his shield wall doubled its pace. They began beating their swords against their shields as they advanced, driving the fugitives in front of them. 'Let them go,' I called to my son, 'but keep them in the centre of the fort!' He understood immediately and wheeled his horse away, taking his men to the northern side of the fortress. 'Berg?' I summoned him. 'We'll manage this southern flank.'

'What are we doing, lord?'

'Letting the women and children go to their men,' I said, 'but make them go straight ahead.'

It is a hard and bloody task to break a shield wall. Two lines of men must clash together and try to break the other with axes, spears, and swords, but for every enemy who is struck down there is another ready to take his place. Whoever commanded Haesten's men in the fort had three ranks of warriors waiting for us, while Finan only had two ranks. Our shield wall was too thin, it was outnumbered, but if we could break their line then we would turn the hilltop's turf dark with their blood. And that was why I shepherded the women and children straight towards the enemy's shield wall. Those fugitives would be frantic to escape the grim noise of our swords beating a rhythm on the painted shields, and they would claw their way through Haesten's wall, their panic would infect his men, their desperate attempts to escape our blades would open gaps in Haesten's wall, and we would use the gaps to split the wall into small groups that could be slaughtered.

And so our few horsemen galloped out of the space between the two shield walls and the women and children, seeing escape, ran for the refuge of their own menfolk's shields. Berg and I made sure they could not run around the end of the enemy's wall, but were forced to go straight towards Haesten's shields, and Finan, seeing what was happening, quickened his pace still further. My men were chanting, beating blades on willow, cheering.

And I knew we had an easy victory.

I could smell the enemy's fear and see their panic. They had been left here by Ragnall and told to keep Eads Byrig safe till his return, and Haesten was relying on trickery and lies to keep the fort secure. The new wall had looked formidable, but it was a sham, the logs had not been sunk deep enough and so it had toppled. Now we were inside the fort, and Æthelflaed had scores more men outside, and Haesten's troops saw annihilation coming. Their families were clawing at them, desperate to open the locked shields and get behind the wall, and Finan saw the gaps appear and ordered the charge.

'Kill the men!' I shouted.

We are cruel. Now that I am old and the brightest sunlight is dim and the roar of the waves crashing on rocks is muted, I think of all the men I have sent to Valhalla. Bench after bench is filled by them, brave men, spear-Danes, staunch fighters, fathers and husbands, whose blood I loosed and bones I shattered. When I remember that fight on Eads Byrig's hilltop I know I could have demanded their surrender and the skull banner would have fallen and the swords would have been tossed to the turf, but we were fighting Ragnall the Cruel. That was the name he craved for himself, and a message had to be given to Ragnall the Cruel, or rather to his men, that we were to be feared even more than Ragnall. I knew we would have to fight him, that eventually our shield wall would have to meet his shield wall, and I wanted his men to have fear in their hearts when they faced us.

And so we killed. The enemy's panic broke his own shield wall. Men, women, and children fled for the gate behind them, and they were too many to get through the narrow entrance and so they crowded behind it, and my men killed them there. We are cruel, we are savage, we are warriors.

I let Tentrig pick his own path. Some few men tried to escape by climbing over the wall and I slashed them off the logs with Serpent-Breath. I wounded rather than killed. I wanted dead men, but I also wanted crippled men to stagger north and take a message to Ragnall. The screams clawed at my ears. Some of the enemy tried to shelter in the half-built hall, but Finan's shield-warriors were in a slaughtering mood. Spears took men in the back. Children watched their fathers die, women shrieked for their husbands, and still my wolf-soldiers went on killing, hacking down with swords and axes, lunging with spears. Our shield wall was no more, there was no need for it because the enemy was not fighting back, but trying to escape. Some few men tried to fight. I saw two turn on Finan, and the Irishman shouted at his companions to stand back, and I watched him throw down his shield and taunt the two. He parried their clumsy attacks and used his speed to first pierce one in the waist and plunge the blade deep, and then duck the other man's savage blow, rip the sword free, and thrust it two-handed into the second assailant's throat. He made it look easy.

A spearman charged me, face contorted, shouting that I was a turd, and he aimed his spear at Tintreg's belly, knowing that if he could bring the stallion down then I would be easy meat for his blade. He could see from my helmet, from the gold and silver that adorned my belt, bridle, boots, and scabbard, that I was a warrior of renown, but to kill me at his own dying would give his name glory. A poet might even sing of him, might sing the lay of Uhtred's death, and I let him come, then touched my heels to Tintreg and he leaped ahead and the spearman was forced to swing the blade, which, instead of opening the stallion's belly, scored a bloody cut along his flank, and I cut back with Serpent-Breath, breaking the spear's ash shaft and the man leaped after me, seizing my right leg and tried to haul me down from the saddle. I stabbed Serpent-Breath down, the blade scraping his helmet's rim to rake his face, slashing off nose and chin, and his blood soaked my right boot as he twisted back in sudden pain, releasing me, and I gave him another blow, this time splitting his helmet. He made a gurgling sound, half crying, clutching his hands to his ruined face as I kicked Tintreg on.

Men were surrendering. They were throwing down their shields, dropping their weapons, and kneeling on the grass. Their women shielded them, shrieking at my killers to stop their madness, and I decided the women were right. We had killed enough.

'Finan,' I called, 'take prisoners!'

And the horn sounded from beyond the gate.

* * *

The fight, which had begun so suddenly, ended abruptly, almost as if the horn were a signal to both sides. It sounded again, urgently, and I saw the crowd at the gate push back into the fort to make way.

Bishop Leofstan appeared, mounted on his gelding with his legs almost dangling to the ground. A rather more impressive band of warriors followed the priest, led by Merewalh, and all of them surrounding Æthelflaed. Haesten and his men came next, while behind them were still more of Æthelflaed's Mercians. 'You have broken the truce!' Father Ceolnoth accused me, more in sorrow than in anger. 'Lord Uhtred, you broke the solemn promise we made!' He looked at the bodies sprawled on the turf, bodiesthat were gutted, their intestines mangled with shattered mail, bodies with brains leaking from split helmets, bodies red with blood that was already attracting flies. 'We made a promise before God,' he said sadly.

Father Haruld, his face taut with anger, knelt and took the hand of a dying man. 'You have no honour,' he spat at me.

I kicked Tintreg forward and dropped Serpent-Breath's bloody point so it touched the Danish priest's neck. 'You know what they call me?' I asked him. 'They call me the priest-killer. Speak to me of honour again and I'll make you eat your own turds.'

'You . . .' he began, but I slapped his head hard

with the flat of Serpent-Breath's blade, knocking him to the turf.

'You lied, priest,' I said, 'you lied, so don't talk to me of honour.'

He went silent.

'Finan,' I snarled, 'disarm them all!'

Æthelflaed pushed her horse to the front of the defeated Northmen. 'Why?' she asked me bitterly. 'Why?'

'They are enemies.'

'The fort would have surrendered on Easter day.'

'My lady,' I said tiredly, 'Haesten has never told a truth in his life.'

'He swore an oath to me!'

'And I never released him from his oath to me,' I snapped back at her, suddenly angry. 'Haesten is my man, sworn to me! No amount of priests or praying can change that!'

'And you,' she said, 'are sworn to me. So your men are my men, and I made a pact with Haesten.'

I turned my horse. Bishop Leofstan had come close, but recoiled from me. Both Tintreg and I were smeared with blood, we stank of it, my sword blade glittered with it. I stood in the stirrups and shouted at Haesten's men, those who survived. 'All of you who are Christians, step forward!' I waited. 'Hurry!' I shouted. 'I want all the Christians over here!' I pointed my sword towards an empty patch of turf between two of the log stacks.

Haesten opened his mouth to speak and I swept Serpent-Breath around to point at him. 'One word from you,' I said, 'and I'll cut your tongue out!' He closed his mouth. 'Christians,' I bellowed, 'over here, now!'

Four men moved. Four men and perhaps thirty women. That was all. 'Now look at the rest,' I said to Æthelflaed, pointing at the men who had not moved. 'See what's hanging at their necks, my lady? Do you see crosses or hammers?'

'Hammers,' she said the word quietly.

'He lied,' I said. 'He told you that all but a few of his men were Christians, that they were waiting for Eostre's feast to convert the others, but look at them! They're pagans like me, and Haesten lies. He always lies.' I pushed Tintreg through her men, speaking as I went. 'He was told to hold onto Eads Byrig until Ragnall returns, and that will be soon. And so he lied because he can't speak the truth. His tongue is bent. He breaks oaths, my lady, and he swears black is white and white is black, and men believe him because he has honey on his bent tongue. But I know him, my lady, because he's my man, he's sworn to me.' And with that I leaned down from the saddle and took hold of Haesten's mail coat, shirt, and cloak, and hauled him up. He was much heavier than I expected, but I heaved him over the saddle and then turned Tintreg back. 'I've known him all my life, my lady,' I said, 'and in all that time he has never spoken one true word. He twists like a serpent, he lies like a weasel, and he has the courage of a mouse.'

Bruna, Haesten's wife, began screaming at me

from the back of the crowd, then pushed her way through with her big meaty fists. She was calling me a murderer, a heathen, a creature of the devil, and she was a Christian, I knew. Haesten had even encouraged her conversion because it had persuaded King Alfred to treat him leniently. He twisted on my saddle and I thumped his arse with Serpent-Breath's heavy hilt. 'Uhtred,' I shouted at my son, 'if that fat bitch lays a finger on me or my horse, break her damned neck!'

'Lord Uhtred,' Leofstan half moved to stop me, then looked at the blood on Serpent-Breath and on Tintreg's flank and stepped back.

'What, father?' I asked.

'He knew the creed,' he spoke hesitantly.

'I know the creed, father, does that make me a Christian?'

Leofstan looked heartbroken. 'He's not?'

'He's not,' I said, 'and I'll prove it to you. Watch.' I threw Haesten off the horse, then dismounted. I threw the reins to Godric, then nodded at Haesten. 'You have your sword, draw it.'

'No, lord,' he said.

'You won't fight?'

The bastard turned to Æthelflaed. 'Doesn't our Lord command us to love our enemies? To turn the other cheek? If I am to die, my lady, I die a Christian. I die as Christ died, willingly. I die as a witness to . . .'

Whatever he was a witness to he never managed to say because I hit him over the back of his helmet with the flat of Serpent-Breath. The blow knocked him flat on the ground. 'Get up,' I said.

'My lady,' he said, looking up at Æthelflaed.

'Get up!' I shouted.

'Stand,' Æthelflaed commanded him. She was watching very closely.

Haesten stood. 'Now fight, you slime turd,' I told him.

'I will not fight,' he said. 'I forgive you.' He made the sign of the cross, then had the gall to drop to his knees and clasp the silver cross in both his hands, which he held up in front of his face as though he was praying. 'Saint Werburgh,' he called, 'pray for me now and at the hour of my death!'

I swung Serpent-Breath so hard that Æthelflaed gasped. The blade whistled in the air, aiming for Haesten's neck. It was a wild swing, lavish and fast, and I checked it at the very last instant so that the bloodied blade stopped just short of Haesten's skin. And he did what I knew he would do. His right hand, that had been clutching the cross, dropped to the hilt of his sword. He gripped it, though he made no attempt to draw it.

I touched Serpent-Breath's blade to his neck. 'Are you frightened,' I asked him, 'that you won't go to Valhalla? Is that why you gripped the sword?'

'Let me live,' he begged, 'and I'll tell you what Ragnall plans.'

'I know what Ragnall plans.' I pressed Serpent-Breath against the side of his neck and he shuddered. 'You're not worth fighting,' I said, and I looked past

Æthelflaed to her nephew. 'Prince Æthelstan! Come here!'

Æthelstan looked at his aunt, but she just nodded, and he slid from his saddle. 'You'll fight Haesten,' I told Æthelstan, 'because it's time you killed a jarl, even a pathetic jarl like this one.' I took my sword from Haesten's neck. 'Get up,' I ordered him.

Haesten stood. He glanced at Æthelstan. 'You'd make me fight a boy?'

'Beat the boy and you live,' I promised him.

And Æthelstan was little more than a boy, slender and young, while Haesten was experienced in war, yet Haesten must have known I would not risk Æthelstan's life unless I was confident that the youngster would win and, knowing that, Haesten tried to cheat. He drew his sword and ran at Æthelstan, who had been waiting for my command to start the fight. Haesten roared as he charged, then swung his blade, but Æthelstan was fast, sidestepping the charge and ripping his own long blade free of its scabbard. He parried the backswing and I heard the clangour of swords and watched as Haesten turned to deliver an overhead blow designed to split Æthelstan's skull in two, but the young man just swayed back, let the blade pass him, then mocked his older enemy with laughter. He lowered his own sword, inviting another attack, but Haesten was cautious now. He was content to circle Æthelstan, who kept turning to keep his sword facing his foe.

I had reason to let Æthelstan fight and win. He might have been King Edward's oldest son and therefore the ætheling of Wessex, but he had a younger half-brother, and there were powerful men in Wessex who favoured the younger boy as their next king. That was not because the younger boy was better, stronger, or wiser, but simply because he was the grandson of Wessex's most powerful ealdorman, and to fight the influence of those wealthy men I would pay a poet bright gold to make a song of this fight, and it would not matter that the song bore no resemblance to the fight, only that it made Æthelstan into a hero who had fought a Danish chieftain to the death in the woods of northern Mercia. Then I would send the poet south into Wessex to sing the song in firelit mead halls so that men and women would know that Æthelstan was worthy.

My men were jeering Haesten now, shouting that he was frightened of a lad, goading him to attack, but Haesten stayed cautious. Then Æthelstan advanced a step and cut at the Dane, his stroke almost casual, but he was judging the swiftness of the older man's responses and what he discovered he liked because he began attacking with short, sharp strokes, forcing Haesten back, not trying to wound him yet, but simply to force Haesten onto his back foot and give him no time to make his own assault. Then suddenly he stepped back, flinching as though he had pulled a muscle and Haesten lunged at him and Æthelstan stepped aside and chopped down hard, viciously hard, the stroke fast as a swift's wingbeat, and the blade struck Haesten's right knee with savage force and the older man stumbled and Æthelstan hacked down hard to cut through the mail of Haesten's shoulder and so drove the Dane to the turf. I saw the battle-joy on Æthelstan's face and heard Haesten cry out in despair as the young man stepped over him with his sword raised for the killing blow.

'Hold!' I shouted. 'Hold! Step back!'

My watching men fell silent. Æthelstan looked puzzled, but nevertheless obeyed me and stepped back from his defeated enemy. Haesten was flinching with pain, but managed to struggle to his feet. He staggered unsteadily on his wounded right leg. 'You will spare my life, lord?' he asked me. 'I will be your man!'

'You are my man,' I said and I took hold of his right arm.

He understood then what I was about to do and his face was distorted with despair. 'No!' he shouted. 'I beg you, no!'

I gripped his wrist, then twisted the sword out of his hand. 'No!' he wailed. 'No! No!'

I tossed the sword away and stepped back. 'Finish your work,' I told Æthelstan curtly.

'Give me my sword!' Haesten cried and limped a painful step towards the fallen blade, but I stood in his path.

'So you can go to Valhalla?' I sneered. 'You think you can share ale with those good men who wait for me in the bone hall? Those brave men? And why does a Christian believe in Valhalla?'

He said nothing. I looked at Æthelflaed, then at Ceolnoth. 'Did you hear?' I demanded. 'This good Christian wants to go to Valhalla. You still think he's a Christian?' Æthelflaed nodded to me, accepting the proof, but Ceolnoth would not meet my gaze.

'My sword!' Haesten said, tears on his cheeks, but I just beckoned Æthelstan forward and stepped aside. 'No!' Haesten wailed. 'My sword! I beg you!' He gazed at Æthelflaed. 'My lady, give me my sword!'

'Why?' she asked coldly, and Haesten had no answer.

Æthelflaed nodded to her nephew, and Æthelstan skewered Haesten with his blade, lunging the steel straight into Haesten's belly, straight through mail and skin and sinew and flesh and he ripped the sword up, grunting with the effort as he looked his enemy in the eye, and the blood was gushing with the man's guts as they spilled on Eads Byrig's thin turf.

So died Haesten the Dane.

And Ragnall was coming.

He would be harder to kill.

CHAPTER 6

We had taken too many prisoners and too many of those prisoners were warriors who, if they lived, were likely to fight us again. Most were Ragnall's followers, a few had been Haesten's men, but all were dangerous. If we had just let them loose they would have rejoined Ragnall's army that was already powerful enough, so my advice was to kill every last one of them. We could not feed almost two hundred men, let alone their families, and I had youngsters in my ranks who needed practice with sword or spear, but Æthelflaed shrank from the slaughter. She was not a weak woman, far from it, and in the past she had watched impassively as other prisoners had been killed, but she was in a merciful or perhaps a squeamish mood. 'So what would you have me do with them?' I asked.

'The Christians can stay in Mercia,' she said, frowning at the handful who had confessed to her faith.

'And the rest?'

'Just don't kill them,' she said brusquely.

So in the end I had my men hack off the

prisoners' sword hands that we collected in sacksful. There were also forty-three dead men on the hilltop, and I ordered all of their corpses beheaded and the severed heads brought to me. The prisoners were then released, along with the older captives, all of them sent east along the Roman road. I told them they would find a crossroads a half-day's walk away and if they turned north it would take them across the river and back into Northumbria. 'You'll meet your master coming the other way,' I told them, 'and you can give him a message. If he comes back to Ceaster he'll lose more than one hand.' We kept the young women and children. Most would be sent to the slave markets of Lundene, but a few would probably find new husbands among my men.

We carted all the captured weapons to Ceaster where they would be given to the fyrd, replacing hoes or sharpened spades. Then we pulled down Eads Byrig's newly-made wall. It fell easily and we used the logs to make a great funeral pyre on which we burned the headless bodies. The corpses shrivelled in the fire, curling up as they shrank and sending the stench of death east with the plume of smoke. Ragnall, I thought, would see that smoke and wonder if it was an omen. Would it deter him? I doubted it. He would surely realise that it was Eads Byrig that burned so fiercely, but his ambition would persuade him to ignore the omen. He would be coming.

And I wanted to welcome him, and so I left

forty-three logs standing like pillars spaced about Eads Byrig's perimeter and we pegged a severed head to each of those and next day I had the bloody hands nailed onto trees either side of the Roman road so that when Ragnall returned he would be greeted first by the hands and then by the raven-pecked heads ringing the slighted fort. 'You really think he'll come?' Æthelflaed asked me.

'He's coming,' I said firmly. Ragnall needed a victory, and to defeat Mercia, let alone Wessex, he needed to capture a burh. There were other burhs he could attack, but Ceaster had to tempt him. Control Ceaster and he would command the seaways to Ireland and dominate all of north-western Mercia. It would be an expensive victory, but Ragnall had men to spend. He would come.

It was night-time, two days after we had taken Eads Byrig, and the two of us were standing above Ceaster's northern gate staring at a sky filled with bright stars. 'If he wants Ceaster so badly,' Æthelflaed asked after a moment's quiet, 'why didn't he come here as soon as he landed? Why go north first?'

'Because by taking Northumbria,' I said, 'he doubled the size of his army. And he doesn't want an enemy at his back. If he had besieged us without taking Northumbria then he would have given Ingver time to assemble troops.'

'Ingver of Eoferwic is weak,' she said scornfully.

I resisted the temptation to ask why, if she believed that, she had resolutely refused to invade Northumbria. I knew the answer. She wanted to secure the rest of Mercia first and she would not invade the north without her brother's support. 'He might be weak,' I said instead, 'but he's still King of Jorvik.'

'Eoferwic,' she corrected me.

'And Jorvik's walls are formidable,' I went on, 'and Ingver still has followers. If Ragnall gave him time then Ingver could probably gather a thousand men. By going north Ragnall panics Ingver. Men in Northumbria face a choice now, Ingver or Ragnall, and you know who they'll choose.'

'Ragnall,' she said quietly.

'Because he's a beast and a fighter. They're scared of him. If Ingver has any sense he's on a ship now, going back to Denmark.'

'And you think Ragnall will come here?' she said.

'Within a week,' I guessed. 'Maybe as soon as tomorrow?'

She stared at the glow of fire on the eastern horizon. Those campfires had been lit by our men who were still at Eads Byrig. They had to finish the fortress's destruction, and then, I hoped, find a way to capture the handful of ships Ragnall had left on the Mærse's northern bank. I had put young Æthelstan in command there, though I made sure he had older men to advise him, yet even so I touched the hammer that hung from my neck and prayed to the gods that he did nothing foolish.

'I should make Eads Byrig a burh,' Æthelflaed said.

'You should,' I said, 'but you won't have time before Ragnall gets here.'

‘I know that,’ she said impatiently.

‘But without Eads Byrig,’ I said, ‘he’ll be in trouble.’

‘What’s to stop him making new walls?’

‘We stop him,’ I said firmly. ‘Do you know how long it will take to make a proper wall around that hilltop? Not that fake thing Haesten put up, but a real wall? It will take all summer! And you have the rest of the army coming here, we have the fyrd, we’ll outnumber him within a week and we’ll give him no peace. We raid, we kill, we haunt him. He can’t build walls if his men are constantly in mail and waiting to be attacked. We slaughter his forage parties, we send big war-bands into the forest, we make his life a living hell. He’ll last two months at most.’

‘He’ll assault us here,’ she said.

‘Eventually he will,’ I said, ‘and I hope he does! He’ll fail. These walls are too strong. I’d be more worried about Brunanburh. Put extra men there and dig the ditch deeper. If he takes Brunanburh then he has his fortress and we have problems.’

‘I’m strengthening Brunanburh,’ she said.

‘Dig the ditch deeper,’ I said again, ‘deeper and wider, and put two hundred extra men into the garrison. He’ll never capture it.’

‘It will all be done,’ she said, then touched my elbow and smiled. ‘You sound very confident.’

‘By summer’s end,’ I said vengefully, ‘I’ll have Ragnall’s sword and he’ll have a grave in Mercia.’

I touched the hammer at my neck, wondering

whether by saying that aloud I had tempted the three Norns who weave our fate at the foot of Yggdrasil. It was not a cold night, but I shivered.

Wyrd bið ful āræd.

On the night before Eostre's feast there was another fight outside the Pisspot. A Frisian in Æthelflaed's service was killed, while a second man, one of mine, lost an eye. At least a dozen other men were hurt badly before my son and Sihtric managed to end the street battle. It was my son who brought me the news, waking me in the middle of the night. 'We've managed to stop the fighting,' he said, 'but it was damned close to being a slaughter.'

'What happened?' I asked.

'Mus happened,' he said flatly.

'Mus?'

'She's too pretty,' my son said, 'and men fight over her.'

'How many is it now?' I snarled.

'Three nights in a row,' my son said, 'but this is the first death.'

'It won't be the last unless we stop the little bitch.'

'What little bitch?' Eadith asked. She had woken and now sat up, clutching the bed pelts to her breasts.

'Mus,' he said.

'Mouse?'

'She's a whore,' I explained, and looked back to

my son, 'so tell Byrdnoth that if there's another fight I'll close his damned tavern down!'

'She doesn't work for Byrdnoth any more,' my son spoke from the doorway where he was just a shadow against the darkness of the courtyard behind. 'And Lady Æthelflaed's men are wanting to keep the fight going.'

'Mus doesn't work for Byrdnoth now?' I asked. I had climbed out of bed and was groping on the floor for something to wear.

'Not any more,' Uhtred said, 'she did, but I'm told the other whores don't like her. She was too popular.'

'So if the other girls don't like her what's she doing in the Pisspot?'

'She's not. She's working her magic in a shed next door.'

'Her magic?' I sneered at that, then pulled on trews and a stinking jerkin.

'An empty shed,' my son ignored my question. 'It's one of those old hay stores that belong to Saint Peter's church.'

A church building! That was hardly surprising. Æthelflaed had granted half the city's property to the church, and half those buildings were unused. I assumed that Leofstan would be putting his cripples and orphans into some of them, but I planned to use most to shelter the fyrd who would garrison Ceaster. Many of the fyrd had already arrived, country men and boys bringing axes, spears, hoes, and hunting bows. 'A whore in a church building?'

I asked as I dragged on boots. 'The new bishop won't like that.'

'He might love it,' my son said, amused, 'she's a very talented girl. But Byrdnoth wants her out of the shed. He says she's ruining his business.'

'So why doesn't he hire her back? Why doesn't he smack the other girls into line and hire the bitch?'

'She won't be hired now, she says she hates Byrdnoth, she hates the other girls, and she hates the Pisspot.'

'And idiots like you keep her busy,' I said savagely.

'She's a pretty little mouse,' he said wistfully. Eadith giggled.

'Expensive?' I asked.

'Anything but! Give her a duck egg and she'll bounce you off the shed walls.'

'Got bruises, have you?' I asked him. He did not answer. 'So they're fighting over her now?'

He shrugged. 'They were.' He looked over his shoulder. 'She seems to favour our men over Æthelflaed's and that causes the trouble. Sihtric has a dozen men keeping them apart for now, but for how long?'

I had covered my clothes with a cloak, but now hesitated. 'Godric!' I shouted, then shouted again until the boy came running. He was my servant, and a good one, but he was of an age when I needed to find another so Godric could stand in the shield wall. 'Bring me my mail coat, my sword and a helmet,' I said.

'You're going to fight?' my son sounded astonished.

'I'm going to frighten the mouse-bitch,' I said. 'If she's setting our men against Lady Æthelflaed's then she's doing Ragnall's work.'

There was a crowd of men outside the Pisspot, their angry faces lit by flaming torches bracketed to the tavern's walls. They were jeering Sihtric who, with a dozen men, guarded the alley that apparently led to the mouse's shed. The crowd fell silent as I arrived. Merewalh appeared at the same moment and looked askance at my mail, helmet, and sword. He was soberly dressed in black with a silver cross hanging at his neck. 'Lady Æthelflaed sent me,' he explained, 'and she's not happy.'

'Nor am I.'

'She's at the vigil, of course. So was I.'

'The vigil?'

'The vigil before Easter,' he said, frowning. 'We pray in church all night and greet the dawn with song.'

'What a wild life you Christians do lead,' I said, then looked at the crowd. 'All of you,' I shouted, 'go to bed! The excitement's over!'

One man, with more ale inside him than sense, wanted to protest, but I stalked towards him with my hand on Serpent-Breath's hilt and his companions dragged him away. I stood, malevolent and glowering, waiting until the crowd had dispersed, then turned back to Sihtric. 'Is the wretched girl still in her shed?'

'Yes, lord.' He sounded relieved that I had come.

Eadith had also arrived, tall and striking in a long green dress and with her flame-red hair loosely tied on top of her head. I beckoned her into the alley and my son followed. There had been a dozen men waiting in the narrow space, but they had vanished as soon as they heard my voice. There were five or six sheds at the alley's end, all of them low wooden buildings that were used to store hay, but only one showed a glimmer of light. There was no door, just an opening that I ducked under, and then stopped.

Because, by the gods, the mouse was beautiful.

Real beauty is rare. Most of us suffer the pox and so have faces dotted with scars, and what teeth we have left go yellow, and our skin has warts, wens, and carbuncles, and we stink like sheep dung. Any girl who survives into womanhood with teeth and a clear skin is accounted a beauty, but this girl had so much more. She had a radiance. I thought of Frigg, the mute girl who had married Cnut Ranulfson and who now lived on my son's estate, though he thought I did not know. Frigg was glorious and beautiful, but where she was dark and lithe, this girl was fair and generous. She was stark naked, her thighs lifted, and her flawless skin seemed to glow with health. Her breasts were full, but not fallen, her blue eyes lively, her lips plump, and her face full of joy until

I hauled the man out from between her thighs. 'Go and piss it into a ditch,' I snarled at him. He was one of my men and he pulled up his trews and scuttled out of the shed as if twenty demons were at his arse.

The mus fell backwards on the hay. She bounced there, giggling and smiling. 'Welcome again, Lord Uhtred,' she spoke to my son, who said nothing. There was a shielded lantern perched on a pile of hay and I saw my son blush in its dim and flickering light.

'Talk to me,' I growled, 'not him.'

She stood and brushed pieces of straw from her perfect skin. Not a scar, not a blemish, though when she turned to me I saw there was a birthmark on her forehead, a small red mark shaped like an apple. It was almost a relief to see that she was not perfect, because even her hands were unscarred. Women's hands grow old fast, burned by pots, worn out by distaffs, and rubbed raw by scrubbing clothes, yet Mus had hands like a baby, soft and flawless. She seemed utterly unworried by her nakedness. She smiled at me and half bobbed down respectfully. 'Greetings, Lord Uhtred,' she spoke demurely, her eyes showing amusement at my anger.

'Who are you?'

'I'm called Mus.'

'What did your parents name you?'

'Trouble,' she said, still smiling.

'Then listen to me, Trouble,' I snarled, 'you have

a choice. Either you work for Byrdnoth in the Plover next door, or you leave Ceaster. Do you understand?'

She frowned and bit her lower lip as she pretended to think, then gave me her bright smile again. 'I was only celebrating Eostre's feast,' she said slyly, 'as I'm told you like it celebrated.'

'What I don't like,' I said, biting back my annoyance at her cleverness, 'is that a man died fighting over you tonight.'

'I tell them not to fight,' she said, all wide-eyed and innocent. 'I don't want them to fight! I want them to . . .'

'I know what you want,' I snarled, 'but what matters is what I want! And I'm telling you to either work for Byrdnoth or leave Ceaster.'

She wrinkled her nose. 'I don't like Byrdnoth.'

'You'll like me even less.'

'Oh, no,' she said, and laughed, 'oh no, lord, never!'

'You work for Byrdnoth,' I insisted, 'or you leave!'

'I won't work for him, lord,' she said, 'he's so fat and slimy!'

'Your choice, bitch,' I said, and I was having trouble from keeping my eyes from those beautiful plump breasts and from her small body that was both compact and generous, and she knew I was having trouble and it amused her.

'Why Byrdnoth?' she asked.

'Because he won't let you cause trouble,' I said. 'You'll hump who he tells you to hump.'

'Including him,' she said, 'and it's disgusting! It's like being bounced by a greased pig.' She gave a shiver of horror.

'If you won't work at the Plover,' I ignored her exaggerated shudder, 'then you're leaving Ceaster. I don't care where you go, but you're leaving.'

'Yes, lord,' she said meekly, then glanced at Eadith. 'May I dress, lord?' she asked me.

'Get dressed,' I snapped. 'Sihtric?'

'Lord?'

'You'll guard her tonight. Lock her up in one of the granaries and see her on the road south tomorrow.'

'It's Easter tomorrow, lord, no one will be travelling,' he said nervously.

'Then keep her quiet till someone does go south! Then pack her off and make certain she doesn't come back.'

'Yes, lord,' he said.

'And tomorrow,' I turned on my son, 'you'll pull down these sheds.'

'Yes, father.'

'And if you do come back,' I looked back to the girl, 'I'll whip the skin off your back till your ribs are showing, you understand?'

'I understand, lord,' she said in a contrite voice. She smiled at Sihtric, her jailer, then stooped into a gap between the piles of hay. Her clothes had been carelessly dropped into the gap and she went down on all fours to retrieve them. 'I'll just get dressed,' she said, 'and I won't cause you any trouble! I promise.' And with those words she suddenly shot forward and vanished through a hole in the shed's back wall. A small hand snaked back and snatched a cloak or dress, and then she was gone.

'After her!' I said. She had wriggled through the mousehole, leaving a small pile of coins and hack-silver beside the lantern. I stooped, but saw the hole was too small for me to negotiate, so I ducked back into the alley. There was no passage to the rear of the shed and by the time we had made our way through the neighbouring house she had long disappeared. I stood at an alley's mouth, staring down an empty side street, and swore in frustration. 'Someone must know where the bitch lives,' I said.

'She's a mouse,' my son said, 'so you need a cat.'

I growled. At least, I thought, I had scared the girl, so perhaps she'd stop her nonsense. And why did she favour my men over Æthelflaed's? Mine were no cleaner or richer. I guessed she was just a trouble-maker who enjoyed having men fight over her.

'You pull the sheds down tomorrow,' I told my son, 'and look for the bitch. Find her and lock her up.'

Eadith and I walked back towards our house. 'She's beautiful,' Eadith said wistfully.

'With that birthmark on her forehead?' I asked in a hopeless attempt to pretend I did not agree.

'She is beautiful,' Eadith insisted.

‘And so are you,’ I said, and so she was.

She smiled at the compliment, though her smile was dutiful, even touched by sadness. ‘She’s what? Sixteen? Seventeen? When you find her you should marry her off.’

‘What man would marry a whore like her?’ I asked savagely, thinking that what I truly wanted was to take the whore to bed and plough her ripe little body.

‘Maybe a husband would tame her,’ Eadith said.

‘Maybe I should marry you,’ I said impulsively.

Eadith stopped, looked at me. We were just outside the big church where the Easter vigil was being kept, and a wash of candlelight came through the open door to shadow her face and to glint off the tears on her cheeks. She reached up with both hands and held the cheek-pieces of my helmet, then stood on tiptoe to kiss me.

God, what fools women make of us.

I always liked to make something special of Eostre’s feast, hiring jugglers, musicians, and acrobats, but Ragnall’s appearance a few days before the feast had deterred such folk from coming to Ceaster. The same fear meant that many of the guests invited to Leofstan’s enthronement had also failed to appear, though Saint Peter’s church was still full.

Enthronement? Who in the cloud-filled heavens did these people think they were? Kings sat on thrones. Lady Æthelflaed should have had a throne, and sometimes used her dead husband’s throne in

Gleawecestre, and when, as a lord, I sat in judgement I used a throne, not because I was royal, but because I represented royal justice. But a bishop? Why would some weasel-brained bishop need a throne? Wulfheard had a throne larger than King Edward's, a high-backed chair carved with gormless saints and bellowing angels. I asked the fool once why he needed so large a chair for his skinny backside, and he told me he was God's representative in Hereford. 'It is God's throne, not mine,' he had said pompously, though I noted that he screeched in anger if anyone else dared park their bum on the carved seat.

'Does your god ever visit Hereford?' I asked him.

'He is omnipresent, so yes, he sits on the throne.'

'So you sit on his lap? That's nice.'

I somehow doubted that the Christian god would be visiting Ceaster because Leofstan had chosen a milking-stool as his throne. It was a three-legged stool that he had bought at the market, and it now stood waiting for him in front of the altar. I had wanted to sneak into the church the night before Eostre's feast to saw a finger's width off two of the legs, but the vigil had thwarted that plan. 'A stool?' I had asked Æthelflaed.

'He's a humble man.'

'But Bishop Wulfheard says it's your god's throne.'

'God is humble too.'

A humble god! You might as well have a toothless wolf! The gods are the gods, ruling thunder and commanding storms, they are the lords of night and day, of fire and ice, the givers of disaster and of triumph. To this day I do not understand why folk become Christians unless it's simply that the other gods enjoy a joke. I have often suspected that Loki, the trickster god, invented Christianity because it has his wicked stench all over it. I can imagine the gods sitting in Asgard one night, all of them bored and probably drunk, and Loki amuses them with a typical piece of his nonsense, 'Let's invent a carpenter,' he suggests, 'and tell the fools that he was the son of the only god, that he died and came back to life, that he cured blindness with lumps of clay, and that he walked on water!' Who would believe that nonsense? But the trouble with Loki is that he always takes his jests too far.

The street outside the church was piled with weapons, shields, and helmets belonging to the men who attended the enthronement. They needed to be armed, or at least to stay close to their weapons, because our scouts had come back from the upper Mærse to tell us that Ragnall's army was approaching. They had seen his campfires in the night, and dawn had brought the sight of smoke smeared across the eastern sky. By now, I reckoned, he should be discovering the remnants of Eads Byrig. He would come to Ceaster next, but we would see him approaching, and the neat piles of weapons and shields were ready for the men inside the church. When they heard the alarm they would have to abandon the bishop's sermon and take to the ramparts.

There had been some good news that morning. Æthelstan had succeeded in taking two ships from the hulls Ragnall had left on the Mærse's northern bank. Both were wide-bellied, high-prowed fighting ships, one with benches for sixty oars and the other for forty. 'The rest of the ships were beached,' Æthelstan reported to me, 'and we couldn't drag them off.'

'They weren't guarded?'

'Probably sixty or seventy men there, lord.'

'How many did you have?'

'Seven of us crossed the river, lord.'

'Seven!'

'None of the others could swim.'

'You can swim?'

'Like a herring, lord!'

Æthelstan and his six companions had stripped naked, and, in the dead of night, crossed the river at the height of the tide. They had managed to cut the lines of the two moored boats, which had then drifted down the Mærse and were now safely tied to the remnants of the pier at Brunanburh. I wanted to put Æthelstan back in charge of that fort, but Æthelflaed insisted that Osferth, her half-brother, should command there, and that decision meant that Æthelstan, poor boy, was now condemned to endure the interminable service that turned Father Leofstan into Bishop Leofstan.

I peered into the church a couple of times. There was the usual chanting, while a dozen priests wafted smoke from swinging censers. An abbot with a waist-length beard gave an impassioned sermon that must have lasted two hours and which drove me to a tavern across the street. When I next looked I saw Leofstan prostrate on the church's floor with his arms outspread. All his cripples were there, while the moon-touched lunatics gibbered and scratched at the back of the church, and the white-robed orphans fidgeted. Most of the congregation was kneeling, and I could see Æthelflaed next to the bishop's wife who, as usual, was swathed in layers of clothing and was now rocking backwards and forwards with her clasped hands held high above her head as though she was experiencing an ecstatic vision. It was, I thought, a sad way to celebrate Eostre's feast.

I walked to the northern gate, climbed the ramparts, and stared at the empty countryside. My son joined me, but said nothing. He was in command of the guard this morning, which meant he was excused from attending the church service, and the two of us stood in companionable silence. There should have been a busy fair in the strip of pastureland between the city ditch and the Roman cemetery, but instead the few market stalls had been placed in the main street. Eostre would not be pleased, though perhaps she would be forgiving because she was not a vengeful goddess. I had heard stories of her when I was a small child, though the stories had been whispered because we were supposed to be Christians, but I heard how she skipped through the dawn, scattering flowers, and how the animals followed her two by two, and how the elves and sprites gathered around with pipes made from reeds and with drums made of thistle-heads, and played their wild music as Eostre sang the world into a new creation. She would look like Mus, I thought, remembering the firm body, the glow of her skin, the glint of joy in her eyes, and the mischief in her smile. Even the memory of her one flaw, the apple-shaped birthmark, seemed attractive now. 'Did you find the girl?' I broke the silence.

'Not yet,' he sounded disconsolate. 'We searched everywhere.'

'You're not keeping her hidden yourself?'

'No, father, I promise.'

'She has to live somewhere!'

'We've asked. We've looked. She just vanished!' He made the sign of the cross. 'I'm thinking she doesn't really exist. That she's a night-walker?'

'Don't be an idiot,' I scoffed. 'Of course she exists! We saw her. And you've more than seen her!'

'But no one saw her last night,' he said, 'and she was naked when she vanished.'

'She took a cloak.'

'Even so, someone would have seen her! A half-naked girl running through the streets? How could she just disappear? But she did!' He paused, frowning. 'She's a night-walker! A shadow-walker!'

A shadow-walker? I had scorned the idea, but shadow-walkers did exist. They were ghosts and spirits and goblins, malevolent creatures who only appeared in the night. And Mus, I thought, was truly malevolent, she was causing trouble by setting my men against Æthelflaed's warriors. And she was too perfect to be real. So was she an apparition sent by the gods to taunt us? To taunt me, anyway, as I remembered the lantern light on her plump breasts. 'She has to be stopped,' I said, 'unless you want a nightly battle between our men and Lady Æthelflaed's.'

'She won't appear again tonight,' my son said uncertainly, 'she won't dare.'

'Unless you're right,' I said, 'and she is a shadow-walker,' I touched the hammer at my neck.

And then I kept my hand on the talisman.

Because from the far woods, from the forest that shrouded the land all around distant Eads Byrig, Ragnall's army was coming.

Ragnall's men came in a line, and that was impressive because the line did not trail out of the forest on the Roman road in a long procession, but instead appeared altogether at the edge of the trees and so suddenly filled the land. One moment the fields were empty, then a great line of horsemen emerged from the woodlands. It must have taken time to arrange that display and it was intended to awe us.

One of my men hammered the iron bar that hung above the gate's fighting rampart. The bar served as a makeshift alarm bell and its harsh sound was brutal and loud, summoning the defenders to the walls. 'Keep hitting it,' I told him. I could see men pouring out of the church, hurrying to snatch up the shields, helmets, and weapons that were stacked in the street.

'Five hundred of them?' my son suggested.

I turned back to stare at the enemy. I divided the far line into half, then half again and counted horses, then multiplied my answer by four. 'Six hundred,' I reckoned. 'Maybe that's all the horses he has.'

'He'll have more men, though.'

'Two thousand, at least.'

Six hundred horsemen were no threat to Ceaster, but I still kept the iron bar's clangour sounding across the town. Men were climbing the ramparts now, and Ragnall would see our spear-points thickening above the high stone walls. I wished he would attack. There is no easier way to kill an enemy than when he is trying to assault a well-defended rampart.

'He'll have been to Eads Byrig,' my son suggested. He was staring eastwards to where the smoke of our corpse-burning fire still smeared the sky. He was thinking that Ragnall would be enraged by the severed heads I had left to greet him and hoping, I think, that those bloodied heads would prompt Ragnall into a foolish assault on the city.

'He won't attack today,' I said. 'He might be headstrong, but he's no fool.'

A horn sounded from that long line of men who

now advanced slowly across the pastureland. The sound of the horn was as harsh as the clangour of my iron bar. I could see men on foot behind the horsemen, but even so there were not more than seven hundred enemy in sight. That was not nearly enough to assault our walls, but I was not summoning the defenders in expectation of any attack, but rather to show Ragnall that we were ready for him. We were both making a display.

'I wish he'd make an assault,' my son said wistfully.

'Not today.'

'He'll lose men if he does!' He was hoping I was wrong, hoping he would have a chance to kill men trying to scale stone walls.

'He has men to lose,' I said drily.

'If I was him,' my son began, then checked.

'Go on.'

'I wouldn't want to lose two hundred men on these walls. I'd raid deeper into Mercia. I'd go south. There are rich pickings down south, but here?'

I nodded. He was right, of course. To attack Ceaster was to assault one of Mercia's strongest fortresses, and the country around Ceaster would be poor territory for plunder or slaves. Folk had gone to their nearest burh, taking their families and livestock with them. We were ready for war, even wanting battle, but a sudden march south into the heartland would find plump farms and easy plunder. 'He will raid deeper into Mercia,' I said, 'but he still wants Ceaster. He won't attack today, but he will attack.'

'Why?'

'Because he can't be King of Britain without capturing the burhs,' I said. 'And because Ceaster is Lady Æthelflaed's achievement. There are plenty of men who still think a woman shouldn't rule a land, but they can't argue with her success. She's fortified this whole district! Her husband was scared of the place. All he did was piss into the wind, but she drove the Danes out. If she does nothing else, then Ceaster stands as her victory! So take this city from her and you make her look weak. Take Ceaster and you've opened up all western Mercia to invasion. If Ragnall wins here he could destroy all Mercia, and he knows it. He won't just be King of Northumbria, but of Mercia too, and that's worth losing two hundred men.'

'But without Eads Byrig . . .'

'Losing Eads Byrig has made life difficult for him,' I interrupted him, 'but he still needs Ceaster! The Irish are driving the Norse out of Ireland, and where will they go? Here! But they can't come here if we hold the rivers.' Indeed it was our failure to hold the rivers that had let Ragnall into Britain in the first place. 'So, yes,' I went on, 'the battle we fight here isn't just for Ceaster, but for everything! For Mercia and in the end for Wessex too.'

The great line of horsemen had stopped, and a smaller group now rode towards the city. There were perhaps a hundred horsemen in the smaller group, followed by some footmen, all of them beneath two great banners. One showed the red axe of Ragnall, the same symbol that his brother Sigtryggr flew, but the second banner was new to me. It was a flag, a big flag, and it was black. Just that, a black flag, except it was made more sinister because the flag's trailing edge had been ripped to tattered shreds so that it blew ragged in the sea wind. 'Whose flag is that?' I asked.

'Never seen it,' my son said.

Finan, Merewalh, and Æthelflaed came to the rampart. None of them recognised the flag. What made it strange was that the flag was every bit as big as Ragnall's axe, suggesting that whoever marched beneath the ragged black banner was his equal.

'There's a woman there,' Finan said. He had eyes like a falcon.

'Ragnall's wife?' Æthelflaed asked.

'Could be,' Merewalh said, 'they say he has four.'

'It's a woman in black,' Finan said. He was shading his eyes as he peered at the approaching enemy. 'She's on the small horse right in front of the flag.'

'Unless it's a priest?' Merewalh suggested uncertainly.

The great line of horsemen had begun beating their swords against their shields, a rhythmic and threatening sound, harsh in the day's warm sunlight. I could see the woman now. She was swathed in black, with a black hood over her head, and she rode a small black horse that was dwarfed by the stallions of the men who surrounded her. 'He won't have a priest with him,' Finan said, 'it's a woman, sure enough.'

'Or a child,' I said. The rider of the small horse was also small.

The horsemen stopped. They were some two hundred paces away, well beyond the distance we could hurl a spear or an axe. Some members of the fyrd carried bows, but they were short hunting bows that were not powerful enough to pierce mail. Such bows forced an enemy to keep his exposed face below his shield, and they were useful at very short distances, but to loose an arrow at two hundred paces was a waste, provoking the enemy to jeer. Two archers did loose and I bellowed at them to put their weapons down. 'They've come to talk,' I shouted, 'not to fight.'

'Yet,' Finan muttered.

I could see Ragnall clearly enough. He was flamboyant as ever, his long hair blowing in the wind and his inked chest bare. He kicked his stallion a few paces forward and stood in his stirrups. 'Lord Uhtred,' he shouted, 'I bring you gifts!' He turned back towards his standard as the men on foot threaded their way between the horses and came towards the ramparts.

'Oh no,' Æthelflaed said, 'no!'

'Forty-three,' I said bitterly. I did not even need to count.

'Play with the devil,' Finan said, 'and you get burned.'

Forty-three men carrying drawn swords were pushing forty-three prisoners towards us. The swordsmen spread into a rough line and stopped, then thrust the prisoners down onto their knees. The prisoners, all of whose hands were bound behind their backs, were mostly men, but there were women among them, women who stared in desperation at our banners that hung from the ramparts. I had no idea who the prisoners were, except they must be Saxon and Christian. They were revenge.

Ragnall must have been told of the forty-three heads waiting on the summit of Eads Byrig and this was his answer. There was nothing we could do. We had manned the walls of Ceaster, but I had not thought to mount men on horses to make any sally out of the gate. We could only listen as the victims wailed and only watch as the swords fell, as the bright blood splashed the morning, and as the heads rolled on the thin turf. Ragnall mocked us with his handsome smile as the swordsmen wiped their blades on the clothes of their victims.

And then there was one last gift, one last prisoner.

That prisoner could not walk. He or she was brought draped over the back of a horse and at first I could not see if it was a man or a woman, I could only see that it was a person dressed in white who was heaved off the horse onto the blood-wet grass. None of us spoke. Then I saw it was a man and I thought him dead until he slowly rolled over and I saw he was dressed in the white robes of a priest, but what was strange was that the front of his skirt was panelled in bright red.

'Christ,' Finan breathed.

Because the skirt was not panelled. It was coloured by blood. The man curled up as if to crush the pain in his groin, and at that moment the black-robed rider spurred her horse forward.

She came close, careless of the threat of our throwing spears, our arrows, or axes. She stopped just yards away from the ditch and pushed back the hood of her cloak and stared up at us. She was an old woman, her face lined and harsh, her hair sparse and white, her lips a thin grimace of hatred. 'What I did to him,' she said, pointing at the wounded man lying behind her, 'I shall do to you! To all of you. One at a time!' She suddenly produced a small curved knife. 'I shall geld your boys, your women shall be whores, and your children slaves, because you are cursed. All of you!' She shrieked those last three words and swept the gelding knife in a curve as if to point to all of us watching from the ramparts. 'You will all die! You are cursed by day and by night, by fire and by water, by fate!'

She spoke our language, the English tongue.

She rocked backwards and forwards in her saddle as if gathering strength and then she took a deep breath and pointed the knife at me. 'And you, Uhtred of Bebbanburg, Uhtred of Nothing, will die last and die slowest because you have betrayed the gods. You are cursed. You are all cursed!' She cackled then, a mad sound, before pointing the blade at me again. 'The gods hate you, Uhtred! You were their son, you were their favourite, you were loved by them, but you chose to use your gifts for the false god, for the filthy Christian god, and now the real gods hate you and curse you! I speak to the gods, they listen to me, they will give you to me and I will kill you so slowly that your death will last till Ragnarok!' And with that she hurled the small knife at me. It fell short, clattering on the wall and dropping to the ditch. She turned away, and all the enemy went with her, back to the trees.

'Who is she?' Æthelflaed asked, her voice scarce above a whisper.

'Her name,' I said, 'is Brida.'

And the gelded priest turned an agonised face towards me and called for help. 'Father!'

He was my son.

PART II

THE GHOST FENCE

CHAPTER 7

Brida.

She was a Saxon who was raised a Christian; a wild-child, my first lover, a girl of passion and fire, and Brida, like me, had found the older gods, but where I have always accepted that the god of the Christians has power like all the other gods, Brida had convinced herself that the Christian god was a demon and that Christianity was an evil that must be eradicated if the world was ever to be good again. She had married my dear friend, Ragnar, she had become more Danish than the Danes, and she had tried to suborn me, to tempt me, to persuade me to fight for the Danes against the Saxons, and she had hated me ever since I had refused. She was a widow now, but she still ruled Ragnar's great fortress of Dunholm, which, after Bebbanburg, was the most formidable stronghold in Northumbria. She had now sided with Ragnall and, as I was later to learn, her declaration of support was enough to drive poor King Ingver into exile. Brida had brought Ragnar's army south, she had added her men to Ragnall's, and the

Northmen now had the strength to attack Ceaster and to accept the deaths that would soak the Roman walls with northern blood.

Beware the hatred of a woman.

Love curdles into hate. I had loved Brida, but she possessed an anger I could never match, an anger she believed came directly from the rage of the gods. It had been Brida who gave Serpent-Breath her name, who had cast a spell on the sword because, even as a child, she had believed the gods spoke directly to her. She had been a black-haired girl, thin as a twig, with a fierceness that burned like the fire that had killed the elder Ragnar and which we had watched together from the high trees. The only child Brida ever bore was mine, but the boy was born dead and she had never had another, so now her offspring were the songs she made and the curses she uttered. Ragnar's father, the blind Ravn, had prophesied that Brida would grow to be a skald and a sorceress, and so she had, but of the bitterest kind. She was an enchantress, white-haired and wizened now, chanting her skald's songs about dead Christians and of Odin triumphant. Songs of hate.

'What she wants,' I told Æthelflaed, 'is to take your god and nail him back to his tree.'

'He came back to life once,' she said piously, 'and he would rise again.'

I ignored that. 'And she wants all Britain worshipping the old gods.'

'A stale old dream,' Æthelflaed said scornfully.

'Just because it's been dreamed before,' I said, 'doesn't mean it can't come true.'

The old dream was the Northmen's vision of ruling all Britain. Again and again their armies had marched, they had invaded Mercia and Wessex, they had slaughtered the Saxons in battle, yet they had never succeeded in taking the whole island. Æthelflaed's father, King Alfred, had defeated them, he had saved Wessex, and ever since we Saxons had been fighting back, thrusting the Northmen ever further northwards. Now a new leader, stronger than any who had come before, threatened us with the old dream.

For me the war was about land. Perhaps that was because my uncle had stolen my land, had stolen the wild country around Bebbanburg, and to take back that land I first needed to defeat the Danes who surrounded it. My whole life has been about that windswept fortress beside the sea, about the land that is mine and was taken from me.

For King Alfred, for his son Edward, and his daughter Æthelflaed, the war was also about land, about the kingdoms of the Saxons. Alfred had saved Wessex, and his daughter was now thrusting the Northmen from Mercia while her brother, Edward of Wessex, took back the lands of East Anglia. But for both of them there was another cause worthy of death, their god. They fought for the Christian god, and in their minds the land belonged to their god and they would only reclaim it by doing his will. 'Englaland,' King Alfred had once said, 'will be God's land. If it exists it will exist because of Him, because He wishes it.' For a time he had even called it Godland, but the name had not stuck.

For Brida there was only one cause, her hatred of that Christian god. For her the war was a battle between the gods, between truth and falsehood, and she would happily have allowed the Saxons to kill every Northman if only they would abandon their religion and turn back to the old gods of Asgard. And now, at last, she had found a champion who would use sword and spear and axe to fight for her gods. And Ragnall? I doubt he cared about the gods. He wanted land, all of it, and he had wanted Brida's hardened warriors to come from their stronghold at Dunholm to add their blades to his army.

And my son?

My son.

I had disowned him, disinherited him, and spurned him, and now he had been returned to me by an enemy and he was no longer a man. He was gelded. The blood on his gown was crusted. 'He's dying,' Bishop Leofstan said sadly and made the sign of the cross over Uhtred's pale face.

His name had been Uhtred, the name always given to the eldest son of our family, but I had taken the name from him when he became a Christian priest. I had named him Judas instead, though he called himself Oswald. Father Oswald, famous for his honesty and piety, and famous too for being my son. My prodigal son. Now I knelt beside him and called him by his old name. 'Uhtred? Uhtred!'

But he could not answer. There was sweat on his forehead and he was shivering. After that one despairing cry of 'Father!' he seemed unable to speak. He tried, but no words came, just a whimper of excruciating pain. 'He's dying,' Bishop Leofstan said again, 'he has the death fever, lord.'

'Then save him,' I snarled.

'Save him?'

'That's what you do, isn't it? Heal the god-damned sick? So heal him.'

He stared at me, suddenly frightened. 'My wife . . .' he began, then faltered.

'What of her?'

'She heals the sick, lord,' he said, 'she has the touch of God in her hands. It is her calling, lord.'

'Then take him to her.'

Folcbald, one of my Frisian warriors and a man of prodigious strength, lifted Uhtred in his arms like a baby and so we took him into the city, following the bishop, who scurried ahead. He led us to one of the more substantial Roman houses on the main street, a house with a deep-arched gateway leading into a pillared courtyard from which a dozen doors led into large rooms. It was not unlike my own house in Ceaster and I was about to make some scornful remark about the bishop's taste for luxury when I saw that the arcade around the courtyard was filled with sick folk lying on straw pallets. 'There's not room for them all inside,' the bishop explained, then watched as the crippled gatekeeper picked up a short metal bar and struck a second bar that was hanging from the gateway's ceiling. Like my alarm bell it made a harsh sound and the gatekeeper went on striking it and I saw robed and hooded women scurrying away into the shadowed doorways. 'The sisters have abjured the company of men,' the bishop explained, 'unless the men are sick, dying, or wounded.'

'They're nuns?' I asked.

'They are a lay sisterhood,' he said, 'and one close to my heart! Most are poor women who wish to dedicate their lives to God's service, while others among them are sinners.' He made the sign of the cross. 'Fallen women,' he paused as though unable to bring himself to say the next words, 'women of the streets, lord! Of the alleyways! But all of them dear creatures we have brought back to God's grace.'

'Whores, you mean.'

'Fallen women, lord, yes.'

'And you live here with them?' I asked sarcastically.

'Oh no, lord!' He was amused rather than offended by the question. 'That would not be seemly! Dear me, no! My dear wife and I have a small dwelling in the alley behind the smithy. Praise God I am not sick, dying or wounded.' The gatekeeper finally put the small iron bar down and the last echo of the clangour died away as a tall, gaunt woman stalked across the courtyard. She had broad shoulders, a grim face, and hands like shovels. Leofstan was a tall man, but this woman towered over him.

'Bishop?' she demanded harshly. She faced Leofstan squarely, arms crossed, glaring down at him.

'Sister Ymma,' Leofstan said humbly as he pointed to the blood-drenched figure in Folcbald's arms, 'here is a grievously wounded priest. He needs my wife's care.'

Sister Ymma, who looked as if she might be useful in a shield wall, looked around and finally pointed to a corner of the arcade. 'There's space over . . .'

'He will be given his own room,' I interrupted her, 'and a bed.'

'He will . . .'

'Have his own room and a bed,' I repeated harshly, 'unless you want my men to scour this damned place clear of Christians? I command in this town, woman, not you!'

Sister Ymma bridled and wanted to protest, but the bishop placated her. 'We shall find room, sister!'

'You'll need room,' I said. 'In the next week you'll have at least a hundred more wounded.' I turned and poked a finger at Sihtric. 'Find space for the bishop. Two houses, three! Space for the wounded!'

'Wounded?' Leofstan asked, concerned.

'There's going to be a fight, bishop,' I told him angrily, 'and it won't be pretty.'

A room was cleared and my son was carried across the courtyard and through a narrow door into a small chamber where he was placed gently on a bed. He muttered something and I stooped to listen, but his words made no sense and then he curled himself by drawing up his legs and whimpered.

'Heal him,' I snarled at Sister Ymma.

'If it is God's will.'

'It's my will!'

'Sister Gomer will tend him,' the bishop told Sister Ymma who, it seemed, was the one sister allowed to confront men, a task she evidently undertook with relish.

'Sister Gomer is your wife?' I asked, remembering the strange name.

'Praise God, she is,' Leofstan said, 'and a dear darling creature she is too.'

'With a strange name,' I said, staring at my son, who moaned on the bed, still curled around his agony.

The bishop smiled. 'She was named Sunngifu by her mother, but when the dear sisters are born again into Christ Jesus they are given a new name, a baptismal name, and so my dear Sunngifu is now known as Sister Gomer. And with her new name God granted her the power of healing.'

'He did indeed,' Sister Ymma said grimly.

'And she will tend him,' the bishop assured me, 'and we shall pray for him!'

'As will I,' I said, and touched the hammer hanging at my neck.

I left. I turned at the gate and saw the cloaked, hooded sisters scurry out of their hiding places. Two went into my son's room and I fingered the hammer again. I had thought I hated my eldest son, but I did not. And so I left him there, lying tight about his cruel wound, and he shivered and he sweated and he moaned strange things in his fever, but he did not die that day, nor the next.

And I took revenge.

The gods loved me because that evening they sent grim clouds rolling from the west. They were sky-darkening clouds, heavy and black, and they came suddenly, building higher, looming in the evening sky to shroud the sunset, and with the clouds came rain and wind. Those grim clouds also brought opportunity, and with the opportunity came argument.

The argument raged inside Ceaster's Great Hall, while the paved Roman street outside was loud with the noise of horses. It was the noise of great war stallions crashing their hooves on stone paving, horses whinnying and snorting as men struggled to saddle the beasts in the seething rain. I was assembling horsemen, warriors of the storm.

'It will leave Ceaster undefended!' Merewalh protested.

'The fyrd will defend the city,' I said.

'The fyrd needs household warriors!' Merewalh insisted. He rarely disagreed with me, indeed he had always been one of my strongest supporters even when he had served Æthelred who had hated me, but my proposal that stormy night alarmed Merewalh. 'The fyrd can fight,' he allowed, 'but they need trained men to help them!'

'The city won't be attacked,' I snarled. Thunder crashed across the night sky to send the dogs that lived in the Great Hall slinking off to the dark corners. The rain was beating on the roof and leaking through a score of places in the old Roman tiles.

'Why else has Ragnall returned,' Æthelflaed asked, 'if not to attack us?'

'He won't attack tonight and he won't attack tomorrow,' I said. 'Which gives us a chance to claw the bastard.'

I was dressed for battle. I wore a knee-length leather jerkin beneath my finest mail coat that was cinched by a thick sword belt from which hung Serpent-Breath. My leather trews were tucked into tall boots reinforced by iron strips. My forearms were thick with warrior rings. Godric, my servant, held my wolf-crested helmet, a thick-hafted spear, and my shield with the snarling wolf's head of Bebbanburg painted on the iron-bound willow-boards. I was dressed for a killing and most in the hall were shrinking from the prospect.

Cynlæf Haraldson, Æthelflaed's young favourite,

who was rumoured to be marrying her daughter, sided with Merewalh. So far he had taken care to avoid antagonising me, using flattery and agreement to avoid any confrontation, but what I was now suggesting drove him to disagreement. 'What has changed, lord?' he asked respectfully.

'Changed?'

'When Ragnall was here before you were reluctant to lead men into the forest.'

'You feared ambush,' Merewalh put in.

'His men were in Eads Byrig,' I said. 'It was his refuge, his fortress. What was the point of leading men through ambush to die on its walls?'

'He still has . . .' Cynlæf began.

'No, he doesn't!' I snapped. 'We didn't know the walls were false! We thought it a fortress! Now it's just a hilltop.'

'He outnumbers us,' Merewalh said unhappily.

'And he always will outnumber us,' I said, 'until we kill enough of his men, and then we'll outnumber him.'

'The safe thing,' Æthelflaed began, then faltered. She sat in the great chair, a throne really, lit by the flickering fire in the central hearth. She had been listening carefully, her eyes looking from speaker to speaker, her face worried. Priests were gathered behind her and they too thought my plans rash.

'The safe thing?' I prompted her, but she just shook her head as if to suggest she had thought better of whatever she had been about to say.

'The safe thing,' Father Ceolnoth said firmly, 'is to make certain Ceaster does not fall!' Men murmured agreement and Father Ceolnoth, emboldened by the support, stepped forward to stand in the firelight beside Æthelflaed's chair. 'Ceaster is our newest diocese! It controls great areas of farmland! It protects the seaway. It is a bulwark against the Welsh! It protects Mercia from the pagan north! It must not be lost!' He stopped abruptly, maybe remembering the savagery with which I usually greeted military advice from priests.

'Take note of the bulwarks!' his brother lisped through his missing teeth, 'that you can tell it to the next generation!'

I stared at him, wondering if he had lost his brains along with his teeth, but the other priests all muttered and nodded approval. 'The words of the psalmist,' blind Father Cuthbert explained to me. Cuthbert was the one priest who supported me, but then he had always been eccentric.

'We cannot tell the next generation,' Father Ceolberht hissed, 'if the bulwarks are lost! We must protect the bulwarks! We cannot abandon Ceaster's walls.'

'It is the word of the Lord, praise be the Lord,' Ceolnoth said.

Cynlæf smiled at me. 'Only a fool ignores your advice,' he said with patronising flattery, 'and the defeat of Ragnall is our aim, of course, but the protection of Ceaster is just as important!'

'And to leave the walls undefended . . .' Merewalh said unhappily, but did not finish the thought.

Another rumble of thunder sounded. Rain was pouring through the hole in the roof and hissing in the hearth. 'God speaks!' Father Ceolnoth said.

Which god? Thor was the god of thunder. I was tempted to remind them of that, but saying as much would only antagonise them.

'We must shelter from the storm,' Ceolberht said, 'and the thunder is the sign that we must stay within these walls.'

'We should stay . . .' Æthelflaed began, but then was interrupted.

'Forgive me,' Bishop Leofstan said, 'dear lady, please, forgive me!'

Æthelflaed looked indignant at the interruption, but managed a gracious smile. 'Bishop?'

'What did our Lord say?' the bishop asked as he limped to the open space by the hearth where rain spattered on his robe. 'Did our Lord say that we should stay at home? Did he encourage us to crouch by the cottage fire? Did he tell his disciples to close the door and huddle by the hearth? No! He sent his followers forth! Two by two! And why? Because he gave them power over the overpowering enemy!' he spoke passionately, and, with astonishment, I realised he was supporting me. 'The kingdom of heaven is not spread by staying at home,' thc bishop said fervently, 'but by going forth as our Lord commanded!'

'Saint Mark,' a very young priest ventured.

'Well spoken, Father Olbert!' the bishop said. 'The commandment is indeed found in the gospel of Mark!' Another peal of thunder crashed in the night. The wind was rising, howling in the dark as the hall dogs whined. The rain was falling harder now, glinting in the firelight where it slanted down to hiss in the bright flames. 'We are commanded to go forth!' the bishop said. 'To go forth and conquer!'

'Bishop,' Cynlæf began.

'The ways of the Lord are strange,' Leofstan ignored Cynlæf. 'I cannot explain why our God has blessed us with the Lord Uhtred's presence, but one thing I do know. The Lord Uhtred wins battles! He is a mighty warrior for the Lord!' He paused suddenly, flinching, and I remembered the sudden pains that assailed him. For a moment he looked in agony, one hand clutched to the robe above his heart, then the pain vanished from his face. 'Is anyone here a greater warrior than the Lord Uhtred?' he asked. 'If so, let them stand up!' Most of the men were already standing, but they seemed to know what Leofstan meant. 'Does anyone here know more of war than Lord Uhtred? Is there anyone here who strikes more fear into the enemy?' He paused, waiting, but no one spoke or stirred. 'I do not deny that he is grievously mistaken about our faith, that he is in need of God's grace and of Christ's forgiveness, but God has sent him to us and we must not reject the gift.' He bowed to Æthelflaed. 'My lady, forgive my humble opinions, but I urge you to listen to the Lord Uhtred.'

I could have kissed him.

Æthelflaed looked about the hall. A spike of lightning lit the roof-hole, followed by a monstrous clap of thunder that shook the sky. Men shuffled their feet, but no one spoke to contradict the bishop. 'Merewalh,' Æthelflaed stood to show that the discussion was finished, 'you will stay in the city with one hundred men. All the rest,' she hesitated a moment, glancing at me, then made her decision, 'will ride with Lord Uhtred.'

'We leave two hours before dawn,' I said.

'Vengeance is mine!' the bishop said happily.

He was wrong. It was mine.

We were leaving Ceaster to attack Ragnall.

I led almost eight hundred men into the darkness. We rode out through the north gate into a storm as wild as any I remembered. Thunder filled the sky, lightning splintered across the clouds, the rain seethed and the wind howled like the shrieks of the damned. I led my men and Æthelflaed's men, the warriors of Mercia, soldiers of the storm, all mounted on good stallions, all in mail and armed with swords, spears, and axes. Bishop Leofstan had stood on the gate's rampart shouting blessings down on us, his voice snatched away by the gale. 'You do the Lord's work!' he had called. 'The Lord is with you, His blessing is upon you!'

The Lord's work was to break Ragnall. And of course it was a risk. Maybe even now Ragnall's warriors were filing through the wet darkness towards Ceaster, carrying ladders and readying themselves to fight and die on a Roman wall. But probably not. I needed neither omens nor scouts to tell me that Ragnall was not ready to assault Ceaster yet.

Ragnall had moved fast. He had taken his large army and lunged towards Eoferwic, and that city, key to the north, had fallen without a fight, and so Ragnall had turned back to make his assault on Ceaster. His men had marched unceasingly. They were tired. They had reached Eads Byrig to find it blood-soaked and ruined, and now they faced a Roman fort packed with defenders. They needed a day or two, more even, to ready themselves, to make the ladders and to find forage and to allow the laggards to catch up with the army.

Merewalh and the others were right, of course. The easiest and safest way to preserve Ceaster was to stay inside the high walls and let Ragnall's men die against the stones. And they would die. Much of the fyrd had arrived, bringing their axes, hoes, and spears. They had brought their families and livestock too, so the streets were filled with cattle, pigs, and sheep. The walls of Ceaster would be well defended, though that would not stop Ragnall making an attempt to cross the ramparts. But if we just stayed inside the walls and waited for that attempt we would yield all the surrounding countryside to his mercy. He would make an assault, and the assault would probably fail, but such was the size of his army that he could afford that failure and attack again. And all the time his troops would be raiding deep into Mercia, burning and killing, taking slaves and capturing livestock, and Æthelflaed's army would be locked into Ceaster, helpless to defend the land it was sworn to protect.

So I wanted to drive him away from Ceaster. I wanted to hit him hard now.

I wanted to hit him in the dark of the night's ending, hit him in the thunder of Thor's providential storm, hit him under the lash of Thor's lightning, strike him in the wind and the rain of the gods. I would bring him chaos. He had hoped to have Eads Byrig as a refuge, but he had no refuge now except for the shields of his men, and those men would be cowering in the storm, chilled and tired, and we rode to kill them.

And to kill Brida. I thought of my son, my gelded son, lying curled on his bed of pain, and I touched Serpent-Breath's hilt and promised myself her blade would taste blood before the sun was risen. I wanted to find Brida, the sorceress who had cut my son, and I swore I would make that vile creature scream till her voice drowned out even Thor's loud thunder.

Cynlæf led Æthelflaed's men. I would have preferred Merewalh, but Æthelflaed wanted someone reliable to guard Ceaster's walls and she had insisted Merewalh stayed, and sent Cynlæf in his place. She had told her favourite that he was to obey me. Æthelflaed, of course, had wanted to come herself and for once I had won that argument, telling her that the chaos of a fight in the half-light of a storm-ridden dawn was no place for her. 'It will be a killing, my lady,' I had told her, 'nothing but killing. And if you're there I'll have to give you a bodyguard, and those men can't join the slaughter. I need them all and I don't need to be worrying whether you're safe or not.' She had reluctantly accepted the argument, sending Cynlæf in her place, and he now rode close to me, saying nothing. We went slowly, we could not hurry. The only light came from the intermittent flashes of lightning that streaked to earth and silvered the sky, but I did not need light. What we did was simple. We would make chaos, and to make it we only needed to reach the forest's edge and wait there until the first faint wolf-light of dawn revealed the trees among the night's shadows and so let us ride safely to a slaughter.

A bolt of lightning showed when we reached the end of the pastureland. In front of us all was black, trees and bushes and ghosts. We stopped and the rain pounded about us. Finan moved his horse next to mine. I could hear his saddle creaking and the thump as his stallion pawed the wet ground. 'Make sure they're well spread out,' I said.

'They are,' Finan responded.

I had ordered the horsemen to form eight groups. Each would advance on its own, careless of what the others did. We were a rake with eight tines, a rake to claw through the forest. The only rules of the morning were that the groups were to kill, they were to avoid the inevitable shield wall that would eventually form, and they were to obey the sound of the horn when it called for withdrawal. I planned to be back in Ceaster for breakfast.

Unless the enemy knew we were coming. Unless their sentries had seen us approach, had seen us silvered in the wet darkness by the bright streaks of Thor's lightning. Unless they were already touching iron-rimmed shields together to make the wall that would be our death. It is during the time of waiting that the mind crawls into a coward's cave and whines to be spared. I thought of all that could go wrong and felt the temptation to be safe, to take the troops back to Ceaster and man the walls and let the enemy die in a furious assault. No one would blame me, and if Ragnall died beneath Ceaster's stones then his death would provide another song of Uhtred that would be chanted in mead halls across all Mercia. I touched the hammer hanging at my neck. All along the forest's edge men were touching their talismans, saying prayers to their god or gods, feeling the creep of fear chill their bones more thoroughly than the soaking rain and gusting wind.

'Almost,' Finan said in a low voice.

'Almost,' I answered. The wolf-light is the light between dark and light, between the night and the dawn. There are no colours, just the grey of a sword blade, of mist, the grey that swallows the ghosts and elves and goblins. Foxes seek their dens, badgers go to earth, and the owl flies home. Another bellow of thunder shook the sky and I looked up, the rain pelting on my face, and I prayed to Thor and to Odin. I do this for you, I said, for your amusement. The gods watch us, they reward us, and sometimes they punish us. At the foot of Yggdrasil the three hags were watching and smiling, and were they sharpening the shears? I thought of Æthelflaed, sometimes so cold and sometimes so desperate for warmth. She hated Eadith, who was so loyal to me and so loving and so fearful of Æthelflaed, and I thought of Mus, that creature of the dark who drove men wild, and I wondered if she feared anyone, and was instead a messenger from the gods.

I looked back to the woods and could see the shape of trees now, dark in the darkness, see the slash of rain. 'Almost,' I said again.

'In the name of God,' Finan muttered. I saw him make the sign of the cross. 'If you see my brother,' he said louder, 'he's mine.'

'If I see your brother,' I promised, 'he's yours.' Godric had offered me the heavy spear, but I preferred a sword, and so I pulled Serpent-Breath from her scabbard and held her straight out, and I could see the sheen of her blade like a shimmer of misted light in the dark. A horse whinnied. I raised the blade and kissed the steel. 'For Eostre,' I said, 'for Eostre and for Mercia!'

And the shadows beneath the trees dissolved into shapes, into bushes and trunks, of leaves thrashing in the wind. It was still night, but the wolf-light had come.

'Let's go,' I said to Finan, then raised my voice to a shout. 'Let's go!'

The time for hiding was over. Now it was speed and noise. I crouched in the saddle, wary of low branches, letting Tintreg pick his own way, but urging him on. The small light grew. The rain was beating on the leaves, the woods were full of the noise of horses, the wind was tossing high branches like mad things in torment. I waited to hear a horn calling to summon our enemies, but none sounded. Lightning flickered to the north, casting stark black shadows among the trees, then the thunder sounded and just then I saw the first pale light of a fire ahead. Campfires! Ragnall's men were in the clearings, and if he had set sentries they had not seen us, or we had passed them, and the flicker of fires fighting the drenching rain became brighter. I saw shadows among the fires. Some men were awake, presumably feeding the flames and oblivious that we were riding to their deaths. Then far off to my right, where the Roman road led into the forest, I heard shouts and knew our killing had begun.

That dawn was savage. Ragnall had thought we were sheltering behind Ceaster's walls, cowed there by his killings on Eostre's feast, but instead we burst on his men, coming with the thunder, and they were not ready. I crashed out of the trees into a wide clearing and saw miserable shelters hastily made from branches, and a man crawled from one, looked up and took Serpent-Breath in his face. The blade struck bone, jarred up my arm, and another man was running and I speared him in the back with the sword's tip. All around me horsemen were wounding and killing. 'Keep going,' I bellowed, 'keep going!' This was just one encampment in a clearing, the main camp was still ahead. A glow above the dark trees showed where fires were lit on the summit of Eads Byrig and I rode that way.

Back into the trees. The light was growing, shrouded by storm clouds, but ahead I could see the wide swathe of land cleared of trees that surrounded the slopes of Eads Byrig and it was there, among the stumps, that most of Ragnall's men were camped, and it was there we killed them. We burst from the woods with bloodied swords and we rode among the panicked men and we cut them down. Women screamed, children cried. My son led men from my right, slicing into fugitives fleeing from our swords. Tintreg thumped into a man, throwing him down into a fire that erupted sparks. His hair caught the flames. He shrieked and I back-handed Serpent-Breath to chop down another man running with wide eyes, his mail coat in his arms, and ahead of me a warrior bellowed defiance and waited with a spear for my charge and then turned, hearing hooves behind him, and died under a Frisian axe that clove his skull. Newly woken men were scrambling through the first ditch and over the earth wall and a horn was now sounding from the old fort's summit. I spurred into a group of men, slashing Serpent-Breath down savagely as Godric rode in with his levelled spear to slice a man's belly open. Tintreg snapped at a man, biting his face, then plunged on as thunder ripped the sky above us. Berg galloped past me, whooping, with a length of entrails dragging from his sword. He chopped the weapon down, turned his horse, and chopped again. The man Tintreg had bitten reeled away, hands clutched to his ruined face and blood seeping through his fingers. The brightest thing in that wolf-light was not the fires, but the blood of enemies reflecting the sudden glare of lightning.

I spurred towards the entrance of the ruined fort and saw a shield wall had formed across the track there. Men were running to join it, pushing their way into the ranks and lining their round shields to make the wall wider. Banners flew above them, but the flags were so soaked by rain that even that dawn's strong wind could not lift them. My son spurred past me, riding for the track, and I called him back. 'Leave them!' There were at least a hundred men guarding the entrance path. Horses could not break them. I was certain Ragnall was there, as was Brida, both beneath their waterlogged banners, but their deaths must wait for another day. We had come to kill, not to fight against a shield wall.

I had told my men that each had only to kill one man and that killing would almost halve

Ragnall's army. We were wounding more than we were killing, but a wounded man is more trouble to an enemy than a dead man. A corpse can be buried or burned, he can be mourned and abandoned, but the wounded need care. The sight of men with missing eyes or with bellies welling blood or with splintered bones showing through flesh will give fear to an enemy. A wounded army is a slow army, full of terror, and we slowed Ragnall even more by driving his horses back into the forest. We drove women and children too, encouraging them by killing any that defied us. Ragnall's men would know their womenfolk were in our hands and their children were destined for our slave markets. War is not kind, but Ragnall had brought war to Mercia in expectation that a land ruled by a woman would be easy to conquer. Now he was discovering just how easy.

I watched Cynlæf hunt down three men, all armed with spears and all trying to gut his horse before killing him. He dealt with them easily, using his skills as a horseman as well as his sword-craft to wound two and kill the third. 'Impressive,' Finan said grudgingly as we watched the young West Saxon turn his stallion, cut fast with his blade to open a man's arm from elbow to shoulder, then use the horse's weight to drive the last enemy down to the turf where he casually finished him off by leaning from the saddle and stabbing. Cynlæf saw we had watched him and grinned at us. 'Good hunting this morning, lord!' he called.

'Sound the horn,' I told Godric, who was grinning because he had killed and survived.

It was time to leave. We had ripped Ragnall's encampments apart, soaked the wolf-light in blood, and hurt the enemy grievously. Bodies lay among the campfires that now died under the lash of rain. A good part of Ragnall's army had survived, and those men were on the summit of Eads Byrig where they could only watch as our rampaging horsemen hunted down the last few survivors from the lower encampments. I gazed through the pelting downpour and thought I saw Ragnall standing next to a diminutive figure cloaked in black, and that could have been Brida. 'My brother's there,' Finan said bitterly.

'You can see him?'

'See him and smell him.' He rammed his sword back into its scabbard. 'Another day. I'll kill him yet.'

We turned away. We had come, we had killed, and now we left, driving horses, women and children ahead of us through the storm-drenched forest. No one pursued us. Ragnall's men, imbued with confidence because of their leader's arrogance, had been sheltering from the storm, and we had come with the thunder and now left with the dawn.

We lost eleven men. Just eleven. Two, I know, drove their horses across the ditches and up into the shield wall on Eads Byrig's summit, but the rest? I never discovered what happened to those nine men, but it was a small price to pay for the havoc we had inflicted on Ragnall's army. We had killed or wounded three or four hundred men and, once back in Ceaster, we discovered we had captured one hundred and seventeen horses, sixty-eight women, and ninety-four children. Even Ceolberht and Ceolnoth, the priests whose hatred for me was so fierce, stood applauding as the captives were driven through the gate. 'Praise God!' Father Ceolnoth exclaimed.

'Praise Him in the highest!' his brother hissed through missing teeth. A captive woman screamed at him and he stepped forward to slap her hard about the head. 'You're fortunate, woman,' he told her, 'you are in God's hands! You will be a Christian now!'

'All the little ones brought to Christ!' Bishop Leofstan exclaimed, looking eagerly at the crying children.

'Brought to Frankish slave markets,' Finan muttered.

I dropped from Tintreg's saddle, unbuckled the sword belt, and gave Serpent-Breath to Godric. 'Clean it well,' I told him, 'and grease it. Then find Father Glædwine and send him to me.'

Godric stared at me. 'You want a priest?' he asked in disbelief.

'I want Father Glædwine,' I said, 'so fetch him.'

Then I went to find breakfast.

Father Glædwine was one of Æthelflaed's priests, a young man with a high pale forehead and a perpetual frown. He was said to be learned, the product of one of King Alfred's schools in Wessex, and Æthelflaed used him as a clerk. He wrote her letters, copied her laws, and drew up land-charters, but his reputation went far beyond such menial duties. He was a poet, famed for the hymns he composed. Those hymns were chanted by monks in church and by harpists in halls, and I had been forced to listen to some, mainly when harpists sang in Æthelflaed's palace. I had expected them to be dull, but Father Glædwine liked his songs to tell stories and, despite my distaste, I had enjoyed listening. One of his better songs told of the woman blacksmith who had forged the nails used to crucify the nailed god. There had been three nails and three curses, the first of which resulted in one of her children being eaten by a wolf, the second doomed her husband to drowning in a Galilean cesspit, and the third gave her the shaking disease and turned her brain to pottage, all of which evidently proved the power of the Christian god.

It was a good story and that was why I summoned Glædwine, who looked as if his own brain had been turned to pottage when he came to the courtyard of my house where Godwin was plunging my mail coat into a barrel. The water had turned pink. 'That's blood,' I told a nervous Glædwine.

'Yes, lord,' he stammered.

'Pagan blood.'

'God be praised,' he began, then remembered I

was a pagan, 'that you lived, lord,' he added hastily and cleverly.

I struggled out of the leather jerkin that I wore beneath the mail coat. It stank. The courtyard was full of petitioners, but it always was. Men came for justice, for favours, or simply to remind me that they existed. Now they waited in the shelter of the roofed walkway that edged the courtyard. It still rained, though much of the storm's malevolence had faded. I saw Gerbruht, the big Frisian, among the petitioners. He was forcing a prisoner to his knees. I did not recognise the man, but assumed he was one of Æthelflaed's men who had been caught stealing. Gerbruht caught my eye and began to speak.

'Later,' I told him, and looked back to the pale priest. 'You will write a song, Glædwine.'

'Yes, lord.'

'A song of Eads Byrig.'

'Of course, lord.'

'This song will tell how Ragnall the Sea King, Ragnall the Cruel, came to Ceaster and was defeated there.'

'He was defeated, lord,' Glædwine repeated. He blinked as the rain fell into his eyes.

'You will tell how his men were cut down, how his women were captured, and his children enslaved.'

'Enslaved, lord,' he nodded.

'And how the men of Mercia carried their blades to an enemy and made them crawl in the mud.'

'The mud, lord.'

'It will be a song of triumph, Glædwine!'

'Of course, lord,' he said, frowning, then looked nervously around the courtyard. 'But don't you have your own poets, lord? Your harpists?'

'And what will my poets chant of Eads Byrig?'

He fluttered his ink-stained hands, wondering what answer I wanted. 'They will tell of your victory, lord, of course—'

'And that's what I don't want!' I interrupted him. 'This will be a song of Lady Æthelflaed's victory, you understand? Leave me out of it! Say the Lady Æthelflaed led the men of Mercia to their slaughter of the pagans, say your god led her and inspired her and gave her the triumph.'

'My God?' he asked astonished.

'I want a Christian poem, you idiot.'

'You want a . . .' the idiot began, then bit off the rest of his question. 'The Lady Æthelflaed's triumph, yes, lord.'

'And Prince Æthelstan,' I said, 'mention him too.' Æthelstan had ridden with my son and acquitted himself well.

'Yes, lord, Prince Æthelstan too.'

'He killed scores! Say that! That Æthelstan made corpses of the pagans. This is a song of Æthelflaed and Æthelstan, you don't even need to mention my name. You can say I stayed in Ceaster with a sore toe.'

'A sore toe, lord,' Glædwine repeated, frowning. 'You want this victory ascribed to Almighty God?'

'And to Æthelflaed,' I insisted.

'And it's Eastertide,' Glædwine said, almost to himself.

'Eostre's feast,' I corrected him.

'I can say it is the Easter victory, lord!' he sounded excited.

'It can be whatever you like,' I snarled, 'but I want that song chanted in every hall. I want it shouted in Wessex, heard in East Anglia, told to the Welsh, and sung in Frankia. Make it good, priest, make it bloody, make it exciting!'

'Of course, lord!'

'The song of Ragnall's defeat,' I said, though of course Ragnall was not defeated, not yet. More than half his army remained, and that half probably still outnumbered us, but he had been shown to be vulnerable. He had come across the sea and he had taken most of Northumbria with speed and daring, and the stories of those exploits would spread until men believed that Ragnall was fated to be a conqueror, so now was the time to tell folk that Ragnall could be beaten and that he would be beaten. And it was better that it was Æthelflaed who was shown to be Ragnall's doom because many men would not allow songs of Uhtred to be sung in their halls. I was a pagan, they were Christian. They would hear Glædwine's song, though, which would give the nailed god all the credit and take away some of the fear of Ragnall. And there were still fools who thought a woman should not rule, so let the fools hear a song about a woman's triumph.

I gave Glædwine gold. Like most poets he claimed he invented his songs because he had no choice, 'I never asked to be a poet,' he had told me once, 'but the words just come to me, lord. They come from the Holy Ghost! He is my inspiration!' That might have been true, though I noticed the Holy Ghost was a lot more inspiring when it smelt gold or silver. 'Write well,' I told him, then waved him away.

The moment that Glædwine scuttled to the gate all the petitioners surged forward to be checked by my spearmen. I nodded to Gerbruht. 'You're next.'

Gerbruht kicked his prisoner towards me. 'He's a Norseman, lord,' he said, 'one of Ragnall's scum.'

'Then why does he have both hands?' I asked. We had taken some men prisoner along with the women and children and I had ordered their sword hands chopped off before we let them go. 'He should be back at Eads Byrig,' I said, 'with a bloody stump for a wrist.' I took a pot of ale from one of the maids and drank it all. When I looked back I saw that the prisoner was crying. He was a good-looking man, maybe in his middle twenties, with a battle-scarred face and cheeks marked with inked axes. I was used to boys crying, but the prisoner was a hard-looking man and he was sobbing. That intrigued me. Most men face mutilation bravely or with defiance, but this man was weeping like a child. 'Wait,' I told Gerbruht, who had drawn a knife.

'I wasn't going to chop him here!' Gerbruht protested, 'Not here. Your lady Eadith doesn't like blood all over the courtyard. Remember that sow we butchered at Yule? She wasn't happy at all!' He kicked the sobbing prisoner. 'And we didn't capture this one in the dawn fight, lord, he only just arrived.'

'He only just arrived?'

'He rode his horse to the gate, lord. There were bastards chasing him, but he got here first.'

'Then we won't chop him or kill him,' I said, 'yet.' I used my boot to raise the prisoner's chin. 'Tell me your name?'

'Vidarr, lord,' he said, trying to control his sobs.

'Norse? Dane?'

'Norse, lord.'

'Why are you here, Vidarr?'

He took a huge breath. Gerbruht evidently thought he would not answer and slapped him around the head. 'My wife!' Vidarr said hurriedly.

'Your wife.'

'My wife!' he said again, and his face crumpled into grief. 'My wife, lord.' He seemed incapable of saying anything else.

'Leave him alone,' I told Gerbruht, who was about to hit the prisoner again. 'Tell me about your wife,' I ordered Vidarr.

'She's your prisoner, lord.'

'So?'

His voice was little more than a whisper. 'She's my wife, lord.'

'And you love her?' I asked harshly.

'Yes, lord.'

'God in His heaven,' Gerbruht mocked. 'He loves her! She's probably been . . .'

'Quiet,' I snarled. I looked at Vidarr. 'Who has your oath?'

'Jarl Ragnall, lord.'

'So what do you expect me to do? Give you back your wife and let you go?'

He shook his head. 'No, lord.'

'A man who breaks his oath,' I said, 'can't be trusted.'

'I swore an oath to Askatla too, lord.'

'Askatla? She's your wife?'

'Yes, lord.'

'And that oath is greater than the one to Jarl Ragnall?'

He knew the answer to that and did not want to say it aloud, so instead he raised his head to look at me. 'I love her, lord,' he pleaded. He sounded pathetic and he knew it, but he had been driven to this humiliation by love. A woman can do that. They have power. We might all say that the oath to our lord is the strong oath that guides our lives, the oath that binds us and rules all the other oaths, but few men would not abandon every oath under the sun for a woman. I have broken oaths. I am not proud of that, but almost every oath I broke was for a woman.

'Give me one reason I should not have you taken to the ditch and killed,' I said to Vidarr. He said nothing. 'Or have you sent back to Jarl Ragnall,' I added. We dare not admit that women have such power, and so I was harsh with him.

He just shook his head, not knowing how to answer me. Gerbruht leered happily, but then Vidarr tried one last desperate appeal. 'I know why your son came to Ragnall!'

'My son?'

'The priest, lord.' He gazed up at me, despair on his face. I said nothing, and he mistook that silence for anger. 'The priest the sorceress cut, lord,' he added in a low voice.

'I know what she did to him,' I said.

His face dropped. 'Spare me, lord,' he almost whispered the words, 'and I will serve you.'

He had intrigued me. I lifted his head with my right hand. 'Why did my son go to Ragnall?' I asked.

'He was an emissary of peace, lord.'

'An emissary?' I asked. That made little sense. 'From whom?'

'From Ireland, lord!' he said in a tone suggesting he thought I already knew. 'From your daughter.'

For a moment I was too astonished to speak. I just stared at him. The rain fell on his face, but I was oblivious of the weather. 'Stiorra?' I finally asked. 'Why would she send an emissary for peace?'

'Because they're at war, lord!'

'They?'

'Ragnall and his brother!'

I still just stared at him. Vidarr opened his mouth

to say more, but I silenced him by shaking my head. So Sigtryggr was Ragnall's enemy too? My son-in-law was an ally?

I shouted to Godric. 'Bring me Serpent-Breath! Now!'

He gave me the sword. I looked into Vidarr's eyes, raised the blade and saw him flinch, then I brought the weapon down hard so that her tip struck into the soft earth between two of the paving stones. I clasped my hands around the hilt. 'Swear loyalty to me,' I ordered him.

He put his hands around mine and swore to be my man, to be loyal to me, to serve me, to die for me. 'Find him a sword,' I commanded Gerbruht, 'and a coat of mail, a shield, and his wife.'

Then I went to find my son. My eldest son.

Wyrd bið ful āræd.

CHAPTER 8

Later that morning Finan led two hundred and fifty horsemen into the country south of Eads Byrig where they discovered two of Ragnall's foraging parties. They killed every man of the first and put the second to panicked flight, capturing an eleven-year-old boy who was the son of a Northumbrian jarl. 'He'll pay a ransom for the boy,' Finan predicted. He had also brought back sixteen horses and a dozen coats of mail, along with weapons, helmets, and shields. I had sent Vidarr with Finan's men to test the newcomer's loyalty. 'Aye, he killed well enough,' Finan told me, 'and he knows his trade.' Out of curiosity I had summoned Vidarr and his wife to my house so I could see for myself what kind of woman drove a man to treason and tears, and discovered she was a small, plump creature with beady eyes and a shrill tongue. 'Will we get land?' she demanded of me, and, when her husband tried to silence her, turned on him like a vixen. 'Don't you hush me, Vidarr Leifson! Jarl Ragnall promised us land! I didn't cross an ocean to die in a Saxon ditch!' She might have driven me to tears, though never to treason, yet Vidarr gazed at her as though she were the queen of Asgard.

Finan's tired horsemen were elated as they returned. They knew they were beating Ragnall's horde and knew that any ransom and the sale of the captured weapons would bring gold to their purses. Men clamoured to ride, and that evening Sihtric led another hundred men to scour the same countryside. I wanted to keep Ragnall embattled, to let him know there would be no peace so long as he stayed close to Ceaster. We had hurt him badly on the day after Eostre's feast and I wanted the pain to continue.

I also wanted to speak to my son, but he seemed incapable of speech. He lay heaped with blankets and furs, sweating and shivering at the same time. 'His fever must burn out,' Ymma, the gaunt woman who seemed to be the only sister allowed to talk to men, told me, 'he needs prayer and sweat,' she said, 'a lot of sweat!' When I had arrived at the house, the crippled gatekeeper had bashed the iron bar to announce a male visitor and there had been a scurrying of hooded women rushing to hide themselves as Sister Ymma emerged grimly from wherever she lurked. 'His bleeding has stopped, thank God,' she said, making the sign of the cross, 'thanks to Saint Werburgh's breastcloth.'

'Thanks to what?'

'The Lady Æthelflaed lent it to us,' she said, 'it is a holy relic.' She shuddered. 'I was privileged to touch it!'

‘Breastcloth?’

‘The blessed Saint Werburgh bound her breasts with a strip of cloth,’ Sister Ymma explained sternly. ‘She bound them tightly, so she would not tempt men. And she put thorns beneath the cloth as a reminder of her Lord’s suffering.’

‘She put pricks on her tits?’ I said aghast.

‘That is one way of glorifying God!’ Sister Ymma replied.

I will never understand Christians. I have seen men and women whip themselves till their backs were nothing but strips of flesh hanging from exposed ribs, watched pilgrims limp on bleeding broken feet to worship the tooth of the whale that swallowed Jonah, and seen a man hammer nails through his own feet. What god wants such nonsense? And why prefer a god who wants you to torture yourself instead of worshipping Eostre who wants you to take a girl into the woods and make babies?

‘The bishop himself prayed over him last night,’ Sister Ymma said, stroking my son’s forehead with a surprisingly gentle touch, ‘and he brought the tongue of Saint Cedd and laid it on his wound. And, of course, Sister Gomer tends him. If anyone can work God’s miracle it is Sister Gomer.’

‘The bishop’s wife,’ I said.

‘A living saint,’ Sister Ymma said reverently.

My son needed a living saint, or at least a miracle. He no longer lay curled about his pain, yet he still seemed incapable of speech. I spoke his name aloud and I thought he recognised it, but I could not be certain. I was not even sure he was awake. 'You bloody damned fool,' I told him, 'what were you doing in Ireland?' Of course he did not answer.

'We can be certain he was doing Christ's work,' Sister Ymma said confidently, 'and now he is a martyr for the faith. He has the privilege of suffering for Christ!'

My son was suffering, but it seemed Sister Gomer was indeed working miracles because next morning the bishop sent me a message that my son was recovering. I went back to the house, waited while the courtyard was cleared of women, then went to the small room where Uhtred lay. Except he was no longer Uhtred. He called himself Father Oswald now and I found him propped up in his bed with colour in his cheeks. He looked up at me and I looked down at him. 'You damned fool,' I said.

'Welcome, father,' he answered weakly. He had evidently eaten because an empty bowl and a wooden spoon lay on the fur covering. He was clutching a crucifix.

'You almost died, you stupid bastard,' I growled.

'Would you have cared?'

I did not answer, but stood in the doorway and glowered out into the courtyard. 'Do these damned women talk to you?'

'They whisper,' he said.

'Whisper?'

'As little as possible. Silence is their gift to god.'

'A silent woman,' I said. 'It's not a bad thing, I suppose.'

'They are just obeying the scripture.'

'The scripture?'

'In his letter to Timothy,' my son said primly, 'Saint Paul says a woman should "be in silence".'

'He was probably married to some dreadful creature who nagged him,' I said, thinking of Vidarr's shrill wife, 'but why would a god want silence?'

'Because his ears are battered by prayers. Thousands of prayers. Prayers from the sick, from the lonely, from the dying, the miserable, the poor and the needy. Silence is a gift to those souls, allowing their prayers to reach God.'

I watched sparrows bicker on the courtyard's grass. 'And you think your god answers those prayers?'

'I'm alive,' he said simply.

'So am I,' I retorted, 'and enough damned Christians have prayed for my death.'

'That's true.' He sounded amused, but when I turned back I saw that his face was a grimace of pain.

I watched him, not knowing what to say. 'That must hurt,' I finally said.

'It hurts,' he agreed.

'How did you get yourself captured by Ragnall? That was a stupid thing to do!'

'I went to him with authority,' my son said tiredly, 'as an emissary. It wasn't stupid, he had agreed to receive me.'

'You were in Ireland?'

'Not when I met him, no. But I'd come from there.'

'From Stiorra?'

'Yes.'

A dwarf woman arrived with a pot of water or ale and whimpered as a way of getting my attention. She wanted me to move from the doorway. 'Get out,' I snarled at her, then looked back to my son. 'Did that bitch Brida cut off your cock as well?'

He hesitated, then nodded. 'Yes.'

'I don't suppose it matters. You're a damned priest. You can piss like a woman.'

I was angry. I might have disowned Uhtred, I might have disinherited him and spurned him, but he was still my son, and an attack on him was an attack on my family. I glowered at him. His hair was cut very short. He had always been a good-looking boy, thin-faced and quick to smile, though doubtless his smile had vanished with his cock. He was better looking than my second son, I decided, who was said to resemble me, blunt-faced and scarred.

He stared back at me. 'I still honour you as my father,' he said after a pause.

'Honour me as the man who'll take revenge for you,' I said, 'and tell me what's happened to Stiorra.'

He sighed, then flinched in pain as he moved under the bed covers. 'She and her husband are under siege.'

'From?'

'From the Uí Néill,' he frowned, 'they're a clan, a tribe, a kingdom in Ireland.' He paused, evidently wanting to explain more, then just shrugged as if any explanation would be too tiring. 'Things are different in Ireland.'

'And they're Ragnall's allies?'

'They are,' he said carefully, 'but they don't trust each other.'

'Who would trust Ragnall?' I asked savagely.

'He takes hostages. That's how he keeps his men loyal.'

I was finding it difficult to understand what he was trying to say. 'Are you telling me the Uí Néill gave him hostages?'

He nodded. 'Ragnall yielded them his land in Ireland, but part of the price was one crew's service for one year.'

'They're mercenaries!' I said, surprised.

'Mercenaries,' he repeated the word, 'and their service is part of the land price. But another part was the death of Sigtryggr. If the Uí Néill don't give him that?'

'If they fail,' I said, 'he has a crew of their men in his power. You think he'd kill them as revenge?'

'What do you think? Conall and his men are mercenaries, but they're hostages too.'

And that, at last, made sense. Neither Finan nor I could understand why there were Irish warriors serving Ragnall, and none of the prisoners we had taken had been able to offer an explanation. They were hired warriors, mercenaries, and a surety of Sigtryggr's death.

'What's the quarrel between Ragnall and his brother?' I asked.

'Sigtryggr refused to join his brother's army.'

'Why?'

'They don't like each other. When their father died he divided his land between them and Ragnall resented that. He thinks it all ought to be his.' He paused to give a mirthless snort of laughter. 'And, of course, Ragnall wants Stiorra.'

I stared at him. 'He what?'

'Ragnall wants Stiorra,' he said again. I still stared at him and said nothing. 'She's grown to be a beautiful woman,' he explained.

'I know what she is! And she's a pagan too.'

He nodded sadly. 'She says she's a pagan, but I think she's like you, father. She says it to annoy people.'

'I am a pagan!' I said angrily. 'And so is Stiorra!'

'I pray for her,' he said.

'So do I,' I growled.

'And Ragnall wants her,' he said simply. 'He has four wives already, now he wants Stiorra as well.'

'And the Uí Néill are supposed to capture her?'

'They're supposed to capture her,' he agreed, 'and to kill Sigtryggr. It's all part of the land price.'

I prowled back to the door and gazed into the courtyard. A weak sun was casting shadows from the remains of a stone-walled ornamental pool that had long lost its water. The edge of the pool's wall was carved with running nymphs and goat-legged men. The eternal chase. 'Finan tells me the Uí Néill are the most powerful tribe in Ireland,' I spoke from the door, 'and you tell me they're pursuing Stiorra?'

'They were,' my son said.

'Were?' I asked, but he only sighed again and seemed reluctant to speak. I turned and looked at him. 'Were?' I repeated harshly.

'They're frightened of her,' he really was reluctant to speak, unable to meet my gaze.

'Why would a powerful tribe fear Stiorra?' I asked.

He sighed. 'They believe she's a sorceress.'

I laughed. My daughter a sorceress! I was proud of her. 'So Sigtryggr and Stiorra are under siege,' I said, 'but the Uí Néill won't attack because they think Stiorra has the gods on her side?'

'The devil, perhaps,' he said primly.

'You think she commands Satan?' I asked harshly.

He shook his head. 'The Irish are superstitious,' he said more energetically. 'God knows there's too much superstition in Britain! Too many folk won't wholly abandon the old beliefs . . .'

'Good,' I said.

'But it's worse in Ireland! Even some of the priests there visit the old shrines. So yes, they're scared of Stiorra and her pagan gods.'

'And how did you come to be mixed up in it? I thought you were safe in Wessex.'

'An abbot in Ireland sent me the news. The monasteries of Ireland are different. They're larger, they have more power, the abbots are like lesser kings in some ways. He wanted the Uí Néill gone from his land because they were slaughtering his livestock and eating his grain. I went there, as he requested . . .'

'What did they think you could do?' I interrupted him impatiently.

'They wanted a peacemaker.'

I sneered at that. 'So you did what? Crawled to Ragnall and begged him to be a nice man and leave your sister alone?'

'I carried an offer to Ragnall,' he said.

'Offer?'

'Sigtryggr offered two helmets filled with gold if Ragnall would ask the Uí Néill to lift their siege.'

'And Ragnall cut your balls off.'

'He refused the offer. He laughed at it. He was going to send me back to Ireland with his reply, but then Brida of Dunholm came to his camp.'

'That bitch,' I said vengefully. I looked back into the courtyard. The women must have decided my presence was not too corrupting because a few of them were carrying linens and food across the worn grass. 'Brida,' I said, 'was my first lover and she hates me.'

'Love can turn to hatred,' he said.

'Can it?' I asked savagely. I looked back to him. 'She cut you because you're my son.'

'And because I'm a Christian. She hates Christians.'

'She's not entirely bad then,' I said, then regretted the jest. 'She hates Christians because they're spoiling the land!' I explained. 'This land belonged to Thor and to Odin, every stream, every river, every field had a spirit or a nymph, now it has a foreign god.'

'The one God,' he said quietly.

'I'll kill her,' I said.

'Father . . .'

'Don't give me your Christian shit about forgiveness,' I snarled. 'I don't turn the other cheek! The bitch cut you and I'll cut her. I'll cut her damned womb out and feed it to my dogs. Where is Sigtryggr?'

'Sigtryggr?' He was not really asking, just recovering from my blast of anger.

'Yes, Sigtryggr and Stiorra! Where are they?'

'On the other side of the Irish Sea.' He sounded tired now. 'There's a great inlet of the sea called Loch Cuan. On its western side is a fort on a hill, it's almost an island.'

'Loch Cuan,' I repeated the unfamiliar name.

'Any shipmaster who knows Ireland can take you to Loch Cuan.'

'How many men does Sigtryggr lead?'

'There were a hundred and forty when I was there.'

'And their wives?'

'And their wives and children, yes.'

I grunted and looked back to the courtyard where two of the bishop's hunchbacks were laying out heavy flax sheets to dry on the grass. As soon as they were gone a small dog wandered out of the shadows and pissed on one of the sheets.

'What are you laughing at?' my son asked.

'Nothing,' I said. 'So there must be five hundred people in his fort?'

'Close to that, yes, if . . .' he hesitated.

'If what?'

'If they have enough food.'

'So the Uí Néill,' I said, 'won't attack, but they will starve them out?'

He nodded. 'Sigtryggr has enough food for a while, and there are fish, of course, and there's a spring on the headland. I'm no soldier . . .'

'More's the pity,' I interrupted.

'But Sigtryggr's fort is defensible. The land approach is narrow and rocky. Twenty men can hold that path, he says. Orvar Freyrson attacked with ships, but he lost men on the only beach.'

'Orvar Freyrson?' I asked.

'He's one of Ragnall's shipmasters. He has four ships in the loch.'

'And Sigtryggr has none?'

'None.'

'So in the end he'll lose. He'll run out of food.'

'Yes.'

'And my granddaughter will be slaughtered.'

'Not if God wills otherwise.'

'I wouldn't trust your god to save a worm.' I looked down at him. 'What happens to you now?'

'Bishop Leofstan has offered to make me his chaplain, if God wills it.'

'If you live, you mean?'

'Yes.'

'And that means you'll stay in Ceaster?'

He nodded. 'I assume so.' He hesitated. 'And you command the garrison here, father, so I assume you don't want me here.'

'What I want,' I said, 'is what I've always wanted. Bebbanburg.'

He nodded. 'So you won't stay here,' he sounded hopeful. 'You won't stay in Ceaster?'

'Of course not, you damned fool,' I said, 'I'm going to Ireland.'

'You will not go to Ireland,' Æthelflaed said. Or rather commanded me.

It was early afternoon. The sun had vanished again, replaced by another mass of low and ominous clouds that promised a hard rain before nightfall. It was a day to stay indoors, but instead we were well to the east of Eads Byrig and south of the Roman road along which I had led three hundred men from Ceaster. Almost half were my men, the rest were Æthelflaed's. We had turned south off the road long before reaching its closest point to Eads Byrig, hoping to find more foraging parties, but we saw none.

'Did you hear me?' Æthelflaed demanded.

'I'm not deaf.'

'Except when you want to be,' she said tartly. She was mounted on Gast, her white horse, and dressed for war. I had not wanted her to come, telling her that the country around Ceaster was still too dangerous for anyone except warriors, but as usual she had scorned the advice. 'I am the ruler of Mercia,' she had told me grandly, 'and I ride wherever I wish in my own country.'

'At least you'll be buried in your own country.'

There seemed no likelihood of that. If Ragnall had sent foraging parties they must have gone directly eastwards because there were none to the south. We had ridden overgrown pastures, crossed streams, and now sat our horses among the remnants of a coppiced wood, though it must have been at least ten years since the last forester had come to trim the oaks that were growing ragged again. I was debating whether to turn back when Berg called that one of our scouts was returning from the north. I had sent half a dozen men to take another look at the Roman road, but the afternoon seemed so quiet that I expected them to find nothing.

I was wrong. 'They're leaving, lord!' Grimdahl, a Mercian, was the scout, and he shouted the news as he spurred his tired horse closer to us. He was grinning. 'They're leaving!' he called again.

'Leaving?' Æthelflaed asked.

'All of them, my lady.' Grimdahl curbed his horse and jerked his head eastwards. 'They're taking the road out and going!'

Æthelflaed kicked her horse forward. 'Wait!' I called, then spurred ahead of her. 'Finan! Twenty-five men. Now!'

We chose men on the fastest horses and I led them across pastureland that was rich with spring grass. These lands had been abandoned for years because the Northmen were too close and anyone farming here could only face raids and killings. It was good land, but the fields were choked with weeds and thick with hazel saplings. We followed an overgrown cattle path eastwards, forced our way through a wood dense with brambles, and so out onto a stretch of heath. There was another belt of woodland ahead, and Grimdahl, who was riding beside me, nodded at the trees. 'The road's not far beyond those pines, lord.'

'We should attack!' Æthelflaed called. She had followed us, spurring Gast to catch up.

'You shouldn't be here,' I told her.

'You do like wasting your breath,' she retorted.

I ignored her. Tintreg plunged into the pine trees. There was little undergrowth and thus little concealment and so I went cautiously, walking the stallion forward until I could see the Roman road. And there they were. A long line of men, horses, women, and children, all trudging eastwards.

'We should attack,' Æthelflaed said again.

I shook my head. 'They're doing what we want them to do. They're leaving. Why disturb them?'

'Because they shouldn't have come here in the first place,' she said vengefully.

I should talk to the priest Glædwine again, I thought. His song of Æthelflaed's victory could now end with the enemy slinking away like whipped dogs. I watched Ragnall's army retreat eastwards and I knew this was triumph. The largest northern army to invade Mercia or Wessex since the days of King Alfred had come, it had flaunted its power in front of Ceaster's walls, and now it was running away. There were no banners flying, no defiance, they were abandoning their hopes of capturing Ceaster. And Ragnall, I thought, was in real trouble.

His army could even fall apart. The Danes and the Norse were terrible enemies, fearsome in battle and savage fighters, but they were opportunists too. When things went well, when land and slaves and gold and livestock fell into their hands they would follow a leader gladly, but as soon as that leader failed they would melt away. Ragnall, I thought, would have a struggle on his hands. He had taken Eoferwic, I knew, but how long could he hold that city? He had needed a great victory and he had been whipped.

'I want to kill more of them,' Æthelflaed said.

I was tempted. Ragnall's men were strung along the road and it would have been simple to ride among them and slaughter the panicked fugitives. But they were still on Mercian soil, and Ragnall must have given orders that they were to march in mail, with shields and weapons ready. If we attacked they would make shield walls, and help would come from the front and the rear of the long column. 'I want them gone,' Æthelflaed said, 'but I also want them dead!'

'We won't attack them,' I said, and saw her bridle with indignation, so held up a hand to calm her. 'We'll let them attack us.'

'Attack us?'

'Wait,' I said. I could see some thirty or forty of Ragnall's men on horseback, all of them riding on the flanks of the column as if they shepherded the fugitives to safety. At least as many other men led their horses, and all those horses were worth gold to an army. Horses allowed an army to move fast and horses were riches. A man was judged by the quality of his gold, his armour, his weapons, his woman, and his horses, and Ragnall, I knew, was still short of horses, and to deprive him of more would hurt him. 'Grimdahl,' I turned in the saddle, 'go back to Sihtric. Tell him to bring everyone to the far wood.' I pointed to the trees on the other side of the heathland. 'He's to bring everyone! And they're to stay hidden.'

'Yes, lord.'

'The rest of you!' I raised my voice. 'We're not attacking them! We're just insulting them! I want you to mock them, jeer them! Laugh at them! Taunt them!' I lowered my voice. 'You can come, my lady, but don't ride too near the road.'

Allowing Æthelflaed to show herself so close to a humiliated enemy was a risk, of course, but I reckoned her presence would drive some of the Norsemen to fury, while others would see a chance to capture her and thus snatch an unlikely victory from their humiliating defeat. She was my bait. 'You hear me?' I demanded of her. 'I want you to show yourself, but be ready to retreat when I give the order.'

'Retreat?' She did not like the word.

'You want to give the orders instead of me?'

She smiled. 'I will behave myself, Lord Uhtred,' she said with mock humility. She was enjoying herself.

I waited until I saw Sihtric's warriors among the far trees and then I led my few men and one woman out onto the open ground beside the road. The enemy saw us, of course, but at first assumed we were just a patrol that did not want trouble, but gradually we veered closer to the road, always keeping pace with the beaten troops. Once within earshot we shouted our insults, we mocked them, we called them frightened boys. I pointed to Æthelflaed, 'You were beaten by a woman! By a woman!' And my men began chanting the words, 'Beaten by a woman! Beaten by a woman!'

The enemy looked sullen. One or two shouted back, but without enthusiasm, and we edged still closer, laughing at them. One man spurred away from the column, his sword drawn, but sheered away when he realised that no one was following him. Yet I saw that men who had been leading their horses were now pulling themselves into their saddles, and other horsemen were returning from the front of the column while still more spurred from the rear. 'Berg!' I called to the young Norseman.

'Lord?'

'You'll stay close beside the Lady Æthelflaed,' I said, 'and make sure she rides away safely.'

Æthelflaed gave an indignant snort, but did not argue. My men were still jeering, but I angled slightly away from the road and turned them back so we were now riding towards the place where Sihtric's men were hidden. We had got as close as forty paces to the beaten army, but I widened the gap now as I watched the enemy horsemen gather. I reckoned there were over a hundred of them, more than enough to slaughter my twenty-five men, and of course they were tempted. We had ridiculed them, they were slinking away from a defeat, and our deaths would be a small consolation.

'They're coming,' Finan warned me.

'Go!' I called to Æthelflaed, then twisted in the saddle. 'We run away!' I called to my men and put my spurs to Tintreg's flanks. I slapped Gast's rump to make her leap away.

Now it was Ragnall's men who jeered. They saw us fleeing and the horsemen quickened as they pursued us. We plunged back into the pines and I saw Æthelflaed's white horse race ahead with Berg close behind her. I touched the spurs again, putting Tintreg to a full gallop so I could get ahead of Æthelflaed and, once in the ragged stretch of heathland beyond the pine wood, I led my fleeing men directly westwards between the two strips of trees. We were sixty or seventy paces ahead of our pursuers, who were whooping and shouting as they urged their horses ever faster. I snatched a backwards glimpse and saw the glint of steel, the flashing sunlight reflecting from swords and spears, and then Sihtric came from the southern trees. The ambush was perfect.

And we slewed around, turf and torn bracken flying from the hooves of our stallions, and the enemy saw the trap and realised they had seen it too late and Sihtric's men crashed into them and the swords fell and the spears lunged. I spurred back, Serpent-Breath alive in my hand. A black horse went down, hooves thrashing. Godric, my servant, who had stayed with Sihtric, was leaning from the saddle to plunge a spear into a fallen rider's breast. A Norseman saw him and rode towards him, his sword ready to lance into Godric's spine, but Finan was faster and the Irishman's blade hissed in a savage cut and the Norseman fell away.

'I want their horses!' I bellowed. 'Take their horses!'

The rearmost men of the pursuing enemy had managed to turn and were trying to escape, but a rush of my men caught them and the swords fell again. I looked for Æthelflaed, but could not see her. A man bleeding from the head was leading his horse northwards and I rode him down, letting Tintreg trample him. I snatched the reins of his horse and turned it back, then slapped its rump with Serpent-Breath to send it into the southern trees and it was then I saw the glint of steel among the thick undergrowth and kicked my horse into the woodland.

Berg was on foot, fighting off two men who had also dismounted. The trees and the bushes were too thick and the branches too low to let men fight on horseback and the two men had seen Æthelflaed ride into the wood and pursued her. She was just behind Berg, still mounted on Gast. 'Ride away!' I shouted at her.

She ignored me. Berg parried a sword cut and was struck by the second man with a lunge that started blood from his thigh, then I was on them,

Serpent-Breath slammed down and the man who had wounded Berg was staggering away with his helmet split. I followed him, pushing a low branch out of my face, and hacked again, this time cleaving Serpent-Breath into his neck. I dragged her back savagely, sawing her edge through blood and flesh, and he half fell against the trunk of a hornbeam. I clambered out of the saddle. I was furious, not because of the enemy, but because of Æthelflaed, and my fury made me hack at the wounded man who was too hurt to resist. He was an older man, doubtless an experienced warrior. He was mumbling and I suspected afterwards that he was asking for mercy. He had a thick beard flecked with white, three arm rings, and finely wrought mail. Such mail had value, but I was angry and careless, disembowelling him with a savage thrust and a two-handed rip upwards that ruined the mail coat. I shouted at him, cut him clumsily across his helmeted head, then finally killed him with a lunge to the throat. He died with his sword in his hand and I knew he would be waiting for me in Valhalla, another enemy who would welcome me to the feasting-hall and pour ale as we retold our stories.

Berg had killed his man, but was bleeding from his thigh. The wound looked deep. 'Lie down,' I told him, then snarled at Æthelflaed, 'I said you shouldn't have come!'

'Be quiet,' she said dismissively, then dismounted to tend Berg's wound.

We took thirty-six horses. The enemy left sixteen dead men among the bracken, and twice that number of wounded men. We abandoned those wounded after taking their weapons and mail. Ragnall could either look after his injured men or leave them to die, either way we had hurt him again.

'Will he have left a garrison at Eads Byrig?' Æthelflaed asked as we rode away.

I thought for a moment. It was possible that Ragnall had left a small garrison on the hilltop, but the more I considered that idea the more unlikely it seemed. There were no walls to defend such a garrison, and no prospect for them except death at Mercian hands. Ragnall had been trounced, driven out, defeated, and any men left at Eads Byrig would meet the same fate as Haesten's force. 'No,' I said.

'Then I want to go there,' Æthelflaed demanded, and so, as the sun began to sink behind the thickening western clouds, I led our horsemen up the ridge and thus back to the ancient fort.

Ragnall had left men there. There were some twenty-seven men who were too wounded to be moved. They had been stripped of their mail and their weapons, then left to die. Some older women were with them and those women fell to their knees and wailed at us. 'What do we do?' Æthelflaed asked, appalled by the stench of the wounds.

'We kill the bastards,' I said. 'It will be a mercy.' The first heavy drops of rain fell.

'There's been enough killing,' Æthelflaed said, evidently forgetting her bitter demands to kill more of Ragnall's men earlier in the afternoon. Now, as the rain began to fall harder, she walked among the injured and stared into their inked faces and desperate eyes. One man reached out to her and she took his hand and held it, then looked at me. 'We'll bring wagons,' she said, 'and move them to Ceaster.'

'And what will you do with them when they're healed?' I asked, though I suspected most would die before they ever reached the city.

'By then,' she said, relinquishing the wounded man's hand, 'they will have been converted to Christ.' I swore at that. She half smiled and took my arm, leading me past the ashes of the buildings that had been burned on the hilltop. We walked to the wall where the palisade had stood and she gazed northwards into the rain-smeared haze that was Northumbria. 'We will go north,' she promised me.

'Tomorrow?'

'When my brother is ready.' She meant Edward, King of Wessex. She wanted his army alongside hers before she pierced the pagan north. She squeezed my forearm through my stiff mail. 'And you're not to go to Ireland,' she said gently.

'My daughter . . .' I began.

'Stiorra made a choice,' she interrupted me firmly. 'She chose to abandon God and marry a pagan. She chose! And she must live with the choice.'

'And you wouldn't rescue your own daughter?' I asked harshly.

She said nothing to that. Her daughter was so unlike her. Ælflæd was flighty and silly, though I liked her well enough. 'I need you here,' Æthelflaed said instead of answering my question, 'and I need your men here.' She looked up at me. 'You can't leave now, not when we're so close to victory!'

'You have your victory,' I said sullenly. 'Ragnall's defeated.'

'Defeated here,' she said, 'but will he leave Mercia?'

Lightning flickered far to the north and I wondered what omen that was. No sound of thunder followed. The clouds were darkening to black as the dusk drew nearer. 'He'll send some men to Eoferwic,' I guessed, 'because he dare not lose that city. But he won't send all his men there. No, he won't leave Mercia.'

'So he's not defeated,' she said.

She was right, of course. 'He's going to keep most of his army here,' I said, 'and look for plunder. He'll move fast, he'll burn, he'll take slaves, he'll pillage. He has to reward his men. He needs to capture slaves, gold, and livestock, so yes, he'll raid deep into Mercia. His only chance of holding onto what's left of his army is to reward them with land, cattle, and captives.'

'Which is why I need you here,' she said, still holding my arm. I said nothing, but she knew I was thinking about Stiorra. 'You say she's trapped by the sea?'

'In a sea loch.'

'And you'd bring her back? If you could?'

'Of course I would.'

She smiled. 'You can send the fishing boat we use to provision Brunanburh.' She was talking of a small boat with room enough for perhaps ten men, but well-made and a good sea boat. It had belonged to a stubborn Mercian who had settled in the empty land west of Brunanburh. We had told him that Norse raiders regularly crossed the mouth of the Mærse to steal cattle or sheep, but he had insisted he would survive. He did survive too, for all of a week, after which he and his family had all been killed or enslaved, but for some reason the raiders had left the man's boat tied to its post in the river's mud, and we now used it to send heavy supplies from Ceaster to Brunanburh. It was much easier to float ten barrels of ale around to the fort by sea than lumber them across the land by wagon.

'Send men in that boat,' she told me. 'They can give Stiorra and her daughter the chance to escape.' I nodded, but said nothing. Ten men in a small boat? When Ragnall had left dragon-ships crammed with sea-warriors in Loch Cuan? 'We can spare a few men,' Æthelflaed went on, 'but if we're to catch Ragnall and kill him? You must stay.' She paused. 'You think like Ragnall so I need you here to fight him. I need you.'

So did my daughter.

And I needed a shipmaster who knew Ireland.

We had sent scouts to follow the retreating army and, just as I had predicted, Ragnall's force divided into two parts. The smaller part went north, presumably towards Eoferwic, while the other, about seven hundred strong, travelled on eastwards. The next day, the day after we had ambushed his retreat, we saw the first pillars of smoke smudge the distant sky, which told us that Ragnall was burning homesteads and barns in northern Mercia.

'He needs to be harassed,' Æthelflaed told me as we watched the far smoke.

'I know what needs to be done,' I said testily.

'I'll give you two hundred men,' she said, 'to add to your men. And I want you to pursue him, harry him, make his life hell.'

'It will be hell,' I promised her, 'but I need a day to prepare.'

'A day?'

'I'll be ready to leave before dawn tomorrow,' I promised her, 'but I need a day to get things ready. The horses are tired, the weapons are blunt, we have to carry our own food. And I have to equip *Blesian*.'

And all of that was true. *Blesian*, which meant blessing, was the fishing boat the Norse had left behind in the Mærse, perhaps because they thought the vessel cursed by the big wooden cross mounted at its prow. 'I'm sending Uhtred to Ireland,' I told Æthelflaed.

'He's well enough to travel?'

'Not him! My younger son.' I made sure she heard the resentment in my voice. 'The boat needs food, supplies.'

She frowned. 'It's not a long voyage, is it?'

'A day if the wind is good,' I said, 'two days if it's calm, but you don't go to sea without provisions. If they get hit by a storm they could be a week at sea.'

She touched my arm. 'I'm sorry about Stiorra,' she began.

'So am I.'

'But defeating Ragnall is our first duty,' she said firmly. 'Once he's finally beaten, you can go to Ireland.'

'Stop worrying,' I told her, 'I'll be ready to leave before dawn tomorrow.'

And I was.

CHAPTER 9

One hundred and twenty-two of us rode before dawn, our hoofbeats loud in the stone tunnel of Ceaster's northern gateway where two torches blazed and smoked. Servants followed with thirteen packhorses loaded with shields, spears, and sacks of hard-baked bread, smoked fish, and flitches of bacon. We were riding to war.

My helmet hung from my saddle's pommel, Serpent-Breath was at my side, Finan rode to my right and Sihtric to my left. Behind me my standard-bearer carried Bebbanburg's flag of the wolf's head. We followed the Roman road that took us north through the cemetery where the spectres watched from their shadowed stones and from their dark grave mounds. The road turned sharply east just before it reached the bank of the Mærse, and it was there I stopped and looked back. Ceaster was a dark shape, its ramparts outlined by the small glow of torches inside the city. There was no moonlight, clouds hid the stars, and I reckoned no one on the city walls could see us.

Ragnall's men were somewhere far to the east. Dawn would reveal great smears of smoke to show where they plundered and burned plump homesteads. Those fires had moved steadily southwards the previous day, showing that his army was moving away from the northern burhs into land that was less protected.

That war was being waged to the east of Ceaster. And we turned west.

We rode west to Brunanburh, following the dyked path that edged the river's southern bank. The darkness forced us to go slowly, but as the wolf-light slowly grew behind us we quickened our pace. The tide was ebbing and the river made gurgling noises as it drained from the mudbanks. Sea birds cried to welcome the dawn. A fox raced across our path with a broken-winged gull in its jaws and I tried to find some good omen in that sight. The river shimmered like dull silver, stirred by the smallest wind. I had been hoping for more wind, for a half gale of wind, but the air was almost still.

And then we came to Brunanburh and the fort was a dark shape, its rampart's top edged with a line of red to show that fires burned in the courtyard. The track turned left here, going to the fort's main gate, but we swerved right, heading for the river where dark shapes showed against the silvered water. They were the two ships that Æthelstan and his companions had loosed from their moorings north of Eads Byrig. The larger one was named *Sæbroga*, the Sea-Terror, and she was now mine.

I had chosen the name because I did not know what the Norsemen had called her. Some ships have a name carved into a strake of the bow, but *Sæbroga* had no such carving. Nor was a name scratched into her mast. All seamen will tell you that it is bad luck to change a ship's name, though I have done it often enough, but never without the necessary precaution of having a virgin piss into the bilge. That averts the ill luck, and so I had made certain a child had peed into the *Sæbroga*'s ballast stones. The newly baptised ship was the largest of the two, and she was a beauty; wide-bellied, sleek in her long lines, and high-prowed. A great axe blade carved from a massive piece of oak was mounted on her rearing prow where most pagan ships flaunted a dragon, a wolf, or an eagle, and the axe made me wonder if this had been Ragnall's own ship. The axe blade had once been painted bright red, though now the paint had largely faded. She had benches for sixty oarsmen, a finely woven sail, and a full set of oars.

'God save us,' Dudda said, then hiccuped, 'but she's lovely.'

'She is,' I agreed.

'A good ship,' he said, sketching a shape with his hands, 'is like a woman.' He said that very seriously, as if no one had ever had the thought before, then slid from his saddle with all the grace of a stunned ox. He grunted as he hit the ground, then lumbered onto the mud at the river's edge where he lowered his hose and pissed. 'A good ship,' he said again, 'is like a woman.' He turned, still pissing mightily. 'Did you ever see that Mus, lord? Little girl Mus? The one with the apple mark on her forehead? Talk about lovely! I could chew her apple down to the core!'

Dudda was, or had been, a shipmaster who had sailed the Irish sea since boyhood. He had also probably drunk the equivalent of that sea in ale and mead, which had left him bloated, red-faced and unsteady on his feet, but he was sober that morning, an unnatural state, and trying to impress me with his knowledge. 'We need,' he said, waving vaguely towards the *Sæbroga*, 'to bring her closer. Warp her in. Lord, warp her in.' She was moored to one of the few pilings that had survived Ragnall's first attack. A new pier was being built, but it had not yet reached the deeper water.

'Why don't you swim out to her?' I suggested to Dudda.

'Christ on his little wooden cross,' he said, alarmed, 'I don't swim, lord! I'm a sailor! Fish swim, not me!' He suddenly sat at the track's edge, tired out by the effort of walking five paces. We had searched Ceaster's taverns for a man who knew the Irish coast, and Dudda, hopeless as he seemed, was the only one we discovered. 'Loch Cuan?' he had slurred when I had first questioned him, 'I could find Loch Cuan blindfolded on a dark night, been there a hundred times, lord.'

'But can you find it when you're drunk?' I had asked him savagely.

'I always have before, lord,' he had replied, grinning.

Two of my younger men were stripping off their mail and boots, readying themselves to wade out to the *Sæbroga* that tugged on her piling as the ebbing tide tried to carry her to sea. One of them nodded towards the fort, 'Horsemen, lord.'

I turned to see Osferth approaching with four companions. He was now commanding Brunanburh's garrison, placed there by Æthelflaed, his half-sister. He was one of my oldest friends, a man who had shared many a shield wall, and he smiled when he saw me. 'I wasn't expecting to see you, lord!'

I had last seen him a few days before when I had ridden to Brunanburh to see the two prizes for myself. Now I jerked my head at *Sæbroga*. 'The Lady Æthelflaed wants that one moved to the Dee,' I said. 'She thinks it will be safer there.'

'It's safe enough here!' he said confidently. 'We haven't seen a pagan ship in a week now. But if the Lady Æthelflaed wishes it . . .' He left the thought unfinished as he looked east to where the dawn was blushing the sky with a pale pink glow. 'You've got a good day for your voyage, lord!'

'You want to come with us?' I asked, praying he refused.

He smiled, evidently amused at the thought of taking a day away from his duties. 'We must finish the wharf.'

'You're making good progress!' I said, looking to where the sturdily rebuilt pier crossed the muddy foreshore.

'We are,' Osferth said, 'though the difficult part

of the work is still ahead, but with God's help?' He made the sign of the cross. He had inherited all of his father's piety, but also Alfred's sense of duty. 'You're leaving the smaller ship here?' he asked anxiously.

I had thought of taking both ships, but decided *Sæbroga* should sail alone. 'Lady Æthelflaed said nothing about the smaller ship,' I said.

'Good! Because I plan to use it to drive the pilings into the deeper water,' he explained. He watched as my two men tied a long hempen line to *Sæbroga*'s bow. One of them brought the line ashore while the other unmoored the ship from her piling, then a score of my men chanted enthusiastically as they hauled *Sæbroga* in to the beach.

'Load her up!' Finan shouted when her high bow slid onto the mud.

I gave Osferth what news I had as my men heaved sacks of provisions onto the ship. I told him how Ragnall had fled eastwards and was now raiding deep into Mercia. 'He won't be coming back here,' I told him, 'at least not for a while, so Lady Æthelflaed might want some of your men back in Ceaster.'

Osferth nodded. He was watching *Sæbroga*'s loading and seemed puzzled. 'You're taking a lot of supplies for a short voyage,' he said.

'You never go to sea without precautions,' I told him. 'Everything might look calm this morning, but that doesn't mean a storm couldn't blow us off course by midday.'

'I pray that doesn't happen,' he said piously, watching the last sack being heaved on board.

I tossed Godric a small purse filled with hack-silver. 'You'll take the horses back to Ceaster,' I ordered him.

'Yes, lord.' Godric hesitated. 'Can't I come with you, lord? Please?'

'You'll look after the horses,' I said harshly. I was taking no one except my shield-wall warriors. No servants were coming, only men who could pull an oar or wield a sword. I suspected I would need all the space I could find in *Sæbroga* if we were to bring Sigtryggr's men off their fort, and however heavily we loaded her we still would not have enough space for all his people. That might have been a good reason to take the smaller ship as well, but I feared dividing my small force into two. We only had the one shipmaster, only one man who claimed to know how to reach Loch Cuan, and if the smaller ship lost touch with *Sæbroga* in the night I might never see her crew again. 'I'll see you tonight,' I lied to Godric for Osferth's benefit, then waded out to *Sæbroga*'s waist and waited as the massive Gerbruht hauled Dudda over the ship's side. Dudda grunted and gasped, then collapsed onto a rowers' bench like an exhausted seal. Gerbruht grinned, held out a meaty hand, and pulled me up onto the ship. Godric had also waded out and now handed me my helmet, sword, and shield. Finan was already standing beside the steering oar. 'Pole us off,' I told my men, and a half-dozen of them used the long oars to thrust *Sæbroga* off the shelving bank and into deeper water.

I called farewell to Osferth. Away to the east I could see three horsemen hurrying along the track from Ceaster. Too late, I thought, too late. I grinned, watching as my men found their places on the benches and thrust the oars into their tholes, and then we turned that high, proud axe towards the distant sea. I took hold of the steering oar and Finan thumped his foot on the deck. 'On my command!' he called. 'Now!'

And the oar-blades bit and the long hull surged and the wildfowl scattered like scraps in the small wind. I felt the steering oar respond, felt the shudder of a ship in my hand, and felt my heart lift to the song of a boat on the sea. The tide was ebbing fast, rippling the river with glittering new sunlight, and Finan shouted the rhythm, stamping his foot, and the sixty rowers pulled harder and I felt the ship coming alive, pulsing with the oar beats, the steering loom resisting me now, and I heard the sound of water sluicing along the hull and saw a wake spreading behind. The three messengers, I assumed they had come from Ceaster, had reached Osferth and he was now galloping along the bank, waving and shouting. I thought I heard him call that we were to come back, that we were ordered back, but *Sæbroga* was moving fast into the river's centre, going ever further from the shore, and I just waved to him. He beckoned frantically and I waved again.

What did Æthelflaed think I would do? In the name of her so-called merciful god, what? Did she think I would abandon my daughter to Ragnall's hunger? Let him slaughter my grandchild so he could plant his own seed in Stiorra? He had already gelded my son, now he would rape my daughter? I vowed I would hear him screaming, I would watch him bleed, I would tear his flesh piece by piece before I would worry about Æthelflaed. This was family. This was revenge.

The *Sæbroga* reared her prow to the larger seas as we left the river. To my left now were the wide treacherous mudbanks that edged Wirhealum, the land between the rivers. In a hard gale and a high tide those flats were a maelstrom of whipping waves and wind-blown foam, a place where ships died, and the bones of too many vessels stood stark and black where the tide sluiced out across the rippled shallows. The wind was rising, but coming from the west, which was not what we needed, but ahead of me was the *Blesian*, hove to about a mile offshore.

My younger son, the one I had renamed Uhtred, was waiting in the smaller ship. He and six men had waited all night, their boat laden with ale barrels, the one thing we could not have carried from Ceaster on our horses. We drew alongside, lashed the two boats together, then rigged a whip from the yardarm and hoisted ale, more food, and a bundle of heavy spears aboard the *Sæbroga*. Dudda, who was watching the ale barrels come aboard, had assured me the voyage should not take longer than a day, perhaps a day and a half, but the Irish Sea was notorious for its sudden storms. I was taking enough ale to last us a week just in case a malevolent fate drove us out to the wider ocean.

'What do we do with the *Blesian*?' my son asked. He looked cheerful for a man who had just spent a nervous night keeping his boat away from the sound of waves seething across a nearby mudflat.

'Just let her go.'

'It seems a pity,' he said wistfully, 'she's a good ship.'

I had thought of towing her and had immediately rejected the thought. The *Blesian* was heavy and her weight would slow us by half. 'Just let her go,' I said again, and we retrieved the lines that had held her close and let her drift. The wind would eventually strand her on Wirhealum's mudflats where she would be pounded to death. We rowed on, driving the *Sæbroga* into the wind and waves until Dudda, reckoning we were far enough offshore, turned us north-westwards. 'We'll come to Mann if you hold this course,' he said, sitting on the deck and leaning against the side of the ship. 'Will you be opening one of those barrels?' he looked longingly at the ale that had been lashed to the base of the mast.

'Soon,' I said.

'Be careful at the island,' he said, meaning Mann. 'There's nothing they like better than capturing a ship.'

'Do I go west of it or east?'

'West.' He glanced up at the rising sun. 'Just stay as you are. We'll get there.' He closed his eyes.

The wind backed by mid-morning and we could raise *Sæbroga*'s great sail, and the sight of it convinced me that we had indeed captured Ragnall's own ship because the sail flaunted a great red axe blade. The sail itself was made from heavy linen, an expensive cloth, close woven and double layered. The axe was a third layer, sewn onto the other two, which were reinforced by a criss-cross pattern of hemp ropes. We shipped the oars when the sail was sheeted home and the boat leaned over, driven by the freshening wind that was flicking the wave-tops white. 'She's a beautiful thing,' I said to Finan as I felt the sea's pressure on the steering-oar.

He grinned. 'To you, yes. But you love ships, lord.'

'I love this one!'

'Me,' he said, 'I'm happiest when I can touch a tree.'

We saw two other ships that morning, but both fled from the sight of the great red axe on our sail. They were either fishing or cargo vessels and they rightly feared a sea-wolf seething northwards with the waves foaming white at her jaws. Dudda might have warned me of the pirates of Mann, but it would take a brave fool to tackle *Sæbroga* with her full crew of savage warriors. Most of those savage warriors were sleeping now, slumped between the benches.

'So,' Finan said, 'your son-in-law.'

'My son-in-law.'

'The fool's got himself trapped, is that right?'

'So I'm told.'

'With nigh-on five hundred folk?'

I nodded.

'It's just that I'm thinking,' he said, 'that we might cram another forty people on board this bucket, but five hundred?'

Sæbroga dipped her bows and a spatter of spray flicked down the hull. The wind was rising, but I sensed no malice in it. I leaned on the oar to turn our bows slightly westwards, knowing that the wind would be pressing us ever to the east. A mound of clouds showed far ahead of our bows, and Dudda reckoned they were heaping above the island called Mann. 'Just hold your course, lord,' he said, 'hold your course.'

'Five hundred people,' Finan reminded me.

I grinned. 'Have you ever heard of a man called Orvar Freyrson?'

'Never,' he shook his head.

'Ragnall left him in Ireland,' I said, 'with four ships. He's already attacked Sigtryggr once and got a bloody nose for his trouble. So now, I suspect, he's content to make sure no one supplies Sigtryggr with food. He's keeping other ships away, hoping to starve the fort into surrender.'

'Makes sense,' Finan said.

'But why does Orvar Freyrson need four ships?' I asked. 'That's just greedy. He'll have to learn to share, won't he?'

Finan smiled. He looked back, but the land had vanished. We were out in the wide sea now, reaching on a brisk wind and splitting the green waves white. We were a sea-wolf given her freedom. 'Her ladyship won't be happy with you,' he remarked.

'Æthelflaed? She'll be spitting like a wildcat,' I said, 'but it's Eadith I feel sorry for.'

'Eadith?'

'Æthelflaed hates her. Eadith won't like being left alone in Ceaster.'

'Poor lass.'

'But we'll be back,' I said.

'And you think either woman will forgive you?'

'Eadith will.'

'And Lady Æthelflaed?'

'I'll just have to take her a gift,' I said.

He laughed at that. 'Christ, but it will have to be some gift! It's not as if she needs any more gold or jewels! So what were you thinking of giving her?'

I smiled. 'I was thinking of giving her Eoferwic.'

'Holy Mary!' Finan said, suddenly coming alert. He sat up straight and stared at me for a heartbeat. 'You're serious! And how in God's name are you going to do that?'

'I don't know,' I said, then laughed.

Because I was at sea and I was happy.

The weather worsened that afternoon. The wind veered, forcing us to lower the great sail and lash it to the yard, and then we rowed into a short sharp sea, struggling against wind and current, while above us the clouds rolled from the west to darken the sky. Rain spattered the rowers and dripped from the rigging. *Sæbroga* was a beautiful craft, elegant and sleek, but as the wind rose and the seas shortened I saw she had a bad habit of burying her head to shatter spray along the deck. 'It's the axe,' I said to Finan.

'Axe?'

'On the prow! It's too heavy.'

He was huddled in his cloak beside me. He peered forward. 'It's a massive piece of wood, that's for sure.'

'We need to move some of the ballast stones aft,' I said.

'But not now!' he sounded alarmed at the thought of wet men struggling with heavy stones while *Sæbroga* pitched in the pounding seas.

I smiled. 'Not now.'

We made landfall at Mann and I kept the island well to our east as the night fell. The wind calmed with the darkness and I held *Sæbroga* off the island's coast, unwilling to journey further in the blackness of night. Not that the night was all black. There were gleams of firelight from the island's distant slopes, faint lights that kept us safe by letting us judge our position. I let my son take the steering-oar and slept till dawn. 'We go west now,' a bleary-eyed Dudda told me in the wolf-light, 'due west, lord, and we'll come to Loch Cuan.'

'And Christ only knows what we find there,' Finan said.

Sigtryggr dead? My daughter abducted? An ancient fort smeared with blood? There are times when the demons persecute us, they give us doubts, they try to persuade us that our fate is doom unless we listen to them. I am convinced that this middle earth swarms with demons, invisible demons, Loki's servants, wafting on the wind to make mischief. I remember, years ago, how dear Father Beocca, my childhood tutor and old friend, told me that Satan sent demons to tempt good Christians. 'They try to keep us from doing God's purpose,' he had told me earnestly. 'Did you know that God has a purpose for all of us, even for you?'

I had shaken my head. I was perhaps eight years old and even then I thought my purpose was to learn sword-craft, not to master the dull skills of reading and writing.

'Let me see if you can discover God's purpose on your own!' Beocca had said enthusiastically. We had been sitting on a ledge of Bebbanburg's rock, staring at the wild sea as it foamed about the Farnea Islands. He had been making me read aloud from a small book that told how Saint Cuthbert had lived on one of those lonely rocks and had preached to the puffins and seals, but then Beocca started bouncing up and down on his scrawny bum as he always did when he became excited. 'I want you to think about what I say! And perhaps you can find the answer on your own! God,' his voice had become very earnest, 'made us in His own image. Think of that!'

I remember thinking that was very strange of God because Beocca was club-footed, had a cock-eyed squint, a squashed nose, wild red hair, and a palsied hand. 'So God's a cripple?' I had asked.

'Of course not,' he had said, slapping me with his good right hand, 'God is perfect!' He slapped me again, harder. 'He is perfect!' I remember thinking that perhaps God looked like Eadburga, one of the kitchen maids, who had taken me behind the fortress chapel and shown me her tits. 'Think!' Father Beocca had urged me, but all I could think of was Eadburga's breasts, so I shook my head. Father Beocca had sighed. 'He made us look like Him,' he explained patiently, 'because the purpose of life is to be like Him.'

'To be like Him?'

'To be perfect! We must learn to be good. To be good men and women!'

'And kill children?' I had asked earnestly.

He had squinted at me. 'And kill children?'

'You told me the story!' I had said excitedly. 'How the two bears killed all the boys! And God made them do it. Tell me again!'

Poor Beocca had looked distraught. 'I should never have read that story to you,' he had said miserably.

'But it is true?'

He had nodded unhappily. 'It is true, yes. It's in our scripture.'

'The boys were rude to the prophet?'

'Elisha, yes.'

'They called him baldie, yes?'

'So the scripture tells us.'

'So God sent two bears to kill them all! As a punishment?'

'Female bears, yes.'

'And forty boys died?'

'Forty-two children died,' he had said miserably.

'The bears tore them apart! I like that story!'

'I'm sure God wanted the children to die quickly,' Beocca had said unconvincingly.

'Do the scriptures say that?'

'No,' he had admitted, 'but God is merciful!'

'Merciful? He killed forty-two children . . .'

He had cuffed me again. 'It's time we read more about the blessed Saint Cuthbert and his mission to the seals. Start at the top of the page.'

I smiled at the memory as *Sæbroga* slammed her prow into a green-hearted sea and slung cold spray down the length of her deck. I had liked Beocca, he was a good man, but so easy to tease. And in truth that story in the Christians' holy book proved that their god was not so unlike my own. The Christians pretended he was good and perfect, but he was just as capable of losing his temper and slaughtering children as any god in Asgard. If the purpose of life was to be an unpredictable, murderous tyrant then it would be easy to be godlike, but I suspected we had a different duty and that was to try to make the world better. And that too was confusing. I thought then and think still that the world would be a better place if men and women worshipped Thor, Woden, Freya, and Eostre, yet I drew my sword on the side of the child-slaughtering Christian god. But at least I had no doubts about the purpose of this voyage. I sailed to take revenge. If I discovered that Sigtryggr had been defeated and Stiorra captured then we would turn *Sæbroga* back eastwards and hunt Ragnall down to the last shadowed corner on earth, where I would rip the guts out of his belly and dance on his spine.

We fought weather all that day, butting *Sæbroga*'s heavy prow into a west wind. I had begun to think the gods did not want me to make this voyage, but late in the afternoon they sent a raven as an omen. The bird was exhausted and landed on the small platform in the ship's prow where, for a time, it just huddled in misery. I watched the bird, knowing it was sent by Odin. All my men, even the Christians, knew it was an omen, and so we waited, pulling oars into short seas, swept by showers, waited for the bird to reveal its message. That message came at dusk as the wind dropped and the seas settled and the Irish coast appeared off our bows. To me the far coast looked like a green blur, but Dudda preened. 'Just there, lord!' he said, pointing a shade or two to the right of our bows. 'That's the entrance, right there!'

I waited. The raven strutted two steps one way, two steps the other. *Sæbroga* pitched as a larger wave rolled under her hull, and just then the raven took to the air and, with renewed energy, flew straight as a spear for the Irish coast. The omen was favourable.

I leaned on the steering oar, turning *Sæbroga* northwards.

'It's there. Lord!' Dudda protested as I turned the ship's head past the place he had indicated and kept on turning her. 'The entrance, lord! There! Just beyond the headland. We'll make the narrows before dark, lord!'

'I'm not taking a ship into enemy waters at dusk,' I growled.

Orvar Freyrson had four ships in Loch Cuan, four warships manned by Ragnall's warriors. When I entered the loch I needed to take him by surprise, not row in and immediately be forced to look for somewhere safe to anchor or moor. Dudda had warned me that the loch was full of ledges, islands, and shallows, so it was no place to arrive in the near darkness while enemy ships that were familiar with the dangers might lurk nearby. 'We enter at dawn,' I told Dudda.

He looked nervous. 'Better to wait for slack water, lord. By dawn the tide will be flooding.'

'Is that what Orvar Freyrson would expect?' I asked. 'That we'd wait for slack water?'

'Yes, lord.' He sounded nervous.

I clapped him on a meaty shoulder. 'Never do what an enemy expects, Dudda. We'll go in at dawn. On the flood.'

That was a bad night. We were close to a rockbound coast, the sky was clouded, and the seas choppy. We rowed, always heading north, and I worried that one of Orvar's men might have recognised *Sæbroga*'s distinctive prow when we first made landfall. That was unlikely. We had turned northwards well offshore and had been under oars so no one on land could have seen the much larger red axe on the big sail. But if the ship had been recognised then Orvar would be wondering why we had turned away rather than seek shelter for the night.

The wind fretted in the darkness, blowing us towards the Irish shore, but I had twelve men pulling on the oars to hold us steady. I listened for the dreaded sound of surf breaking or of seas crashing on rocks. Sometimes I thought I heard those noises and felt a surge of panic, but that was likely a sea-demon playing tricks, and Ran, the sea-goddess, who can be a jealous and savage bitch, was in a good mood that night. The sea sparkled and glimmered with her jewels, the strange lights that flicker and glow in the water. When an oar-blade dipped the sea would shatter into thousands of glowing droplets that faded slowly. Ran only sent the jewels when she was feeling kind, but even so I was fearful. Yet there was no need to be nervous because when the dawn broke grey and slow we were still well offshore. 'Sweet Jesus,' Dudda said when at last he could make out the coast, 'sweet mother of God. Thank Christ!' He too had been nervous, drinking steadily through the night, and now he gazed bleary-eyed at the green strip of land. 'Just go south, lord, just go south.'

'How far?'

'One hour?'

It took longer, not because Dudda was wrong, but because I gave my men time to eat, then to pull on their mail coats. 'Keep your helmets and weapons close,' I told them, 'but I don't want anyone in a helmet yet. And put cloaks over your mail!' We could not arrive at the loch looking ready for war, but rather like men tired from a voyage and wanting nothing more than to join their comrades. I called Vidarr, the Norseman who had deserted to join his wife, back to the stern. 'What can you tell me of Orvar Freyrson?' I asked him.

Vidarr frowned. 'He's one of Ragnall's ship-masters, lord, and a good one.'

'Good at what?'

'Seamanship, lord.'

'Good at fighting too?'

Vidarr shrugged. 'We're all fighters, lord, but Orvar's older now, he's cautious.'

'Does he know you?'

'Oh yes, lord. I sailed with him in the northern islands.'

'Then you'll hail him, or hail whoever we meet, understand? Tell him we're sent to attack Sigtryggr. And if you betray me . . .'

'I won't, lord!'

I paused, watching him. 'Have you been into the loch?'

'Yes, lord.'

'Tell me about it.'

He told me what Dudda had already described to me, that Loch Cuan was a massive sea-lake dotted with rocks and islets, and entered by a long and very narrow channel through which the tide flowed with astonishing speed. 'There's plenty of water in the channel's centre, lord, but the edges are treacherous.'

'And the place where Sigtryggr is trapped?'

'It's almost an island, lord. The land bridge is narrow. A wall of ten men can block it easily.'

'So Orvar would attack by sea?'

'That's difficult too, lord. The headland is surrounded by rocks, and the channel to the beach is narrow.'

Which explained why Orvar was trying to starve Sigtryggr into submission unless, of course, he had already captured the fort.

We were close to the land now, close enough to see smoke drifting up from cooking fires and close enough to see the waves breaking on rocks and then draining white to the foam-scummed sea. An east wind had livened after the dawn and allowed us to raise the sail again, and *Sæbroga* was moving fast as she dipped her steerboard strakes towards the brisk waves. 'When we get there,' I told Dudda, 'I want to sail or row straight through the channel. I don't want to stop and feel my way through shallows.'

'It's safer . . .' he began.

'Damn safer!' I snarled. 'We have to look as if we know what we're doing, not as if we're nervous! Would Ragnall look nervous?'

'No, lord.'

'So we go in fast!'

'You can sail in, lord,' he said, 'but for Christ's sake stay in the channel's centre.' He hesitated. 'The narrows run almost straight north, lord. The wind and tide will carry us through, but the hills confuse the wind. It's no place to be taken aback.' He meant that the hills would sometimes block the wind altogether, or veer it unexpectedly, and such a change could drive *Sæbroga* onto the rocks that evidently lined the narrows, or drive her into the whirlpool that Dudda described as 'vicious'.

'So we use oars as well as sail,' I said.

'The current is frightening, lord,' Vidarr said warningly.

'Best to go really fast then,' I said. 'Do you know where Orvar keeps his men when they're ashore?' I asked him.

'Just off the channel, lord. On the western bank. There's a bay that offers shelter.'

'I want to run straight past him,' I told Dudda, 'as fast as we can.'

'The tide will help,' he said, 'it's flooding nicely, but Vidarr's right. The current will take you like the wind, lord. It runs like a deer.'

We hit rough water south of the headland that protected the entrance to the narrows. I suspected there were rocks not far beneath *Sæbroga*'s keel, but Dudda was unworried. 'It's a bad place when the tide ebbs, lord, but safe enough on the flood.' We were running before the wind now, the big red axe sail bellied out to drive *Sæbroga*'s prow hard into the churning water. 'Before we sail back,' I said, 'I want to move ballast stones aft.'

'If we live,' Dudda said quietly, then sketched the sign of the cross.

We turned north, slewing the sail around to keep the ship moving fast and I felt her picking up speed as the tide caught her. I could see Dudda was nervous. His hands were clenching and unclenching as he gazed ahead. The waves seemed to be racing northwards, lifting *Sæbroga*'s stern and hurling her forward. Water seethed at the hull, waves shattered white at the prow, and the sound of seas crashing on rocks was incessant. 'Loch Cuan,' Finan had to speak loudly, 'means the calm lake!' he laughed.

'We call it Strangrfjörthr!' Vidarr shouted.

The sea was thrusting us as if she wanted to dash us onto the great rocks either side of the channel's entrance. Those rocks were wreathed in huge plumes of white spray. The steering-oar felt slack. 'Oars!' I shouted. We needed speed. 'Row harder!' I bellowed. 'Row as if the devil were up your arse!'

We needed speed! We already had speed! The tide and wind were carrying *Sæbroga* faster than any boat I had ever sailed, but most of that speed was the current, and we needed to be faster than the seething water if the long steering-oar was to control the hull. 'Row, you ugly bastards,' I shouted, 'row!'

'Sweet Jesus,' Finan muttered.

My son made a whooping noise. He was grinning, holding onto the boat's side. The waves were broken, slapping into white caps, shredding the heaving rowers with spray. We were racing into a cauldron of rock and churning seas. 'When you're past the entrance,' Dudda was shouting, 'you'll see an island! Go to the east of it!'

'Does it get calmer inside?'

'It gets worse!'

I laughed. The wind was rising, whipping my hair across my eyes. Then suddenly, we were in the entrance, in the jaws of rock and wind-driven foam, and I could see the island and I pulled to steerboard, but the blade had no bite. The current was stronger than ever, sweeping us towards the rocks ahead. 'Row!' I bellowed. 'Row!' I heaved on the steering-oar and *Sæbroga* slowly responded. Then the hills caused a wind shadow and the huge sail flapped like a crazy thing, but still we raced inland. To right and left were maelstroms where the water eddied and broke over hidden rocks, where white birds shrieked at us. The waves no longer heaved us forward, but the current was rushing us through the narrow channel. 'Row!' I shouted at my sweating men. 'Row!'

The green hills on either bank looked so calm. The day promised to be fine. The sky was blue with just a few tattered white clouds. There were sheep grazing on a green meadow. 'Glad to be home?' I called to Finan.

'If I ever get home!' he said morosely.

I had never seen a channel so rockbound or so treacherous, but by staying in the centre where the current ran strongest, we stayed in deep water. Other ships had died here, their black ribs stark above the hurrying water. Dudda guided us, pointing out the whirlpool that ripped the sea's surface into turmoil. 'That'll kill you,' he said, 'sure as eggs are eggs. I've seen that thing tear the bottom out of a good ship, lord! She went down like a stone.' The pool was to our right and still we seethed on, leaving it safely behind.

'The harbour, lord!' Vidarr shouted, and he pointed to where two masts could be seen above a low rocky headland.

'Row!' I shouted. The channel was at its narrowest and the current was sliding us at astonishing speed. A gust of wind bellied the sail, adding speed, and we cleared the point of land and I saw the huts above a shingle beach and a dozen men standing on the rocky shore. They waved and I waved back. 'Orvar has four ships, yes?' I asked Vidarr.

'Four, lord.'

So two were probably ahead of us, somewhere in the long reaches of the loch, and that lay not far ahead, just beyond a low grassy island.

'Don't go near the island, lord,' Dudda said, 'there are rocks all around it.'

Then suddenly, amazingly, *Sæbroga* shot into calm water. One moment she was in the grip of an angry sea, the next she was floating as placid as a swan on a sun-dappled lake. The sail that had beaten dementedly now filled tamely, the hull slowed, and my men slumped on their oars as we gently coasted on a limpid calm. 'Welcome to Loch Cuan,' Finan said with a crooked smile.

I felt the tension go from my arms. I had not even realised I was gripping the steering-oar so hard. Then I stooped and took the pot of ale from Dudda's hand and drained it. 'You're still not safe, lord,' he said with a grin.

'No?'

'Ledges! Reefs! This place can claw your hull to splinters! Best put a man on the prow, lord. It looks calm enough but it's full of sunken rocks!'

And full of enemies. Those who had seen us did not pursue us because they must have thought we had been sent by Ragnall and they were content to wait to discover our business. The great axe on the prow and the huge axe on the sail had lulled them, and I trusted those blood-dark symbols to deceive the other ships that waited somewhere ahead.

And so we rowed into a heaven. I have rarely seen a place so beautiful or so lush. It was a sea-lake dotted by islands with seals on the beaches, fish beneath our oars, and more birds than a god could count. The hills were gentle, the grass rich, and the loch's edges lined with fish traps. No man could starve here. The oars dipped slowly and *Sæbroga* slid through the gentle water with scarcely a tremor. Our wake widened softly, rocking ducks, geese, and gulls.

There were a few small crude fishing boats being paddled or rowed, none with more than three men, and all of them hurried out of our path. Berg, who had refused to stay in Ceaster despite his wounded thigh, stood high in the prow with one arm hooked over the axe head, watching the water. I kept glancing behind, looking to see if either of the two ships we had seen in the narrows would put to sea and follow us, but their masts stayed motionless. A cow lowed on shore. A shawled woman collecting shellfish watched us pass. I waved, but she ignored the gesture. 'So where's Sigtryggr?' I asked Vidarr.

'The western bank, lord.' He could not remember precisely where, but there was a smear of smoke on the loch's western side and so we rowed towards that distant mark. We went slowly, wary of the sunken ledges and rocks. Berg made hand signals to guide us, but even so the oars on the steerboard side of the ship scraped stone twice. The small wind dropped, letting the sail sag, but I left it hanging as a signal that this was Ragnall's ship.

'There,' Finan said, pointing ahead.

He had seen a mast behind a low island. Orvar, I knew, had two ships on the loch and I guessed one was north of Sigtryggr and the other south. They had evidently failed to assault Sigtryggr's fort, so the task of the ships now was to stop any small craft from carrying food to the besieged garrison. I strapped Serpent-Breath at my waist, then covered her with a rough brown woollen cloak. 'I want you by my side, Vidarr,' I said, 'and my name is Ranulf Godricson.'

'Ranulf Godricson,' he repeated.

'A Dane,' I told him.

'Ranulf Godricson,' he said again.

I gave the steering-oar to Dudda, who, though half hazed by ale, was a competent enough helmsman. 'When we reach that ship,' I said, nodding towards the distant mast, 'I'll want to go alongside. If he doesn't let us then we'll have to break some of his oars, but not too many because we need them. Just put our bow alongside his.'

'Bow to bow,' Dudda said.

I sent Finan with twenty men to *Sæbroga*'s bow where they crouched or lay. No one wore a helmet, our mail was covered by cloaks, and our shields were left flat on the deck. To a casual glance we were unprepared for war.

The far ship had seen us now. She appeared from behind the small island and I saw the sunlight flash from her oar banks as the blades rose wet from the water. A ripple of white showed at her prow as she turned towards us. A dragon or an eagle, it was hard to tell which, reared at that prow. 'That's Orvar's ship,' Vidarr told me.

'Good.'

'The *Hræsvelgr*,' he said.

I smiled at the name. Hræsvelgr is the eagle that sits at the topmost branch of Yggdrasil, the world tree. It is a vicious bird, watching both gods and men, and ever ready to stoop and rend with claws or beak. Orvar's job was to watch Sigtryggr, but it was *Hræsvelgr* that was about to be rended.

We brailed up the sail, tying it loosely to the great yard. 'When I tell you,' I called to the rowers, 'bring the oars in slow! Make it ragged! Make it look as if you're tired!'

'We are tired,' one of them called back.

'And Christians,' I called, 'hide your crosses!' I watched as the talismans were kissed, then tucked beneath mail coats. 'And when we attack we go in fast! Finan!'

'Lord?'

'I want at least one prisoner. Someone who looks as if he knows what he's talking about.'

We rowed on, rowing slow as weary men would, and then we were close enough for me to see that it was an eagle on *Hræsvelgr*'s bow and the bird's eyes were painted white and the tip of her hooked beak red. A man was in her bows, presumably watching for sunken rocks just as Berg did. I tried to count the oars and guessed there were no more than twelve on each side. 'And remember,' I shouted, 'look dozy. We want to surprise them!'

I waited through ten more lazy oar beats. 'Ship oars!'

The oars came up clumsily. There was a moment's confusion as the long looms were brought inboard and laid in *Sæbroga*'s centre, then the ship settled as we coasted on. Whoever commanded the other ship saw what we intended and shipped his oars too. It was a lovely piece of seamanship, the two great boats gliding softly together. My men were slumped on their benches, but their hands were already gripping the hilts of swords or the hafts of axes.

'Hail them,' I told Vidarr.

'Jarl Orvar!' he shouted.

A man waved from the stern of the *Hræsvelgr*. 'Vidarr!' he bellowed. 'Is that you? Is the Jarl with you?'

'Jarl Ranulf is here!'

The name could not have meant anything to Orvar, but he ignored it for the moment. 'Why are you here?' he called.

'Why do you think?'

Orvar spat over the side. 'You've come for Sigtryggr's bitch? You go and fetch her!'

'The Jarl wants her!' I shouted in Danish. 'He can't wait!'

Orvar spat again. He was a burly man, grey-bearded, sun-darkened, standing beside his own steersman. *Hræsvelgr* had far fewer men than *Sæbroga*, a mere fifty or so. 'He'll have the bitch soon enough,' he called back as the two ships closed on each other, 'they must starve soon!'

'How does a man starve here?' I demanded, just as a fish leaped from the water with a flash of silver scales. 'We have to attack them!'

Orvar strode between his rowers' benches, going to *Hræsvelgr*'s prow to see us better. 'Who are you?' he demanded.

'Ranulf Godricson,' I called back.

'Never heard of you,' he snarled.

'I've heard of you!'

'The Jarl sent you?'

'He's tired of waiting,' I said. I did not need to

shout because the ships were just paces apart now, slowly coming together.

'So how many men must die just so he can get between that bitch's thighs?' Orvar demanded, and at that moment the two boats touched and my men seized *Hrœsvelgr*'s upper strake and hauled her into *Sæbroga*'s steerboard flank.

'Go!' I shouted. I could not leap the gap from the stern, but I hurried forward as the first of my men scrambled across, weapons showing. Finan led, jumping across the gap with a drawn sword.

Jumping to slaughter.

The crew of *Hrœsvelgr* were good men, brave men, warriors of the north. They deserved better. They were not ready for battle, they were grinning a welcome one moment and dying the next. Few even had time to find a weapon. My men, like hounds smelling blood, poured across the boats' sides and started killing. They gutted the centre of *Hrœsvelgr* instantly, clearing a space in her belly. Finan led his men towards her stern while I took mine towards the eagle-proud bows. By now some of Orvar's crew had seized swords or axes, but none was dressed in mail. A blade thumped on my ribs, did not cut the iron links, and I chopped Serpent-Breath sideways, striking the man on the side of his neck with the base of the blade. He went down and my son finished him with a thrust of his sword Raven-Beak. Men retreated in front of us, tripping over the benches, and some leaped overboard rather than face our wet blades. I could not see Orvar, but I could hear a man roaring, 'No! No! No! No!'

A youngster lunged at me from the deck, plunging his sword two-handed at my waist. I turned the lunge away with Serpent-Breath and kneed him in the face, then stamped on his groin.

'No! No!' the voice still roared. The youngster kicked me and I tripped on a stiff coil of rope and sprawled onto the deck, and two of my men stepped protectively over me. Eadger slid his sword point into the youngster's mouth, then drove the point hard down to the deck beneath. Vidarr gave me his hand and hauled me upright. The voice still shouted, 'No! No!'

I rammed Serpent-Breath at a man readying to strike at Eadger with an axe. The man fell backwards. I was ready to slide Serpent-Breath into his ribcage when the axe was snatched from his hand and I saw that Orvar had pushed his way from the ship's prow and now stood on a bench above the prone axeman. 'No, no!' Orvar shouted at me, then realised he had been bellowing the wrong message because he dropped the axe and spread his hands wide, 'I yield!' he called, 'I yield!' He was staring at me, shock and pain on his face, 'I yield!' he cried again. 'Stop fighting!'

'Stop fighting!' It was my turn to shout. 'Stop!'

The deck was slippery with blood. Men groaned, men cried, men whimpered as the two ships, tied together now, rocked slightly on the lake's placid water. One of Orvar's men lurched to *Hræsvelgr*'s side and vomited blood.

'Stop fighting!' Finan echoed my shout.

Orvar still stared at me, then he took a sword from one of his men, stepped down from the bench and held the sword's hilt to me. 'I yield,' he said again, 'I yield, you bastard.'

And now I had two ships.

CHAPTER 10

A smear of red discoloured the water. It drifted away, turned pink and slowly vanished. The deck of *Hræsvelgr* was thick with blood, while the air stank of blood and shit. There were sixteen dead men, eight prisoners, and the rest of Orvar's crew were in the bloodied water clinging to oars that floated close by the hull. We hauled those men aboard, then searched both them and the dead for coins, hacksilver, or anything else of value. We piled the plunder and the captured weapons by *Sæbroga*'s mast, close to which Orvar sat watching as the first of his dead crewmen were thrown overboard from *Hræsvelgr*, which was still lashed to our larger ship. 'Who are you?' he asked me.

'I'm the bitch's father,' I said.

He flinched, then closed his eyes for a second. 'Uhtred of Bebbanburg?'

'I'm Uhtred.'

He laughed, which surprised me, though it was a bitter laugh, bereft of any amusement. 'Jarl Ragnall sacrificed a black stallion to Thor as a pledge of your death.'

'Did it die well?'

He shook his head. 'They bodged it. It took three blows of the hammer.'

'I was given a black stallion not long ago,' I said.

He flinched again, recognising that the gods had favoured me and that Ragnall's sacrifice had been rejected. 'The gods love you then,' he said, 'lucky you.' He was about my age, which meant he was old. He looked grizzled, lined and hard. His beard, grey with dark streaks, had ivory rings woven into the hair, he wore golden rings in his ears, and had worn a thick golden chain with a golden hammer until my son took it from him. 'Did you have to kill them?' he asked, looking at the corpses of his men floating naked in the reddened water.

'You have my daughter under siege,' I said angrily, 'she and my granddaughter. What was I supposed to do? Kiss you?'

He nodded reluctant acceptance of my anger. 'But they were good boys,' he said, grimacing as another corpse was tossed over *Hræsvelgr*'s side. 'How did you capture the *Øxtívar*?' he asked.

'*Øxtívar*?'

'His ship!' He rapped the mast. 'This ship!'

So that had been *Sæbroga*'s name, *Øxtívar*. It meant axe of the gods and it was a good name, but *Sæbroga* was better. 'The same way I sent Ragnall running away from Ceaster,' I said, 'by beating him in battle.'

He frowned at me as if assessing whether I told the truth, then gave another of his mirthless laughs. 'We've heard nothing from the Jarl,' he said, 'not since he left. Does he live?'

'Not for long.'

He grimaced. 'Nor me, I suppose?' He waited for a response, but I said nothing, so he just patted the mast. 'He loves this ship.'

'Loved,' I corrected him. 'But he kept too much weight forward.'

He nodded. 'He always did. But he likes to see his oarsmen get soaked because it amuses him. He says it toughens them. His father was the same.'

'And Sigtryggr?' I asked.

'What of him?'

'Does he like toughening his crew?'

'No,' Orvar said, 'he's the good brother.'

That answer surprised me, not because I thought Sigtryggr bad, but because Orvar served Ragnall and loyalty alone would have suggested a different response. 'The good brother?' I asked.

'People like him,' Orvar said, 'they've always liked him. He's generous. Ragnall's cruel and Sigtryggr's generous. You should know that, he married your daughter!'

'I like him,' I said, 'and it sounds as if you do too.'

'I do,' he said simply, 'but Ragnall has my oath.'

'You had a choice?'

He shook his head. 'Their father ordered it. Some of us were sworn to Ragnall, some to Sigtryggr. I think Jarl Olaf thought they'd divide his lands peaceably, but once he died they fell out with each other instead.' He looked at the floating bodies. 'And here I am.' He watched as I sorted through the captured weapons, weighing the swords one by one. 'So now you'll kill me?' he asked.

'You have a better idea?' I asked sarcastically.

'Either you kill me or the Irish will,' Orvar said gloomily.

'I thought they were your allies?'

'Some allies!' he said scornfully. 'They agreed to attack the land side of the fort while we assaulted the beach, but the bastards never came. I lost twenty-three men! The damned Irish said the omens were bad.' He spat. 'I don't believe they ever did intend to attack! They just lied.'

'And they won't attack,' I suggested, 'because of my daughter's sorcery?'

'She's got them scared, right enough, but I also think they want us to do all the fighting for them so they can move in and kill the survivors. Then take your daughter to . . .' he did not finish that sentence. 'We fight,' he said wryly, 'and they win. They're not fools.'

I looked up, seeing small white clouds sailing serene in a perfect blue. The sun lit the land almost a luminous green. I could see why men lusted after this land, but I had known Finan long enough to learn that it was no easy place to settle. 'I don't understand,' I told Orvar. 'You like Sigtryggr, you mistrust your allies, so why didn't you just make a truce with him? Why not join Sigtryggr?'

Orvar had been gazing at the water, but now raised his eyes to look into mine. 'Because Ragnall has my wife as a hostage.'

I winced at that.

'My children too,' Orvar went on. 'He took my wife and he took Bjarke's woman too.'

'Bjarke?'

'Bjarke Neilson,' he said, 'shipmaster on the *Nidhogg*,' he jerked his head northwards and I realised the *Nidhogg* must be the second ship that was blockading Sigtryggr's fastness, and the jerk of Orvar's head told me she was somewhere to the north of the loch. If Hræsvelgr was the eagle perched at the top of the life tree then Nidhogg was the serpent coiled at its roots, a vile creature that gnawed at the corpses of dishonoured men. It was a strange name for a ship, but one, I supposed, that would strike fear into enemies. Orvar frowned. 'I suppose you'll want to capture her too?'

'Of course.'

'And you can't risk any of us warning *Nidhogg* by shouting,' he said, 'but at least let us die with swords in our hands?' He looked at me pleadingly. 'I beg you, lord, let us die like warriors.'

I found the best sword from among the captured weapons. It was long-bladed with a fine hilt of carved ivory and crosspieces shaped like hammers. I weighed it in my hand, liking its heft. 'Was this yours?'

'And my father's before me,' he said, staring at the blade.

'So tell me,' I said, 'what must you do to get your family back?'

'Give Ragnall your daughter, of course. What else?'

I turned the sword around, holding it by the blade to offer him the hilt. 'Then why don't we do just that?' I asked.

He stared at me.

So I explained.

I needed men. I needed an army. For years Æthelflaed had refused to cross the frontier into Northumbria except to punish the Norse or Danes who had stolen cattle or slaves from Mercia. Such revenge raids could be brutal, but they were just raids, never an invasion. She wanted to secure Mercia first, to build a chain of burhs along its northern border, but by refusing to capture Northumbrian land she was also doing her brother's bidding.

Edward of Wessex had proved to be a good enough king. He was not the equal of his father, of course. He lacked Alfred's intense cleverness and Alfred's single-minded determination to rescue the Saxons and Christianity from the pagan Northmen, but Edward had continued his father's work. He had led the West Saxon army into East Anglia where he was winning back land and building burhs. The land ruled by Wessex was being pushed slowly northwards, and Saxons were settling estates that had belonged to Danish jarls. Alfred had dreamed of one kingdom, a kingdom of Saxon Christians, ruled by a Saxon Christian king and speaking the language of the Saxons. Alfred had called himself the King of the English-Speaking people, which was not quite the same thing as being

King of Englaland, but that dream, the dream of a united country, was slowly coming true.

But to make it wholly true meant subduing the Norse and the Danes in Northumbria, and that Æthelflaed was reluctant to do. She did not fear the risks, but rather feared the displeasure of her brother and of the church. Wessex was far richer than war-torn Mercia. West Saxon silver supported Æthelflaed's troops and West Saxon gold was poured into Mercian churches, and Edward did not want his sister to be reckoned a greater ruler than himself. If Northumbria was to be invaded, then Edward would lead the army and Edward would gain the reputation, and so he forbade his sister from invading Northumbria without him, and Æthelflaed, knowing how reliant she was on her brother's gold and, besides, reluctant to offend him, was content to reclaim Mercia's northern lands. The time would come, she liked to tell me, when the combined armies of Mercia and Wessex would march triumphantly to the Scottish border and when that happened there would be a new country, not Wessex, not Mercia, not East Anglia, not Northumbria, but Englaland.

All of which might have been true, but it was too slow for me. I was growing old. There were aches in my bones, grey hairs in my beard, and an old dream in my heart. I wanted Bebbanburg. Bebbanburg was mine. I was and am the Lord of Bebbanburg. Bebbanburg belonged to my father and to his father, and it will belong to my son and to his son. And Bebbanburg lay deep inside

Northumbria. To besiege it, to capture it from my cousin whose father had stolen it from me, I needed to be in Northumbria. I needed to lay siege and I could not hope to do that with a horde of bitter Norsemen and vengeful Danes surrounding me. I had already tried to capture Bebbanburg once by approaching the fortress from the sea, and that attempt had failed. Next time, I vowed, I would take an army to Bebbanburg, and to do that I first had to capture the land around the fortress, and that meant defeating the Northmen who ruled that territory. I needed to invade Northumbria.

Which meant I needed an army.

The idea had come to me when I had light-heartedly told Finan that my forgiveness gift to Æthelflaed would be Eoferwic, by which I had meant that one way or the other I would rid that city of Ragnall's forces.

But now, suddenly, I saw the idea clearly.

I needed Bebbanburg. To gain Bebbanburg I needed to defeat the Northmen of Northumbria, and to defeat the Northmen of Northumbria I needed an army.

And if Æthelflaed would not let me use the Mercian army then I would use Ragnall's.

Sigtryggr's fortress was almost an island. It was a steep hump of rock-strewn land rearing from the lough's water and protected from a sea approach by ledges, islets, and rocks. The land approach was even worse. The only path to the hump of rock was a low and narrow neck, scarce wide enough for six men to walk abreast. Even if men could cross the neck they faced a steep climb to the summit of Sigtryggr's fort, the same climb that any attackers from the sea would find beyond the thin beach. To reach that beach a ship first had to negotiate a twisting channel that dog-legged from the south, but once the troops had leaped off the boat's prow they would be confronted by high bluffs and precipitous slopes above which the defenders waited. The headland was like Bebbanburg, a place made to frustrate an attacker, though, unlike Bebbanburg, there was no palisade because none was needed, just the rocky heights above which cooking fires smoked on the hill's wide green summit.

Sæbroga approached the fort from the south, picking a delicate path between the hidden ledges and rocks. Gerbruht stood in the prow, probing the water with an oar and shouting when its blade struck rock. I had just twelve men rowing, there was no need for more because we dared not travel fast. We could only creep through the dangers.

Sigtryggr's garrison saw a boat crammed with men, glinting with weapons and displaying Ragnall's big red axe at its prow. They would recognise *Sæbroga* and think that either Ragnall himself had come to finish them or else sent one of his more trusted war chiefs. I watched as the garrison formed a shield wall on the slope and I listened to the harsh clash of war-blades striking willow-boards. Sigtryggr's banner, a red axe just like his brother's symbol, was unfurled higher on the hill and I thought I saw Stiorra standing beside the banner. Her husband, blond hair bright in the sunlight, pushed through his shield wall and strode halfway down to the beach. 'Come and die!' he bellowed from the summit of one of the headland's many rock bluffs. 'Come join your friends!' He gestured with his drawn sword and I saw human heads had been placed on rocks along the shore. Just as I had welcomed Ragnall with the severed heads at Eads Byrig, so Sigtryggr was welcoming visitors to his refuge.

'It's a corpse fence,' Finan said.

'A what?'

'The heads! You think twice before crossing a corpse fence.' He made the sign of the cross.

'I need more heads!' Sigtryggr shouted. 'So bring me yours! I beg you!' Behind him the swords clattered on shields. No attacker could hope to survive an assault on that rock, not unless he could bring an army to the shore and so overwhelm the few defenders, and that would be impossible. There was only room for three or perhaps four ships on the beach, and those ships would be forced to approach single file between the hazards. We inched our way, and more than once the *Sæbroga*'s bows touched rock and we had to back water and try again as Gerbruht bellowed instructions.

'To make it easy for you,' Sigtryggr shouted, 'we'll let you land!' He stood on the bluff beside one of the heads. His long golden hair hung below his shoulders around which a chain of gold was looped three times. He was in mail, but wore no helmet nor carried a shield. He had his long-sword in his right hand, the blade naked. He was grinning, looking forward to a battle he knew he would win. I remembered young Berg describing him as a lord of war, and even though he was trapped and besieged, he looked magnificent.

I went forward and told Gerbruht to make way for me, then climbed onto the small platform just beneath the axe-head prow. I wore a plain helmet with closed cheek-pieces and Sigtryggr mistook me for Orvar. 'Welcome back, Orvar! You brought me more men to be killed? You didn't lose enough last time?'

'Do I look like Orvar?' I bellowed back. 'You half-blind idiot! You spawn of a goat! Do you want me to take your other eye?'

He stared.

'Can't a father visit his daughter without being insulted by some shit-brained, one-eyed arse-dropping Norseman?' I called.

He held up his free hand, indicating that his men should stop beating their shields. And still he stared. Behind him the clatter of blades on willow slowly faded.

I took the helmet off and tossed it back to Gerbruht. 'Is this the welcome a loving father-in-law gets?' I demanded. 'I come all this way to rescue your worthless arse and you threaten me with your feeble insults? Why aren't you showering me with gold and gifts, you wall-eyed piece of ungrateful toad shit?'

He began to laugh, then he danced. He capered for a few heartbeats, then stopped and spread his arms wide. 'It's amazing!' he shouted.

'What's amazing, you goat dropping?'

'That a mere Saxon should bring a boat safe from Britain! Was the voyage very frightening?'

'About as scary as facing you in battle,' I said.

'So you pissed yourself then?' he asked, grinning.

I laughed. 'We borrowed your brother's boat!'

'So I see!' He sheathed his sword. 'You're safe now! You've got deep water all the way to the beach!'

'Pull!' I called to the rowers, and they tugged on the looms and *Sæbroga* surged across the last few yards to grind her bow on the shingle. I stepped back off the platform and clambered over the steerboard bow strake. I dropped into water that came up to my thighs and almost lost my balance, but Sigtryggr had come down from his boulder, stretched out a hand, and pulled me ashore. He embraced me.

Even without an eye he was still a handsome man, hawk-faced and fair-haired, quick to smile, and I understood so well why Stiorra had sailed with him from Britain. I had been seeking a husband for her, looking among the warriors of Mercia and Wessex for a man who could match her intelligence and fierce passion, but she had taken the choice from me. She had married my enemy and now he was my ally. I was pleased to see him, even surprised by the surge of pleasure I felt.

'You took your time coming, lord,' he said happily.

‘I knew you weren’t in real trouble,’ I said, ‘so why should I hurry?’

‘Because we were running out of ale, of course.’ He turned and shouted up the rocky slope. ‘You can put your swords away! These ugly bastards are friends!’ He plucked my elbow. ‘Come and meet your granddaughter, lord.’

Stiorra came to me instead, leading a small child by the hand, and I confess the breath caught in my throat. It was not the child that misted my eyes. I have never liked small children, not even my own, but I loved my daughter and I could see why Ragnall would go to war for her. Stiorra had become a woman, graceful and confident, and so like her mother that it hurt just to look at her. She smiled as she approached, then offered me a dutiful curtsey. ‘Father,’ she said.

‘I’m not crying,’ I said, ‘dust got in my eye.’

‘Yes, father,’ she said.

I embraced her, then held her at arm’s length. She wore a dark dress of finely woven linen beneath a woollen cloak dyed black. An ivory hammer hung at her neck and a golden torque circled it. She wore her hair high, pinned by combs of gold and ivory. She took a step back, but only so she could draw her daughter forward. ‘This is your granddaughter,’ she said, ‘Gisela Sigtryggdottir.’

‘That’s a mouthful.’

‘She’s a handful.’

I glanced at the girl who looked like her mother and grandmother. She was dark, with large eyes and long black hair. She looked back at me very solemnly, but neither of us had anything to say and so said nothing. Stiorra laughed at our tongue-tied silence, then turned away to greet Finan. My men were securing the *Sæbroga* to the shore, using long lines that they lashed around boulders.

'You might want to leave men aboard,' Sigtryggr warned me, 'because two of my brother's ships are patrolling the loch. *Hræsvelgr* and *Nidhogg*.'

'*Hræsvelgr* is already ours,' I told him, 'and *Nidhogg* soon will be. We'll capture the other two as well.'

'You captured *Hræsvelgr*?' he asked, evidently astonished at the news.

'You didn't see it?' I asked, and looked south and saw that islands would have hidden the *Sæbroga*'s meeting with the *Hræsvelgr*. 'We should have five ships by tomorrow,' I said brusquely, 'but with their crews, my crew, and your people? They'll be crowded! But if the weather stays calm like this, we should be safe enough. Unless you want to stay here?'

He was still trying to comprehend what I was saying. 'Their crews?'

'Your crews, really,' I said, deliberately confusing him with a flood of good news. He looked over my shoulder and I turned to see that the *Hræsvelgr* had just appeared around the headland. Orvar was back in command of her. I watched and, sure enough, a second ship was following in her wake, 'That must be the *Nidhogg*,' I said to Sigtryggr.

'It is.'

'Orvar Freyrson,' I told him, 'is going to swear loyalty to you. I assume Bjarke is too, and every man of their crews as well. If any of them refuse, I suggest we strand them on an island here, unless you'd rather kill them.'

'Orvar will swear loyalty?' he asked.

'And Bjarke too, I suspect.'

'If Orvar and Bjarke swear,' he said, frowning as he tried to comprehend the significance of all I was telling him, 'their crews will too. All of them.'

'And Orvar is confident he can persuade the other two ships to do the same,' I said.

'How did you persuade . . .' he began, then just stopped, still trying to understand how fate had turned that morning. He had woken trapped and besieged, now he was commanding a small fleet.

'How?' I asked. 'Because I offered him land, a lot of land. Your land, as it happens, but I didn't think you'd mind.'

'My land?' he asked, now totally confused.

'I'm making you King of Eoferwic,' I explained, as if that was something I did every day, 'and of Northumbria too. Don't thank me!' He had made no sign of thanking me, he was just staring at me in astonishment. 'Because there will be conditions! But for now we should get the ships ready for a voyage. I'm reckoning we must empty some of their ballast because they're going to be loaded to the upper strake. I'm told the weather on this coast can change in an eyeblink, but this looks settled enough and we should leave as soon as we can.

And Dudda tells me we should leave the lough at slack water, so perhaps tomorrow morning?'

'Dudda?'

'My shipmaster,' I explained, 'and usually drunk, but it doesn't seem to make much difference to him. So tomorrow morning?'

'Where are we going?' Sigtryggr asked.

'To Cair Ligualid.'

He stared at me vacantly. It was plain he had never heard of the place. 'And Cair whatever it is,' he asked, 'is where?'

'Over there,' I said, pointing east, 'a day's voyage.'

'King of Northumbria?' he asked, still trying to understand what I was telling him.

'If you agree,' I said, 'then I'm making you King of Northumbria. King of Jorvik, really, but whoever holds that throne usually calls himself King of Northumbria too. Your brother reckons he's the king there now, but you and I should be able to give him a grave instead.' *Hræsvelgr* had just beached, and Orvar leaped off the prow to stumble awkwardly on the rocky shore. 'He's either going to kill you,' I said, watching Orvar, 'or else kneel to you.'

Orvar, his golden chain restored, just as all his men had been given back their weapons, coins, hacksilver, and talismans, crossed the short stretch of beach. He gave Stiorra a respectful and embarrassed nod, then looked Sigtryggr in the eye. 'Lord?' he said.

'You gave my brother your oath,' Sigtryggr said harshly.

'And your brother took my family hostage,' Orvar said, 'which no oath-lord should ever do.'

'True,' Sigtryggr said. He looked away as the *Nidhogg* grounded, her prow scraping on the shingle. Her master, Bjarke, leaped off the bow and stood watching Sigtryggr, who drew his long-sword. The blade hissed as it scraped through the scabbard's throat. For a heartbeat Sigtryggr seemed to threaten Orvar with the long blade, then he let the sword fall so that its tip was planted in the shingle. 'You know what to do,' he told Orvar.

The crews of *Hræsvelgr* and *Nidhogg* watched as Orvar knelt and clasped his hands around Sigtryggr's hands, which, in turn, held the sword. Orvar took a breath, but before speaking the oath he looked up at me. 'You promise my family will live, lord?'

'What I promise,' I said carefully, 'is that I will do everything I can to make certain that they live and are unharmed.' I touched the hammer at my neck, 'and I swear that by Thor and by the lives of my own family.'

'And how do you keep that oath?' Sigtryggr asked me.

'By giving Ragnall your wife, of course. Now let Jarl Orvar swear you loyalty.'

And on a beach, beside a placid lough, under a sky of blue and white, the oaths were made.

It is not difficult to be a lord, a jarl, or even a king, but it is difficult to be a leader.

Most men want to follow, and what they demand

of their leader is prosperity. We are the ring-givers, the gold-givers. We give land, we give silver, we give slaves, but that alone is not enough. They must be led. Leave men standing or sitting for days at a time and they get bored, and bored men make trouble. They must be surprised and challenged, given tasks they think beyond their abilities. And they must fear. A leader who is not feared will cease to rule, but fear is not enough. They must love too. When a man has been led into the shield wall, when an enemy is roaring defiance, when the blades are clashing on shields, when the soil is about to be soaked in blood, when the ravens circle in wait for the offal of men, then a man who loves his leader will fight better than a man who merely fears him. At that moment we are brothers, we fight for each other, and a man must know that his leader will sacrifice his own life to save any one of his men.

I learned all that from Ragnar, a man who led with joy in his soul, though he was feared too. His great enemy, Kjartan, knew only how to lead by fear, and Ragnall was the same. Men who lead by fear might become great kings and might rule lands so great that no man knows their boundaries, but they can be beaten too, beaten by men who fight as brothers.

'What my brother offered,' Sigtryggr told me that night, 'was that I should be king of the islands and he would be king of Britain.'

'The islands?'

'All the sea islands,' he explained, 'everything along the coast.' He waved northwards. I had sailed those waters and knew that everything north of the Irish Sea is a tangle of islands, rocks and wild waves.

'The Scots might not have liked that,' I said, amused. 'And the Scots are nothing but trouble.'

He grinned. 'That, I think, was in Ragnall's mind. I would keep the Scots off his back while he conquered the Saxon lands.' He paused, watching the sparks whirl up into the darkness. 'I'd get the rocks, the seaweed, the gulls, and the goats, and he'd get the gold, the wheat, and the women.'

'You said no?'

'I said yes.'

'Why?'

He looked at me with his one eye. The other was a pucker of sunken scar tissue. 'It's family,' he said, 'it's what our father wanted. Life has become hard here in Ireland and it's time to find new lands.' He shrugged. 'Besides, if I was Lord of the Islands I could turn their rocks into gold.'

'Rocks, seaweed, gulls, and goats?' I asked.

'And ships,' he said wolfishly. He was thinking piracy. 'And they say there are lands beyond the sea.'

'I've heard those stories,' I said dubiously.

'But think of it! New lands! Waiting to be settled.'

'There's nothing but fire and ice out there,' I said. 'I sailed it once, out to where the ice glitters and the mountains spill fire.'

'Then we use the fire to melt the ice.'

'And beyond that?' I asked. 'Men say there are other lands, but haunted by monsters.'

'Then we slaughter the monsters,' he said happily.

I smiled at his enthusiasm. 'So you said yes to your brother?'

'I did! I would be the Sea King and he would be King of Britain,' he paused, 'but then he demanded Stiorra.'

There was silence around the fire. Stiorra had been listening, her long face grave, and now she caught my eye and smiled slightly, a secret smile. Men leaned in beyond the inner circle, trying to hear what was being said and relaying the words to those who were out of earshot.

'He wanted Stiorra,' I said flatly.

'He always wants hostages,' Orvar said.

I grimaced. 'You hold your enemies' families hostage, not your friends.'

'We're all enemies to Ragnall,' Bjarke put in. He was *Nidhogg*'s shipmaster, a tall and lean Norseman with a long plaited beard and a face marked with an inked ship on either cheek.

'He holds your wife too?' I asked.

'My wife, two daughters, and my son.'

So Ragnall ruled by fear, and only by fear. Men were scared of him and so they should be because he was a frightening man, but a leader who rules by fear must also be successful. He must lead his men from victory to victory because the moment he shows himself weak then he is vulnerable, and Ragnall had been beaten. I had thrashed him in the woods about Eads Byrig, I had driven him from the lands around Ceaster, and it was no wonder, I thought, that the men he had left in Ireland were so ready to betray the oaths they had sworn to him.

And that was another question. If a man swears an oath of loyalty and afterwards the lord takes hostages for the fulfilment of that oath, is the oath valid? When a man clasped hands with me, when he said the words that bound his fate to mine, then he became like a brother. Ragnall trusted no one, it seemed. He took oaths and he took hostages. Every man was his enemy, and a man owes no loyalty to an enemy.

Svart, a huge man who was Sigtryggr's second-in-command, growled, 'He didn't want the Lady Stiorra as a hostage,' he said.

'No,' Sigtryggr agreed.

'I was to be his wife,' Stiorra said, 'his fifth wife.'

'He told you that?' I asked.

'Fulla told me,' she said. 'Fulla is his first wife. She showed me her scars too.' She spoke very calmly. 'Did you ever beat your wives, father?'

I smiled at her through the flames. 'I'm weak that way, no.'

She smiled back. 'I remember you telling us that a man does not beat a woman. You said it often.'

'Only a weak man beats a woman,' I said. Some of the listening men looked uncomfortable, but none of them argued. 'But it might take a strong man to have more than one wife?' I went on, looking at Sigtryggr, who laughed.

'I wouldn't dare,' he said, 'she'd beat me to a pulp.'

'So Ragnall demanded Stiorra?' I prompted him.

'He brought his whole fleet to take her! Hundreds of men! It was his right, he said. And so we came here.'

'Fled here,' Stiorra said drily.

'We had six ships,' Sigtryggr explained, 'and he had thirty-six.'

'What happened to the six ships?'

'We bribed the Irish with them, exchanged them for grain and ale.'

'The same Irish who were paid to kill you?' I asked. Sigtryggr nodded. 'So why haven't they killed you?'

'Because they don't want to die on these rocks,' Sigtryggr said, 'and because of your daughter.'

I looked at her. 'Because of your sorcery?'

Stiorra nodded, then stood, her face cast into stern shadows by the flames. 'Come with me, father,' she said and I saw that Sigtryggr's men were grinning, enjoying some secret jest. 'Father?' Stiorra beckoned westwards. 'It's time, anyway.'

'Time?'

'You'll see.'

I followed her westwards. She gave me her hand to guide me down the slope because the night was dark and the path off the hilltop was steep. We went slowly, our eyes adjusting to the night's blackness. 'It's me,' she called softly as we reached the foot of the hill.

'Mistress,' a voice acknowledged from the dark. There were evidently sentries beside the crude stone wall that had been built to bar the narrow neck of land that led away from the fort. I could see fires now, campfires, a long way off on the mainland.

'How many men around those fires?' I asked.

'Hundreds,' Stiorra said calmly. 'Enough to overwhelm us, so we needed to use other methods to keep them away.' She climbed onto the wall's top and let go of my hand. I could hardly see her now. She wore a cloak as black as the night, as black as her hair, but I was aware of her standing straight and tall, facing the distant enemy.

And then she began to sing.

Or rather she crooned and she moaned, her voice sliding up and down eerily, crying in the darkness, and sometimes pausing to yelp like a vixen. Then she would stop and there would be silence in the night except for the sigh of wind across the land. She started again, yelping again, short sharp barks that she spat westwards before letting her voice slide up into a desperate scream that slowly, slowly faded into a whimper and then to nothing.

And then, as if in answer, the western horizon was lit by lightning. Not the sharp stabs of Thor's thunderbolts, not the jagged streaks of anger that split the sky, but flickering sheets of silent summer lightning. They showed, distant and bright, then went, leaving darkness again and a stillness that felt full of menace. There was one last burst of far light and I saw the white skulls of the death fence arrayed along the wall where Stiorra stood.

'There, father,' she held out a hand, 'they're cursed again.'

I took her hand and helped her down from the wall. 'Cursed?'

'They think I'm a sorceress.'

'And are you?'

'They fear me,' she said. 'I call the spirits of the dead to haunt them and they know I speak to the gods.'

'I thought they were Christians?'

'They are, but they fear the older gods, and I keep them frightened.' She paused, staring up into the dark. 'There's something different here in Ireland,' she said, sounding puzzled, 'as if the old magic still clings to the earth. You can feel it.'

'I can't.'

She smiled. I saw the white of her teeth. 'I learned the runesticks. Fulla taught me.'

I had given her the runesticks that her mother had used, the slender polished shafts that, when cast, made intricate patterns that were said to tell the future. 'Do they speak to you?' I asked.

'They said you'd come, and they said Ragnall will die. They said a third thing . . .' she stopped abruptly.

'A third thing?' I asked.

'No,' she shook her head. 'Sometimes they're hard to read,' she said dismissively, taking my arm and leading me back towards the fire on the hilltop. 'In the morning the Christian sorcerers will try to undo my magic. They'll fail.'

'Christian sorcerers?'

'Priests,' she said dismissively.

'And did the runesticks tell you that your eldest brother would be gelded?'

She stopped and looked up at me in the darkness. 'Gelded?'

'He almost died.'

'No!' she said. 'No!'

'Brida did it.'

'Brida?'

'A hell-bitch,' I said bitterly, 'who has joined Ragnall.'

'No!' she protested again. 'But Uhtred was here! He went to Ragnall in peace!'

'He's called Father Oswald now,' I said, 'and that's what he'll never be, a father.'

'This Brida,' she asked fiercely, 'is she an enchantress?'

'She thinks so, she says so.'

She breathed a sigh of relief. 'And that was the third thing the runesticks said, father, that an enchantress must die.'

'The runesticks said that?'

'It must be her,' she said vengefully. She had plainly feared the sticks had foretold her own death. 'It will be her,' she said.

And I followed her back to the fire.

* * *

In the morning three Irish priests approached the narrow neck of land where the skulls stood on the low stone wall. They stopped at least fifty paces from the skulls, where they held their hands in the air and chanted prayers. One of them, a wild-haired man, danced in circles as he chanted. 'What do they hope to do?' I asked.

'They're praying that God will destroy the skulls,' Finan said. He made the sign of the cross.

'They really fear them,' I said in wonder.

'You wouldn't?'

'They're just skulls.'

'They're the dead!' he said fiercely. 'Didn't you know that when you put the heads around Eads Byrig?'

'I just wanted to horrify Ragnall,' I said.

'You gave him a ghost fence,' Finan said, 'and it's no wonder he left the place. And this one?' He nodded downhill to where Stiorra had arranged the skulls to face the mainland. 'This ghost fence has power!'

'Power?'

'Let me show you.' He led me across the hilltop to a stone-lined pit. It was not large, perhaps six feet square, but every inch of space had been crammed with bones. 'God knows how long they've been there,' Finan said, 'they were covered with that slab.' He pointed to a stone slab that had been shoved away from the pit. The surface of the slab had a cross scratched into it, the cross now filled with lichen. The bones had been sorted so that the long yellowed leg bones were all stacked together and the ribs carefully piled. There were pelvises, knucklebones, arm bones, but no skulls. 'I reckon the skulls were the top layer,' Finan said.

'Who were they?' I stooped to look into the pit.

'Monks probably. Maybe slaughtered when the first Norsemen came?' He turned and stared westwards. 'And those poor bastards are terrified of them. It's an army of the dead, their own dead! They'll be wanting more gold before they cross this ghost fence.'

'More gold?'

Finan half smiled. 'Ragnall paid the Uí Néill gold to capture Stiorra. But if they have to fight the dead as well as the living they'll want a lot more than the gold he's given them so far.'

'The dead don't fight,' I said.

Finan scorned that. 'You Saxons! I sometimes think you know nothing! No, the dead don't fight, but they take revenge! You want your milk sour from the udder? You want your crops to shrivel? Your cattle to have the staggers? Your children sick?'

I could hear the Irish priests making yelping noises and I wondered if the air was filled with unseen spirits fighting a battle of magic. The thought made me touch the hammer about my neck, then I forgot the phantoms as my son shouted from down the hill. 'Father!' he called. 'The ships!'

I saw that the last two ships were coming from the south, which meant Orvar had talked their crews into betraying Ragnall. I had my fleet now and the beginnings of an army. 'We have to rescue Orvar's family,' I said.

'We made that promise,' Finan agreed.

'Ragnall won't have them with his horsemen,' I guessed. 'You don't want women and children slowing you down when you're raiding deep in hostile country.'

'But he'll have them kept safe,' Finan said.

Which meant, I thought, that they were in Eoferwic. That city was Ragnall's base, his stronghold. We knew he had sent part of his army back there, presumably to hold the Roman walls while the rest of his men ravaged Mercia. 'Let's just hope they're not in Dunholm,' I said. Brida's fortress was formidable, perched on its crag above the river.

'That place would be a bitch to capture again,' Finan said.

'They'll be in Eoferwic,' I said, praying I was right.

And Eoferwic, I thought, was where my story had all begun. Where my father had died. Where I had become the Lord of Bebbanburg. Where I had met Ragnar and learned of the ancient gods.

And it was time to go back.

PART III

WAR OF THE BROTHERS

CHAPTER 11

I have endured nightmare voyages. I was a slave once, pulling a heavy oar in tumbling seas, freezing in the spray, fighting waves and wind, dragging a boat towards a rock-bound shore rimmed with ice. I had almost wished that the sea would take us. We were whimpering with fear and cold.

This was worse.

I had been aboard Alfred's ship *Heahengel* when Guthrum's fleet had died in a sudden storm that whipped the sea off the West Saxon coast to frenzy. The wind had shrieked, the waves were white devils, masts went overboard, sails were ripped to crazed tatters, and the great boats had sunk one after the other. The cries of the drowning had lived with me for days.

But this was worse.

This was worse even though the sea was calm, the waves placid and what small wind did blow wafted gently from the west. We saw no enemies. We crossed a sea as tame as a duck pond, yet every moment of that voyage was terrifying.

We left the lough at high water when the savage currents that streamed through the narrows were sullen and still. We had five ships now. All of Ragnall's crews in Loch Cuan had sworn their loyalty to Sigtryggr, but that meant we had their families and all Sigtryggr's people and all my men. Ships that were meant to carry no more than seventy crew had close to two hundred people aboard. They rode low in the water, the small waves constantly slopping over the upper strakes so that those men not rowing had to bail. We had thrown some of the ballast stones overboard, but that made the ships perilously top heavy so they rocked alarmingly whenever an errant breath of wind came from the north or south, and even the smallest cross-sea threatened to sink us. We crept across that gentle sea, but never for one moment did I feel out of danger. Even in the worst storm men can row, they can fight the gods, but those fragile five ships in a calm sea felt so vulnerable. The worst moments were in the night-time. The wind dropped to nothing, which might have been our salvation, but in the dark we could not see the small waves, only feel them as they spilled over the boats' sides. We pulled slow and steady through the darkness and we hammered the ears of the gods with prayers. We watched for oar-splashes, straining to stay close to the other ships, and still we prayed to every god known to us.

The gods must have listened because next day all five ships came safely to Britain's coast. There was a mist on the beach, just thick enough to shroud the headlands north and south so that

Dudda frowned in puzzlement. 'God knows where we are,' he finally admitted.

'Wherever it is,' I said, 'we're going ashore.' And so we rowed the boats straight at the beach where small waves slopped and the sound of the keel grating on sand was the sweetest sound I ever heard. 'Sweet Jesus,' Finan said. He had leaped ashore and now dropped to his knees. He crossed himself. 'I pray to God I never see another ship.'

'Just pray we're not in Strath Clota,' I said. All I knew was that by rowing eastwards we had crossed the sea to where Northumbria bordered Scotland, and that the coast of Scotland was inhabited by savages who called their country Strath Clota. This was wild country, a place of raiding parties, grim forts, and pitiless skirmishes. We had more than enough men to fight our way south if we had landed on Scottish soil, but I did not want to be pursued by wild-haired tribesmen wanting revenge, plunder, and slaves.

I gazed into the mist, seeing grass on dunes and the dim slopes of a hill beyond, and I thought this was how my ancestor must have felt when he brought his ship across the North Sea and landed on a strange beach in Britain, not knowing where he was or what dangers waited for him. His name was Ida, Ida the Flamebearer, and it was Ida who had captured the great crag beside the grey sea where Bebbanburg would be built. And his men, like the men who now landed from the five ships, must have waded through the small surf to bring their weapons to a strange land and gazed inland wondering what enemies waited for them. They had defeated those enemies, and the land Ida's warriors had conquered was now our land. Ida the Flamebearer's enemies had been driven from their pastures and valleys, hunted to Wales, to Scotland, or to Cornwalum, and the land they left behind was now ours, the land we wanted one day to be called Englaland.

Sigtryggr leaped ashore. 'Welcome to your kingdom, lord,' I said, 'at least I hope it's your kingdom.'

He gazed at the dunes where pale grass grew. 'This is Northumbria?'

'I hope so.'

He grinned. 'Why not your kingdom, lord?'

I confess I had been tempted. To be King of Northumbria? To be lord of the lands that had once been my family's kingdom? Because my family had been kings once. Ida the Flamebearer's descendants had been rulers of Bernicia, a kingdom that embraced Northumbria and the southern parts of Scotland, and it had been a king of Bernicia who had reared Bebbanburg on its grim rock beside the sea. For a moment, standing on that mist-shrouded beach beside the slow breaking waves, I imagined a crown on my head, and then I thought of Alfred.

I had never liked him any more than he had liked me, but I was not such a fool as to think him a bad king. He had been a good king, but being a king meant nothing but duty and responsibility, and those had weighed Alfred down and put furrows on his face and callouses on his knees worn out by praying. My temptation came from a child's view of kingship, as if by being king I could do whatever I wished, and for some reason I had a vision of Mus, the night-child in Ceaster, and I must have smiled and Sigtryggr mistook the smile for acceptance of his suggestion. 'You should be king, lord,' he said.

'No,' I responded firmly, and for a heartbeat I was tempted to tell him the truth, but I could not make him King of Northumbria and tell him, at the same instant, that Northumbria was doomed.

We cannot know the future. Perhaps some, like my daughter, can read the runesticks and find prophecies in their tangle, and others, like the bitch hag in the cave who had once foretold my life, might get dreams from the gods, but for most of us the future is a mist and we only see as far ahead as the mist allows, yet I was certain Northumbria was doomed. To its north was Scotland, and the people of that land are wild, savage, and proud. We are fated to fight them, probably for ever, but I had no wish to lead an army into their bitter hills. To stay in the valleys of Scotland meant ambush, while to march on the heights meant starvation. The Scots were welcome to their land, and if they thought to take ours then we would kill them as we always did just as they slaughtered us if we invaded their hills.

And to the south of Northumbria were the Saxons and they had a dream, Alfred's dream, the dream I had served for almost my whole life, and that dream was to unite the kingdoms where Saxons lived and call it one country, and Northumbria was the last part of that dream, and Æthelflaed passionately wanted that dream to come true. I have broken many oaths in my life, but I had never broken an oath to Æthelflaed. I would make Sigtryggr king, but the condition was that he lived in peace with Æthelflaed's Mercia. I would make him king to destroy his brother and to give me a chance to attack Bebbanburg, and I would make him king even as I sowed the seeds of his kingdom's destruction, because while he must swear to live in peace with Mercia I could not and would not demand that Æthelflaed live in peace with him. Sigtryggr's Northumbria would be trapped between the savagery of the north and the ambitions of the south.

And I told Sigtryggr none of that. Instead I put my arm around his shoulder and walked him to the top of a dune from where we watched men and women come ashore. The mist was lifting, and all along the beach I could see weapons and shields being carried through the low surf. Children, released from the tightly-packed ships, raced about the sand shrieking and tumbling. 'We'll march under your banner,' I told Sigtryggr.

'The red axe.'

'Because men will think you serve your brother.'

'And we go to Jorvik,' he said.

'To Eoferwic, yes.'

He frowned, thinking. A sea breeze had started

and it stirred his fair hair. He gazed at the ships and I knew he was thinking that it would be a pity to abandon them, but there was no choice. A small boy climbed the dune and stared open-mouthed at Sigtryggr. I growled and the child looked terrified, then ran away. 'You don't like children?' Sigtryggr asked, amused.

'Hate them. Noisy little bastards.'

He laughed. 'Your daughter says you were a good father.'

'That's because she hardly ever saw me,' I said. I felt a slight pang. I had been fortunate in my children. Stiorra was a woman any man would be proud to call his daughter, while Uhtred, who was carrying spears through the shallows and laughing with his companions, was a fine man and a good warrior, but my eldest? My gelded son? He, I thought, was the cleverest of my three, and perhaps the best of them, but we would never be friends. 'My father never liked me,' I said.

'Nor did mine,' Sigtryggr said, 'not till I was a man, anyway.' He turned and looked inland. 'So what do we do now?' he asked.

'We find out where we are. With any luck we're close to Cair Ligualid, so we'll go there first and find places for the families. Then we march on Eoferwic.'

'How far's that?'

'Without horses? It'll take us a week.'

'Is it defensible?'

'It has good walls,' I said, 'but it lies in flat land. It needs a large garrison.'

He nodded. 'And if my brother's there?'

'We'll have a fight on our hands,' I said, 'but we have that anyway. You're not safe till he's dead.'

I doubted that Ragnall would have returned to Eoferwic. Despite his defeat at Eads Byrig he still possessed a large army, and he needed to give that army plunder. I suspected he was still ravaging Mercia, but I also suspected he would have sent a force back to Eoferwic to hold the city till he returned. I also suspected I could be wrong. We were marching blind, but at least our ships had landed in Northumbria because late that morning, when the mist had cleared entirely, I climbed a nearby hill and saw smoke rising from a substantial town to our north. It could only be Cair Ligualid, for there was no other large settlement in Cumbraland.

Cumbraland was that part of Northumbria west of the mountains. It had always been a wild and lawless place. The kings who ruled in Eoferwic might claim to rule in Cumbraland, but few would travel there without a large army, and even fewer would see any advantage in making the journey at all. It was a region of hills and lakes, deep valleys, and deeper woods. The Danes and the Norse had settled it, building steadings protected by stout palisades, but it was no land to make a man rich. There were sheep and goats, a few paltry fields of barley, and enemies everywhere. The old inhabitants, small and dark, still lived in the high valleys where they worshipped gods that had been forgotten elsewhere, and always there were Scots crossing the River Hedene to steal cattle and slaves. Cair Ligualid guarded that river, and even that town would not have existed if it had not been for the Romans who had built it, fortified it, and left a great church at its centre.

It might have been a daunting fortress once, as formidable as Ceaster or Eoferwic, but time had not been kind to Cair Ligualid. The stone walls had partly fallen, the Roman buildings had mostly collapsed, and what was left was an untidy collection of timber huts with roofs of mossy thatch. The church still stood, though almost all of its walls had fallen to be replaced with timber, and the old tiled roof had long gone. Yet I loved that church because it was there that I had first seen Gisela. I felt the pang of her loss as we came into Cair Ligualid, and I stole a glance at Stiorra who so resembled her mother.

There were still monks in the town, though at first I thought they were beggars or vagabonds in strange robes. The brown cloth was patched, the hems tattered, and it was only the tonsures and the heavy wooden crosses that betrayed the half-dozen men as monks. The oldest, who had a wispy beard stretching almost to his waist, strode to meet us. 'Who are you?' he demanded. 'What do you want? When are you leaving?'

'Who are you?' I retorted.

'I am Abbot Hengist,' he said in a tone that suggested I should recognise the name.

'Who rules here?' I asked.

'Almighty God.'

'He's the jarl?'

'He is the mighty jarl of all the earth and everything in it. He is the jarl of creation!'

'Then why hasn't he repaired the walls here?'

Abbot Hengist frowned at that, not sure what to answer. 'Who are you?'

'The man who's going to pull the guts out of your arsehole if you don't tell me who rules in Cair Ligualid,' I said pleasantly.

'I do!' Hengist said, backing away.

'Good!' I said briskly. 'We're staying two nights. Tomorrow we'll help repair your wall. I don't suppose you have enough food for all of us, but you'll supply us with ale. We'll be leaving the women and children here under your protection, and you will feed them till we send for them.'

Abbot Hengist gaped at the crowd who had come into his town. 'I can't feed that . . .'

'You're a Christian?'

'Of course!'

'You believe in miracles?' I asked, and he nodded. 'Then you'd better fetch your five loaves and two fishes,' I went on, 'and pray that your wretched god provides the rest. I'm leaving some warriors here too, they need feeding as well.'

'We can't . . .'

'Yes, you can,' I growled. I walked up to him and seized the front of his grubby robe, grabbing a handful of white beard at the same time. 'You will feed them, you horrible little man,' I said, 'and you will protect them,' I shook him as I spoke, 'and if I find one child missing or one child hungry when I send for them I'll strip the flesh off your scrawny bones and feed it to the dogs. You have fish traps? You have seed grain? You have livestock?' I waited until he gave a reluctant nod to each question. 'Then you will feed them!' I shook him again, then let him go. He staggered and fell back on his arse. 'There,' I said happily, 'that's agreed.' I waited till he had scrambled to his feet. 'We'll also need timber to repair the walls,' I told him.

'There is none!' he whined.

I had noticed few trees close to the town, and those few were stunted and wind-bent, no good for filling the gaps in the ancient ramparts. 'No timber?' I asked. 'So what's your monastery built from?'

He stared at me for a moment. 'Timber,' he finally whispered.

'There!' I said cheerfully. 'You have an answer for all our problems!'

I could not take the wives and children to Eoferwic. The women could march as well as the men, but children would slow us down. Besides, we carried no food, so everything we ate on our journey would have to be bought, stolen, or scrounged, so the fewer mouths we had to feed the better. We were liable to end up in Eoferwic hungry, but I was certain that once there we would find storehouses filled with grain, smoked meat, and fish.

Yet before we could march we needed to protect the families we would leave behind. Men will fight willingly enough, but need to know their women and children are safe, and so we spent a day filling the gaps in Cair Ligualid's wall with heavy timbers pulled down from the monastery. There were only seven monks and two small boys who lived in buildings that could have sheltered seventy, and the rafters and pillars made stout palisades. To man the wall we left thirty-six warriors, mostly the older men or the wounded. They had no hope of resisting a full-scale assault by a horde of shrieking warriors from Strath Clota, but such an attack was unlikely. The Scottish war-bands were rarely more than forty or fifty strong, all of them vicious fighters mounted on small horses, but they did not cross the river to die on Roman walls. They came to snatch slaves from the fields and cattle from the hill pastures, and the few men we left, along with the townspeople, should be more than enough to deter an attack on the town. Just to make sure, we lifted a slab in the church to find an ancient crypt stacked with bones from which we took sixty-three skulls that we placed around the town's ramparts with their empty eyes staring outwards. Abbot Hengist objected. 'They are monks, lord,' he said nervously.

'You want an enemy raping your two novices?' I asked.

'God help us, no!'

'It's a ghost fence,' I said. 'The dead will protect the living.'

Stiorra, swathed in black, chanted strange incantations to each of the sixty-three guardians, then daubed their foreheads with a symbol that meant nothing to me. It was just a swirl of dampened soot, but Hengist saw the swirl and heard the chant and feared a pagan magic that was too powerful for his feeble faith. I almost felt sorry for him because he was trying to keep his religion alive in a place of paganism. The nearest farmlands were owned by Norsemen who worshipped Thor and Odin, who sacrificed beasts to the old gods and had no love for Hengist's nailed redeemer. 'I'm surprised they didn't kill you,' I told him.

'The pagans?' he shrugged. 'Some wanted to, but the strongest jarl here is Geir,' he jerked his head towards the south, indicating where Geir's land lay, 'and his wife was sick unto death, lord, and he brought her to us and instructed us to use our God to save her. Which, in His great mercy, He did.' He made the sign of the cross.

'What did you do?' I asked. 'Pray?'

'Of course, lord, but we also pricked her buttocks with one of Saint Bega's arrows.'

'You pricked her arse?' I asked, astonished.

He nodded. 'Saint Bega defended her convent's land with a bow, lord, but didn't aim to kill. Just to frighten away the wrongdoers. She always said God aimed her arrows, and we're lucky to own just one of them.'

'God shot the bastards in the arse?'

'Yes, lord.'

'And now you live under Geir's protection?' I asked.

'We do, lord, thanks to the blessed Saint Bega and her holy arrows.'

'So where is Geir?'

'He joined Ragnall, lord.'

'And what news do you have of Ragnall or Geir?'

'None, lord.'

Nor did I expect any news. Cumbraland was too remote, but it was significant that Geir had thought it worth his while to cross the hills and join Ragnall's forces. 'Why did he go to Jarl Ragnall?' I asked the monk.

Abbot Hengist shivered and his hand twitched as if he was about to cross himself. 'He was frightened, lord!' He looked at me nervously. 'Jarl Ragnall sent word that he'd slaughter every man here if they didn't march to join him.' He made the sign of the cross and momentarily closed his eyes. 'They all went, lord! All the landowners who had weapons. They fear him. And I hear the Jarl Ragnall hates Christians!'

'He does.'

'God preserve us,' he whispered.

So Ragnall was ruling purely by fear, and that would work so long as he was successful, and I had a moment's pang of guilt as I thought what his forces would be doing in Mercia. They would be slaughtering and burning and destroying anything and anyone not protected by a burh, but Æthelflaed should have attacked northwards. She was defending Mercia when she should have been attacking Northumbria. A man does not rid his home of a plague of wasps by swatting them one by one, but by finding the nest and burning it. I was Ida the Flamebearer's descendant and, just as he had brought fire across the sea, I would carry flames across the hills.

We set out next morning.

It was a hard journey across hard country. We had found three ponies and a mule close to Cair Ligualid, but no horses. Stiorra, with her daughter, rode one of the ponies, but the rest of us travelled on foot and carried our own mail, weapons, food, and shields. We drank from mountain streams, slaughtered sheep for supper, and roasted their ribs over paltry fires of bracken and furze. We were all either used to riding to war or else rowing, and our boots were not fit for the journey. By the second day the stony tracks threatened to rip the boots apart and I ordered men to walk barefoot and save the boots for battle. That slowed us as men limped and stumbled. There were no convenient Roman roads showing the way, just goat paths and sheep tracks and high hills and wind from the north bringing rain in vicious gusts. There was no shelter the first two nights and little food, but on the third day we descended into a fertile valley where a rich steading offered warmth. A woman and two elderly servants watched us arrive. There were over three hundred and fifty of us, all carrying weapons, and the woman left the gate of her palisade wide open to show that she could offer no resistance. She was grey-haired, straight-backed, and blue-eyed, the mistress of a hall, two barns, and a rotting cattle shed. 'My husband,' she greeted us icily, 'is not here.'

'He went to Ragnall?' I asked.

'To Jarl Ragnall, yes,' she sounded disapproving.

'With how many men?'

'Sixteen,' she said, 'and who are you?'

'Men summoned by Jarl Ragnall,' I said evasively.

'I hear he needs more men,' she said scornfully.

'Mistress,' I asked, intrigued by her tone, 'what have you heard?'

'Njall will tell you,' she said. 'I suppose you're about to rob me?'

'I'll pay for whatever we take.'

'Which will still leave us hungry. I can't feed my people on your hacksilver.'

Njall proved to be one of the sixteen warriors who had gone south to join Ragnall's army. He had lost his right hand at Eads Byrig and had returned to this lonely valley where he farmed a few thin fields. He came to the hall that night, a morose man with a red beard and a bandaged stump and a thin, resentful wife. Most of my men were eating in the largest barn, dining on three slaughtered pigs and two goats, but Lifa, who was the mistress of the steading during her husband's absence, insisted that some of us join her in the hall where she served us a meal of beef, barley, bread, and ale. 'We have a harpist,' she told me, 'but he went south with my husband.'

'And won't return,' Njall said.

'He was killed,' Lifa explained. 'What kind of enemy kills harpists?'

'I was there,' Njall said gloomily, 'I saw him take a spear in the back.'

'So tell your story, Njall,' our hostess commanded imperiously, 'tell these men what enemy they will face.'

'Uhtred,' Njall snarled.

'I've heard of him,' I said.

Njall looked at me resentfully. 'But you haven't fought him,' he said.

'True.' I poured him ale. 'So what happened?'

'He has a witch to help him,' Njall said, touching the hammer at his neck, 'a sorceress.'

'I'd not heard that.'

'The witch of Mercia. She's called Æthelflaed.'

'Æthelflaed is a witch?' Finan put in.

'How else can she rule Mercia?' Njall asked resentfully. 'You think a woman can rule unless she uses witchcraft?'

'So what happened?' Sigtryggr asked.

We coaxed the tale from him. He claimed that Ragnall had us all trapped in Ceaster, though he could not remember the name of that town, only that it was a place that had stone walls, which he assumed had been built by spirits working for Æthelflaed. 'Even so, they were trapped in the city,' he said, 'and the Jarl said he would keep them there while he captured the rest of Mercia. But the witch sent a storm and Uhtred rode the morning wind.'

'Rode the wind?'

'He came with the storm. A horde of them came,

but he led. He has a sword of fire and a shield of ice. He came with the thunder.'

'And Jarl Ragnall?' I asked.

Njall shrugged. 'He lives. He still has an army, but so does Uhtred.' He knew little more because, captured at Eads Byrig, he had been one of the men we had released after severing his hand. He had walked home, he said, but then added one more scrap of news. 'The Jarl could be dead for all I know. But he planned to raid Mercia till his own witch worked her magic.'

'His own witch?' I asked.

He touched the hammer again. 'How do you fight a sorceress? With another sorceress, of course. The Jarl has found a powerful one! An old hag, and she's making the dead.'

I just stared at him for a moment. 'She's making the dead?'

'I journeyed north with her,' he said, clutching the hammer now, 'and she explained.'

'Explained what?' Sigtryggr asked.

'The Christians worship the dead,' Njall said. 'All their churches have an idol of a dead man and they keep bits of dead people in silver boxes.'

'I've seen those,' I said.

'Relics,' Finan put in.

'And they talk to the pieces of dead people,' Njall said, 'and the dead people talk to their god.' He looked around the table, fearing that no one believed him. 'It's how they do it!' he insisted. 'It's how they talk to their god!'

'It makes sense,' Sigtryggr said cautiously, looking at me.

I nodded. 'It's hard for the living to talk to the gods,' I said.

'But not for Christians,' Njall said. 'That's why they win! That's why their witch is so powerful! Their god listens to the dead.'

Finan, the only Christian at the table, smiled wryly. 'Maybe the Christians win because they have Uhtred?'

'And why do they have Uhtred?' Njall asked forcefully. 'Men say he worships our gods, yet he fights for the Christian god. The witch has charmed him!'

'That's true,' Finan said rather too enthusiastically, and I almost kicked him beneath the table.

'He must be a lonely god,' Lifa, our hostess, said thoughtfully. 'Our gods have company. They feast together, fight together, but their god? He has no one.'

'So he listens to the dead,' Sigtryggr said.

'But only to the Christian dead,' Njall insisted.

'But what can Jarl Ragnall's witch,' I almost named Brida, but avoided it at the last moment, 'do to change that?'

'She's sending a message to their god,' Njall said.

'A message?'

'She says she'll send him a host of dead people. They'll tell him to take away the Mercian witch's power or else she'll kill every Christian in Britain.'

I almost laughed aloud. Only Brida, I thought, would be mad enough to threaten a god! And then

I shuddered. She wanted to send a cloud of messengers? And where would she find those messengers? They had to be Christians or else their nailed god would not listen to them, and in many parts of Northumbria the monasteries and convents had been burned down and their monks and nuns either killed or driven to exile. But there was one place the church still flourished. One place where she could find enough Christians to send screaming into the afterlife with a defiant message to the nailed god.

She had gone to Eoferwic.

And there we went too.

I had told Sigtryggr that Eoferwic lay in flat land and that was true, though that flat land was raised slightly above the rest of the plain where the city lay. It also lay between the junction of two rivers, and that alone made it a difficult city to attack. The walls made it almost impossible because they were twice the height of the walls at Ceaster. There had been great gaps in the wall when my father had led an assault on the city, but those gaps had been baits for a trap, and he had died in the trap's jaw. Those gaps were filled now, the new masonry looking much lighter than the old. Jarl Ragnall's flag of the blood-red axe hung from the walls and stirred idly on a tall pole above the southernmost gate.

We were a ragged band, still mostly on foot though we had stolen or bought a dozen horses as we journeyed from Lifa's steading in the hills. Most of us were barefoot, weary, and dusty. Some thirty men had fallen behind, but the rest still carried their mail, their weapons, and shields. Now, as we approached the city, we flew Sigtryggr's banner, which was identical to his brother's flag, and we mounted Orvar and his men on the stallions. Stiorra, dressed in a white gown, rode a small black mare with her daughter perched in front of her. She appeared to be guarded by Finan and by two of Orvar's Norsemen, who rode either side of her. Sigtryggr and I walked among the mass of men who followed the horsemen towards the city's gate.

The wall was high, and built atop a bank of earth. 'This is where your grandfather died,' I told my son, 'and where I was captured by the Danes.' I pointed to one of the paler stretches of new masonry. 'Your grandfather led an attack right there. I thought we'd won! There was a gap in the wall there and he stormed the mound and went into the city.'

'What happened?'

'They'd built a new wall behind it. It was a trap, and once our army was inside they attacked and slew them all.'

He stared ahead, noting the church towers topped by crosses. 'But if it's been Danish for so long why is it still Christian?'

'Some of the Danes converted,' I said. 'Your uncle for one.'

'My uncle?'

'Your mother's brother.'

'Why?'

I shrugged. 'He ruled here. Most of his people were Saxons, Christian Saxons. He wanted them to fight for him, so he changed his religion. I don't think he was a very good Christian, but it was convenient.'

'There are a lot of Danish Christians here,' Sigtryggr put in. He sounded gloomy. 'They marry Saxon girls and convert.'

'Why?' my son asked again.

'Peace and quiet,' Sigtryggr said. 'And a good pair of tits will persuade most men to change their religion.'

'Missionaries,' Finan said happily. 'Show us your missionaries!'

The city gate opened. Our leading horsemen were still two hundred paces away, but the sight of Sigtryggr's great banner had reassured the guards. Just two horsemen galloped to meet us, and Orvar, who was pretending to be the leader of our small army, held up his hand to halt us as they approached. I edged forward to listen.

'Orvar!' One of the approaching horsemen recognised him.

'I've brought the Jarl his girl,' Orvar said, jerking a thumb towards Stiorra. She sat straight-backed in her saddle, her hands clasped protectively about Gisela.

'You did well!' One of the horsemen pushed through Orvar's men to look at Stiorra. 'And what of her husband?'

'Feeding the fish in Ireland.'

'Dead?'

'Cut to pieces,' Orvar said.

'Leaving a pretty widow.' The man chuckled and reached out a gloved hand to lift Stiorra's chin. Sigtryggr growled beside me and I put a cautionary hand on his arm. I had made him wear a helmet with closed cheek-pieces that hid his face. He also wore old mail, no arm rings and no gold, appearing to be a man not worth a second glance. The horseman who had come from the city smiled nastily at Stiorra. 'Oh, very pretty,' he said. 'When the Jarl has finished with you, darling, I'll give you a treat you won't forget.'

Stiorra spat in his face. The man immediately brought back his hand to hit her, but Finan, who was mounted on one of our few horses, caught the man's wrist. 'What's your name?' he asked, sounding friendly.

'Brynkætil,' the man said sullenly.

'Touch her, Brynkætil,' Finan said pleasantly, 'and I'll feed her your balls,' he smiled, 'fried, as a treat.'

'Enough!' Orvar kicked his horse to come between the two men. 'Is the Jarl here?'

'The Jarl is raping Mercia,' Brynkætil said, still glowering, 'but the old bitch is here.' He gave the rest of us a cursory glance and was evidently not impressed by what he saw.

'The old bitch?' Orvar asked.

'She's called Brida of Dunholm,' he growled. 'You'll meet her. Just follow me.' He jerked his head towards the gate.

And so, after many years, I came to Eoferwic again. I had known the city as a child, I had visited it often when I was young, but fate had taken me to Wessex, and Eoferwic lay far to the north. It was the second most important city in Britain, at least if you judge a city by size and wealth, though in truth Eoferwic was a poor place compared to Lundene, which grew fatter and richer and dirtier with every passing year. Yet Eoferwic had its wealth, brought to it by the rich farmlands that surrounded it, and by the ships that could sail all the way up the rivers to where a bridge stopped them. A Roman bridge, of course. Most of Eoferwic had been built by the Romans, including the great walls that surrounded the city.

I walked through the gate tunnel and came into a street with houses that had stairways! Lundene had such houses too, and they always amaze me. Houses that have one floor piled on another! I remembered that Ragnar had a house in Eoferwic with two stairways, and his son Rorik and I used to race around and around, up one stair and down the other, whooping and shouting, leading a pack of barking dogs in a mad chase to nowhere until Ragnar would corner us, thump us about the ears, and tell us to go and annoy someone else.

Most of the houses had shops opening onto the street, and, as we followed Orvar and his horsemen, I saw that the shops were full of goods. I saw leatherware, pottery, cloth, knives, and a goldsmith with two mailed warriors guarding his stock, but though the goods were plentiful the streets were strangely empty. The city had a sullen air. A beggar scuttled away from us, hiding in an alley, a woman peered at us from an upper floor, then closed the shutters. We passed two churches though neither had an open door, which suggested that the Christians of the city were fearful. And no wonder if Brida was ruling the place. She who hated Christians had come to one of the only two places in Britain that had an archbishop. Contwaraburg was the other. An archbishop is important to the Christians, he knows more sorcery than ordinary priests, even more than the bishops, and he has more authority. I have met several archbishops over the years and there was not one of them I would trust to run a market stall selling carrots. They are all sly, two-faced, and vindictive. Æthelflaed, of course, thought them the holiest of men. If Plegmund, Archbishop of Contwaraburg, so much as farted she chanted amen.

Finan must have been thinking much the same thoughts as me because he turned in his saddle. 'What happened to the archbishop here?' he asked Brynkætil.

'The old man?' Brynkætil laughed. 'We burned him alive. Never heard a man squeal so much!'

The palace at Eoferwic's centre must have been the place from which a Roman lord ruled the north. It had decayed over the years, but what great buildings left by the Romans had not crumbled to ruin? It had become the palace of the kings of Northumbria, and I remembered seeing King Osbert, the last Saxon to rule without Danish support, being slaughtered by drunken Danes in the great hall. His belly had been sliced open and his guts had spilled out. They had let the dogs eat his intestines while he lived, though the dogs had taken one bite and then been repelled by the taste. 'It must have been something he ate,' blind Ravn had told me when I described the scene to him, 'or else our dogs just don't like the taste of Saxons.' King Osbert had died weeping and screaming.

There was an open space in front of the palace. Six huge Roman pillars had stood there when I was a child, though to what purpose I never did discover, and as we came out of the street's dark shadow I saw that just four of them remained like great markers at the edge of the wide space. And I heard my son gasp.

It was not the high carved pillars that prompted the gasp, nor the pale stone facade of the palace with its Roman statues, not even the size of the church that had been built to one side of the open space. Instead it was what filled the great square that shocked him. Crosses. And on each cross a naked body. 'Christians!' Brynkætil said in curt explanation.

'Does Brida rule here?' I asked him.

'Who's asking?'

'A man who deserves an answer,' Orvar growled.

'She rules for Ragnall,' Brynkætil said sullenly.

'It will be a pleasure to meet her,' I said. He just sneered at that. 'Is she pretty?' I asked.

'Depends how desperate you are,' he answered, amused. 'She's old, dried up, and as vicious as a wildcat.' He looked down at me. 'Ideal for an old man like you. I'd better tell her you're coming so she can get herself ready.' He spurred his horse towards the palace.

'Jesus,' Finan said, crossing himself and looking at the crucifixions. There were thirty-four crosses and thirty-four naked bodies, both men and women. Some had torn hands, the dried blood black on their wrists, and I realised that Brida, it had to be Brida, had tried to nail them by the hands to the crossbars, but the hands could not take the weight and the bodies must have fallen. Now the thirty-four were lashed to the crosses with leather ropes, though all had nailed hands and feet as well. One, a young woman, was still alive, though barely. She stirred and groaned. So this was how Brida sent a message to the Christian god? What a fool, I thought. I might share her distaste for the Christian god, lonely and vengeful as he was, but I had never denied his power, and what man or woman spits in a god's face?

I pushed alongside Stiorra's horse. 'Are you ready for this?'

'Yes, father.'

'I'll stay close,' I said, 'so will Sigtryggr.'

'Don't be recognised!' she said.

I had a helmet like the one which Sigtryggr wore

and I now closed the face-pieces, hiding my face. Like him I wore none of my finery. To a casual glance we both looked like lowly warriors, men who could fill a shield wall, but had never filled our own purses with plunder. Orvar was the best-dressed of us and, for the moment, Orvar pretended to be our leader.

'No weapons in the hall!' a man shouted as we approached the palace. 'No weapons!'

That was customary. No ruler let men carry weapons in a hall, except for his own housecarls who could be trusted with blades, and so we ostentatiously threw down our spears and swords, clattering them into a pile that we would leave our own warriors to guard. I laid Serpent-Breath down, but that did not leave me weaponless. I wore a homespun brown cloak that was long enough to hide Wasp-Sting, my seax.

Every shield wall warrior carries two swords. The long one, the sword that is scabbarded in silver or gold and that carries a noble name, is the sword we treasure. Mine was Serpent-Breath, and to this day I keep her close so that by the help of her hilt I will be carried to Valhalla when death comes for me. But we carry a second sword too, a seax, and a seax is a short, stubby blade, less flexible than the long-sword and less beautiful, but in the shield wall, when you can smell the stink of your enemy's breath and see the lice in his beard, a seax is the weapon to use. A man stabs with a seax. He puts it between the shields and thrusts it into an enemy's guts. Serpent-Breath was too long for a shield wall, her reach too distant, and in that lover's embrace of death a man needs a short-sword that can stab in the press of sweating men struggling to kill each other. Wasp-Sting was just such a sword, her stout blade no longer than my hand and forearm, but in the crushed space of a shield wall she was lethal.

I hid her sheathed at my spine beneath the cloak because, once in the hall, Wasp-Sting would be needed.

Sigtryggr and I hung back with our men, letting Orvar and his crews go first because they would be recognised by any of Ragnall's men who might be waiting inside the palace. Those men would not look to see who came in last and, even if they did, Sigtryggr's face, like mine, was hidden by a helmet. I left Sihtric and six men to guard our weapons. 'You know what to do?' I muttered to Sihtric.

'I know, lord,' he said wolfishly.

'Do it well,' I said, and then, when the last of Orvar's men had filed into the building, Sigtryggr and I followed.

I remembered the hall so well. It was larger than the Great Hall of Ceaster and far more elegant, though its beauty had faded as water leached into the walls, collapsing most of the marble sheets that had once sheathed the thin red bricks. In other places the water had peeled away the plaster, though patches remained with faint pictures showing men and women draped in what appeared to be shrouds. Great columns supported a high roof. Sparrows flew between the beams, some darting out through holes in the roof tiles. Some of the holes were patched with straw thatch, but most were open to the sky and let in shafts of sunlight. The floor had once been covered in small tiles, none bigger than a fingernail, which had shown Roman gods, but most of the tiles had long disappeared, leaving dull grey stones covered in dried rushes. At the hall's far end was a wooden dais some three feet high, approached by steps, and on the dais was a throne draped in a black cloth. Warriors flanked the throne. They must have been Brida's men because they were allowed weapons in the hall, each of them carrying a long-hafted broad-bladed spear. There were eight guards on the dais, and more standing down the shadowed sides of the hall. The throne was empty.

Courtesy said we should have been greeted with ale and with basins of water to wash our hands, though there were so many of us that I hardly expected we would all be so treated. Even so a steward should have sought our leaders to offer a welcome, but instead a thin man dressed all in black came from a door that led onto the dais and rapped a staff on the wooden floor. He rapped again, frowning at us. He had black hair oiled tight to his scalp, a haughty face, and a short beard that had been carefully trimmed. 'The Lady of Dunholm,' he announced when the hall was silent, 'will be here soon. You will wait!'

Orvar took a step forward. ‘My men need food,’ he said, ‘and shelter.’

The thin man stared at Orvar. ‘Are you,’ he asked after a long pause, ‘the one they call Orvar?’

‘I am Orvar Freyrson, and my men . . .’

‘Need food, you said so.’ He looked at the rest of us, distaste on his face. ‘When the Lady of Dunholm arrives, you will kneel.’ He shuddered. ‘So many of you! And you smell!’ He stalked back the way he had come, and the guards on the dais exchanged smirks.

More men were coming to the hall, some pushing in behind us, others using doors in the side walls until there must have been close to four hundred men under the high roof. Sigtryggr looked at me quizzically, but I just shrugged. I did not know what was happening, only that Brynkætil must have announced our arrival and that Brida was coming. I edged through the men in front, making my way to Stiorra, who stood beside Orvar, her hand holding her daughter’s hand.

And just as I reached her the drum sounded.

One beat, loud and sudden, and the newcomers, those who had followed us into the hall and knew what was expected of them, dropped to their knees.

And the drum sounded again. One slow beat after another. Ominous, regular and remorseless, a heartbeat of doom.

We knelt.

CHAPTER 12

Only the guards remained standing.

The drumbeat went on. The drum itself was in a room beyond the hall, but from its sound I knew it to be one of the great goatskin-covered tubs that were so massive that they needed to be carried to war on carts, which was why they were so rarely heard on a battlefield, though if they were present then their deep, heart-pounding sound could strike fear into an enemy. The beat was slow, each ominous blow fading to silence before another sounded, and the beat became slower so that I continually thought the drummer had stopped altogether, then there would be another pounding and we all watched the dais, waiting for Brida to appear.

Then the drumbeat did stop and the silence that followed was even more ominous. No one spoke. We were kneeling, and I sensed the terror in the room. No one even moved, but just waited.

Then there was a suppressed gasp as an ungreased hinge squealed. The door that led onto the dais was pushed open and I watched, expecting to see Brida, but instead two small children came into the hall, both girls and both in black dresses with long skirts that brushed the floor. They were perhaps five or six years old, each with black hair that fell to their waists. They could have been twins, maybe they were, and their appearance made Stiorra gasp.

Because both girls had been blinded.

It took me a moment to see that their eyes were nothing but scarred, gouged pits; wrinkled holes of dark horror in faces that had once been lovely. The two girls walked onto the dais and then hesitated, unsure which way to turn, but the thin man hurried behind them and used his black staff to guide them. He placed one on each side of the throne, then stood behind it, his dark eyes watching us, despising us.

Then Brida entered.

She shuffled in, muttering under her breath and hurrying as though she were late. She wore a great swathing black cloak pinned at her neck with a golden brooch. She stopped beside the black-draped throne and darted glances into the hall where we knelt. She looked indignant, as if our presence was a nuisance.

I stared at her under the rim of my helmet and I could not see the girl I had loved in the crone who had entered the hall. She had saved my life once, she had conspired with me and laughed with me and she had watched Ragnar die with me, and I had thought her beautiful, fascinating and so full of life, but her beauty had soured into rancor, and her love into hatred. Now she gazed at us and I sensed a shiver of apprehension in the hall. The guards stood straighter and avoided looking at her. I ducked down, fearing she would recognise me even with the helmet's cheek-pieces closed.

She sat on the throne, which dwarfed her. Her face was malignant, her eyes bright, and her sparse hair white. The thin man moved a footstool, the scrape of its wooden legs unexpectedly loud in the hall. She rested her feet on the stool and placed a black bag on her lap. The two blind girls did not move. The thin man bent to the throne and whispered in Brida's ear and she nodded impatiently. 'Onarr Gormson,' she called in a husky voice, 'is Onarr Gormson here?'

'My lady,' a man answered from the body of the hall.

'Approach, Onarr Gormson,' she said.

The man stood and walked to the dais. He climbed the steps and knelt in front of Brida. He was a big man with a brutally scarred face on which ravens had been inked. He looked like a warrior who had carved his way through shield walls, yet his nervousness was apparent as he bowed his head in front of Brida.

The thin man had been whispering again and Brida nodded. 'Onarr Gormson brought us twenty-nine Christians yesterday,' she announced, 'twenty-nine! Where did you find them, Onarr?'

'A convent, my lady, in the hills to the north.'

'They were hiding?' Her voice was a croak, harsh as a raven's call.

'They were hiding, my lady.'

'You have done well, Onarr Gormson,' she said. 'You have served the gods and they will reward you. As will I.' She fumbled in the bag and brought out a pouch clinking with coins that she handed to the kneeling man. 'We will cleanse this country,' she said, 'cleanse it of the false god!' She waved Onarr away, then suddenly stopped him by holding up a claw-like hand. 'A convent?'

'Yes, my lady.'

'Are they all women?'

'All of them, my lady,' he said. I saw he had not raised his face once to meet Brida's gaze, but had kept his eyes on her small feet.

'If your men want the young ones,' she said, 'they are yours. The rest will die.' She waved him away again. 'Is Skopti Alsvartson here?'

'My lady!' another man answered, and he too had found Christians, three priests who he had brought to Eoferwic. He too received a purse and he too did not raise his eyes as he knelt at Brida's feet. It seemed that this gathering in the hall was a daily occurrence, a chance for Brida to reward the men who were doing her bidding and to encourage the ones who were laggards.

One of the two blind girls suddenly gasped, then made a pathetic mewing noise. I thought Brida would be angry with the child's interruption, but instead she leaned down and the girl whispered into Brida's ear. Brida, straightening, offered us a grimace that was intended to be a smile. 'The gods have spoken!' she announced, 'and tell us that the

Jarl Ragnall has burned three more towns in Mercia!' The second child now whispered, and again Brida listened. 'He has taken captives by the score,' she seemed to be repeating what the child had told her, 'and he is sending the treasure of ten churches north to our keeping.' A murmur of appreciation sounded in the hall, but I was puzzled. What towns? Any town of size in Mercia was a burh and it defied the imagination to believe that Ragnall had captured three. 'The foul Æthelflaed still cowers in Ceaster,' Brida went on, 'protected by the traitor Uhtred! They will not last long.' I almost smiled when she mentioned my name. So she was inventing the stories and pretending they came from the two blinded children. 'The man who calls himself king in Wessex has retreated to Lundene,' Brida declared, 'and soon Jarl Ragnall will scour him from that city. Soon all Britain will be ours!'

The thin man welcomed that claim by thumping his staff on the wooden dais, and the men in the hall, those who were accustomed to this ritual, responded by slapping the floor. Brida smiled, or at least she bared her yellow teeth in another grimace. 'And I am told that Orvar Freyrson has returned from Ireland!'

'I have!' Orvar said. He sounded nervous.

'Come here, Orvar Freyrson,' Brida ordered.

Orvar stood and went to the dais. The two men who had received purses had gone back to the crowd, and Orvar knelt alone in front of the black-draped throne with its malevolent occupant.

'You bring the girl from Ireland?' Brida asked, knowing the answer because she was staring at Stiorra.

'Yes, lady,' Orvar spoke in a whisper.

'And her husband?'

'Is dead, lady.'

'Dead?'

'Cut down by our swords, lady.'

'Did you bring me his head?' Brida asked.

'I didn't think, lady. No.'

'A pity,' she said, still gazing at Stiorra. 'But you have done well, Orvar Freyrson. You have brought us Stiorra Uhtredsdottir and her spawn. You have fulfilled the Jarl's bidding, your name will be told in Asgard, you will be beloved of the gods! You are blessed!' She gave him a purse, much heavier than the two she had already presented, then peered into the body of the hall again. For a moment I thought her old eyes looked straight into mine and I felt a shiver of fear, but her gaze moved on. 'You bring men, Orvar!' she said. 'Many men!'

'Five crews,' he muttered. He, like the men who had knelt to her before, stared down at her footstool.

'You will take them to Jarl Ragnall,' Brida ordered. 'You will leave tomorrow and march to help his conquest. Go now,' she waved him away, 'back to your place.' Orvar seemed relieved to be off the dais. He came back to the stone floor and knelt beside Stiorra.

Brida turned in the throne. 'Fritjof!' The thin man

hurried to offer his mistress an arm to help her out of the throne. 'Take me to the girl,' she ordered.

There was not a sound in the Great Hall as she shuffled down from the dais and across the rush-covered stones. Fritjof, smiling, held her arm until she shook him off when she was five paces from Stiorra. 'Stand, girl,' she ordered.

Stiorra stood.

'And your whelp,' Brida snarled, and Stiorra tugged Gisela to her feet. 'You will go south with Orvar,' Brida told Stiorra, 'to your new life as a wife to Jarl Ragnall. You are fortunate, girl, that he chose you. If your fate was mine?' She paused and shuddered. 'Fritjof!'

'My lady,' the thin man murmured.

'She must go arrayed as a bride. That grubby smock won't do. You will find suitable clothes.'

'Something beautiful, my lady,' Fritjof said. He looked Stiorra up and down. 'As beautiful as the lady herself.'

'How would you know?' Brida asked nastily. 'But find her something fit for a queen of all Britain,' Brida almost spat the last four words. 'Something fit for the Jarl. But if you disappoint the Jarl,' she was talking to Stiorra again, 'you will be mine, girl, do you understand?'

'No,' Stiorra said, not because that was true, but because she wanted to annoy Brida.

She succeeded. 'You're not queen yet!' Brida screeched. 'Not yet, girl! And if Jarl Ragnall tires of you then you'll wish you were a slave girl in the lowest brothel of Britain.' She shuddered. 'And that will happen, girl, it will happen! You are your father's daughter and his rotten blood will show in you.' She cackled suddenly. 'Go to your queendom, girl, but know you will end as my slave and then you will wish your mother had never opened her thighs. Now give me your daughter.'

Stiorra did not move. She just clutched Gisela's hand tighter. There was not a sound in the Great Hall. It seemed to me that every man there held his breath.

'Give me your daughter!' Brida hissed each word separately, distinctly.

'No,' Stiorra said.

I was slowly, carefully, moving Wasp-Sting's scabbard so my right hand could reach her hilt. I grasped it and went still again.

'Your daughter is fortunate,' Brida said, crooning now as if she wanted to seduce Stiorra into obedience. 'Your new husband doesn't want your spawn! And you can't keep her! But I will give her a new life of great wisdom, I will make her an enchantress! She will be given the power of the gods!' She held out her hand, but Stiorra stubbornly held onto her daughter. 'Odin,' Brida said, 'sacrificed an eye so he could learn wisdom. Your child will have the same wisdom! She will see the future!'

'You'd blind her?' Stiorra asked, horrified.

I slowly, so slowly, eased the short blade from its scabbard. Stiorra's dark cloak hid me from Brida.

‘I won’t blind her, fool,’ Brida snarled, ‘but open her eyes to the gods. Give her to me!’

‘No!’ Stiorra said. I held Wasp-Sting by the blade.

‘Fritjof,’ Brida said, ‘take the child.’

‘Blind her now?’ Fritjof asked.

‘Blind her now,’ Brida said.

Fritjof laid down his staff and took an awl from a pouch at his belt. The awl had a bulbous wooden handle that held a short and stout metal spike, the kind used by leather-workers to punch holes. ‘Come child,’ he said, and stepped forward, reaching, and Stiorra took a pace backwards. She thrust Gisela behind her and I took the child’s hand and, at the same moment, pushed Wasp-Sting’s hilt into Stiorra’s grasp. Fritjof, not yet understanding what was happening, leaned forward to snatch the child from behind Stiorra’s back, and she stabbed Wasp-Sting up and forward.

The first Brida knew of any trouble was when Fritjof gave a shriek. He recoiled, the awl clattering on the stones, and then he clutched at his groin and moaned as blood spilled down his legs. I thrust Gisela back into the crowd and stood myself. All around me men were producing seaxes or knives, Sigtryggr was pushing through the throng, and Sihtric came with him, carrying Serpent-Breath. ‘We killed the two outside, lord,’ he said, giving me the sword.

Fritjof collapsed. Stiorra’s thrust had glanced off his ribs, scored down his belly and cut him to the groin, and he was now mewing pathetically, his legs kicking beneath his long robe. My men were all standing now, swords or seaxes in hand. One guard was foolish enough to level his spear and he went down under a welter of sword-blows. I thrust Sigtryggr forward. 'Get to the dais,' I told him, 'the throne is yours!'

'No!' the shriek was Brida's. It had taken her a shocked moment to understand what was happening, to understand that her Great Hall had been invaded by an outnumbering enemy. She stared at Fritjof for a heartbeat then launched herself at Stiorra, only to be caught by Sigtryggr, who thrust her backwards so violently that she tripped on the stones and sprawled on her back.

'The dais!' I called to Sigtryggr. 'Leave her!'

My men, I counted Orvar's crews among my men now, far outnumbered the rest. I saw my son striding down one side of the hall, using his sword to knock the guards' spears to the floor. Sihtric had his sword at Brida's throat, keeping her down. He looked at me quizzically, but I shook my head. It would not be his privilege to kill her. Sigtryggr had reached the dais where the two blind girls were crying hysterically, and the guards, still with spears in their hands, stared in shock at the chaos beneath them. Sigtryggr stood beside the throne and looked at the guards one by one, and one by one their spears were lowered. He plucked the black cloth from the throne, tossed it aside, then kicked the footstool away and sat. He reached out and gathered the two girls, holding them close to his knees and soothing them. 'Keep the bitch there,' I told Sihtric, then joined Sigtryggr on the dais. 'You,' I snarled at the eight spearmen who had guarded the throne, 'leave your spears here and join the others,' I pointed to the body of the hall, then waited as they obeyed me. Only one of Brida's men had put up any kind of fight and even he, I reckoned, had raised his weapon from panic rather than out of loyalty. Brida, like Ragnall, ruled by terror, and her support had vanished like mist under a burning sun.

'My name,' I stood at the front of the dais, 'is Uhtred of Bebbanburg.'

'No!' Brida screeched.

'Keep her quiet,' I told Sihtric. I waited as he shifted the tip of his sword, and Brida went utterly still. I looked at the men in the hall, those I did not know, and I saw no defiance among them. 'I present to you,' I said, 'your new king, Sigtryggr Ivarson.'

There was silence. I sensed that many of Brida's supporters were relieved, but naming Sigtryggr as king did not make him the ruler, not while his brother lived. Every one of Brida's followers was thinking the same thing, wondering which brother they should support.

'I present to you,' I said again, making my voice threatening, 'your new king, Sigtryggr Ivarson.'

My men cheered, and, slowly, hesitantly, the others joined the clamour. Sigtryggr had taken off his helmet and was smiling. He listened to the acclaim for a moment, then held up his hand for silence. When the hall was quiet he said something to one of the blind girls, but spoke too low for me to catch his words. He stooped to hear the child's answer and I looked back to the nervous hall. 'Oaths will be sworn,' I said.

'But first!' Sigtryggr stood. 'That thing,' he pointed to the wounded Fritjof, 'blinded these girls and would have blinded my daughter.' He strode to the edge of the dais and drew his long-sword. He still smiled. He was tall, striking, confident, a man who looked as if he should be king. 'A man who blinds children,' he said as he descended the stone steps, 'is not a man.' He walked to Fritjof, who gazed up in terror. 'Did the girls scream?' Sigtryggr asked him. Fritjof, who was in pain rather than grievously wounded, did not answer. 'I asked you a question,' Sigtryggr said, 'did the girls scream when you blinded them?'

'Yes,' Fritjof's answer was a whisper.

'Then listen, girls!' Sigtryggr called. 'Listen well! Because this is your revenge.' He placed the tip of his sword on Fritjof's face, and the man did scream in pure terror.

Sigtryggr paused, letting the scream echo in the hall, then his sword struck three times. One piercing stab for each eye, a third for the throat, and Fritjof's blood pooled on the floor to be diluted by his piss. Sigtryggr watched the man die. 'Quicker than he deserved,' he said bitterly. He stooped and cleaned the tip of his sword on Fritjof's cloak, then sheathed the long blade. He drew his seax instead and nodded to Sihtric who still guarded Brida. 'Let her stand.'

Sihtric stepped away. Brida hesitated, then suddenly scrambled to her feet and lunged at Sigtryggr as if trying to snatch the seax from his hand, but he held her at arm's length with contemptuous ease. 'You would have blinded my daughter,' he said bitterly.

'I would have given her wisdom!'

Sigtryggr held her with his left hand and raised the seax with his right, but Stiorra intervened. She touched his right arm. 'She's mine,' she said.

Sigtryggr hesitated, then nodded. 'She's yours,' he agreed.

'Give her the sword,' Stiorra said. She still held Wasp-Sting.

'Give her the sword?' Sigtryggr asked, frowning.

'Give it to her,' Stiorra commanded. 'Let's discover who the gods love. Uhtredsdottir or her.'

Sigtryggr held the seax hilt first to Brida. 'Let's see who the gods love,' he agreed.

Brida was darting her eyes around the hall, looking for support that was not there. For a heartbeat she ignored the proffered seax, then suddenly snatched it from Sigtryggr's hand and immediately lunged it at his belly, but he just knocked it contemptuously aside with his right hand. A seax rarely has a sharpened edge, it is a weapon made to pierce, not to slash, and the blade left no mark on Sigtryggr's wrist. 'She's yours,' he said to Stiorra again.

And so died my first lover. She did not die well because there was an anger in my daughter. Stiorra had inherited her mother's beauty, she looked so calm, so graceful, but under that loveliness was a soul of steel. I had watched her kill a priest once and seen the joy on her face, and now I saw the joy again as she hacked Brida to death. She could have killed the old woman quickly, but she chose to kill her slowly, reducing her to a whimpering, piss-soaked, blood-spattered mess, before finishing her with a hard lunge to the gullet.

And thus did Sigtryggr Ivarson, Sigtryggr One-Eye, become King of Jorvik.

Most of the men in Eoferwic had sworn oaths to Ragnall, but almost all now knelt to his brother, clasped his hands, and once again I felt their relief. The Christians who had been captured and held ready for Brida's next mass slaughter were released. 'There will be no rape,' I told Onarr Gormson. He, like almost all the men in the city, had knelt to Sigtryggr, though a handful of warriors refused to abandon their oath to his brother. Skopti Alsvartson, the man who had found three priests and brought them to Eoferwic for Brida's amusement, was one. He was a stubborn Norseman, wolf-faced, experienced in battle, his long hair plaited to his waist. He led thirty-eight men, his crew, and Ragnall had given him land south of the city. 'I made an oath,' he told me defiantly.

'To Ragnall's father, Olaf.'

'And to his son.'

'You were commanded to make that oath,' I said, 'by Olaf.'

'I gave it willingly,' he insisted.

I would not kill a man for refusing to abandon an oath. Brida's followers had been freed of their obligation by her death, and most of those followers were confused by the fate that had changed their lives so suddenly. Some had fled, doubtless going to the grim fort at Dunholm where one day they would need to be scoured out by steel, but most knelt to Sigtryggr. A few, no more than a dozen, cursed us for killing her and those few died. Brynkætil, who had tried to strike my daughter and then insulted me, was among those few. He offered his oath, but he had made an enemy of me and so he died. Skopti Alsvartson did not curse us, he did not challenge us, but simply said he would keep his oath to Ragnall. 'So do what you wish with me,' he growled, 'just let me die like a man.'

'Have I taken your sword away?' I asked him, and he shook his head. 'So keep your sword,' I told him, 'but make me one promise.'

He looked at me cautiously. 'A promise?'

'That you will not leave the city till I give you permission.'

'And when will that be?'

'Soon,' I said, 'very soon.'

He nodded. 'And I can join Jarl Ragnall?'

'You can do whatever you like,' I said, 'but not till I give you leave.'

He thought for a heartbeat, then nodded again. 'I promise.'

I spat on my hand and held it to him. He spat on his and we shook.

Orvar had found his wife. We found all the hostages kept prisoner in what had been a convent, and all said they had been well-treated, though that did not stop some of them sighing with obvious relief when Sigtryggr told them of Brida's death. 'How many of you,' he asked, 'have husbands serving with my brother?' Eight women raised their hands. Their men were far to the south, riding in Ragnall's service, raiding and raping, stealing and burning. 'We shall be going south,' Sigtryggr told those women, 'and you will come with us.'

'But your children must stay here,' I insisted. 'They will be safe.'

'They will be safe,' Sigtryggr echoed. The eight women protested, but Sigtryggr cut their indignation short. 'You will come with us,' he decreed, 'and your children will not.'

We now had over seven hundred men, though despite their oaths we could not be certain that all would prove loyal. Many, I knew, had sworn to follow Sigtryggr simply to avoid trouble, and maybe those men would return to their steadings at the first opportunity. The city was still frightened, scared of Ragnall's revenge or perhaps fearful that Brida, an enchantress, was not really dead, which was why we paraded her corpse through the streets. We laid her body on a handcart with her black banner dragging behind, and we took it to the river bank south of the city where we burned her corpse. We gave a feast that night, roasting three whole oxen on great fires made from Brida's crosses. Four men died in fighting started by the ale, but that was a small price. Most were content to listen to the songs, drink, and look for Eoferwic's whores.

And while they sang, drank, and whored, I wrote a letter.

Alfred had insisted that I learn to read and write. I had never wanted to. As a boy I had wanted to learn horsemanship, sword-craft and shield-skill, but my tutors had beaten me until I could read their tedious tales of dull men who preached sermons to seals, puffins, and salmon. I could write too, though my letters were crabbed. I did not have the patience to make them neat that night, instead I scratched them across the page with a blunt quill, but reckoned the words were readable.

I wrote to Æthelflaed. I told her I was in Eoferwic, which had a new king who had forsworn Northumbria's ambitions against Mercia and was ready to sign a truce with her. First, though, Ragnall must be destroyed, to which end we would be marching south within a week. 'I will bring five hundred warriors,' I wrote, though I hoped it would be more. Ragnall, I insisted, would outnumber us, which he would, though I did not tell her that I doubted the loyalty of many of his men. He commanded jarls whose wives had been held hostage in Eoferwic and those women would travel with us. Ragnall ruled by terror and I would turn the terror against him by showing his men that we now held their families, but I told

Æthelflaed none of that. 'What I would wish,' I wrote laboriously, 'is that you follow Ragnall's horde as they march towards us, which they most surely will, and that you help us to destroy him even if that destruction takes place in Northumbria.' I knew she would be reluctant to lead an army across the Northumbrian border because of her brother's insistence that she not invade the northern kingdom without him, so I suggested she would simply be leading a large raid in retaliation for the damage being done to Mercia by Ragnall's army.

I sent my son to carry the letter, telling him that we would follow him south in three or four days. 'We'll march to Lindcolne,' I told him. From that city there was a choice of roads, one going on south towards Lundene, the other slanting south-west into Mercia's centre. 'We'll probably take the road to Ledecestre,' I told him, meaning the route that headed into the heart of Mercia.

'And Ragnall will march to meet you,' my son said.

'So tell Æthelflaed that! Or tell whoever commands her army. Tell them they're to follow hard on his heels!'

'If they've even left Ceaster,' my son said dubiously.

'We're all in trouble if they haven't,' I said, touching the hammer.

I gave my son an escort of thirty men and one of the priests we had saved from Brida's mad challenge to the Christian god. The priest was called Father Wilfa, an earnest young man whose sincerity and apparent piety I thought would impress Æthelflaed. 'Tell her your story,' I ordered him, 'and tell her what happened here!' I had shown him the bodies we had taken down from Brida's crosses and I had seen the horror on his face and made sure he knew that it was a pagan army of Norse and Danes that had stopped the massacres. 'And tell her,' I said, 'that Uhtred of Bebbanburg has done all this in her service.'

'I will tell her, lord,' Father Wilfa said. I liked him. He was respectful, but not subservient. 'Do you know, lord, what happened to Archbishop Æthelbald?'

'He was burned alive,' I told Wilfa.

'God help us,' he said, wincing. 'And the cathedral was desecrated?'

'Tell the Lady Æthelflaed that his death is revenged, that the churches are open again, and the cathedral is being cleansed.' Brida had stabled horses in the cavernous church. She had hacked the altars apart, torn down the sacred banners, and pulled the dead from their graves. 'And tell her that King Sigtryggr has promised his protection to Christians.'

It seemed strange to call him King Sigtryggr. A circlet of gilt bronze had been discovered in the palace treasury, and I made him wear it as a crown. On the morning after the feast, the Great Hall was filled with petitioners, many of them men whose land had been taken away by Ragnall to be given to his supporters. They brought charters to prove their ownership, and Stiorra, because she could read, sat at a table by her husband's throne and deciphered the ancient documents. One had even been signed by my father, ceding land I never knew he owned. Many men had no charter, just the indignant claim that their fields had been owned by their father, grandfather and great-grandfather back to the dawn of time. 'What do I do?' Sigtryggr asked me, 'I don't know who's telling the truth!'

'Tell them nothing will be done till Ragnall is dead. Then find a priest who can read and have him make a list of all the claims.'

'What good will that do?'

'It delays,' I said. 'It gives you time. And when your brother's dead you can assemble a Witan.'

'Witan?'

'A council. Have all the men who claim land gather in the hall, have them present their claims one by one, and let the council vote. They know who really owns the land. They know their neighbours. They'll also know what land belongs to the men who support your brother, and that land is now yours to give away. But wait till your brother's dead.'

To kill him we needed horses. Finan had searched the city and sent men into the wide valley of the Use and had collected four hundred and sixty-two horses. Many had belonged to Brida's men, but others we purchased using coin and hacksilver from Brida's treasury. They were not good horses, there was not one I would want to ride into battle, but they would carry us south faster than our own legs, and that was all we needed. I took a dozen of the poorest animals and gave them to Skopti Alsvartson who had kept his promise to stay in the city till I gave him permission to leave. 'You can go,' I told him two days after my son had ridden south.

Skopti was no fool. He knew I was using him. He would ride into Mercia and give Ragnall news of what had happened to Brida and to Ragnall's own supporters in Eoferwic, and he would warn Ragnall that we were coming. That was what I wanted. I deliberately let Skopti see the horses we had collected and even gave him time to count them so he could tell Ragnall that our army was small, fewer than five hundred men. I had told Æthelflaed I would march with more than five hundred, but that hope was fading and I knew our army would be perilously small, but the army of Mercia would make up the numbers. 'Tell him,' I said, 'that we will meet him and kill him. And we'll kill you too if you stay loyal to him.'

'He has my oath,' Skopti said stubbornly.

He rode south. Most of his crew had to walk, and they would follow Skopti, who, I reckoned, should reach Ragnall within three or four days. It was possible Ragnall already knew what had happened in Eoferwic, already knew of his brother's return and the death of Brida. A steady trickle of slaves had made their way northwards, always escorted by Ragnall's warriors, and it was more than possible that fugitives from the city had met one such group, who would then have turned to carry word back to Ragnall. One way or another he either knew or would know soon, and what would he do about Sigtryggr's return? He knew Æthelflaed's army was seeking him, or at least I hoped it was, and now he had a new enemy coming from the north. 'If he has any sense,' Finan told me, 'he'll go east. Find ships and sail away.'

'If he has any sense,' I said, 'he'd turn on Æthelflaed and destroy her, then come to defeat us. But he won't.'

'No?'

I shook my head. 'He hates his brother too much. He'll look for us first.'

And two days after Skopti left to warn Ragnall, we also rode south.

We were a small army. In the end only three hundred and eighty-four men rode, the rest we left in Eoferwic under Orvar's command. I had wanted to take more, far more, but we had too few horses and some of those horses were needed to carry supplies. Sigtryggr was also concerned that Brida's followers, too many of whom had escaped north immediately after their mistress's death, could summon enough help to assault Eoferwic. I thought it more likely that those fugitives would barricade themselves behind Dunholm's high walls, but I yielded to Sigtryggr's wishes to leave a substantial garrison in Eoferwic. He was, after all, the king.

Three hundred and eighty-four men rode, but

also nine women. Stiorra was one. Like Æthelflaed, she would not be denied, and I think she was also wary of being left behind with Orvar who, so recently, had been Ragnall's man. I trusted Orvar, as did Sigtryggr who had insisted that his daughter, my granddaughter, stay in the city under Orvar's protection. Stiorra was unhappy, but agreed. The remaining eight women had all been Ragnall's hostages, the wives of men who were the Sea King's jarls, and they were now my weapon.

We followed the Roman road south. Ragnall, if he had learned anything of the Roman network of roads that laced Britain, would guess we were riding from Eoferwic to Lindcolne, because that route offered us the quickest journey, but I doubted he would have had the time to move his army to block our path. The last I had seen of him, admittedly many days before, he had been moving further south into Mercia, and so I did not expect to see the smoke of his fires until we had passed Lindcolne and were well on the road to Ledecestre, a Mercian town that had been in Danish hands for all my lifetime. Ledecestre lay in that great swathe of northern Mercia that remained unconquered by the Saxons, land that Æthelflaed had sworn to retake. Once south of Ledecestre we would approach country that neither Dane nor Saxon ruled, a place of raids and ruin, the land that lay between two tribes and two religions.

We had scouts ahead. We might be in Northumbria still and flying Ragnall's own banner of the red axe, but I still treated the country as enemy land. We lit no campfires at night, but instead sought a place well away from the road to sleep, eat, and rest the horses. We stayed to the west of Lindcolne, though Sigtryggr and I crossed the Roman bridge with a dozen men and climbed the steep hill into the town where we were met by a steward wearing a silver chain of office. He was elderly, grey-bearded, and had lost one arm. 'Lost it fighting the West Saxons,' he told us cheerfully, 'but the bastard who took it lost both of his!'

The steward was a Dane called Asmund whose master was a jarl named Steen Stigson. 'He joined Ragnall a month ago,' Asmund told us, 'and you're on your way to join him too?'

'We are,' Sigtryggr answered.

'But where is he?' I asked.

'Who knows?' Asmund said, still cheerful. 'Last we heard they were way down south. What I can tell you is that Jarl Steen sent us fifty head of cattle a week ago and the drovers said it took them four days' journey.'

'And the Mercians?' I asked.

'Haven't seen any! Haven't heard anything.' We were talking by one of the gates that led through the Roman walls, and from their ramparts a man could look far across the countryside, but no plume of smoke smeared the sky. The land looked peaceful, lush, green. It was hard to imagine that armies sought each other in that tangle of woods, pasture, and arable.

'Ragnall was sending slaves to Eoferwic,' I said. We had been hoping to meet some of Ragnall's men bringing those slaves out of Mercia and discover from them where Ragnall might be, but we had seen none.

'Haven't seen anyone pass for a week now! Maybe he's collecting the poor bastards at Ledecestre? Bring it here!' The last three words were called to a maidservant who had brought a tray heaped with pots of ale. Asmund took two of the pots and handed them up to us, then beckoned the girl to carry the rest to our men. 'Best thing you can do, lords, is keep riding south!' Asmund urged us a little too enthusiastically. 'You'll find someone!'

The enthusiasm intrigued me. 'Did you see Skopti Alsvartson?' I asked.

'Skopti Alsvartson?' There was a slight hesitation. 'Don't know him, lord.'

I put the ale into my left hand and used my right to touch Serpent-Breath's hilt, and Asmund took a hurried step backwards. I pretended I was just shifting the sword for comfort, then finished the ale and gave the pot to the maid. 'We'll keep riding south,' I said to Asmund's relief.

Asmund had been telling us lies. He had done it well, convincingly, but Skopti Alsvartson must have come through Lindcolne. Skopti, like us, would have taken the swiftest route south, and that would explain why we had met none of Ragnall's men coming the other way, because they had been warned by Skopti. It was possible, of course, that Skopti and his men had ridden straight past the city, but not likely. They would have wanted food and they had probably demanded fresh horses to replace the tired nags I had given them. I looked into Asmund's eyes and thought I saw nervousness. I smiled. 'Thank you for the ale.'

'You're welcome, lord.'

'How many men do you have here?' I asked.

'Not enough, lord.' He meant not enough to defend the walls. Lindcolne was a burh, but I suspected that most of the garrison had marched south with Jarl Steen, and one day, I thought, men would have to die on these Roman walls to make Englaland.

I took a last look southwards from the vantage point offered by Lindcolne's hill. Ragnall was out there, I could feel it. And by now he knew Brida was dead and Eoferwic was taken and he would want revenge.

He was coming to kill us. And I gazed at that great spread of rich land where cloud shadows slid over copse and pasture, over the bright green of new crops, over orchards and fields, and knew that death was hidden there. Ragnall was coming north.

We rode on south.

'Two days,' I said when we had left Lindcolne behind.

'Two days?' Sigtryggr asked.

'Ragnall will find us in two days,' I said.

'With seven hundred men.'

'More, probably.'

We had seen no sign of Ragnall's marauding army, nor of any Mercian forces. There had been no far smear of smoke to show where an army lit campfires. There was smoke, of course, there is always smoke in the sky. Villagers kept their cooking fires burning and there were charcoal burners in the woods, but there was no massive haze of smoke betraying an army's existence. The campfires of the Mercian army, if it even existed, would be far to the west, and that afternoon we left the Roman road and turned west. I was no longer marching to bring Ragnall to battle, but rather looking for help. I needed Æthelflaed's warriors.

Late that afternoon we came to a woodland clearing where an abandoned hovel decayed. It might have been a forester's home once, but now it was little more than a great heap of thatch covering a hole scraped into the clearing's thin soil. We spent an hour chopping branches and heaping them over the thatch, then rode on westwards leaving two scouts behind. We followed no road, just cattle tracks that led forever towards the setting sun. We stopped at dusk and, looking back into the night-encroaching east, I saw the fire blaze sudden among the trees. The scouts had lit the thatch, and the blaze was a beacon to our enemies. My hope was that Ragnall would see the smoke besmirching the dawn sky and would ride eastwards in search of us while we rode on westwards.

The smoke was still there next morning, grey

against a blue sky. We left it far behind as we travelled away from the rising sun. Our scouts rode well to the south of our path, but saw no enemy. They saw no friends either, and I remembered the argument in Ceaster's Great Hall when I had wanted to ride out against the enemy, and every man there, except for Bishop Leofstan, had argued to remain in Ceaster. Was that what Æthelflaed had done? My son, if he had survived, must have reached Æthelflaed by now even if she was still sheltering in Ceaster, and was she so angry with me that she would leave us to die in these low hills?

'What are we doing, father?' Stiorra asked me.

The truthful answer? We were running away. The truthful answer was that I was heading west towards distant Ceaster in hopes of finding Mercian forces. 'I want to draw Ragnall north,' I said instead, 'to where he's caught between us and the Mercian army.' That was also true. That was why I had led these men south from Eoferwic, but ever since Lindcolne I had been assailed by the fear that we were alone, that no Mercians stalked Ragnall, and we would have to face him alone. I tried to sound cheerful. 'We just have to avoid Ragnall till we know the Mercians are close enough to help!'

'And the Mercians know that?'

That was the proper question, of course, a question to which I had no proper answer. 'If your brother reached them,' I said, 'yes.'

'And if he didn't?'

'And if he didn't,' I said, no longer cheerful,

'then you and Sigtryggr go north as fast as you can. Go and rescue your daughter, then find somewhere safe. Go across the sea! Just go!' My last few words were spoken in anger, but I was not angry with my daughter, but at myself.

'My husband doesn't run away,' Stiorra said.

'Then he's a fool,' I said.

But I was the bigger fool. I had hammered young Æthelstan with advice, telling him not to be headstrong, to use his brain before he used his sword, and now I had led a small army into disaster by not thinking. I had thought to join a Mercian army, thought we could trap Ragnall between two forces, but I was the one who would be trapped. I knew Ragnall was coming. I could not see him or smell him, but I knew it. Every hour the suspicion grew that we were not alone in this innocent-looking countryside. Instinct was shrieking at me, and I had learned to trust instinct. I was being stalked, and there was no help at hand. There was no smoke from an army's campfires in the sky, but nor would there be. Ragnall would rather freeze to death than betray his presence. He knew where we were, and we did not know where his army marched. That morning we saw his scouts for the first time. We had glimpses of far distant horsemen, and Eadger, who was the best of my scouts, led half a dozen men in pursuit of two such riders, but he was headed off by a score of mounted men. All he could report to me was that the larger group had been to the south. 'We couldn't get past the bastards, lord,' he told me. He had tried, wanting to catch a glimpse of Ragnall's army, but the enemy had baulked him. 'But they can't be far off, lord,' Eadger said, and he was right. I thought of turning north, of going back to Eoferwic and hoping to outpace Ragnall's pursuit, but even if we reached Eoferwic we would merely be trapped inside that city. Æthelflaed's forces would never march that far into Northumbria to help us, there would be no rescue, just an assault on Eoferwic's walls and a merciless slaughter in its narrow streets.

What had I thought? I had assumed that Æthelflaed would have sent men to harass Ragnall, that somewhere close to his army was a Mercian force of at least four or five hundred men who would join us. I had thought to astonish Æthelflaed with the capture of Eoferwic, to give her a new King of Northumbria sworn to keep peace with her and to offer her Ragnall's blood-red banner as a trophy. I had thought to give Mercia a new song of Uhtred, but instead I was giving Ragnall's poets a new song.

So I did not tell Stiorra the truth, which was that I had led her into disaster, but at midday it was surely obvious to all my men. We were riding a crest above a wide river valley. The river curled in great loops, running quietly to the sea between meadows thick with grass where sheep grazed. This was what we fought for, for this rich land. We were still heading west, following the ridge line above the river, though I had no idea of where we were. We asked a shepherd, but all he could say was 'home', as if that explained everything. Then, moments later as we paused at the top of a small rise, I saw horsemen far ahead. There were three of them. 'Not ours,' Finan grunted.

So Ragnall's scouts were ahead of us. They were to our west, to our south, and doubtless behind us too. I glanced at the river. We were south of it. I supposed we could cross it somewhere and head north, but our horses were poor beasts, and if Ragnall was as close as I now suspected then he would easily overtake us and fight us on ground of his own choosing. It was time to go to earth and so I sent Finan and a score of men to find a place we could defend. Like a hunted beast I would turn on our pursuers and choose a place where we could maul the enemy before he overwhelmed us. A place, I thought, where we would die unless the Mercians came. 'Look for a hilltop,' I told Finan, who hardly needed the advice.

He found something better. 'You remember that place where Eardwulf had us trapped?' he asked me on his return.

'I remember.'

'It's like that, only better.'

Eardwulf had led a rebellion against Æthelflaed, and he had trapped us in the remains of an old Roman fort built where two rivers met. We had survived that trap, saved by Æthelflaed's arrival, but I was abandoning any hopes of rescue now.

'The river bends ahead,' Finan told me. 'We have

to cross it, but there's a ford. And on the other bank there's a fort.' He was right. The place he had found was as good as I could have hoped for, a place made for defence, a place made, once again, by the Romans and, like Alencestre where Eardwulf had trapped us, a place where two rivers met. Both rivers were too deep for men to cross on foot, and between them was a square Roman earthwork that stood atop higher ground. The only approach was from the ford to the north, from the direction we had come, which meant Ragnall would be forced to march around the fort and cross the ford, and that would take time, time for a Mercian army to come and save us. And if no Mercian army came then we had a fort to defend and a wall on which to kill our enemies.

It was almost dusk when we filed our horses through the fort's northern entrance. That entrance had no gate, it was just a track through the remains of the earthwork which, like the old walls around Eads Byrig, had decayed under the assault of rain and time. There was no trace of any Roman buildings inside the fort, just a steading with a thickly thatched hall of dark timber and next to it a barn and a cattle shed, but there was no sign of any cattle, nor of any people except for an old man who lived in one of the hovels outside the fort wall. Berg brought him to me. 'He says the place belongs to a Dane called Egill,' he said.

'Used to belong to a Saxon,' the old man said.

He was a Saxon himself, 'Hrothwulf! I remember Hrothwulf! He was a good man.'

'What's this place called?' I asked him.

He frowned. 'Hrothwulf's farm, of course!'

'Where is Hrothwulf?'

'Dead and buried, lord, under the soil. Gone to heaven, I hope. Sent there by a Dane,' he spat. 'I was just a lad! Nothing more than a lad. It was Egill's grandfather that killed him. I saw it! Spitted him like a lark.'

'And Egill?'

'He left, lord, took everything with him.'

'Left today,' Finan said. He pointed to some cattle dung just outside the barn. 'A cow shat that this morning,' he said.

I dismounted and drew Serpent-Breath. Finan joined me, sword in hand, and we pushed open the hall door. The hall was empty except for two crude tables, some benches, a straw-filled mattress, a rusted cooking pot, a broken scythe, and a pile of threadbare, stinking pelts. There was a stone hearth in the hall's centre and I crouched beside it and felt the grey ash. 'Still warm,' I said. I stirred the ash with Serpent-Breath's tip and saw embers glowing. So Egill the Dane had been in the house not long before, but he had left, taking his livestock. 'He was warned,' I told Sigtryggr when I joined him on the earthen rampart. 'Egill knew we were coming.'

And Egill, I thought, had been given time to take his cattle and possessions, which meant he must have been given at least a half-day's warning, and that, in turn, meant Ragnall's scouts must have been watching us since early that morning. I gazed north along the gentle ridge between the rivers. 'You should take Stiorra north,' I told Sigtryggr.

'And leave you and your men here?'

'You should go,' I said.

'I'm king here,' he said, 'no one chases me from my own land.'

The ridge to the north was flat-topped and ran between the two rivers, which joined just south of the fort. The ridge was mostly pastureland that dropped very gently away from us before rising, just as gently, to a band of thick woods where horsemen suddenly appeared. 'They're our scouts,' Finan said as men put their hands on sword hilts.

There were six of them and they rode across the pasture together, and as they drew nearer I saw that two were injured. One slumped in his saddle, the other had a bloody head. The six men rode their tired horses to the fort's entrance. 'They're coming, lord,' Eadger said from his saddle. He jerked his head to the south.

I turned, but the land beyond the rivers was silent, still, sun-warmed, empty.

'What did you see?' Sigtryggr asked.

'There's a farmstead beyond those woods,' Eadger pointed towards trees across the river. 'At least a hundred men are there and more are coming. Coming from all over.' He paused as Folcbald lifted the injured man down from his saddle. 'A half-dozen of them chased us,' Eadger went on, 'and Ceadda took a spear in the belly.'

'We emptied two saddles though,' the man with the bleeding scalp said.

'They're well scattered, lord,' Eadger said, 'like they're coming from east, west, and south, coming from all over, but they're coming.'

For a wild moment I thought of taking our men and attacking the vanguard of Ragnall's forces. We would cross the river, find the newly arrived men beyond the far wood, then slash havoc among them before the rest of their army arrived, but just then Finan grunted and I turned back to see that a single horseman had appeared at the northern tree line. The man rode a grey horse that he stood motionless. He was watching us. Two more men appeared, then a half-dozen.

'They're across the river,' Finan said.

And still more men showed at the distant tree line. They just stood watching us. I turned and looked south, and this time I saw horsemen, streams of horsemen, following the road that led to the ford. 'They're all here,' I said.

Ragnall had found us.

CHAPTER 13

The first fire was lit not long after sunset. It blazed somewhere deep among the woods beyond the ridge's pastureland, its flames flickering lurid shadows among the trees.

More fires were lit, one after the other, fires that burned bright in the northern woods that stretched between the rivers. So many fires that at times it seemed as if the whole belt of trees burned. Then, deep in the firelit night, we heard hooves on the ridge and I saw the shadow of a horseman galloping towards us, then turning away. 'They want to keep us awake,' Sigtryggr said. A second horseman followed, while off to the southern side of the ridge an unseen enemy clashed a blade against a shield.

'They are keeping us awake,' I answered, then looked at Stiorra, 'and why didn't you ride north?'

'I forgot,' she said.

Egill had left two spades in his barn and we were using them to deepen the old trench in front of the earthen wall. It would not be a deep trench, but it would be a small obstacle to an advancing shield wall. I did not have enough men to fight in the open pastureland, so we would make our own shield wall on what remained of the Roman rampart. The Romans, I knew, had made two kinds of fort. There were the great fastnesses like Eoferwic, Lundene or Ceaster that were defended by massive stone walls, and then there were these country forts, scores of them, which were little more than a ditch and a bank topped by a wooden wall. These smaller forts guarded river crossings and road junctions, and though the timbers of this fort had long disappeared, its bank of earth, despite its decay, was still steep enough to make a formidable obstacle. Or so I told myself. Ragnall's men would have to negotiate the ditch, then clamber up the bank into our axes, spears, and swords, and their dead and wounded would make another barrier to trip men coming to kill us. The weakest point was the fort's entrance, which was nothing but a flat track through the bank, but there were thorns growing thick by the river junction and my son took a score of men who hacked the bushes down and dragged them back to make a barricade.

Sigtryggr had looked around the fort before the sun set and the darkness shrouded us. 'We could do with another hundred men,' he had said grimly.

'Pray he attacks us straight on,' I had answered.

'He's no fool.'

We had sufficient men to defend one wall of the fort. If Ragnall came down the track that led across the pastureland and assaulted us head-on then I reckoned we could hold till what the Christians called doomsday. But if he also sent men to either side of the fort to attack the eastern and western walls we would be sorely stretched. Luckily the ground fell away towards the rivers on both sides, but the slopes were not impossibly steep, and that meant I would need men on both flanking walls, and more men on the southern wall if Ragnall's forces surrounded us. The truth, and I knew it, was that Ragnall would overwhelm us. We would put up a fight, we would slaughter some of his best warriors, but by midday we would all be corpses or prisoners unless Ragnall obliged me by simply assaulting the northern wall.

Or unless the Mercians came.

'We do have the hostages,' Sigtryggr said. We were standing on the northern wall, watching the threatening fires and listening to the hacking sound of our spades deepening the ditch. Another enemy rode close to the fort, man and horse outlined by the glare of the fires burning in the distant wood.

'We have the hostages,' I agreed. The eight women were all wives of Ragnall's jarls. The youngest was around fourteen, the oldest perhaps thirty. They were, unsurprisingly, sullen and resentful. We had them all in Egill's hall, guarded there by four men. 'What did he fear?' I asked Sigtryggr.

'Fear?'

'Why did he take hostages?'

'Disloyalty,' he said simply.

'An oath isn't enough to make men loyal?'

'Not for my brother,' Sigtryggr said, then sighed. 'Five years ago, maybe six, father led an army to the south of Ireland. Things didn't go well, and half the army just took to their ships and sailed away.'

'Which happens,' I said.

'If you're capturing land, slaves, cattle,' Sigtryggr said, 'then men stay loyal, but as soon as there are difficulties? They melt away. Hostages are Ragnall's answer.'

'You take hostages from the enemy,' I said, 'not from your own side.'

'Unless you're my brother,' Sigtryggr said. He was stroking a stone down the edge of his long-sword. The sound was monotonous. I gazed at the far woods and knew our enemies were also sharpening their blades. They had to be confident. They knew the dawn would bring them a battle, victory, plunder, and reputation.

'What will you do with the hostages?' Finan asked.

'Show them,' Sigtryggr said.

'And threaten them?' Stiorra asked.

'They're a weapon to use,' Sigtryggr answered unhappily.

'And you'll kill them?' Stiorra demanded. Sigtryggr did not answer. 'If you kill them,' my daughter said, 'then you lose the power of them.'

'It should be enough to just threaten their deaths,' Sigtryggr answered.

'Those men,' Stiorra nodded her head towards the fires in the woodland, 'know you. They know you won't kill women.'

'We might have to,' Sigtryggr said unhappily. 'One, at least.'

None of us spoke. Behind us, in the fort, men sat around campfires. Some of them sang, though the songs were not happy. They were laments. The men knew what faced them and I wondered how many I could rely on. I was sure of my own men and of Sigtryggr's, but a quarter of the warriors had been sworn to Ragnall not a week or two before, and how would they fight? Would they desert? Or would their fear of Ragnall's wrath persuade them to fight even harder for me?

'Remember Eardwulf?' Finan suddenly asked.

I half smiled. 'I know what you're thinking.'

'Eardwulf?' Sigtryggr asked.

'An ambitious man,' I said, 'and he had us trapped like this. Just like this. And moments before he slaughtered us the Lady Æthelflaed arrived.'

'With an army?'

'He thought she had an army,' I said, 'in fact she didn't, but he thought she did and so he left us alone.'

'And tomorrow?' Sigtryggr asked.

'There should be a Mercian army following Ragnall,' I said.

'Should be,' Sigtryggr said flatly.

I still hoped for that Mercian army. I told myself that it could be two hours' march away, somewhere to the west. Perhaps Merewalh was leading it? He would be wise enough not to light campfires, clever enough to march before dawn to assault Ragnall from the rear. I had to cling to that hope, even though every instinct told me it was a vain hope. Without help, I knew, we were doomed.

'There are other hostages,' Finan said unexpectedly. We all looked at him. 'My brother's troops,' he explained.

'You think they won't fight?' I asked him.

'Of course they'll fight,' he said, 'they're Irish. But in the morning, lord, lend me your helmet, your arm rings, and all the gold and silver you can find.'

'They're mercenaries,' I said, 'you're going to buy them?'

He shook his head. 'And I want our best horse too.'

'You can have whatever you want,' I said.

'To do what?' Sigtryggr asked.

And Finan smiled. 'Sorcery,' he said, 'just Irish sorcery.'

We waited for the dawn.

A small mist greeted the wolf-light. The fires in the far wood faded, though they were still there, dim among the misted trees. Finan tried to count those fires, but they were too many. We were all counting. We had just over three hundred and eighty men fit to fight, and the enemy had to have three times that number, maybe four times. We all counted, though no one spoke of it.

The first horsemen came soon after dawn. They were young men from Ragnall's army and they could not resist taunting us. They came from the trees and cantered till they were squarely in front of our northern wall, and there they would simply wait, usually some thirty or forty paces away, daring any one of us to cross the ditch and fight in single combat. I had given orders that no one was to accept such challenges, and our refusal prompted more of Ragnall's young men to provoke us. His army was still hidden in the trees that were a half-mile away, but he permitted his hot-headed warriors to confront us.

'You're cowards!' one bellowed.

'Come and kill me! If you dare!' Another trotted up and down in front of us.

'If you're frightened of me, shall I send my sister to fight one of you?'

They were showing off to each other as much as to us. Such insults have always been a part of battle. It takes time for men to form a shield wall, and even more time to summon the courage to attack another wall, and the ritual of insult and challenge was a part of that summoning. Ragnall had yet to reveal his men, he was keeping them among the trees, though every now and then we would see a glimpse of metal through the far leaves. He would be haranguing his leaders, telling them what he expected and how they would be rewarded, and meanwhile his young men came to mock us.

'Two of you come and fight!' a man shouted. 'I'll kill you both!'

'Pup,' Sigtryggr growled.

'I seem to remember you taunting me at Ceaster,' I said.

'I was young and foolish.'

'You haven't changed.'

He smiled. He was in a mail coat that had been scoured with sand and vinegar so that it reflected the new sunlight. His sword belt was studded with gold buttons, and a gold chain was wrapped three times around his neck and from it hung a golden hammer. He wore no helmet, but around his fair hair he had the gilt-bronze circlet we had discovered in Eoferwic. 'I'll lend Finan the chain,' he offered.

Finan was saddling a tall black stallion. Like Sigtryggr he wore polished mail, and he had borrowed my sword belt with its intricate silver panels riveted to the leather. He had braided his hair and hung it with ribbons, while his forearms were thick with warrior rings. The iron rim of his shield had been scraped free of rust, while the faded paint on the willow-boards had also been scraped down to make a Christian cross out of the fresh wood. Whatever sorcery he planned was evidently Christian, but he would not tell me what it was. I watched as he cinched the stallion's girth tight, then just turned, leaned against the placid horse, and looked out through the thorn-blocked gateway to where a half-dozen of Ragnall's young warriors still taunted us. The rest had become bored and had ridden back to the far trees, but these six had kicked their horses right to the ditch's edge where they sneered at us. 'Are you all so frightened?' one asked. 'I'll fight two of you! Don't be babies! Come and fight!'

Three more horsemen came from the northern trees and cantered to join the six. 'I'd love to go and kill some of them,' Sigtryggr growled.

'Don't.'

'I won't.' He watched the three horsemen, who had drawn their swords. 'Aren't they eager?' he asked scornfully.

'The young always are,' I said.

'Were you?'

'I remember my first shield wall,' I said, 'and I was scared.' It had been against cattle raiders from Wales and I had been terrified. Since then I had fought against the best that the Northmen could send against us, I had clashed shields and smelled my enemy's stinking breath as I killed him, and I still feared the shield wall. One day I would die in such a wall. I would go down, biting against the pain, and an enemy's blade would tear the life from me. Maybe today, I thought, probably today. I touched the hammer.

'What are they doing?' Sigtryggr asked. He was not looking at me, but at the three approaching horsemen who had spurred their stallions into full gallop and now charged the men insulting us. Those men turned, not certain what was happening, and their hesitation was their doom. All three newcomers unhorsed an opponent, the one in the centre charging his enemy's horse and throwing it down by the collision, then turning on a second man and lunging with his sword. I saw the long blade sink through mail, saw the Norseman bend over the blade, saw his own sword drop to the grass, then watched his attacker gallop past and almost get pulled from the saddle because his sword's blade was buried in the dying man's guts. The attacking rider was wrenched backwards by the blade's suction, but managed to drag the weapon free. He turned his horse fast and chopped the blade down on the wounded man's spine. One of the six men who had been jeering us was racing away along the ridge, the other five were either dead or wounded. None was mounted any longer.

The three turned towards us and I saw their leader was my son, Uhtred, who grinned at me as he trotted towards the thorn fence that barred the fort's entrance. We dragged a section of the fence back to let the three men through and they arrived to cheers. I saw that my son was wearing a big iron hammer amulet about his neck. I held his horse while he dismounted, then embraced him. 'You pretended to be a Dane?' I asked, touching his hammer.

'I did!' he said. 'And no one even questioned us! We came last night.' His companions were both Danes who had sworn oaths to me. They grinned, proud of what they had just done. I took two rings from my arms and gave one to each of the Danes.

'You could have stayed with Ragnall,' I told them, 'but you didn't.'

'You're our oath-lord,' one said.

'And you haven't led us to defeat yet, lord,' the other said, and I felt a pang of guilt, because surely they had galloped to their deaths by crossing the wide pasture.

'You were easy to find,' my son said. 'Northmen are swarming here like wasps to honey.'

'How many?' Sigtryggr asked.

'Too many,' my son said grimly.

'And the Mercian army?' I asked.

He shook his head. 'What Mercian army?'

I swore and looked back to the pasture that was empty now except for three corpses and two lamed men who were staggering back towards the trees. 'Lady Æthelflaed didn't pursue Ragnall?' I asked.

'The Lady Æthelflaed,' my son said, 'pursued him, but then went back to Ceaster for Bishop Leofstan's funeral.'

'She did what?' I gaped at him.

'Leofstan died,' Uhtred said. 'One minute he lived and the next he was dead. I'm told he was celebrating mass when it happened. He gave a cry of pain and collapsed.'

'No!' I was surprised by the grief I felt. I had hated Leofstan when he first came to the city, arriving so full of a humility that I thought must be false, but I had come to like him, even to admire him. 'He was a good man,' I said.

'He was.'

'And Æthelflaed took the army back for his funeral?'

My son shook his head, then paused to take a cup of water from Berg. 'Thank you,' he said. 'She went back with a score of men and her usual priests,' he said, when he had drunk, 'but she left Cynlæf commanding the army.'

Cynlæf, her favourite, the man marked to marry her daughter. 'And Cynlæf?' I asked bitterly.

'The last I heard he was well south of Ledecestre,' my son said, 'and refusing to lead troops into Northumbria.'

'Bastard,' I said.

'We went to Ceaster,' he said, 'and pleaded with her.'

'And?'

'She sent orders for Cynlæf to march north and find you, but he's probably only getting those orders today.'

'And he's a day's march away.'

'At least a day's march,' my son said, 'so we have to beat these bastards all on our own.' He grinned, then astonished me one more time by turning and looking at Finan. 'Hey, Irishman!'

Finan looked surprised to be called that, but he took no offence. 'Lord Uhtred?' he responded mildly.

My son was grinning like a madman. 'You owe me two shillings,' he said.

'I do?'

'You said the bishop's wife would look like a toad, remember?'

Finan nodded. 'I remember.'

'She doesn't. So you owe me two shillings.'

Finan snorted. 'I only have your word for it, lord! And what's your word worth? You thought that tavern maid in Gleawecestre was beautiful, and she had a face like a bullock's backside. Even Gerbruht wouldn't touch her and I've seen him hump things a dog wouldn't sniff!'

'Oh, Sister Gomer is beautiful,' my son said, 'just ask my father.'

'Me?' I exclaimed. 'How would I know?'

'Because,' my son said, 'Sister Gomer has an apple birthmark, father. Right here,' and he touched a gloved finger to his forehead.

I was speechless. I just stared at him. I even forgot Ragnall for a moment, thinking only of that ripe body in the hay shed.

'Well?' Finan asked.

'You owe my son two shillings,' I said, and started laughing.

And Ragnall came to give battle.

I remembered how Ragnall had led his horsemen from the trees at Ceaster when he had taken revenge for the heads arrayed around the remnants of the fort at Eads Byrig. He had brought his men from the wood in a line so they appeared all at once, and now he did it again. One moment the far trees were bright with a sun-drenched morning's light, their green leaves peaceful, and then they came. Ranks of men on foot, men with shields, men with weapons, a shield wall that was meant to awe us, and it did.

A shield wall is a terrible thing. It is a wall of wood, iron, and steel with one purpose alone, to kill.

And this shield wall was massive, a wall of

painted round shields stretching wide across the ridge's flat top, and above it were the banners of the jarls, chieftains, and kings who had come to kill us. At the centre, of course, was Ragnall's red axe, but the axe was flanked by forty or fifty other banners bright with ravens, eagles, wolves, serpents, and with creatures that no man had ever seen except in nightmares. The shield-warriors who followed those banners came from the wood and there they stopped and began clashing their shields together, a constant thunder. I counted them as best I could and reckoned they numbered at least a thousand men. The flanks of the wall were on the ridge's slopes, and that suggested they would wrap that great wall around the fort and attack on three sides. My own men were on the fort's wall. They could count too, and they were silent as they watched Ragnall's massive force and listened to the thunder of his shields.

Ragnall was still not ready to attack. He was letting his men see us, letting them realise how few we were. Those men who clashed shields to make the thunder of challenge would see the fort's wall and, on its summit, a much smaller shield wall than their own. They would see we had just two banners, the wolf's head and the red axe, and Ragnall wanted them to know how easy this victory would be. I saw him riding a black horse behind his wall and calling to his men. He was assuring them of victory and promising our deaths. He was filling them with confidence, and it was just moments, I knew, before he came to insult us. He would offer us a chance to surrender, and, when we refused, he would bring his shield wall forward.

But before Ragnall could move, Finan rode towards the enemy.

He rode alone and he rode slowly, his horse high-stepping in the lush pasture. Man and horse were magnificent, gold-hung, silver-shining. He had Sigtryggr's thick golden chain about his neck, though he had removed the hammer, and he wore my helmet with its crouching silver wolf on the crown from which he had hung strips of dark cloth that mimicked the horse's tail plume of his brother's helmet. And it was to his brother that he rode, towards the banner of the dark ship sailing on a blood-red sea. That banner was on the right of Ragnall's line, at the edge of the plateau. The Irish carried other flags decorated with the Christian cross, the same symbol that Finan had scraped into his shield that hung at his left side above the glittering scabbard in which he carried Soul-Stealer, a sword he had taken from a Norseman in battle. Soul-Stealer was lighter than most swords, though its reach was just as long, a blade that I feared could be easily broken by the heavy swords most of us carried. But Finan, who had given the sword its name, loved Soul-Stealer.

Two men rode from Ragnall's ranks to challenge Finan. Their horses must have been kept close behind the shield wall, and I assumed Ragnall had given them permission to fight, and I heard his army cheering as the two men rode. I had no doubt that the two were battle-tested, full of sword-craft and terrible in combat, and Ragnall, and all his men too, must have assumed Finan would accept the challenge of one or the other, but instead he rode past them. They followed him, taunting, but neither attacked him. That too was part of battle's ritual. Finan had ridden alone and he would choose his enemy. He rode on, slow and deliberate, until he faced the Irishmen beneath their banners.

And he spoke to them.

I was much too far away to hear anything he said, and even if I had been at his elbow I would not have understood his tongue. The two champions, perhaps realising that the challenge was from one Irishman to his countrymen, turned away, and Finan spoke on.

He must have taunted them. And in his thoughts there must have been a girl lovely as a dream, a dark-haired girl of the Ó Domhnaill, a girl worth defying fate for, a girl to love and to worship, and a girl who had been dragged through the mud to be his brother's plaything, a girl who had haunted Finan in all the long years since her death.

And a man stepped out of the Irish ranks.

It was not Conall. The enemy shield wall was a long way off, but even I could see that this man was much bigger than Conall, bigger than Finan too. He was a great brute of a man, hulking in his mail, carrying a shield larger than any other in the wall and hefting a sword that looked as if it were made for a god, not for a man, a sword as heavy as a war axe, a sword for butchery. And Finan slid from his saddle.

Two armies watched.

Finan threw away his shield, and I remembered that far-off day, so long ago, when I had faced Steapa in single combat. That was before we became friends, and no man had given me a chance against Steapa. He had been known then as Steapa Snotor, Steapa the Clever, which was a cruel joke because he was not the cleverest of men, but he was loyal, he was thoughtful, and he was unstoppable in battle. He, like the man striding towards Finan, was huge and hugely strong, a giver of death, and I had fought him, supposedly to the death, and one of us would have died that day had the Danes not surged across the frontier that same morning. And when I had fought Steapa I had begun by casting aside my shield and even taking off my mail coat. Steapa had watched me, expressionless. He knew what I was doing. I was making myself fast. I would not be cumbered by weight, I would be quick and I would dance around the larger man like a nimble dog baiting a bull.

Finan kept his mail coat, but he threw the shield down, then just waited.

And we saw the big man charge, using his shield to batter Finan away, and what happened next was so swift that none of us could be certain of what we saw. It was far away, too far to see clearly, but the two figures closed, I saw the big man ram the shield to slam Finan and, thinking he had struck Finan, begin to turn with the massive sword raised to kill. And then he just dropped.

It was fast, so fast, but I have never known a man swifter than Finan. He was not big, indeed he looked skinny, but he was quick. He could carry Soul-Stealer because he rarely needed to parry with the blade, he could dance out of a blow's way. I had fought him in practice often enough and I had rarely got past his guard. The big man, I assumed he was Conall's champion, dropped to his knees, and Finan sliced Soul-Stealer down onto his neck and that was the end of the fight. It had been over in two or three heartbeats and Finan had made it look so easy. The thunder of the far shields stopped.

And Finan spoke to his countrymen again. I never learned what he said, but I saw him walk to the shield wall, walk within the reach of their swords and spears, and there he spoke to his brother. I could see it was his brother because Conall's helmet was brighter than the rest and he stood directly beneath the blood-red banner. The brothers stood face to face. I remembered the hatred between them at Ceaster, and the same hatred must have been there, but Conall did not move. He had seen his champion die and had no wish to follow him down to hell.

Finan took one pace backwards.

Two armies watched.

Finan turned his back on his brother and began walking towards his horse.

And Conall charged.

We gasped. I think every man on the field who saw it gasped. Conall charged, his sword reaching for Finan's spine, and Finan spun.

Soul-Stealer flashed. I did not hear the clash of blades, just saw Conall's sword fly up as it was deflected, saw Soul-Stealer slice at Conall's face, then saw Finan turn his back and walk away again. No one who watched spoke. They saw Conall step back, blood on his face, and watched Finan walk away. And again Conall attacked. This time he lunged for the nape of Finan's neck, and Finan ducked, turned again, and punched Soul-Stealer's hilt into his brother's face. Conall staggered, then tripped on his heel and sat heavily.

Finan walked to him. He ignored his brother's sword, but just held Soul-Stealer at Conall's neck. I expected to see the lunge and the sudden splash of blood, but instead Finan held the blade at his brother's throat and spoke to his brother's men. Conall tried to lift his sword, but Finan kicked it contemptuously aside, then he stooped and, using his left hand, seized his brother's helmet.

He dragged it free.

He still stood over his brother. Now, with even greater contempt, he sheathed Soul-Stealer. He took off my helmet and replaced it with his brother's black horse-tailed helmet with its royal circlet. King Finan.

Then he just walked away and, retrieving his shield from the grass, he climbed back into his saddle. He had humiliated his brother and now he rode the stallion along the face of Ragnall's whole line. He did not hurry. He dared men to come and face him and none did. There was scorn in that ride. The horse-tail of the gold-ringed helmet streamed behind him as at last he kicked his stallion into a canter and rode back to us.

He reached the thorn fence and tossed me my helmet. 'Conall's men won't fight us now,' was all he said.

Which only left about a thousand men who would.

We had given Ragnall a problem and Finan had worsened it. Ragnall had to be confident that he could beat us, but knew he would pay a price for that victory. The Roman fort was old, but its walls were steep, and men climbing those short slopes would be vulnerable. In the end he would break us. He had too many men and we had too few, but too many of Ragnall's men would die in killing us. That is why battles of the shield wall are slow to start. Men have to nerve themselves for the horror. The fort's ditches were not much of an obstacle, but we had hammered short stakes into the ditch during the night, and men advancing behind shields can see little, and, especially if they are pushed on by the rank behind, they can trip, and a man who falls in the shield wall is as good as dead. At Æsc's Hill, so many years ago, I had seen an army of victorious Danes defeated by a ditch that Alfred defended. The rearmost ranks had pushed the shield wall forward and the front ranks had stumbled in the ditch where the West Saxon warriors had killed them till the ditch was brimming red. So Ragnall's men were reluctant to attack, and made more reluctant by the omen of Conall's humiliation. It was Ragnall's task to fire them now, to fill them with anger as well as ale. You can smell the ale on an enemy's breath in the shield wall. We had none. We would fight sober.

The sun was halfway to his summit by the time Ragnall came to insult us. That too was a part of the pattern of battle. First the young fools challenge the enemy to single combat, then the speeches are made to fire men with the lust for blood, and finally the enemy is insulted. 'Maggots!' Ragnall called to us. 'Sow turds! You want to die here?' My men rhythmically clashed seax blades against shields, making the music of death to drown his words. 'Send me my little brother,' Ragnall shouted, 'and you can live!'

Ragnall had donned mail and helmet for battle. He rode his black stallion, and, for a weapon, carried a massive axe. A dozen men accompanied him, grim warriors on big horses, their faces made mysterious by closed cheek-pieces. They were inspecting the ditch and wall, readying to warn their men what difficulties they would face. Two rode towards the thorn fence and only turned away when a spear struck the ground between their horses. One of them seized the quivering haft and carried it away.

'We have ravaged Mercia!' Ragnall shouted. 'Razed farmsteads, taken captives, stripped the fields of cattle! The old hag who calls herself the ruler of Mercia is hiding behind stone walls! Her country is ours and I have her land to give away! You want good land, rich land? Come to me!'

Instead of insulting us he was trying to bribe us. Behind him, across the ridge's wide pasture-land, I could see the ale-skins being passed among the enemy. Shields were resting on the ground, their upper rims against men's thighs, and spears were held upright, their points glinting in the sun. There was a mass of those spear-points beneath Ragnall's banner at the centre of his line, and that told me he planned to use the long spears to shatter the centre of our line. It was what I would have done. He would have assembled his biggest men there, the most savage, the men who revelled in killing and who boasted of the widows they had made, and he would loose those men at the fort's entrance and follow it with a rush of swordsmen to peel our wall apart and kill us like trapped rats.

He tired of shouting. We had not responded, and the clash of blades on shields had not ceased, and besides, his men had seen what obstacles we had waiting and they needed to see no more and Ragnall, after spitting towards us and shouting that we had chosen death instead of life, rode back to his men. And those men, seeing him come, picked up their shields, and I watched as the shields were hefted and overlapped. The spearmen parted to let Ragnall and his companions ride through the wall, then the shields closed again. I saw Ragnall dismount, saw him push through to the front rank. They were coming.

But first Sigtryggr rode.

He rode with eight warriors and with the eight hostages. The women's hands were tied in front of their bodies, and their horses were led by the eight men. Ragnall must have known we had captured the women when we had taken Eoferwic, but it would have been a surprise for him to see them here. A surprise and a shock. And the eight men whose women we had as captives? I remembered Orvar's words that men liked Sigtryggr, but feared Ragnall, and now Sigtryggr, resplendent in his shining mail and with the kingly circlet about his helmet, rode towards them, and behind him came the hostages, each escorted by a man with a drawn sword, and Ragnall's men must have thought they would see blood and I heard a murmur of anger swelling from the pasture's far side.

Sigtryggr stopped halfway between the armies. The women were in a line, each woman threatened with a blade. The message was obvious. If Ragnall attacked, then the women would die, but it was equally clear that if Sigtryggr killed the hostages he would merely provoke an attack. 'He should just bring them back here,' Finan said.

'Why?'

'He can't kill them there! If they're hidden in

the hall then the enemy won't know what's happening to them.'

Instead Sigtryggr raised his right arm in a signal to his eight men, then dropped it fast. 'Now!' he called.

The eight swords were used to cut the bonds that had loosely tied the women's wrists. 'Go,' Sigtryggr told them, 'go find your husbands, just go.'

The women hesitated a moment, then clumsily kicked their horses towards Ragnall's line that had fallen abruptly silent when Sigtryggr, instead of slaughtering the wives, had released them. One woman, unable to control her nervous horse, climbed out of the saddle and ran towards her husband's banner. I saw two men come the other way, hurrying to greet their women, and Ragnall, understanding that he had lost power over men he wanted to fear him, also understood that he had to attack now. I saw him turn and shout, saw him beckon his shield wall forward. Horns brayed, banners were lifted, the spear-points dropped to the attack, and men started forward. They cheered.

But not every man was cheering.

The shield wall did start forward. The men at the centre, the men I feared most, were advancing steadily and, either side of them, other men were coming, but out at the flanks there was hesitation. The Irish had not moved, and the contingents next to them also stayed still. Other men stayed put. I saw a man embracing his wife, and his followers were not moving either. Maybe half of

Ragnall's line was marching towards us, the other half had lost their fear of him.

Sigtryggr was riding back to us, but he paused when he heard the loud horns. He turned his horse and saw how half of his brother's shield wall was reluctant to attack. Horsemen were galloping behind Ragnall's shields, bellowing at reluctant men to advance. The Irish had not even picked up their shields, but stood stubbornly still. We were watching an army in two minds, an army that had lost confidence. The men whose wives had been restored to them were weighing their loyalty, and we could see it in their hesitation.

Sigtryggr turned and looked at me. 'Lord Uhtred!' he called. His voice was urgent. 'Lord Uhtred!' he called again.

'I know!' I shouted.

He laughed. My son-in-law took a delight in war. He was a warrior born, a lord of war, a Norseman, and he had seen what I saw. If a man rules by fear he must succeed. He must keep his followers docile by showing that he cannot be beaten, that his fate is victory and riches. Wyrd bið ful āræd. Fate is inexorable. A man who rules by fear cannot afford a single setback, and Sigtryggr's release of the hostages had loosened the bonds of fear. But the men who hesitated would not stay defiant for long. If they saw Ragnall's spearmen cut their savage way through the thorn fence and through the fort's entrance, if they saw men swarming up the wall, if they saw the axes chopping at our shields on the wall's top, then they would join the battle. Men want to be on the winning side. In a few moments all they would see was Ragnall's men crowding at our defences and outflanking them, and they would fear that Ragnall's victory would bring Ragnall's revenge on those who had hung back.

What Sigtryggr had seen and what I had seen was that they must not be given that glimpse of Ragnall's victory. We could not defend the fort even though it was made for defence, because those of Ragnall's men who advanced were still more than enough to overwhelm us, and the sight of those men forcing their way into the fort would bring the rest of Ragnall's army into the battle.

So we had to give the rest of Ragnall's army a glimpse of Ragnall's defeat.

We had to offer them hope.

We had to leave our refuge.

We had to attack.

'Forward!' I shouted. 'Forward and kill them!'

'Jesus Christ,' Finan said beside me.

My men hesitated for a heartbeat, not out of reluctance, but from surprise. All night we had prepared them to defend the fort and now we were leaving it to carry our blades to the enemy. I jumped down the wall into the ditch. 'Come on!' I shouted. 'We're going to kill them!'

Men kicked the thorn fence aside. Other men scrambled down the fort's wall and through the ditch to reform the shield wall on its far side.

'Keep going!' I shouted. 'Keep going and kill them!'

Sigtryggr and his horsemen scattered from our path. We advanced along the ridge's flat top, still clashing blades on shields. The enemy had stopped, astonished.

Men need a battle cry. I could not ask them to shout for Mercia, because most of my force were not Mercians, they were Norsemen. I could have called Sigtryggr's name and doubtless all my men would have echoed that because we fought for his throne, but some impulse made me offer a different shout. 'For Mus,' I bellowed, 'for the best whore in Britain! For Mus!'

There was a pause, and then my men burst into laughter. 'For Mus!' they shouted.

An enemy sees his attackers laughing? It is better than all the insults. A man who laughs as he goes into battle is a man who has confidence, and a man with confidence is terrifying to an enemy. 'For the whore!' I shouted. 'For Mus!' And the shout spread along my line as men who had never heard of Mus learned she was a whore and a good one too. They loved the idea. They were all laughing or shouting her name now. Shouting for a whore as they went to death's embrace. 'Mus! Mus! Mus!'

'She'd better reward them,' Finan said grimly.

'She will!' my son called from my other side.

Ragnall was shouting for his spearmen to advance, but they were watching Sigtryggr, who had ridden with his horsemen off to their right. He was shouting at the men who had not joined the advance, men who were now lagging behind Ragnall's shield wall. He was encouraging them to turn against Ragnall.

'Just kill them!' I shouted and quickened my pace. We had to close on the enemy before the laggards decided we were doomed. Men love to be on the winning side, so we needed to win! 'Faster,' I shouted, 'for the whore!' Thirty paces, twenty, and you can see the eyes of the men who will try to kill you, and see the spear-blades, and the instinct is to stop, to straighten the shields. We cringe from battle, fear claws at us, time seems to stop, there is silence though a thousand men shout, and at that moment, when terror savages the heart like a trapped beast, you must hurl yourself into the horror.

Because the enemy feels the same.

And you have come to kill him. You are the beast from his nightmares. The man facing me had crouched slightly, his spear levelled and his shield high. I knew he would either raise or lower the blade as I closed, and I wanted him to raise it so I deliberately let my shield down so it covered my legs. I did not think about it. I knew what would happen. I had fought too many battles, and sure enough the spear-blade came up, aimed at my chest or neck as he braced himself, and I lifted the shield so the spear glanced off it to go high in the air, and then we hit.

The crash of the shield walls, the sudden noise, the hammering of wood and steel and men screaming their war cries, and I thrust Wasp-Sting into the gap between two shields and the man behind me had hooked the enemy's shield with his axe and was tugging, and the man was struggling to pull his spear back as I rammed the seax up into his ribs. I felt it burst through the links of his mail, slice through the leather beneath to grate on bone. I twisted the blade and tugged her back as a sword struck my shield a ringing blow. Finan was protecting my right, his own seax stabbing. My opponent let go of his spear, it was far too long a weapon for the shield wall. It was meant to break open another wall and was almost useless in defence. He drew his seax, but before the blade had left the scabbard I raked Wasp-Sting across his face that was inked with ravens. She left an open wound spilling blood that blinded him and turned his short beard red. Another stab, this to his throat and he was down and the man in the rank behind him lunged over the falling body with a sword thrust that turned my shield and sliced into my son's arm. I almost tripped on the fallen man, who still tried to stab up with his seax.

'Kill him!' I shouted to the man behind me and rammed my shield at the swordsman, who snarled as he tried to lunge with the blade again, and my shield slammed into his body and I stabbed Wasp-Sting down to open his thigh from groin to knee. A blade crashed against my helmet. An axe swung overhead and I ducked down fast, raising the shield, and the axe split the iron rim, shattered willow, and tilted the shield over my head, but I could see the bleeding thigh and I stabbed again, upwards this time in the wicked blow that made the man shriek and took him from the fight. Finan ripped the axeman's cheek away from his jaw with his seax and stabbed again, aiming for the eyes. Gerbruht, behind me, seized the axe and turned it against the enemy. He thought, because I was crouching, that I was wounded, and he bellowed in anger as he pushed past me and swung the huge weapon with all the force of his huge strength. A sword pierced his upper chest, but slid upwards as his axe cut a helmet and a skull in two, and there was a mist of blood as a spatter of brains slapped on my helmet. I stood, covering Gerbruht with my shield. My son was heaving forward on my left, stamping his foot on an enemy's face. We had taken down Ragnall's two front ranks and the men behind were stepping back, trying to escape our blood-painted shields, our wet blades, our snarling love of slaughter.

And I heard another clash and heard shouting and though I could not see what happened I felt the shudder from my left and knew that other men had joined the fight. 'For the whore!' I shouted. 'For the whore!'

That was a mad shout! But now the battle-joy had come, the song of slaughter. Folcbald had arrived to the left of my son, and he was as strong as Gerbruht and armed with a short-handled axe that had a massive head, and he was hooking down enemy shields so my son could lunge over them.

A spear slid beneath my shield to strike against the iron strips in my boot. I stamped on the blade, rammed Wasp-Sting between two shields, felt her bite. I was keening a wordless song. Finan was using his seax to give short fast lunges between shields, raking his enemies' forearms with the blade till their weapons dropped, when he would slice the blade up into their ribcage. Folcbald had abandoned his shattered shield and was hacking with the axe, bellowing a Frisian challenge, smashing the heavy blade through helmets and skulls, making a pile of blood-spattered enemy dead and shouting at men to come and be killed. Somewhere ahead, not far, I could see Ragnall's banner. I shouted for him. 'Ragnall! You bastard! Ragnall! You shrivelled piece of shit! Come and die, you bastard! For the whore!'

Oh the madness of battle! We fear it, we celebrate it, the poets sing of it, and when it fills the blood like fire it is a real madness. It is joy! All the terror is swept away, a man feels he could live for ever, he sees the enemy retreating, knows he himself is invincible, that even the gods would shrink from his blade and his bloodied shield. And I was still keening that mad song, the battle song of slaughter, the sound that blotted out the screams of dying men and the crying of the wounded. It is fear, of course, that feeds the battle madness, the release of fear into savagery. You win in the shield wall by being more savage than your enemy, by turning his savagery back into fear.

I wanted to kill Ragnall, but I could not see him. All I could see were shield rims, bearded faces, blades, men snarling, a man spitting teeth from a mouth filled with blood, a boy screaming for his mother, another weeping on the ground and shaking. A wounded man groaned and turned over on the grass, and I thought he was trying to lift a seax to stab me and I slid Wasp-Sting down into his throat and the jet of blood struck warm on my face. I ground the blade downwards, cursing the man, then ripped the blade free as I saw a short man come from my right. I back-handed the blade, striking the man, who sank down and shrieked, 'Father!' It was a boy, not a man. 'Father!' That second call was my son, pulling me backwards. The weeping and shaking boy was crying hysterically, gasping for breath, his face laced with blood. I had put him on the ground. I had not known. I had just seen him coming from my right and struck at him, but he could not have been more than nine years old, maybe ten, and I had half severed his left arm. 'It's over,' my son said, holding my sword arm, 'it's over.'

It was not quite over. Men still clashed shield against shield, the blades still hacked and lunged, but Ragnall's own men had turned on him. The Irish had joined the fight, but on our side. They were keening their battle sound, a high-pitched scream as they savaged Ragnall's remaining warriors. The men whose wives we had released had also turned against Ragnall and, of his thousand men, only a few were left, maybe two hundred or so, but they were surrounded.

'Enough!' Sigtryggr shouted. 'Enough!' He had found a horse from somewhere and hauled himself into the saddle. He carried his bloodied sword as he shouted at the men struggling to kill his brother. 'Enough! Let them live!' His brother was in the centre of the men who still fought for him, the outnumbered and encircled men who now lowered their weapons as the battle died.

'Look after that boy,' I told my son. The boy was crouching over his dead father, weeping hysterically. That had been me, I thought, at Eoferwic, how many years ago? I looked at Finan. 'How old are we?' I asked.

'Too old, lord.' There was blood on his face. His beard was grey, trickling blood.

'Are you hurt?' I asked, and he shook his head. He still wore his brother's helmet with its golden circlet that had been dented by a sword blow. 'Are you going home?' I asked him.

'Home?' he was puzzled by my question.

'To Ireland,' I said. I looked at the circlet, 'King Finan.'

He smiled. 'I am home, lord.'

'And your brother?'

Finan shrugged. 'He'll have to live with the shame of this day for ever. He's finished. Besides,' he made the sign of the cross, 'a man shouldn't kill his own brother.'

Sigtryggr killed his own brother. He offered life

to the men who would surrender, and afterwards, as those men deserted Ragnall, Sigtryggr fought him. It was a fair fight. I did not watch, but afterwards Sigtryggr had a sword slash on one hip and a broken rib. 'He could fight,' he said happily, 'but I fought better.'

I looked at the men in the pasture. Hundreds of men. 'They're all yours now,' I said.

'Mine,' he agreed.

'You should return to Eoferwic,' I told him. 'Give away land, but make sure you have sufficient men to guard the city walls. Four men for every five paces. Some of those men can be butchers, bakers, leather-workers, labourers, but salt them with your warriors. And capture Dunholm.'

'I will.' He looked at me, grinned, and we embraced. 'Thank you,' he said.

'For what?'

'For making your daughter a queen.'

I took my men away next morning. We had lost sixteen in the battle, only sixteen, though another forty were too wounded to move. I embraced my daughter, then bowed to her because she was indeed a queen. Sigtryggr tried to give me his great gold chain, but I refused it. 'I have enough gold,' I told him, 'and you are now the gold-giver. Be generous.'

And we rode away.

I met Æthelflaed six days later. We met in the Great Hall of Ceaster. Cynlæf was there, as were Merewalh, Osferth, and young Prince Æthelstan. The warriors of Mercia were there too, the men who had not pursued Ragnall north of Ledecestre. Ceolnoth and Ceolberht stood among their fellow priests. My other son, Father Oswald, was also there, and he stood protectively close to Bishop Leofstan's widow, Sister Gomer, the Mus. She smiled at me, but the smile vanished when I glared at her.

I had not cleaned my mail. Rain had washed most of the blood away, but the blade-torn gaps in the rings were still there and the leather beneath was stained with blood. My helmet had a gash in one side from an axe blow that I had hardly felt in the heat of battle, though now my head still throbbed with a dull pain. I stalked into the hall with Uhtred, my son, with Finan, and with Rorik. That was the boy's name, the boy I had wounded in battle, and he carried the same name as Ragnar's son, my boyhood friend. This Rorik's arm was healing, indeed was healed well enough for him to hold a big bronze casket that had pictures of saints around its sides and a depiction of Christ in glory on its lid. He was a good boy, fair-haired and blue-eyed, with a strong mischievous face. He had never known his mother and I had killed his father. 'This is Rorik,' I introduced him to Æthelflaed and the company, 'and he is as a son to me.' I touched the golden hammer amulet around Rorik's neck. The amulet had belonged to his father, as did the sword that hung, far too big, at his skinny waist. 'Rorik,' I went on, 'is what you call a pagan, and he will stay a pagan.' I looked at the priests, and only Father Oswald met my eye. He nodded.

'I have a daughter,' I said, looking back to Æthelflaed who sat in the chair that passed for a throne in Ceaster, 'and she is now queen of Northumbria. Her husband is king. He has sworn not to attack Mercia. He will also cede to you some Mercian land that is presently under Danish rule as a gesture of his friendship, and he will make a treaty with you.'

'Thank you, Lord Uhtred,' Æthelflaed said. Her face was unreadable, but she met my gaze and held it for a moment before looking at the boy beside me. 'And welcome, Rorik.'

'It seemed best, my lady,' I said, 'to put a friendly pagan on Northumbria's throne because it seems the men of Mercia are too cowardly to enter that country,' I was looking at Cynlæf, 'even to pursue their enemies.'

Cynlæf bridled. 'I . . .' he began, then faltered.

'You what?' I challenged him.

He looked to Æthelflaed for help, but she offered none. 'I was advised,' he finally said weakly.

'By a priest?' I asked, looking at Ceolnoth.

'We were commanded not to enter Northumbria!' Cynlæf protested.

'You will learn from the Lord Uhtred,' Æthelflaed said, still looking at me even though she spoke to Cynlæf, 'that there are times when you disobey orders.' She turned to him, and her voice was icy. 'You made the wrong decision.'

'But it's of no consequence,' I said, looking at Father Ceolnoth, 'because Thor and Woden answered my prayers.'

Æthelflaed gave a glimmer of a smile. 'You will eat with us tonight, Lord Uhtred?'

'And leave tomorrow,' I said, 'with my men and their families.' I looked to the side of the hall where Eadith stood among the shadows. 'And with you too,' I said, and she nodded.

'Tomorrow! You're leaving?' Æthelflaed asked, surprised and indignant.

'By your leave, lady, yes.'

'To go where?'

'To go north, my lady, north.'

'North?' she frowned.

'But before I leave,' I said, 'I have a gift for you.'

'Where in the north?'

'I have business in the north, lady,' I said, then touched Rorik's shoulder. 'Go, boy,' I said, 'lay it at her feet.'

The boy carried the heavy bronze casket around the hearth, then knelt and dropped his burden with a clang at the foot of Æthelflaed's throne. He backed away to my side, the big sword dragging through the stale rushes on the hall floor. 'I planned to give you Eoferwic, my lady,' I told her, 'but I gave that city to Sigtryggr instead. That gift is in its place.'

She knew what was in the box even before it was opened, but she snapped her fingers and a servant hurried from the shadows, knelt, and opened the heavy lid. Men craned to see what was inside and I heard some of the priests hiss with distaste, but Æthelflaed just smiled. Ragnall's bloody head grimaced at her from the casket. 'Thank you, Lord Uhtred,' she said calmly, 'the gift is most generous.'

'And what you wanted,' I said.

'It is.'

'Then with your permission, lady,' I bowed, 'my work is done and I would rest.'

She nodded. I beckoned to Eadith and walked to the hall's great doors. 'Lord Uhtred!' Æthelflaed called, and I turned. 'What business in the north?' she asked.

I hesitated, then told her the truth. 'I am the Lord of Bebbanburg, lady.'

And I am. I have ancient parchments that say that Uhtred, son of Uhtred, is the lawful and sole owner of the lands that are carefully marked by stones and by dykes, by oaks and by ash, by marsh and by sea. They are wave-beaten lands, wild beneath the wind-driven sky, and they were stolen from me.

I had business in the north.

HISTORICAL NOTE

There was, briefly, a Bishopric of Chester in the eleventh century, but the see proper was not established until 1541, so Leofstan, like his diocese, is entirely fictional. Indeed I confess that much of *Warriors of the Storm* is fictional, a tale woven onto a deep background of truth.

The underlying story of all Uhtred's novels is the tale of England's making, and perhaps the most remarkable thing about that story is how little it is known. When Uhtred's saga began, back before the reign of Alfred the Great, there was no such place as England or, as it came to be called, Englaland. Ever since the Romans left in the early fifth century AD, Britain had been split into many small kingdoms. By the time of Alfred the land that would become England was divided into four; Wessex, Mercia, East Anglia, and Northumbria. The Danes had captured East Anglia and Northumbria, and held most of northern Mercia. At one point it looked as if the Danes would overwhelm Wessex too, and it was Alfred's great achievement to save that last Saxon kingdom from their domination. The story of the subsequent years is how the English gradually reclaimed their land, working gradually northwards from Wessex in the south. Æthelflaed, Alfred's daughter, was the ruler of Mercia, and she was to liberate much of the northern midlands from Danish rule. It was under Æthelflaed's rule that Ceaster, Chester, was brought back under Saxon control, and she built burhs at both Brunanburh and at Eads Byrig, though the latter was occupied only briefly.

The fortresses at Ceaster, Brunanburh, and Eads Byrig did more than defend Mercia against incursions from Danish-ruled Northumbria. The Norsemen had occupied much of Ireland's eastern coast, and, in the early years of the tenth century, they were under severe pressure from the Irish kings. Many abandoned their holdings in Ireland and looked for land in Britain, and Æthelflaed's forts guarded the rivers against their invasion. They landed further north, mostly in Cumbria, and Sigtryggr was one of them. He did indeed, become king in Eoferwic.

Readers who, like me, endured far too many tedious hours in Sunday School might recall that Gomer was the prostitute that the prophet Hosea married. The tale of the two she-bears slaughtering the forty-two children at God's command can be found in the Second Book of Kings, Chapter two.

The story of England's making is blood-drenched. Eventually the Northmen (Danes and Norse) will intermarry with the Saxons, but so long as the two sides compete for ownership of the land then war will continue. Uhtred has marched from Wessex in the south to the northern borders of Mercia. He has further to go, so he will march again.

THE MAKING OF ENGLAND

The background to Uhtred's story

The Uhtred novels are about the making of England. Some countries, like the United States, have a birthday, a date which definitively marks the beginning of their existence, but the origins of England are much murkier, lost somewhere in what we loosely call the Dark Ages. The same is true of Wales, Scotland, Ireland and, indeed, of many other European states.

The start of English history, as taught in many schools, is the Norman invasion of 1066. England, of course, already existed by then, but little attention is paid to pre-Norman England, other than to note that Julius Caesar came, saw and conquered (in fact he came, saw and went away) and that King Alfred was an extremely poor baker of cakes. The Vikings are romantic, murderous adventurers with horns on their helmets (apparently an invention of opera costume designers in the nineteenth century) who came on dragon-headed ships to rape and pillage, but the true relevance of the Vikings to the making of England is rarely taught, let alone understood. Yet the presence of Vikings in the story of England's birth should tell us that it was an extraordinary adventure, shot through with blood, heroes and battles. It is Uhtred's story.

I constantly call Uhtred a Saxon, which annoys purists because he was most likely an Angle, but using the name Saxons for all the tribes which spoke the Anglish language makes for simplicity in the telling of the story. The Angles and the Saxons are two Germanic tribes who invaded Britain in the fifth and sixth centuries and they were not alone; there were also Jutes, Frisians and Franks crossing the North Sea to find land in Britain. The opportunity for this Germanic invasion came when the Romans abandoned Britain, leaving it almost defenceless. The Saxons had been threatening even before the Romans left, which is why the Romans built forts along Britain's east coast, the 'Forts of the Saxon Shore' as they are called, but once the Legions were gone the Germanic tribes came in ever greater numbers.

Very roughly the Angles settled in the north of what would become England and the Saxons the south, which reflects their origins. The Angles and Jutes came from what is now Denmark and the Saxons, Franks and Frisians from what is now the coastal regions of Germany and Holland. They might have been distinct tribes but they shared a language (with marked regional differences) and a pagan religion. They invaded a Christian land

and drove the natives to the margins; to the lowlands of Scotland, to Cornwall, to Wales and across the sea to Brittany. It was a most successful invasion. Within two hundred years the land that would come to be called England was inhabited almost exclusively by the Germanic tribes who spoke a language which they themselves called 'the Anglish tongue'. They had intermarried with the Britons and they kept some British names which is why there are so many River Avons in England; 'afon' was the native word for river and, presumably, when the newcomers inquired what a river was called they were told 'it's a river!', and so it became the River River. Lundene is another name that is probably British in origin, though the city which the invaders discovered on the north bank of the Thames had been built by the Romans.

The native British had been unable to put up an organised resistance to the invaders who, once they secured the land, divided it into squabbling kingdoms which were forever at war with each other. One such kingdom was Bernicia, a name long lost in the mists of time. Bernicia encompassed much of north-east England and southern Scotland and is important to Uhtred because his ancestors were once kings of Bernicia. He traces his lineage back to Ida the Flamebearer, one of the original invaders who established his kingdom in what is now Northumberland. It was there, on the wild coast, that Ida discovered the great rock on which Bamburgh Castle now stands. There was almost certainly an existing fort on the rock, a fort that Ida captured and rebuilt, and which his grandson, Æthelfrith, named for his queen, Bebba. Thus the fort on its daunting rock became Bebbanburg, a name that has changed over the centuries into Bamburgh. Æthelfrith was a hugely successful monarch of Bernicia, the early church historian Bede records that he 'ravaged the Britons more than all the great men of the English', though eventually he was killed in battle and his kingdom was subsumed into Northumbria. Uhtred is his descendant. By the ninth century the descendants of Ida have lost their kingdom of Bernicia, but have held onto Bebbanburg and its lands. They are a formidable presence in the north.

The Saxons took the land from the native Britons and held it, but it was not a peaceful process. They suffered at least one great defeat (Mount Badon), but also won notable victories like the battle at Catraeth (now Caterick), the subject of a famous Welsh poem *Y Gododdin*.

> Men went to Catraeth with a war-cry,
> On fast horses and with grim armour and
>   shields,
> Their spears held high and spear-points
>   sharp,
> And shining coats-of-mail and swords.

The poem, which might have been composed as early as the seventh century, tells of a Welsh defeat at the hands of the Saxons. Interestingly the Welsh army which marched into what is now Yorkshire came from southern Scotland, a reminder that the native Britons had been thrust there by the Saxon invaders. In time those Welsh settlers would take on a new Scottish identity, but when they marched to disaster they still spoke Welsh and thought of themselves as Britons. The poem, though it concerns a defeat, is heroic, and in that it resembles the poetry of the people who defeated them. Anglo-Saxon poetry is rich in warfare and battles, reflecting the times in which our ancestors lived.

He thrust then with his shield so that the
 spear shaft broke,
And the spear-head shattered as it stabbed in
 reply.
The warrior became furious, he pierced
The proud Viking who had given him the
 wound.
He was an experienced fighter, he thrust his
 spear forward
Through the warrior's neck, his hand guiding
So that he would lethally pierce his enemy's
 life.

That is a fragment from a poem called the 'Battle of Maldon', which was fought much later than Catraeth. Again it describes a defeat, this time when Brythnoth, a Saxon leader in East Anglia, is trounced by a force of Vikings who had sailed up the Blackwater River in Essex. That poem, and the many similar poems, are reminders that England was forged by warfare, not only the original war against the native Britons, but a new and terrible struggle against the invaders whom we call the Vikings.

Because, by the ninth century, a new influx of people were trying to capture the Saxon kingdoms. In many ways they were very similar to the old Germanic invaders, indeed some of them came from the same lands that were originally inhabited by the Angles and Jutes. Others came from further north, from what is now Sweden and Norway. We know them all as the Vikings, and their role in England's story is vital. By the ninth century the old Saxon invaders, now the inhabitants of four Saxon kingdoms in Britain, have (largely) been converted to Christianity. The new enemy, though, still adheres to the old religion, the worship of Thor, Woden and the other great gods of the Germanic pantheon, so to the horrors of territorial war is added the fury of religious conflict. A monk, copying a manuscript, wrote a prayer in the margin; 'From the fury of the Northmen, good Lord deliver us.' The assault of the Vikings was savage and, for a time, hugely successful.

The land the Vikings assaulted had settled into four kingdoms. In the north was Northumbria, below which was Mercia (roughly the present English Midlands), East Anglia lay to the east while south of the Thames was Wessex. Uhtred's story begins with *The Last Kingdom*, which is Wessex, and I called it the 'last' kingdom because it was the last Saxon kingdom. The others had fallen to the Vikings, mostly Danes, who had captured Northumbria, East Anglia and much of Mercia. They then invaded Wessex, driving King Alfred to his refuge in the Somerset marshes, and it is from those wetlands that the Saxon fight-back begins. The story of England's making is really a tale of how the Saxons reclaim their lost kingdoms, beginning in the south and working inexorably northwards until, in 937 AD, a West Saxon army under Æthelstan, King Alfred's grandson, inflicts a huge defeat on a combined army of Vikings, Scots and Irish at Brunanburh. Naturally a poem followed;

> Then Aethelstan, king, leader of leaders . . .
> Struck in battle with sword's edge
> At Brunanburh. He broke the shield wall,
> Shattered shields with swords . . .
> Crushed the hated people,
> Scottish-folk and sea raiders fell.
> The field was flooded with blood.
> There lay scores of men killed by blades.
> West-Saxons went forth from dawn till night,
> The mounted warriors pursued the enemy
> The fugitives were slaughtered from behind
> With freshly sharpened swords.

The result of Brunanburh was the acknowledgement by the Saxon peoples that they were ruled by Æthelstan, and so at last one king ruled one people in the lands where the Anglish language was spoken. Englaland, as they called it, was born. The survival of the new kingdom would prove a struggle. The north was slow to be assimilated, it would be lost to the Northmen again, then regained, and for a time Danish kings would rule all of England and then, of course, the Normans would come, but Æthelstan's achievement had been to unite the four kingdoms, reclaim the lost Saxon territory and establish what we take for granted, a kingdom called England.

The new kingdom was not purely a Saxon country, not even an Anglo-Saxon-Jutish-Frisian kingdom. The language its citizens spoke was, or became, English, but it was heavily influenced by the Northmen. We think of the Vikings as raiders, savage men bringing terror on their beast-headed long-ships, but, like the Saxons before them, they were settlers too and they left their mark on both England and England's language. The north and east of England are thick with place names that were given by Viking settlers; any town ending in 'by', like Grimsby, is a Viking settlement. Thorpe, toft and thwaite are other elements found only in the town names of the north and east, all evidence of Viking settlements. Those settlers intermarried with the Saxons and adopted the Saxon religion. They adopted the language too, but introduced many Scandinavian words we still use. King Alfred's burnt cakes might have contained eyren, but thanks to the Northmen we call them eggs instead. Slaughter, sky, window, anger, husband, freckle, leg, trust, dazzle; the list could go on and on, all words donated to English by Scandinavian settlers.

That language has now spread about the world, yet it is extraordinary to think that in 878 AD the Saxon rule of Britain almost ended. That was the year King Alfred was driven to take refuge in the Somerset levels by a Danish invasion. If he had been defeated, if he had not led his army to the victory at Ethandun, it is conceivable that the last kingdom, Wessex, would have fallen to the Danes. There would be no England. Fate, as Uhtred is fond of saying, is inexorable, and the story of England's making is a tale of men and women struggling against inexorable fate to make their homeland. 'Wyrd bið ful aræd!' wrote a Saxon poet in the tenth century, using the English that Uhtred would have known.

Wyrd bið ful aræd!
Swa cwæð eardstapa,
earfeþa gemyndig,
wraþra wælsleahta,
winemæga hryre.

'Fate is inexorable! So spoke the earth-stepper (the wanderer), mindful of hardships, of savage slaughters and the downfall of kinfolk.' Slaughters and hardships; it is the story of England's making.